1 MONTH OF
FREE
READING

at

www.ForgottenBooks.com

By purchasing this book you are eligible for one month membership to ForgottenBooks.com, giving you unlimited access to our entire collection of over 1,000,000 titles via our web site and mobile apps.

To claim your free month visit:
www.forgottenbooks.com/free186086

ISBN 978-0-265-18925-2
PIBN 10186086

THE WINDS
OF CHANCE

BY
REX BEACH
AUTHOR OF
"HEART OF THE SUNSET"
"THE SILVER HORDE" ETC.

Illustrated

HARPER & BROTHERS PUBLISHERS
NEW YORK AND LONDON

ILLUSTRATIONS

THE WINDS OF CHANCE

CHAPTER I

WITH an ostentatious flourish Mr. "Lucky" Broad placed a crisp ten-dollar bill in an eager palm outstretched across his folding-table.

"The gentleman wins and the gambler loses!" Mr. Broad proclaimed to the world. "The eye is quicker than the hand, and the dealer's moans is music to the stranger's ear." With practised touch he rearranged the three worn walnut-shells which constituted his stock in trade. Beneath one of them he deftly concealed a pellet about the size of a five-grain allopathic pill. It was the erratic behavior of this tiny ball, its mysterious comings and goings, that had summoned Mr. Broad's audience and now held its observant interest. This audience, composed of roughly dressed men, listened attentively to the seductive monologue which accompanied the dealer's deft manipulations, and was greatly entertained thereby. "Three tiny tepees in a row and a little black medicine-man inside." The speaker's voice was high-pitched and it carried like a "thirty-

thirty." "You see him walk in, you open the door, and—you double your money. Awfully simple! Simpully awful! What? As I live! The gentleman wins ten more—ten silver-tongued song-birds, ten messengers of mirth—the price of a hard day's toil. Take it, sir, and may it make a better and a stronger man of you. Times are good and I spend my money free. I made it packin' grub to Linderman, four bits a pound, but —easy come, easy go. Now then, who's next? You've seen me work. I couldn't baffle a sore-eyed Siwash with snow-glasses."

Lucky Broad's three-legged table stood among some stumps beside the muddy roadway which did service as the main street of Dyea and along which flowed an irregular stream of pedestrians; incidental to his practised manipulation of the polished walnut-shells he maintained an unceasing chatter of the sort above set down. Now his voice was loud and challenging, now it was apologetic, always it stimulated curiosity. One moment he was jubilant and gay, again he was contrite and querulous. Occasionally he burst forth into plaintive self-denunciations.

Fixing a hypnotic gaze upon a bland, blue-eyed bystander who had just joined the charmed circle, he murmured, invitingly: "Better try your luck, Olaf. It's Danish dice—three chances to win and one to lose."

The object of his address shook his head. "Aye ant Danish, Aye ban Norvegen," said he.

"Danish dice or Norwegian poker, they're both

2

the same. I'll deal you a free hand and it won't cost you a cent. Fix your baby blues on the little ball and watch me close. Don't let me deceive you. Now then, which hut hides the grain?"

Noting a half-dozen pairs of eyes upon him, the Norseman became conscious that he was a center of interest. He grinned half-heartedly and, after a brief hesitation, thrust forth a clumsy paw, lifted a shell, and exposed the object of general curiosity.

"You guessed it!" There was commendation, there was pleased surprise, in Mr. Broad's tone. "You can't fool a foreigner, can you, boys? My, my! Ain't it lucky for me that we played for fun? But you got to give me another chance, Lars; I'll fool you yet. In walks the little pill once more, I make the magic pass, and you follow me attentively, knowing in your heart of hearts that I'm a slick un. Now then, shoot, Kid; you can't miss me!"

The onlookers stirred with interest; with eager fingers the artless Norwegian fumbled in his pocket. At the last moment, however, he thought better of his impulse, grunted once, then turned his back to the table and walked away.

"Missed him!" murmured the dealer, with no display of feeling; then to the group around him he announced, shamelessly: "You got to lead those birds; they fly fast."

One of Mr. Broad's boosters, he who had twice won for the Norseman's benefit, carelessly returned his winnings. "Sure!" he agreed. "They got a head like a turtle, them Swedes."

Mr. Broad carefully smoothed out the two bills and reverently laid them to rest in his bank-roll. "Yes, and they got bony mouths. You got to set your hook or it won't hold."

"Slow pickin's," yawned an honest miner with a pack upon his back. Attracted by the group at the table, he had dropped out of the procession in the street and had paused long enough to win a bet or two. Now he straightened himself and stretched his arms. "These Michael Strogoffs is hep to the old stuff, Lucky. I'm thinking of joining the big rush. They say this Klondike is some rich."

Inasmuch as there were no strangers in sight at the moment, the proprietor of the deadfall gave up barking; he daintily folded and tore in half a cigarette paper, out of which he fashioned a thin smoke for himself. It was that well-earned moment of repose, that welcome recess from the day's toil. Mr. Broad inhaled deeply, then he turned his eyes upon the former speaker.

"You've been thinking again, have you?" He frowned darkly. With a note of warning in his voice he declared: "You ain't strong enough for such heavy work, Kid. That's why I've got you packing hay."

The object of this sarcasm hitched his shoulders and the movement showed that his burden was indeed no more than a cunning counterfeit, a bundle of hay rolled inside a tarpaulin.

"Oh, I got a head and I've been doing some heavy thinking with it," the Kid retorted. "This here Dawson is going to be a good town. I'm getting readied up to join the parade."

"Are you, now?" the shell-man mocked. "I s'pose you got it all framed with the Canucks to let you through? I s'pose the chief of police knows you and likes you, eh? You and him is cousins, or something?"

"Coppers is all alike; there's always a way to square 'em—"

"Lay off that 'squaring' stuff," cautioned a renegade crook, disguised by a suit of mackinaws and a week's growth of beard into the likeness of a stampeder. "A thousand bucks and a ton of grub, that's what the sign says, and that's what it means. They wouldn't let you over the Line with nine hundred and ninety-nine fifty."

"Right!" agreed a third capper. "It's a closed season on broken stiffs. You can't monkey with the Mounted Police. When they put over an edict it lays there till it freezes. They'll make you show your 'openers' at the Boundary. Gee! If I had 'em I wouldn't bother to go 'inside.' What's a guy want with more than a thousand dollars and a ton of grub, anyhow?"

"All the same, I'm about set to hit the trail," stubbornly maintained the man with the alfalfa pack. "I ain't broke. When you boys get to Dawson, just ask for Kid Bridges' saloon and I'll open wine. These woollys can have their mines; me for a hootch-mill on Main Street."

5

Lucky addressed his bevy of boosters. "Have I nursed a serpent in my breast, or has the Kid met a banker's son? Gimme room, boys. I'm going to shuffle the shells for him and let him double his money. Keep your eye on the magic pea, Mr. Bridges. Three tiny tepees in a row—" There was a general laugh as Broad began to shift the walnut-shells, but Kid Bridges retorted, contemptuously:

"That's the trouble with all you wiseacres. You get a dollar ahead and you fall for another man's game. I never knew a faro-dealer that wouldn't shoot craps. No, I haven't met no banker's son and I ain't likely to in this place. These pilgrims have sewed their money in their underclothes, and they sleep with their eyes open. Seems like they'd go blind, but they don't. These ain't Rubes, Lucky; they're city folks. They've seen three-ringed circuses and three-shell games, and all that farmer stuff. They've been 'gypped,' and it's an old story to 'em."

"You're dead right," Broad acknowledged. "That's why it's good. D'you know the best town in America for the shells? Little old New York. If the cops would let me set up at the corner of Broad and Wall, I'd own the Stock Exchange in a week. Madison and State is another good stand; so's Market and Kearney, or Pioneer Square, down by the totem pole. New York, Chicago, 'Frisco, Seattle, they're all hick towns. For every city guy that's been stung by a bee there's a hundred that still thinks honey

6

comes from a fruit. This rush is just starting, and the bigger it grows the better we'll do. Say, Kid, if you mush over to Tagish with that load of timothy on your spine, the police will put you on the wood-pile for the winter."

While Mr. Lucky Broad and his business associates were thus busied in discussing the latest decree of the Northwest Mounted Police, other townsmen of theirs were similarly engaged. Details of this proclamation—the most arbitrary of any, hitherto—had just arrived from the International Boundary, and had caused a halt, an eddy, in the stream of gold-seekers which flowed inland toward the Chilkoot Pass. A human tide was setting northward from the States, a tide which swelled and quickened daily as the news of George Carmack's discovery spread across the world, but at Healy & Wilson's log-store, where the notice above referred to had been posted, the stream slowed. A crowd of new-comers from the barges and steamers in the roadstead had assembled there, and now gave voice to hoarse indignation and bitter resentment. Late arrivals from Skagway, farther down the coast, brought word of similar scenes at that point and a similar feeling of dismay; they reported a similar increase in the general excitement, too. There, as here, a tent city was springing up, the wooded hills were awakening to echoes of unaccustomed life, a thrill and a stir were running through the wilderness and the odor of spruce fires was growing heavier with every ship that came.

Pierce Phillips emerged from the trading-post and, drawn by the force of gravitation, joined the largest and the most excited group of Argonauts. He was still somewhat dazed by his perusal of that Police edict; the blow to his hopes was still too stunning, his disappointment was still too keen, to permit of clear thought.

"A ton of provisions and a thousand dollars!" he repeated, blankly. Why, that was absurd, out of all possible reason! It would bar the way to fully half this rushing army; it would turn men back at the very threshold of the golden North. Nevertheless, there stood the notice in black and white, a clear and unequivocal warning from the Canadian authorities, evidently designed to forestall famine on the foodless Yukon. From the loud arguments round about him Phillips gathered that opinion on the justice of the measure was about evenly divided; those fortunate men who had come well provided commended it heartily, those less fortunate fellows who were sailing close-hauled were equally noisy in their denunciation of it. The latter could see in this precautionary ruling nothing except the exercise of a tyrannical power aimed at their ruin, and in consequence they voiced threats, and promises of violence the which Phillips put down as mere resentful mouthings of no actual significance. As for himself, he had never possessed anything like a thousand dollars at one time, therefore the problem of acquiring such a prodigious sum in the immediate future presented appalling difficulties.

8

He had come north to get rich, only to find that it was necessary to be rich in order to get north. A fine situation, truly! A ton of provisions would cost at least five hundred dollars and the expense of transporting it across summer swamps and tundras, then up and over that mysterious and forbidding Chilkoot of which he had heard so much, would bring the total capital required up to impossible proportions. The prospect was indeed dismaying. Phillips had been ashore less than an hour, but already he had gained some faint idea of the country that lay ahead of him; already he had noted the almost absolute lack of transportation; already he had learned the price of packers, and as a result he found himself at an *impasse.*

One thousand dollars and two hundred pounds! It was enough to dash high hopes. And yet, strangely enough, Phillips was not discouraged. He was rather surprised at his own rebound after the first shock; his reasonless optimism vaguely amazed him, until, in contemplating the matter, he discovered that his thoughts were running somewhat after this fashion:

"They told me I couldn't make it; they said something was sure to happen. Well, it has. I'm up against it—hard. Most fellows would quit and go home, but I sha'n't. I'm going to win .out, somehow, for this is the real thing. This is Life, Adventure. It will be wonderful to look back and say: 'I did it. Nothing stopped me. I landed at Dyea with one hundred and thirty-five dollars, but look at me now!'"

Thoughts such as these were in his mind, and their resolute nature must have been reflected in his face, for a voice aroused him from his meditations.

"It don't seem to faze you much, partner. I s'pose you came heeled?" Phillips looked up and into a sullen, angry face.

"It nearly kills me," he smiled. "I'm the worst-heeled man in the crowd."

"Well, it's a darned outrage. A ton of grub! Why, have you seen the trail? Take a look; it's a man-killer, and the rate is forty cents a pound to Linderman. It 'll go to fifty now—maybe a dollar—and there aren't enough packers to handle half the stuff."

"Things are worse at Skagway," another man volunteered. "I came up yesterday, and they're losing a hundred head of horses a day — bogging 'em down and breaking their legs. You can walk on dead carcasses from the Porcupine to the Summit."

A third stranger, evidently one of the well-provided few, laughed carelessly. "If you boys can't· stand the strain you'd better stay where you are," said he. "Grub's sky-high in Dawson, and mighty short. I knew what I was up against, so I came prepared. Better go home and try it next summer."

The first speaker, he of the sullen visage, turned his back, muttering, resentfully: "Another wise guy! They make me sick! I've a notion to go through anyhow."

"Don't try that," cautioned the man from Skagway. "If you got past the Police they'd follow you to hell but what they'd bring you back. They ain't like our police."

Still meditating his plight, Pierce Phillips edged out of the crowd and walked slowly down the street. It was not a street at all, except by courtesy, for it was no more than an open water-front faced by a few log buildings and a meandering line of new white tents. Tents were going up everywhere and all of them bore painful evidence of their newness. So did the clothes of their owners for that matter—men's garments still bore their price-tags. The beach was crowded with piles of merchandise over which there was much wrangling, barges plying regularly back and forth from the anchored ships added hourly to the confusion. As outfits were dumped upon the sand their owners assembled them and bore them away to their temporary camp sites. In this occupation every man faced his own responsibilities single-handed, for there were neither drays nor carts nor vehicles of any sort.

As Phillips looked on at the disorder along the water's edge, as he stared up the fir-flanked Dyea valley, whither a steady stream of traffic flowed, he began to feel a fretful eagerness to join in it, to be up and going. 'Way yonder through those hills towered the Chilkoot, and beyond that was the mighty river rushing toward Dawson City, toward Life and Adventure, for that was what the gold-fields signified to Phillips. Yes, Life! Adventure! He had set out to seek them, to taste the flavor of the world, and there it lay—his world, at least—just out of reach. A fierce impatience, a hot resentment at that senseless restriction which chained him in his tracks, ran through the boy. What right had any one to stop him here at the very door, when just inside great things were happening? Past that white-and-purple barrier which he could see against the sky a new land lay, a radiant land of promise, of mystery, and of fascination; Pierce vowed that he would not, could not, wait. Fortunes would reward the first arrivals; how, then, could he permit these other men to precede him? The world was a good place —it would not let a person starve.

To the young and the foot-free Adventure lurks just over the hill; Life opens from the crest of the very next divide. It matters not that we never quite come up with either, that we never quite attain the summit whence our promises are realized; the ever-present expectation, the eager straining forward, is the breath of youth. It was that breath which Phillips now felt in his nostrils. It was pungent, salty.

He noted a group of people gathered about some center of attraction whence issued a high-pitched intonation.

"Oh, look at the cute little pea! Klondike croquet, the packer's pastime. Who'll risk a dollar to win a dollar? It's a healthy sport. It's good for young and old—a cheeild can understand it. Three Eskimo igloos and an educated pill!"

12

"A shell-game!" Pierce Phillips halted in his
tracks and stared incredulously, then he smiled.
"A shell-game, running wide open on the main
street of the town!" This *was* the frontier, the
very edge of things. With an odd sense of unreality he felt the world turn back ten years.
He had seen shell-games at circuses and fair-
grounds when he was much younger, but he supposed they had long since been abandoned in
favor of more ingenious and less discreditable
methods of robbery. Evidently, however, there
were some gulls left, for this device appeared to
be well patronized. Still doubting the evidence
of his ears, he joined the group.

"The gentleman wins and the gambler loses!"
droned the dealer as he paid a bet. "Now then,
we're off for another journey. Who'll ride with
me this time?"

Phillips was amazed that any one could be so
simple-minded as to squander his money upon
such a notoriously unprofitable form of entertainment. Nevertheless, men were playing, and
they did not seem to suspect that the persons
whom the dealer occasionally paid were his con-
federates.

The operator maintained an incessant monologue. At the moment of Pierce's arrival he was
directing it at an ox-eyed individual, evidently
selected to be the next victim. The fellow was
stupid, nevertheless he exercised some caution
at first. He won a few dollars, then he lost a
few, but, alas! the gambling fever mounted in

13

him and greed finally overcame his hesitation.
With an eager gesture he chose a shell and Phillips felt a glow of satisfaction at the realization
that the man had once more guessed aright.
Drawing forth a wallet. the fellow laid it on the
table.

"I'll bet the lump," he cried.

The dealer hesitated. "How much you got in
that alligator valise?"

"Two hundred dollars."

"Two hundred berries on one bush!" The proprietor of the game was incredulous. "Boys, he
aims to leave me cleaner than a snow-bird."
Seizing the walnut-shell between his thumb and
forefinger, he turned it over, but instead of exposing the elusive pellet he managed, by an almost imperceptible forward movement, to roll
it out from under its hiding-place and to conceal
it between his third and fourth fingers. The
stranger was surprised, dumfounded, at sight of
the empty shell. He looked on open-mouthed
while his wallet was looted of its contents.

"Every now and then I win a little one," the
gambler announced as he politely returned the
bill-case to its owner. He lifted another shell,
and by some sleight-of-hand managed to replace
the pellet upon the table, then gravely flipped
a five-dollar gold piece to one of his boosters.

Phillips's eyes were quick; from where he stood
he had detected the maneuver and it left him
hot with indignation. He felt impelled to tell
the victim how he had been robbed, but thought

better of the impulse and assured himself that this was none of his affair. For perhaps ten minutes he looked on while the sheep-shearing proceeded.

After a time there came a lull and the dealer raised his voice to entice new patrons. Meanwhile, he paused to roll a cigarette the size of a wheat straw. While thus engaged there sounded the hoarse blast of a steamer's whistle in the offing and he turned his head. Profiting by this instant of inattention a hand reached across the table and lifted one of the walnut-shells. There was nothing under it.

"Five bucks on this one!" A soiled bill was placed beside one of the two remaining shells, the empty one.

Thus far Phillips had followed the pea unerringly, therefore he was amazed at the new better's mistake.

The dealer turned back to his layout and winked at the bystanders, saying, "Brother, I'll bet you ten more that you've made a bad bet." His offer was accepted. Simultaneously Phillips was seized with an intense desire to beat this sharper at his own game; impulsively he laid a protecting palm over the shell beneath which he knew the little sphere to lie.

"I'll pick this one," he heard himself say.

"Better let me deal you a new hand," the gambler suggested.

"Nothing of the sort," a man at Phillips' shoulder broke in. "Hang on to that shell, kid.

You're right and I'm going down for the size of his bankroll." The speaker was evidently a miner, for he carried a bulky pack upon his shoulders. He placed a heavy palm over the back of Phillips' hand, then extracted from the depths of his overalls a fat roll of paper money.

The size of this wager, together with the determination of its owner, appeared briefly to nonplus the dealer. He voiced a protest, but the miner forcibly overbore it:

"Say, I eat up this shell stuff!" he declared. "It's my meat, and I've trimmed every tinhorn that ever came to my town. There's three hundred dollars; you cover it, and you cover this boy's bet, too." The fellow winked reassuringly at Phillips. "You heard him say the sky was his limit, didn't you? Well, let's see how high the sky is in these parts!"

There was a movement in the crowd, whereupon the speaker cried, warningly: "Boosters, stand back! Don't try to give us the elbow, or I'll close up this game!" To Pierce he murmured, confidentially: "We've got him right. Don't let anybody edge you out." He put more weight upon Phillips' hand and forced the young man closer to the table.

Pierce had no intention of surrendering his place, and now the satisfaction of triumphing over these crooks excited him. He continued to cover the walnut-shell while with his free hand he drew his own money from his pocket. He saw that the owner of the game was suffering extreme discomfort at this checkmate, and he enjoyed the situation.

"I watched you trim that farmer a few minutes ago," Phillips' companion chuckled. "Now I'm going to make you put up or shut up. There's my three hundred. I can use it when it grows to six."

"How much are you betting?" the dealer inquired of Phillips.

Pierce had intended merely to risk a dollar or two, but now there came to him a thrilling thought. That notice at Healy & Wilson's store flashed into his mind. "One thousand dollars and a ton of food," the sign had read. Well, why not bet and bet heavy? he asked himself. Here was a chance to double his scanty capital at the expense of a rogue. To beat a barefaced cheater at his own game surely could not be considered cheating; in this instance it was mere retribution.

He had no time to analyze the right or the wrong of his reasoning—at best the question would bear debate. Granting that it wasn't exactly honest, what did such nice considerations weigh when balanced against the stern necessities of this hour? A stranger endeavored to shove him away from the table and this clinched his decision. He'd make them play fair. With a sweep of his free arm, Phillips sent the fellow staggering back and then placed his entire roll of bills on the table in front of the dealer.

"There's mine," he said, shortly. "One hundred and thirty-five dollars. I don't have to count it, for I know it by heart."

"Business appears to be picking up," murmured the proprietor of the game.

Phillips' neighbor continued to hold the boy's hand in a vicelike grip. Now he leaned forward, saying:

"Look here! Are you going to **cover our** coin or am I going to smoke you up?"

"The groans of the gambler is sweet music in their ears!" The dealer shrugged reluctantly and counted out four hundred and thirty-five dollars, which he separated into two piles.

A certain shame at his action swept over Phillips when he felt his companion's grasp relax and heard him say, "Turn her over, kid."

This was diamond cut diamond, of course; nevertheless, it was a low-down trick and—

Pierce Phillips started, he examined the interior of the walnut-shell in bewilderment, for he had lifted it only to find it quite empty.

"Every now and then I win a little one," the dealer intoned, gravely pocketing his winnings. "It only goes to show you that the hand—"

"Damnation!" exploded the man at Phillips' side. "Trimmed for three hundred, **or** I'm a goat!"

As Pierce walked away some one fell into step with him; it was the sullen, black-browed individual he had seen at the trading-post.

"So they took you for a hundred and thirty-five, eh? You must be rolling in coin," the man observed.

Even yet Pierce was **more** than a little dazed.

18

"Do you know," said he, "I was sure I had the right shell."

"Why, of course you had the right one." The stranger laughed shortly. "They laid it up for you on purpose, then Kid Bridges worked a shift when he held your hand. You can't beat 'em."

Pierce halted. "Was he—was *that* fellow with the pack a booster?"

"Certainly. They're all boosters. The Kid carries enough hay on his back to feed a team. It's his bed. I've been here a week and I know 'em." The speaker stared in surprise at Phillips, who had broken into a hearty laugh. "Look here! A little hundred and thirty-five must be chicken feed to you. If you've got any more to toss away, toss it in my direction."

"That's what makes it so funny. You see, I haven't any more. That was my last dollar. Well, it serves me right. Now I can start from scratch and win on my own speed."

The dark-browed man studied Phillips curiously. "You're certainly game," he announced. "I s'pose now you'll be wanting to sell some of your outfit. That's why I've been hanging around that game. I've picked up quite a bit of stuff that way, but I'm still short a few things and I'll buy—"

"I haven't a pound of grub. I came up second-class."

"Huh! Then you'll go back steerage."

"Oh no, I won't! I'm going on to Dawson." There was a momentary silence. "You say

19

you've been here a week? Put me up for the night—until I get a job. Will you?"

The black-eyed man hesitated, then he grinned. "You've got your nerve, but—I'm blamed if I don't like it," said he. "My brother Jim is cooking supper now. Suppose we go over to the tent and ask him."

CHAPTER II

THE headwaters of the Dyea River spring from a giant's punch-bowl. Three miles above timber-line the valley bottom widens out into a flinty field strewn with boulders which in ages past have lost their footing on the steep hills forming the sides of the cup. Between these boulders a thin carpet of moss is spread, but the slopes themselves are quite naked; they are seamed and cracked and weather-beaten, their surfaces are split and shattered from the play of the elements. High up toward the crest of one of them rides a glacier— a pallid, weeping sentinel which stands guard for the great ice-caps beyond. Winter snows, summer fogs and rains have washed the hillsides clean; they are leached out and they present a lifeless, forbidding front to travelers. In many places the granite fragments which still encumber them lie piled one above another in such titanic chaos as to discourage man's puny efforts to climb over them. Nevertheless, men have done so, and by the thousands, by the tens of thousands. On this particular morning an unending procession of human beings was straining up and over and through the confusion. They lifted themselves by foot and by hand; where the slope was steepest they crept on all-fours. They formed an unbroken, threadlike stream extending from timberline to crest, each individual being dwarfed to microscopic proportions by the size of his surroundings. They flowed across the floor of the valley, then slowly, very slowly, they flowed up its almost perpendicular wall. Now they were lost to sight; again they reappeared clambering over glacier scars or toiling up steep, rocky slides; finally they emerged away up under the arch of the sky.

Looking down from the roof of the pass itself, the scene was doubly impressive, for the wooded valley lay outstretched clear to the sea, and out of it came that long, wavering line of ants. They did, indeed, appear to be ants, those men, as they dragged themselves across the meadow and up the ascent; they resembled nothing more than a file of those industrious insects creeping across the bottom and up the sides of a bath-tub, and the likeness was borne out by the fact that all carried burdens. That was in truth the marvel of the scene, for every man on the Chilkoot was bent beneath a back-breaking load.

Three miles down the gulch, where the upward march of the forests had been halted, there, among scattered outposts of scrubby spruce and wind-twisted willow, stood a village, a sprawling, formless aggregation of flimsy tents and green logs known as Sheep Camp. Although it was a temporary, makeshift town, already it bulked big in the minds of men from Maine to California, from the Great Lakes to the Gulf, for it was the last outpost of civilization, and beyond it lay a land of mystery. Sheep Camp had become famous by reason of the fact that it was linked with the name of that Via Dolorosa, that summit of despair, the Chilkoot. Already it had come to stand for the weak man's ultimate mile-post, the end of many journeys.

The approach from the sea was easy, if twelve miles of boulder and bog, of swamp and niggerhead, of root and stump, can be called easy under the best of circumstances; but easy it was as compared with what lay beyond and above it. Nevertheless, many Argonauts had never penetrated even thus far, and of those who had, a considerable proportion had turned back at the giant pit three miles above. One look at the towering barrier had been enough for them. The Chilkoot was more than a mountain, more than an obstacle of nature; it was a Presence, a tremendous and a terrifying Personality which overshadowed the minds of men and could neither be ignored at the time nor forgotten later. No wonder, then, that Sheep Camp, which was a part of the Chilkoot, represented a sort of acid test; no wonder that those who had moved their outfits thus far were of the breed the Northland loves —the stout of heart and of body.

Provisions were cached at frequent intervals all the way up from the sea, but in the open meadow beneath the thousand-foot wall an immense sup-

ply depot had sprung up. This pocket in the hills
had become an open-air commissary, stocked with
every sort of provender and gear. There were
acres of sacks and bundles, of boxes and bales,
of lumber and hardware and perishable stuffs,
and all day long men came and went in relays.
One relay staggered up and out of the cañon and
dropped its packs, another picked up the bundles
and ascended skyward. Pound by pound, ton
by ton, this vast equipment of supplies went forward, but slowly, oh, so slowly! And at such
effort! It was indeed fit work for ants, for it
arrived nowhere and it never ended. Antlike,
these burden-bearers possessed but one idea—to
fetch and to carry; they traveled back and forth
along the trail until they wore it into a bottom-
less bog, until every rock, every tree, every land-
mark along it became hatefully familiar and their
eyes grew sick from seeing them.

The character of their labor and its monotony,
even in this short time, had changed the men's
characters—they had become pack-animals and
they deported themselves as such. All labor-
saving devices, all mechanical aids, all short cuts
to comfort and to accomplishment, had been left
behind; here was the wilderness, primitive, hostile,
merciless. Every foot they moved, every ounce
they carried, was at the cost of muscular exertion.
It was only natural that they should take on the
color of their surroundings.

Money lost its value a mile above Sheep Camp
and became a thing of weight, a thing to carry.

The standard of value was the pound, and men thought in hundredweights or in tons. Yet there was no relief, no respite, for famine stalked in the Yukon and the Northwest Mounted were on guard, hence these unfortunates were chained to their grub-piles as galley-slaves are shackled to their benches.

Toe to heel, like peons rising from the bowels of a mine, they bent their backs and strained up that riven rock wall. Blasphemy and pain, high hopes and black despair, hearts overtaxed and eyes blind with fatigue, that was what the Chilkoot stood for. Permeating the entire atmosphere of the place, so that even the dullest could feel it, was a feverish haste, an apprehensive demand for speed, more speed, to keep ahead of the pressing thousands coming on behind.

Pierce Phillips breasted the last rise to the Summit, slipped his pack-straps, and flung himself full length upon the ground. His lungs felt as if they were bursting, the blood surged through his veins until he rocked, his body streamed with sweat, and his legs were as heavy as if molded from solid iron. He was pumped out, winded; nevertheless, he felt his strength return with magic swiftness, for he possessed that marvelous recuperative power of youth, and, like some fabled warrior, new strength flowed into him from the earth. Round about him other men were sprawled; some lay like corpses, others were propped against their packs, a few stirred and sighed like the sorely wounded after a charge. Those who had lain longest rose, took up their burdens, and went groaning over the sky-line and out of sight. Every moment new faces, purple with effort or white with exhaustion, rose out of the depths—all were bitten deep with lines of physical suffering. On buckled knees their owners lurched forward to find resting-places; in their eyes burned a sullen rage; in their mouths were foul curses at this Devil's Stairway. There were striplings and graybeards in the crowd, strong men and weak men, but here at the Summit all were alike in one particular—they lacked breath for anything except oaths.

Here, too, as in the valley beneath, was another great depot of provision piles. Near where Phillips had thrown himself down there was one man whose bearing was in marked contrast to that of the others. He sat astride a bulging canvas bag in a leather harness, and in spite of the fact that the mark of a tump-line showed beneath his cap he betrayed no signs of fatigue. He was not at all exhausted, and from the interest he displayed it seemed that he had chosen this spot as a vantage-point from which to study the upcoming file rather than as a place in which to rest. This he did with a quick, appreciative eye and with a genial smile. In face, in dress, in manner, he was different. For one thing, he was of foreign birth, and yet he appeared to be more a piece of the country than any man Pierce had seen. His clothes were of a pattern common

26

among the native packers, but he wore them with a free, unconscious grace all his own. From the peak of his Canadian toque there depended a tassel which bobbed when he talked; his boots were of Indian make, and they were soft and light and waterproof; a sash of several colors was knotted about his waist. But it was not alone his dress which challenged the eye—there was something in this fellow's easy, open bearing which arrested attention. His dark skin had been deepened by windburn, his well-set, well-shaped head bore a countenance both eager and intelligent, a countenance that fairly glowed with confidence and good humor.

Oddly enough, he sang as he sat upon his pack. High up on this hillside, amid blasphemous complaints, he hummed a gay little song:

> *"Chanté, rossignol, chanté!*
> *Toi qui à le cœur gai!*
> *Tu as le cœur à rire*
> *Mai j'l'ai-t-à pleurer,"*

ran his chanson.

Phillips had seen the fellow several times, and the circumstances of their first encounter had been sufficiently unusual to impress themselves upon his mind. Pierce had been resting here, at this very spot, when the Canuck had come up into sight, bearing a hundred-pound pack without apparent effort. Two flour-sacks upon a man's back was a rare sight on the roof of the Chilkoot. There were not many who could master that slope with more than one, but this fellow had borne his burden without apparent effort; and what was even more remarkable, what had caused Pierce Phillips to open his eyes in genuine astonishment, was the fact that the man climbed with a pipe in his teeth and smoked it with relish. On that occasion the Frenchman had not stopped at the crest to breathe, but had merely paused long enough to admire the scene outspread beneath him; then he had swung onward. Of all the sights young Phillips had beheld in this new land, the vision of that huge, unhurried Canadian, smoking, had impressed him deepest. It had awakened his keen envy, too, for Pierce was beginning to glory in his own strength. A few days later they had rested near each other on the Long Lake portage. That is, Phillips had rested; the Canadian, it seemed, had a habit of pausing when and where the fancy struck him. His reason for stopping there had been the antics of a peculiarly fearless and impertinent "camp-robber." With a crust of bread he had tolled the bird almost within his reach and was accepting its scolding with intense amusement. Having both teased and made friends with the creature, he finally gave it the crust and resumed his journey.

This was a land where brawn was glorified; the tales told oftenest around the stoves at Sheep Camp had to do with feats of strength or endurance, they were stories of mighty men and mighty packs, of long marches and of grim staying powers.

28

Already the names of certain "old-timers" like Dinsmore and McDonald and Peterson and Stick Jim had become famous because of some conspicuous exploit. Dinsmore, according to the legend, had once lugged a hundred and sixty pounds to the Summit; McDonald had bent a horseshoe in his hands; Peterson had lifted the stem-piece out of a poling-boat lodged on the rocks below White Horse; Stick Jim had run down a moose and killed it with his knife.

From what Phillips had seen of this French Canadian it was plain that he, too, was an "old-timer," one of that Jovian band of supermen who had dared the dark interior and robbed the bars of Forty Mile in the hard days before the El Dorado discovery. Since this was their first opportunity of exchanging speech, Phillips ventured to address the man.

"I thought I had a load this morning, but I'd hate to swap packs with you," he said.

The Frenchman flashed him a smile which exposed a row of teeth snow-white against his tan. "Ho! You're stronger as me. I see you plenty tams biffore."

This was indeed agreeable praise, and Pierce showed his pleasure. "Oh no!" he modestly protested. "I'm just getting broken in."

"Look out you don' broke your back," warned the other. "Dis Chilkoot she's bad bizness. She's keel a lot of dese sof' fellers. Dey get seeck in de back. You hear 'bout it?"

"Spinal meningitis. It's partly from exposure."

29

"Dat's him! Don' never carry too moch; don' be in soch hurry."

Phillips laughed at this caution. "Why, we have to hurry," said he. "New people are coming all the time and they'll beat us in if we don't look out."

His comrade shrugged. "Mebbe so; but s'posin' dey do. W'at's de hodds? She's beeg countree; dere's plenty claims."

"Are there, really?" Phillips' eyes brightened. "You're an old-timer; you've been 'inside.' Do you mean there's plenty of gold for all of us?"

"Dere ain't 'nuff gold in all de worl' for some people."

"I mean is Dawson as rich as they say it is?"

"Um—m! I don' know."

"Didn't you get in on the strike?"

"I hear 'bout 'im, but I'm t'inkin' 'bout oder t'ings."

Phillips regarded the speaker curiously. "That's funny. What business are you in?"

"My bizness? Jus' livin'." The Canadian's eyes twinkled. "You don' savvy, eh—? Wal, dat's biccause you're lak dese oder feller—you're in beeg hurry to be reech. Me—?" He shrugged his brawny shoulders and smiled cheerily. "I got plenty tam. I'm loafer. I enjoy myse'f—"

"So do I. For that matter, I'm enjoying myself now. I think this is all perfectly corking, and I'm having the time of my young life. Why, just think, over there"—Pierce waved his hand toward the northward panorama of white peaks and purple valleys—"everything is unknown!" His face lit up with some restless desire which the Frenchman appeared to understand, for he nodded seriously. "Sometimes it scares me a little."

"W'at you scare' 'bout, you?"

"Myself, I suppose. Sometimes I'm afraid I haven't the stuff in me to last."

"Dat's good sign." The speaker slipped his arms into his pack-harness and adjusted the tumpline to his forehead preparatory to rising. "You goin' mak' good 'sourdough' lak me. You goin' love de woods and de hills wen you know 'em. I can tell. Wal, I see you bimeby at W'ite 'Orse."

"White Horse? Is that where you're going?"

"Yes. I'm batteau man; I'm goin' be pilot."

"Isn't that pretty dangerous work? They say those rapids are awful."

"Sure! Everybody scare' to try 'im. W'en I came up dey pay me fifty dollar for tak' one boat t'rough. By gosh! I never mak' so moch money —t'ree hondred dollar a day. I'm reech man now. You lak get reech queeck? I teach you be pilot. Swif' water, beeg noise! Plenty fun in dat!" The Canadian threw back his head and laughed loudly. "W'at you say?"

"I wouldn't mind trying it," Pierce confessed, "but I have no outfit. I'm packing for wages. I'll be along when I get my grub-stake together."

"Good! I go purty queeck now. W'en you come, I tak' you t'rough de cañon free. In one day I teach you be good pilot. You ask for 'Poleon Doret. Remember?"

"I say!" Phillips halted the cheerful giant as he was about to rise. "Do you know, you're the first man who has offered to do me a favor; you're the only one who hasn't tried to hold me back and climb over me. You're the first man I've seen with—with a smile on his face."

The speaker nodded. "I know! It's peety, too. Dese poor feller is scare', lak' you. Dey don' onderstan'. But bimeby, dey get wise; dey learn to he'p de oder feller, dey learn dat a smile will carry a pack or row a boat. You remember dat. A smile and a song, she'll shorten de miles and mak' fren's wid everybody. Don' forget w'at I tell you."

"Thank you, I won't," said Pierce, with a flicker of amusement at the man's brief sermon. This Doret was evidently a sort of backwoods preacher.

"Adieu!" With another flashing smile and a wave of his hand the fellow joined the procession and went on over the crest.

It had been pleasant to exchange even these few friendly words, for of late the habit of silence had been forced upon Pierce Phillips. For weeks now he had toiled among reticent men who regarded him with hostility, who made way for him with reluctance. Haste, labor, strain had numbed and brutalized them; fatigue had rendered them irritable, and the strangeness of their environment had made them both fearful and suspicious. There was no good-fellowship, no consideration on the Chilkoot. This was a race against time, and the stakes went to him who was most ruthless. Phillips had not exaggerated. Until this morning, he had received no faintest word of encouragement, no slightest offer of help. Not once had a hand been outstretched to him, and every inch he had gained had been won at the cost of his own efforts and by reason of his own determination.

He was yet warm with a wordless gratitude at the Frenchman's cheer when a figure came lurching toward him and fell into the space Doret had vacated. This man was quite the opposite of the one who had just left; he was old and he was far from robust. He fell face downward and lay motionless. Impulsively Phillips rose and removed the new-comer's pack.

"That last lift takes it out of you, doesn't it?" he inquired, sympathetically.

After a moment the stranger lifted a thin, colorless face overgrown with a bushy gray beard and began to curse in a gasping voice.

The youth warned him. "You're only tiring yourself, my friend. It's all down-hill from here."

The sufferer regarded Phillips from a pair of hard, smoky-blue eyes in which there lurked both curiosity and surprise.

"I say!" he panted. "You're the first white man I've met in two weeks."

Pierce laughed. "It's the result of a good example. A fellow was decent to me just now."

"This is the kind of work that gives a man dead babies," groaned the stranger. "And these

33

darned trail-hogs!" He ground his teeth vindictively. "'Get out of the way!' 'Hurry up, old man!' 'Step lively, grandpa!' That's what they say. They snap at your heels like coyotes. Hurry? You can't force your luck!" The speaker struggled into a sitting posture and in an apologetic tone explained: "I dassent lay down or I'll get rheumatism. Tough guys—frontiersmen—Pah!" He spat out the exclamation with disgust, then closed his eyes again and sank back against his burden. "Coyotes! That's what they are! They'd rob a carcass, they'd gnaw each other's bones to get through ahead of the ice."

Up out of the chasm below came a slow-moving file of Indian packers. Their eyes were bent upon the ground, and they stepped noiselessly into one another's tracks. The only sound they made came from their creaking pack-leathers. They paused briefly to breathe and to take in their surroundings, then they went on and out of sight.

When they had disappeared the stranger spoke in a changed tone. "Poor devils! I wonder what they've done. And you?" he turned to Phillips. "What sins have you committed?"

"Oh, just the ordinary ones. But I don't look at it that way. This is a sort of a lark for me, and I'm having a great time. It's pretty fierce, I'll admit, but—I wouldn't miss it for anything. Would you?"

"*Would* I? In a minute! You're young, I'm old. I've got rheumatism and—a partner. He can't pack enough grub for his own lunch, and I

have to do it all. He's a Jonah, too—born on
Friday, or something. Last night somebody stole
a sack of our bacon. Sixty pounds, and every
pound had cost me sweat!" Again the speaker
ground his teeth vindictively. "Lord! I'd like
to catch the fellow that did it! I'd take a drop
of blood for every drop of sweat that bacon cost.
Have you lost anything?"

"I haven't anything to lose. I'm packing
for wages to earn money enough to buy an
outfit."

After a brief survey of Phillips' burden, the
stranger said, enviously: "Looks like you wouldn't
have to make more than a trip or two. I wish I
could pack like you do, but I'm stove up. At that,
I'm better than my partner! He couldn't carry
a tune." There was a pause. "He eats good,
though; eats like a hired man and he snores so I
can't sleep. I just lie awake nights and groan at
the joints and listen to him grow old. He can't
even guard our grub-pile."

"The Vigilantes will put a stop to this stealing,"
Pierce ventured.

"Think so? Who's going to keep an eye on
them? Who's going to strangle the Stranglers?
Chances are they're the very ones that are lifting
our grub. I know these citizens' committees."
Whatever the physical limitations of the rheumatic Argonaut, it was plain that his temper was
active and his resentment strong.

Phillips had cooled off by this time; in fact,
the chill breath of the snow-fields had begun to

penetrate his sodden clothing, therefore he prepared to take up his march.

"Going through to Linderman?" queried the other man. "So am I. If you'll wait a second I'll join you. Maybe we can give each other a hand."

The speaker's motive was patent; nevertheless, Phillips obligingly acceded to his request, and a short time later assisted him into his harness, whereupon they set out one behind the other. Pierce's pack was at least double the weight of his companion's, and it gave him a pleasurable thrill to realize that he was one of the strong, one of the elect; he wondered pityingly how long this feeble, middle-aged man could last.

Before they had tramped far, however, he saw that the object of his pity possessed a quality which was lacking in many of the younger, stronger stampeders—namely, a grim determination, a dogged perseverance—no poor substitute, indeed, for youth and brawn. Once the man was in motion he made no complaint, and he managed to maintain a very good pace.

Leaving the crest of Chilkoot behind them, the travelers bore to the right across the snowcap, then followed the ridge above Crater Lake. Every mile or two they rested briefly to relieve their chafed and aching shoulders. They exchanged few words while they were in motion, for one soon learns to conserve his forces on the trail, but when they lay propped against their packs they talked.

Phillips' abundant vigor continued to evoke

36

the elder man's frank admiration; he eyed the
boy approvingly and plied him with questions.
Before they had traveled many miles he had
learned what there was to learn, for Pierce answered his questions frankly and told him about
the sacrifice his family had made in order to send
him North, about the trip itself, about his landing
at Dyea, and all the rest. When he came to the
account of that shell-game the grizzled stranger
smiled.

"I've lived in wide-open countries all my life,"
said the latter, "but this beats anything I ever saw.
Why, the crooks outnumber the honest men and
they're running things to suit themselves. One of
'em tried to lay me. *Me!*" He chuckled as if
the mere idea was fantastically humorous. "Have
you heard about this Soapy Smith? He's the
boss, the bell-cow, and he's made himself mayor
of Skagway. Can you beat it? I'll bet some of
his men are on our Citizens' Committee at Sheep
Camp. They need a lot of killing, they do, and
they'll get it. What did vou do after you lost
your money?"

"I fell in with two brothers and went to packing."

"Went partners with them?'

"No, they—" Phillips' face clouded, he hesitated briefly. "I merely lived with them and
helped them with their outfit from time to time.
We're at Sheep Camp now, and I share their tent
whenever I'm there. I'm about ready to pull out
and go it alone."

"Right! And don't hook up with anybody."
The old man spoke with feeling. "Look at me.
I'm nesting with a dodo—darned gray-whiskered
milliner! He's so ornery I have to hide the ax
every time I see him. I just yearn to put him out
of his misery, but I dassent. Of course he has his
points—everybody has; he's a game old rooster
and he loves me. That's all that saves him."

Phillips was greatly interested to learn that two
men so unfitted for this life, this country, should
have essayed the hardships of the Chilkoot trail.
It amazed him to learn that already most of their
outfit was at Linderman.

"Do you mean to say that you have done all
the packing for yourself and your partner?" he
inquired.

"N—no. Old Jerry totters across with a package of soda-crackers once in a while. You must
have heard him; he creaks like a gate. Of course
he eats up all the crackers before he gets to Linderman and then gorges himself on the heavy grub
that I've lugged over, but in spite of that we've
managed to make pretty good time." After a
moment of meditation he continued: "Say! You
ought to see that old buzzard eat! It's disgusting,
but it's interesting. It ain't so much the expense
that I care about as the work. Old Jerry ought
to be in an institution—some place where they've
got wheel-chairs and a big market-garden. But
he's plumb helpless, so I can't cut him loose and
let him bleach his bones in a strange land. I
haven't got the heart."

They were resting at the Long Lake outlet, some time later, when the old man inquired:

"I presume you've got a camp at Linderman, eh?"

"No. I have some blankets cached there and I sleep out whenever I can't make the round trip."

"Round trip? Round trip in one day? Why, that's thirty miles!"

"Real miles, too. This country makes a man of a fellow. I wouldn't mind sleeping out if I were sure of a hot meal once in a while, but money is no good this side of the Summit, and these people won't even let a stranger use their stoves."

"You can't last long at that, my boy."

Phillips smiled cheerfully. "I don't have to last much longer. I sent a thousand dollars to Dyea this morning by Jim McCaskey, one of the fellows I live with. He's going to put it in Healy & Wilson's safe for me. Now all I've got to do is to earn a ton of grub and get it over before snow flies. It won't take long."

"You can bunk in our tent as long as we're here," the other man volunteered. "If you get across in time you can travel in our boat, too. But I'll have to warn you about Old Jerry. He's ornery. Nature was cruel when she introduced him into a defenseless world."

"That's the second kind offer I've had this morning," Pierce said, thoughtfully. "A big smiling Canadian made the first one. I found him singing on the Summit. He's an 'old-timer' and

39

he's altogether different to us tenderfeet. He made me rather ashamed of myself."

The elderly man nodded. "Most pioneers are big-calibered. I'm a sort of pioneer myself, but that infernal partner of mine has about ruined my disposition. Take it by and large, though, it pays a man to be accommodating."

CHAPTER III

HAVING crossed the high barrens, Phillips and his companion dropped down to timber-line and soon arrived at Linderman, their journey's end. This was perhaps the most feverishly busy camp on the entire thirty-mile Dyea trail, but, unlike the coast towns, there was no merrymaking, no gaiety, no gambling here. Linderman's fever came from overwork, not from overplay. A tent village had sprung up at the head of the lake, and from dawn until dark it echoed to the unceasing sound of ax and hammer, of plane and saw. The air was redolent with the odor of fresh-cut spruce and of boiling tar, for this was the shipyard where an army of Jasons hewed and joined and fitted, each upon a bark of his own making. Half-way down the lake was the Boundary, and a few miles below that again was the customs station with its hateful red-jacketed police. Beyond were uncharted waters, quite as perilous, because quite as unknown, as those traversed by that first band of Argonauts. Deep lakes, dark cañons, roaring rapids lay between Linderman and the land of the Golden Fleece, but the nearer these men approached those dangers the more eagerly they pressed on.

Already the weeding-out process had gone far and the citizens of Linderman were those who had survived it. The weak and the irresolute had disappeared long since; these fellows who labored so mightily to forestall the coming winter were the strong and the fit and the enduring—the kind the North takes to herself.

In spite of his light pack, Phillips' elderly trail-mate was all but spent. He dragged his feet, he stumbled without reason, the lines in his face were deeply set, and his bearded lips had retreated from his teeth in a grin of exhaustion.

"Yonder's the tent," he said, finally, and his tone was eloquent of relief.

In and out among canvas walls and taut guy-ropes the travelers wound their way, emerging at length upon a gravelly beach where vast supplies of provisions were cached. All about, in various stages of construction, were skeletons of skiffs, of scows, and of barges; the ground was spread with a carpet of shavings and sawdust.

Pierce's companion paused; then, after an incredulous stare, he said: "Look! Is that smoke coming from my stovepipe?"

"Why, yes!"

There could be no mistake about it; from the tent in question arose the plain evidence that a lively fire was burning inside.

"Well, I'll be darned!" breathed the elder man. "Somebody's jumped the cache."

"Perhaps your partner—"

"He's in Sheep Camp." The speaker laboriously loosened his pack and let it fall, then with stiff, clumsy fingers he undid the top buttons of his vest and, to Pierce's amazement, produced a large-calibered revolver, which he mechanically cocked and uncocked several times, the while his eyes remained hypnotically fixed upon the telltale streamer of smoke. Not only did his action appear to be totally uncalled for, but he himself had undergone a startling transformation and Phillips was impelled to remonstrate.

"Here! What the deuce—?" he began.

"Listen to me!" The old man spoke in a queer, suppressed tone, and his eyes, when he turned them upon his fellow-packer, were even smokier than usual. "Somebody's up to a little thievin', most likely, and it looks like I had 'em red-handed. I've been layin' for this!"

Pierce divested himself of his pack-harness, then said, simply, "If that's the case, I'll give you a hand."

"Better stand back," the other cautioned him. "I don't need any help—this is my line." The man's fatigue had fallen from him; of a sudden he had become surprisingly alert and forceful. He stole forward, making as little noise as possible, and Phillips followed at his back. They came to a pause within arm's-length of the tent flaps, which they noted were securely tied.

"Hello inside!" The owner spoke suddenly and with his free hand he jerked at one of the knots.

There came an answering exclamation, a move-

ment; then the flaps were seized and firmly
held.

"You can't come in!" cried a voice.

"Let go! Quick!" The old man's voice was
harsh.

"You'll have to wait a minute. I'm undressed."

Phillips retreated a step, as did the other man;
they stared at each other.

"A woman!" Pierce breathed.

"Lord!" The owner of the premises slowly,
reluctantly sheathed his weapon under his left
arm.

"I invited myself in," the voice explained—it
was a deep-pitched contralto voice. "I was wet
and nobody offered to let me dry out, so I took
possession of the first empty tent I came to.
Is it yours?"

"It is—half of it. I'm mighty tired and I ain't
particular how you look, so hurry up." As the
two men returned for their loads the speaker went
on, irritably. "She's got her nerve! I s'pose
she's one of these actresses. There's a bunch of
'em on the trail. Actresses!" He snorted derisively. "I bet she smells of cologne, and, gosh!
how I hate it!"

When he and Pierce returned they were admitted promptly enough, and any lingering suspicions of the trespasser's intent were instantly
dissipated. The woman was clad in a short,
damp underskirt which fell about to her knees;
she had drawn on the only dry article of apparel
in sight, a man's sweater jacket; she had thrust

her bare feet into a pair of beaded moccasins;
on a line attached to the ridgepole over her head
sundry outer garments were steaming. Phillips'
first thought was that this woman possessed the
fairest, the whitest, skin he had ever seen; it was
like milk. But his first impressions were confused, for embarrassment followed quickly upon
his entrance and he felt an impulse to withdraw.
The trespasser was not at all the sort of person he
had expected to find, and her complete self-
possession at the intrusion, her dignified greeting,
left him not a little chagrined at his rudeness.
She eyed both men coolly from a pair of ice-blue
eyes—eyes that bespoke her nationality quite as
plainly as did her features, her dazzling com-
plexion, and her head of fine, straight flaxen hair.
She was Scandinavian, she was a Norsewoman;
that much was instantly apparent. She appeared
to derive a certain malicious pleasure now from
the consternation her appearance evoked; there
was a hint of contempt, of defiance, in her smile.
In a voice so low-pitched that its quality alone
saved it from masculinity, she said:

"Pray don't be distressed; you merely startled
me, that's all. My Indians managed to get hold
of some hootch at Tagish and upset our canoe
just below here. It was windy and of course
they couldn't swim—none of them can, you know
—so I had hard work to save them. I've already
explained how I happened to select this particular '
refuge. Your neighbors—" her lip curled disdainfully, then she shrugged. "Well, I never got

45

such a reception as they gave me, but I suppose they're cheechakos. I'll be off for Dyea early in the morning. If you can put me up for the night I'll pay you well."

During this speech, delivered in a matter-of-fact, business-like tone, the owner of the tent had managed to overcome his first surprise; he removed his hat now and began with an effort:

"I'm a bad hand at begging pardons, miss, but you see I've been suffering the pangs of bereavement lately over some dear, departed grub. I thought you were a thief and I looked forward to the pleasure of seeing you dance. I apologize. Would you mind telling me where you came from?"

"From Dawson." There was a silence the while the flaxen-haired woman eyed her interrogator less disdainfully. "Yes, by poling-boat and birch-bark. I'm not fleeing the law; I'm not a cache-robber."

"You're—all alone?"

The woman nodded. "Can you stow me away for the night? You may name your own price."

"The price won't cripple you. I'm sorry there ain't some more women here at Linderman, but —there ain't. We had one—a doctor's wife, but she's gone."

"I met her at Lake Marsh."

"We've a lot more coming, but they're not here. My name is Linton. The more-or-less Christian prefix thereto is Tom. I've got a partner named Jerry. Put the two together, and drink hearty.

46

This young man is Mr.—" The speaker turned questioningly upon Phillips, who made himself known. "I'm a family man. Mr. Phillips is a—well, he's a good packer. That's all I know about him. I'm safe and sane, but he's about the right age to propose marriage to you as soon as he gets his breath. A pretty woman in this country has to expect that, as you probably know."

The woman smiled and shook hands with both men, exchanging a grip as firm and as strong as theirs. "I am the Countess Courteau," said she.

"The — which?" Mr. Linton queried, with a start.

The Countess laughed frankly. "It is French, but I'm a Dane. I think my husband bought the title—they're cheap in his country. He was a poor sort of count, and I'm a poor sort of countess. But I'm a good cook—a very good cook indeed—and if you'll excuse my looks and permit me to wear your sweater I'll prepare supper."

Linton's eyes twinkled as he said, "I've never et with the nobility and I don't know as I'd like their diet, for a steady thing, but—the baking-powder is in that box and we fry with bacon grease."

Wood and water were handy, the Countess Courteau had a quick and capable way, therefore supper was not long delayed. The tent was not equipped for housekeeping, hence the diners held their plates in their laps and either harpooned their food from the frying-pan or ladled it from tin cans, but even so it had a flavor to-night so

47

unaccustomed, so different, that both men grasped the poignant fact that the culinary art is mysteriously wedded to female hands. Mr. Linton voiced this thought in his own manner.

"If a countess cooks like this," he observed, "I'd sure love to board with a duke." Later, while the dishes were being washed and when his visitor had shown no intention of explaining her presence in further detail, he said, whimsically: "See here, ma'am, our young friend has been watching you like he was afraid you'd disappear before he gets an eyeful, and it's plain to be seen that he's devoured by curiosity. As for me, I'm totally lacking in that miserable trait, and I abhor it in others; but all the same, if you don't see fit to tell us pretty quick how you came to pole up from Dawson and what in Heaven's name a woman like you is doing here, a lone and without benefit of chaperon, I shall pass away in dreadful agony."

"It's very simple," the Countess told him. "I have important business 'outside.' I couldn't go down the river, for the Yukon is low, the steamers are aground on the flats, and connections at St. Michael's are uncertain at best. Naturally I came up against the stream. I've been working 'up-stream' all my life." She flashed him a smile at this latter statement. "As for a chaperon—I've never felt the need of one. Do you think they're necessary in this country?"

"Does your husband, Count—"

"My husband doesn't count. That's the

trouble." The speaker laughed again and without the faintest trace of embarrassment. "He has been out of the picture for years." She turned to Phillips and inquired, abruptly, "What is the packing price to Sheep Camp?"

"Fifty cents a pound, coming this way. Going back it is nothing," he told her, gallantly.

"I haven't much to carry, but if you'll take it I'll pay you the regular price. I'd like to leave at daylight."

"You seem to be in a rush," Mr. Linton hazarded, mildly.

"I am. Now, then, if you don't mind I'll turn in, for I must be in Dyea to-morrow night."

Pierce Phillips had said little during the meal or thereafter, to be sure, nevertheless, he had thought much. He had indeed used his eyes to good purpose, and now he regretted exceedingly that the evening promised to be so short. The more he saw of this unconventional countess the more she intrigued his interest. She was the most unusual woman he had ever met and he was eager to learn all about her. His knowledge of women was peculiarly elemental; his acquaintance with the sex was extremely limited. Those he had known in his home town were one kind, a familiar kind; those he had encountered since leaving home were, for the most part, of a totally different class and of a type that awoke his disapproval. To a youth of his training and of his worldly experience the *genus* woman is divided into two species—old women and young women.

49

The former are interesting only in ·a motherly way, and demand nothing more than abstract courtesy. They do not matter. The latter, on the contrary, separate themselves again into two families or suborders—viz., good women and bad women. The demarcation between the two branches of the suborder is distinct; there is nothing common to the two. Good women are good through and through—bad ones are likewise thoroughly bad. There are no intermediate types, no troublesome variations, no hybrids nor crosses.

The Countess Courteau, it seemed to him, was a unique specimen and extremely hard to classify, in that she was neither old nor young—or, what was even more puzzling, in that she was both. In years she was not far advanced—little older than he, in fact—but in experience, in wisdom, in self-reliance she was vastly his superior; and experience, he believed, is what makes women old. As to the family, the suborder to which she belonged, he was at an utter loss to decide. For instance, she accepted her present situation with a *sang-froid* equaling that of a camp harpy, a few of whom Pierce had seen; then, too, she was, or had been, married to a no-account foreigner to whom she referred with a calloused and most unwifely flippancy; moreover, she bore herself with a freedom, a boldness, quite irreconcilable to the modesty of so-called "good women." Those facts were enough to classify her definitely, and yet despite them she was anything but

50

common, and it would have taken rare courage indeed to transgress that indefinable barrier of decorum with which she managed to surround herself. There was something about her as cold and as pure as blue ice, and she gave the same impression of crystal clarity. All in all, hers was a baffling personality and Phillips fell asleep with the riddle of it unanswered. He awoke in the morning with it still upon his mind.

The Countess Courteau had been first to arise; she was fully dressed and the sheet-iron stove was glowing when her companions roused themselves. By the time they had returned from the lake she had breakfast ready.

"Old Jerry is going to be awful sore at missing this court function," Mr. Linton told her during the meal. "He's a great ladies' man, Old Jerry is."

"Perhaps I shall meet him."

"You wouldn't like him if you did; nobody likes him, except me, and I hate him." Linton sighed. "He's a handicap to a young man like me."

"Why don't you send him home?"

"Home? Old Jerry would die before he'd turn back. He'd lift his muzzle and bay at the very idea until some stranger terminated him. Well, he's my cross; I s'pose I've got to bear him."

"Who is Mr. Linton?" the Countess inquired, as she and Pierce left the village behind them.

"Just an ordinary stampeder, like the rest of us, I think."

"He's more than that. He's the kind who'll go through and make good. I dare say his partner is just like him."

Phillips approved of the Countess Courteau this morning even more thoroughly than he had on the evening previous, and they had not walked far before he realized that as a traveler she was the equal of him or of any man. She was lithe and strong and light of foot; the way she covered ground awoke his sincere admiration. She did not trouble to talk much and she dispensed with small talk in others; she appeared to be absorbed in her own affairs, and only when they rested did she engage in conversation. The more Phillips studied her and the better acquainted he became with her the larger proportions did she assume. Not only was she completely mistress of herself, but she had a forceful, compelling way with others; there was a natural air of authority about her, and she managed in some subtle manner to invest herself and her words with importance. She was quite remarkable.

Now, the trail breeds its own peculiar intimacy; although the two talked little, they nevertheless got to know each other quite well, and when they reached the Summit, about midday, Phillips felt a keen regret that their journey was so near its end.

A mist was drifting up from the sea; it obscured the valley below and clung to the peaks like ragged garments. Up and out of this fog came the interminable procession of burden-bearers. The Countess paused to observe them

52

and to survey the accumulation of stores which crowned the watershed.

"I didn't dream so many were coming," said she.

"It's getting worse daily," Pierce told her. "Dyea is jammed, and so is Skagway. The trails are alive with men."

"How many do you think will come?"

"There's no telling. Twenty, thirty, fifty thousand, perhaps. About half of them turn back when they see the Chilkoot."

"And the rest will wish they had. It's a hard country; not one in a hundred will prosper."

They picked their way down the drunken descent to the Scales, then breasted the sluggish human current to Sheep Camp.

A group of men were reading a notice newly posted upon the wall of the log building which served as restaurant and hotel, and after scanning it Pierce explained:

"It's another call for a miners' meeting. We're having quite a time with cache-robbers. If we catch them we'll hang them."

The Countess nodded. "Right! They deserve it. You know we don't have any stealing on the 'inside.' Now, then, I'll say good-by." She paid Pierce and extended her hand to him. "Thank you for helping me across. I'll be in Dyea by dark."

"I hope we'll meet again," he said, with a slight flush.

The woman favored him with one of her generous, friendly smiles. "I hope so, too. You're a nice boy. I like you." Then she stepped into the building and was gone.

"A nice boy!" Phillips was pained. A boy! And he the sturdiest packer on the pass, with perhaps one exception! That was hardly just to him. If they did meet again—and he vowed they would—he'd show her he was more than a boy. He experienced a keen desire to appear well in her eyes, to appear mature and forceful. He asked himself what kind of man Count Courteau could be; he wondered if he, Pierce Phillips, could fall in love with such a woman as this, an older woman, a woman who had been married. It would be queer to marry a countess, he reflected.

As he walked toward his temporary home he beheld quite a gathering of citizens, and paused long enough to note that they were being harangued by the confidence-man who had first initiated him into the subtleties of the three-shell game. Mr. Broad had climbed upon a raised tent platform and was presenting an earnest argument against capital punishment. Two strangers upon the fringe of the crowd were talking, and Pierce heard one of them say:

"Of course he wants the law to take its course, inasmuch as there isn't any law. He's one of the gang."

"The surest way to flush a covey of crooks is to whistle for old Judge Lynch," the other man agreed. "Listen to him!"

"Have they caught the cache-robbers?" **Phillips** made bold to inquire.

"No, and they won't catch them, with fellows like that on the committee. The crooks hang together and we don't. If I had my way that's just what they'd do—hang together. I'd start in by bending a limb over that rascal."

Phillips had attended several of these indignation meetings and, remembering that all of them had proved purposeless, he went on toward the McCaskey brothers' tent. He and the McCaskeys were not the closest of friends, in spite of the fact that they had done him a favor—a favor, by the way. for which he had paid many times over—nevertheless, they were his most intimate acquaintances and he felt an urgent desire to tell them about his unusual experience. His desire to talk about the Countess Courteau was irresistible.

But when he entered the tent his greeting fell flat, for Joe, the elder McCaskey, addressed him sharply, almost accusingly:

"Say, it's about time you showed up!"

"What's the matter?" Pierce saw that the other brother was stretched out in his blankets and that his head was bandaged. "Hello!" he cried. "What ails Jim? Is he sick?"

"Sick? Worse than sick," Joe grumbled. "That money of yours is to blame for it. It's a wonder he isn't dead."

"My money? How?" Phillips was both mystified and alarmed.

55

Jim raised himself in his blankets and said, irritably: "After this you can run your own pay-car, kid. I'm through, d'you hear?"

"Speak out. What's wrong?"

"Jim was stuck up, that's what's wrong. That's enough, isn't it? They bent a six-gun over his head and grabbed your coin. He's got a dent in his crust the size of a saucer!"

Phillips' face whitened slowly. "My money! Robbed!" he gasped. "*Jim!* Who did it? How could you let them?"

The younger McCaskey fell back weakly; he waved a feeble gesture at his brother. "Joe 'll tell you. I'm dizzy; my head ain't right yet."

"A stranger stopped him—asked him something or other—and another guy flattened him from behind. That's all he remembers. When he came to he found he'd been frisked. He was still dippy when he got home, so I put him to bed. He got up and moved around a bit this morning, but he's wrong in his head."

Phillips seated himself upon a candle-box. "Robbed!" he exclaimed, weakly. "Broke—again! Gee! That was hard money! It was the first I ever earned!"

Joe McCaskey's dark face was doubly unpleasant as he frowned down upon the youth. "Thinking about nothing except your coin, eh? Why don't you think about Jim? He did you a favor and 'most lost his life."

"Oh, I'm sorry—of course!" Phillips rose heavily and crossed to the bed. "I didn't mean to appear selfish. I don't blame you, Jim. I'll get a doctor for you, then you must describe the hold-ups. Give me a hint who they are and I'll go after them."

The younger brother rolled his head in negation and mumbled, sullenly: "I'm all right. I don't want a doctor."

Joe explained for him: "He never saw the fellows before and he don't seem to remember much about them. That's natural enough. Your money's gone clean, kid, and a yelp won't get you anything. The crooks are organized and if you set up a holler they'll get all of us. They'll alibi anybody you accuse—it's no trick to alibi a pal—"

"Isn't it?" The question was uttered unexpectedly; it came from the front of the tent and startled the occupants thereof, who turned to behold a stranger just entering their premises. He was an elderly man; he possessed a quick, shrewd eye; he had poked the tent flap aside with the barrel of a Colt's revolver. Through the door-opening could be seen other faces and the bodies of other men who had likewise stolen up unheard. During the moment of amazement following his first words these other men crowded in behind him.

"Maybe it 'll be more of a trick than you figure on." The stranger's gray mustache lifted in a grin that was not at all friendly.

"What the blazes—?" Joe McCaskey exploded.

"Go easy!" the intruder cautioned him. "We've been laying around, waiting for your pal to get back." With a movement of the revolver muzzle he indicated Phillips. "Now then, stretch! On your toes and reach high. You there, get up!" He addressed himself to Jim, who rose from his bed and thrust his hands over his bandaged head. "That's nice!" the stranger nodded approvingly. "Now don't startle me; don't make any quick moves or I may tremble this gun off— she's easy on the trigger." To his friends he called, "Come in, gentlemen; they're gentle."

There were four of the latter; they appeared to be substantial men, men of determination. All were armed.

Pierce Phillips' amazement gave way to indignation. "What is this, an arrest or a hold-up?" he inquired.

"It's right smart of both," the leader of the posse drawled, in a voice which betrayed the fact that he hailed from somewhere in the far Southwest. "We're in quest of a bag of rice—a bag with a rip in it and 'W. K.' on the side. While I slap your pockets, just to see if you're ironed, these gentlemen are goin' to look over your outfit."

"This is an outrage!" Jim McCaskey complained. "I'm just getting over one stick-up. I'm a sick man."

"Sure!" his brother exclaimed, furiously. "You're a pack of fools! What d'you want, anyhow?"

"We want you to shut up! See that you do."
The old man's eyes snapped. "If you've got
to say something, tell us how there happens to
be a trail of rice from this man's cache"—he indicated one of his companions—"right up to your
tent."

The McCaskeys exchanged glances. Phillips
turned a startled face upon them.

"It isn't much of a trail, but it's enough to
follow."

For a few moments nothing was said, and
meanwhile the search of the tent went on. When
Pierce could no longer remain silent he broke
out:

"There's some mistake. These boys packed
this grub from Dyea and I helped with some
of it."

"Aren't you partners?" some one inquired.

Joe McCaskey answered this question. "No.
He landed broke. We felt sorry for him and
took him in."

Joe was interrupted by an exclamation from
one of the searchers. "Here it is!" said the man.
He had unearthed a bulging canvas sack which
he flung down for inspection. "There's my
mark, 'W. K.,' and there's the rip. I knew we
had 'em right!"

After a brief examination the leader of the posse
turned to his prisoners, whose hands were still
held high, saying:

"Anything you can think of in the way of explanations you'd better save for the miners'

meeting. It's waitin' to welcome you. We'll put a guard over this plunder till the rest of it is identified. Now, then, fall in line and don't crowd. After you, gentlemen."

Pierce Phillips realized that it was useless to argue, for his words would not be listened to, therefore he followed the McCaskeys out into the open air. The odium of this accusation was hard to bear; he bitterly resented his situation and something told him he would have to fight to clear himself; nevertheless, he was not seriously concerned over the outcome. Public feeling was high, to be sure; the men of Sheep Camp were in a dangerous frame of mind and their actions were liable to be hasty, ill-considered—their verdict was apt to be fantastic—but, secure in the knowledge of his innocence, Pierce felt no apprehension. Rather he experienced a thrill of excitement at the *contretemps* and at the ordeal which he knew was forthcoming.

The Countess Courteau had called him a boy. This wasn't a boy's business; this was a real man-sized adventure.

"Gee! What a day this has been!" he said to himself.

CHAPTER IV

THE story of the first trial at Sheep Camp is an old one, but it differs with every telling. In the hectic hurry of that gold-rush many incidents were soon forgotten and such salient facts as did survive were deeply colored, for those were colorful days. That trial marked an epoch in early Yukon history, for, although its true significance was unsensed at the time, it really signalized the dawn of common honesty on the Chilkoot and the Chilkat trails, and it was the first move taken toward the disruption of organized outlawry—a bitter fight, by the way, which ended only in the tragic death of Soapy Smith and the flight of his notorious henchmen. Although the circumstances of the Sheep Camp demonstration now seem shocking, they did not seem so at the time, and they served a larger purpose than was at first apparent; not only did theft become an unprofitable and an uninteresting occupation thereafter, but also the men who shaped a code and drew first blood in defense of it experienced a beneficial reaction and learned to fit the punishment to the crime—no easy lesson to learn where life runs hot and where might is right.

The meeting was in session and it had been harangued into a dangerous frame of mind when Pierce Phillips and the two McCaskeys were led before it. A statement by the leader of the posse, corroborated by the owner of the missing sack of rice, roused the audience to a fury. Even while these stories were being told there came other men who had identified property of theirs among the provision piles inside the McCaskey tent, and when they, too, had made their reports the crowd began to mill; there were demands for a speedy trial and a swift vengeance.

These demands found loudest echo among the outlaw element for which Lucky Broad had acted as mouthpiece. Although the members of that band were unknown—as a matter of fact, no man knew his neighbor—nevertheless it was plain that there was an organization of crooks and that a strong bond of understanding existed between them. Now, inasmuch as the eye of suspicion had been turned away from them, now that a herring had been dragged across the trail, their obstructive tactics ended and they, too, became noisy in their clamor that justice be done.

The meeting was quickly organized along formal lines and a committee of three was appointed to conduct the hearing. The chairman of this committee—he constituted himself chairman by virtue of the fact that he was first nominated—made a ringing speech in which he praised his honesty, his fairness, and his knowledge of the law. He complimented the miners for their acumen in selecting for such a position of responsibility a man of his distinguished qualifications. It was plain that he believed they had chosen wisely. Then, having inquired the names of his two committeemen, he likewise commended them in glowing terms, although of course he could not praise them quite as unstintedly as he had praised himself. Still, he spoke well of them and concluded by stating that so long as affairs were left in his hands justice would be safeguarded and the rights of this miserable, cringing trio of thieves would be protected, albeit killing, in his judgment, was too mild a punishment for people of their caliber.

"Hear! Hear!" yelled the mob.

Pierce Phillips listened to this speech with a keenly personal and yet a peculiarly detached interest. The situation struck him as unreal, grotesque, and the whole procedure as futile. Under other circumstances it would have been grimly amusing; now he was uncomfortably aware that it was anything but that. There was no law whatever in the land save the will of these men; in their hands lay life or death, exoneration or infamy. He searched the faces round about him, but could find signs neither of friendship nor of sympathy. This done, he looked everywhere for a glimpse of a woman's straw-colored hair and was relieved to discover that the Countess Courteau was not in the audience. Doubtless she had left for Dyea and was already some distance down the trail. He breathed easier, for he did not wish her to witness his humiliation, and her presence would have merely added to his embarrassment.

The prosecution's case was quickly made, and it was a strong one. Even yet the damning trickle of rice grains could be traced through the moss and mire directly to the door of the prisoners' tent, and the original package, identified positively by its owner, was put in evidence. This in itself was enough; testimony from the other men who had likewise recovered merchandise they had missed and mourned merely strengthened the case and further inflamed the minds of the citizens.

From the first there had never been a doubt in Phillips' mind that the McCaskeys were guilty. The facts offered in evidence served only to explain certain things which had puzzled him at various times; nevertheless, his indignation and his contempt for them were tempered with regrets, for he could not but remember that they had befriended him. It was of course imperative that he establish his own innocence, but he determined that in so doing he would prejudice their case as little as possible. That was no more than the merest loyalty.

When it came time to hear the defense, the McCaskeys stared at Pierce coolly; therefore he climbed to the tent platform and faced his accusers.

He made known his name, his birthplace, the ship which had borne him north. He told how he had landed at Dyea, how he had lost his last dollar at the gambling-table, how he had appealed to the McCaskey boys, and how they had given him shelter. That chance association, he took pains to explain, had continued, but had never ripened into anything more, anything closer; it was in no wise a partnership; he had nothing to do with them and they had nothing to do with him. Inasmuch as the rice had been stolen during the previous night, he argued that he could have had no hand in the theft, for he had spent the night in Linderman, which fact he offered to prove by two witnesses.

"Produce them," ordered the chairman.

"One of them is still at Linderman, the other was here in Sheep Camp an hour ago. She has probably started for Dyea by this time."

"A woman?"

"Yes, sir. I brought her across."

"What is her name?"

Phillips hesitated. "The Countess Courteau," said he. There was a murmur of interest; the members of the committee conferred with one an other.

"Do you mean to tell us that you've got a titled witness?" the self-appointed spokesman inquired. His face wore a smile of disbelief; when the prisoner flushed and nodded he called out over the heads of the crowd:

"Countess Courteau!" There was no answer. "Do any of you gentlemen know the Countess Courteau?" he inquired.

His question was greeted by a general laugh.

"Don't let him kid you," cried a derisive voice.

"Never heard of her, but I met four kings last night," yelled another.

"Call the Marquis of Queensberry," shouted still a third.

"Countess Courteau!" repeated the chairman, using his hands for a megaphone.

The cry was taken up by other throats. "Countess Courteau! Countess Courteau!" they mocked. "Come, Countess! Nice Countess! Pretty Countess!" There was a ribald note to this mockery which caused Phillips' eyes to glow.

"She and the count have just left the palace. Let's get along with the hangin'," one shrill voice demanded.

"You won't hang me!" Phillips retorted, angrily.

"Be not so sure," taunted the acting judge. "Inasmuch as your countess appears to be constituted of that thin fabric of which dreams are made; inasmuch as there is no such animal—"

"Hol' up!" came a peremptory challenge. "M'sieu Jodge!" It was the big French Canadian whom Pierce had met on the crest of the divide; he came forward now, pushing his resistless way through the audience. "W'at for you say dere ain't nobody by dat name, eh?" He turned his back to the committee and addressed the meeting. "W'at for you hack lak dis, anyhow? By gosh! I heard 'bout dis lady! She's ol'-timer lak me."

"Well, trot her out! Where is she?"

"She's on her way to Dyea," Pierce insisted. "She can't be far—"

66

'Poleon Doret was angry. "I don' listen to no woman be joke 'bout, you hear? Dis boy spik true. He was in Linderman las' night, for I seen him on top of Chilkoot yesterday myse'f, wit' pack on his back so beeg as a barn."

"Do you know the accused?" queried the spokesman.

'Poleon turned with a shrug. "Non! No! But—yes, I know him li'l bit. Anybody can tell he's hones' boy. By Gar! She's strong feller, too—pack lak hell!"

Pierce Phillips was grateful for this evidence of faith, inconclusive as it was in point of law. He was sorry, therefore, to see the Frenchman, after replying shortly, impatiently, to several senseless cross-questions, force his way out of the crowd and disappear, shaking his head and muttering in manifest disgust at the temper of his townsmen.

But although one friend had gone, another took his place—a champion, by the way, whom Pierce would never have suspected of being such. Profiting by the break in the proceedings, Lucky Broad spoke up.

"Frenchy was right—this kid's on the square," he declared. "I'm the gentleman who gathered his wheat at Dyea—he fairly fed it to me, like he said—so I guess I'm acquainted with him. We're all assembled up to mete out justice, and justice is going to be met, but, say! a sucker like this boy wouldn't *know* enough to steal!"

It was doubtful if this witness, well-intentioned

as he was, carried conviction, for, although his followers took their cue from him and applauded loudly, their very manifestations of faith aroused suspicion among the honest men present.

One of the latter, a red-faced, square-shouldered person, thrust a determined countenance close to Broad's and cried, angrily: "Is that so? Well, I'm for hangin' anybody you boost!"

This sentiment met with such instantaneous second that the confidence-man withdrew precipitately. "Have it your own way," he gave in, with an airy gesture. "But take it from me you're a bunch of boobs. Hangin' ain't a nice game, and the guy that hollers loudest for it is usually the one that needs it worst."

It took some effort on the part of the chairman to bring the meeting to order so that the hearing could be resumed.

Phillips went on with his story and told of spending the night with Tom Linton, then of his return to Sheep Camp to learn that he had been robbed of all his savings. Corroboration of this misfortune he left to the oral testimony of the two brothers McCaskey and to the circumstantial evidence of Jim's bandaged head.

While it seemed to him that he had given a simple, straightforward account of himself which would establish his innocence, so far, at least, as it applied to the theft of the sack of rice, he was uncomfortably aware that evidence of systematic pilfering had been introduced and that evidence he had not met except indirectly. His proof seemed good so far as it went, but it did not go far, and he believed it all too likely that his hearers still considered him an accomplice, at the best.

Jim McCaskey was next called and Pierce made way for him. The younger brother made a poor start, but he warmed up to his own defense, gaining confidence and ease as he talked.

In the first place, both he and Joe were innocent of this outrageous charge—as innocent as unborn babes—and this air of suspicion was like to smother them. This Jim declared upon his honor. The evidence was strong, he admitted, but it was purely circumstantial, and he proposed to explain it away. He proposed to tell the truth, the whole truth, and nothing but the truth; letting the blame fall where it would and leaving the verdict entirely up to his hearers. Joe would substantiate his every statement.

It was quite true that he and his brother had been Good Samaritans; they had opened their doors and had taken in this young man when he was hungry and homeless, but that was their habit. They had fed him, they had shared their blankets with him, they had helped him in a thousand ways, not without serious inconvenience to themselves. Why, only on the day before the speaker himself had volunteered to take the young man's earnings to Dyea for safekeeping, thereby letting himself in for an unmerciful mauling, and suffering a semi-fractured skull, the marks of which would doubtless stay with him for a long time.

Phillips had left camp early the previous morning, to be sure, and he had not come home until an hour or two ago, but where he had gone, how he had occupied himself during his absence, where he had spent the night, of course the speaker had no way of knowing. Phillips was often absent at night; he came and he went at all hours, and neither Joe nor the witness ever questioned him, believing his statements that he was packing for hire. Neither his brother nor he had ever seen that sack of rice until it was uncovered by the posse, and as for the other plunder, it was all part and parcel of an outfit which their guest had been assembling for some time. They supposed, of course, that he had bought it, bit by bit, with his earnings.

Pierce Phillips listened in speechless amazement, scarcely believing his own ears, the while Jim McCaskey struck the fetters from his own and his brother's limbs and placed them upon his. It seemed impossible that such a story could carry weight, but from all indications it did. When Joe McCaskey took the center of the stage and glibly corroborated his brother's statements Pierce interrupted him savagely, only to be warned that he'd better be silent.

"That's all we've got to say," concluded the elder of the precious pair when he had finished. "You can judge for yourselves who did the stealing. Jim and I've got all the grub we want; this fellow hasn't any."

"Have you anything to say for yourself?" The chairman addressed himself to Phillips.

"I have." Pierce again took the stand. "You're making a great mistake," he said, earnestly. "These men have lied; they're trying to save themselves at my expense. I've told you everything, now I demand that you wait to hear the Countess Courteau or Mr. Linton. They'll prove where I spent last night, at least."

"Mr. Chairman!" A stranger claimed general attention. "I've listened to the evidence and it's strong enough for me. The grub didn't get up and walk away by itself; somebody took it. Grub is more than grub in this country; it's more than money; it's a man's life, that's what it is. Now, then, the McCaskeys had an outfit when they landed; they didn't need to steal; but this fellow, this dirty ingrate, he hadn't a pound. I don't swallow his countess story and I don't care a hoot where he was last night. Let's decide first what punishment a thief gets, then let's give it to him."

"Hear! Hear!" came the cry.

"Hanging is good enough for thieves!" shouted the choleric individual who had so pointedly made known his distrust of Lucky Broad. "I say stretch 'em."

"Right! Let's make an example!"

"Hang him!" There rose a hoarse chorus of assent to this suggestion, whereupon the chairman stepped forward.

"All those in favor of hanging—" he began. But again he was interrupted by 'Poleon Doret, who once more bored his way into the crowd, crying:

"Wait! I got somet'ing to say." He was breathing heavily, as if from a considerable exertion; perspiration stood upon his face; his eyes were flashing. He vaulted lightly to the platform, then flung out his long arms, crying: "You hack lak crazee mans. W'at talk is dis 'bout hangin'? You ain't wild hanimals!"

The red-faced advocate of the noose who had spoken a moment before answered him in a loud voice:

"I paid hard money for my grub and I've packed every pound of it on my back. You can take a man's life by stealing his matches the same as by shooting him. I want to see thieves on the end of a rope."

Doret bent down to him. "All right, m'sieu! You want blood; we give it to you. Bring on dat rope. I'll put it on dis boy's neck if you'll do de pullin'. For me, I ain't care 'bout killin' nobody, but you—you're brave man. You hang on tight w'ile dis boy he keeck, an' strangle, an' grow black in de face. It's goin' mak you feel good all over!"

"Rats! *I* won't do the trick, but—"

"Somebody mus' do de pullin'." 'Poleon grinned. "He ain't goin' hang himse'f. Mebbe you got pardner w'at lak give you hand, eh?" He raised his head and laughed at the crowd. "Messieurs, you see how 'tis. It tak' brave man to hang a feller lak dis. Some day policeman's goin' come along an' say: 'By Gar, I been lookin' for you long tam. De new jodge at Dyea he tell me you murder a boy at Sheep Camp. S'pose you come wit' me an' do little hangin' yourse'f.' No, messieurs! We ain't Hinjuns; we're good sensible peoples, eh?"

A member of the committee, one who had hitherto acted a passive part, now stepped forward.

"Frenchy has put it right," he acknowledged. "We'll have courts in this country some day, and we'll have to answer to them. Miners' law is all right, so far as it goes, but I won't be a party to a murder. That's what this would be, murder. If you're going to talk hanging, you can take me off of your committee."

Lucky Broad uttered a yelp of encouragement. "Hangin' sounds better 'n it feels," he declared. "Think it over, you family men. When you make your stakes and go home, little Johnny's going to climb onto your knee and say, 'Papa, tell me why you hung that man at Sheep Camp,' and you'll say, 'Why, son, we hung him because he stole a sack of rice.' Like hell you will!"

'Poleon Doret regained public attention by saying, "Messieurs, I got s'prise for you." He lifted himself to his toes and called loudly over the heads of the assembled citizens, "Dis way, madame." From the direction he was looking there came a swiftly moving figure, the figure of a tall woman with straw-gold hair. Men gave way before her. She hurried straight to the tent platform, where 'Poleon leaned down, took her beneath her arms, and swung her lightly up beside

73

him. "Madame de Countess Courteau," he announced; then with a flourish he swept off his knitted cap and bowed to the new-comer. To those beneath him he cried, sharply, "'Tak' off dose hat or I knock dem off."

The Countess, too, had evidently made haste, for she was breathing deeply. She flashed a smile at Pierce Phillips, then said, so that all could hear: .

"I understand you accuse this young man of stealing something last night. Well, he was in Linderman. He brought me over to-day."

"We don't care so much about the rice; this stealing has been going on for a long time," a bystander explained.

"True. But the rice was stolen last night, wasn't it? The man who stole it probably stole the other stuff."

"They're two to one," Pierce told her. "They're trying to saw it off on me."

The Countess turned and stared at the McCaskey brothers, who met her look defiantly. "Bah!" she exclaimed. "I haven't heard the evidence, for I was on my way to Dyea when Mr.—" She glanced inquiringly at 'Poleon.

He bowed again. "Doret," said he. "Napoleon Doret."

"—when Mr. Doret overtook me, but I'm willing to wager my life that this boy isn't a thief." Again she smiled at Phillips, and he experienced a tumult of conflicting emotions. Never had he seen a woman like this one, who radiated such

74

strength, such confidence, such power. She stood there like a goddess, a splendid creature fashioned of snow and gold; she dominated the assembly. He was embarrassed that she should find him in this predicament, shamed that she should be forced to come to his assistance; nevertheless, he was thrilled at her ready response.

It was the elder McCaskey who next claimed attention. "We've made our spiel," he began; then he launched into a repetition of his former statement of facts.

The Countess stepped to Pierce's side, inquiring, quickly, "What is this, a joke?"

"I thought so at first, but it looks as if I'll be cutting figure eights on the end of a tent-rope."

"What makes them think you did the stealing?"

"The McCaskeys swear I did. You see, I had no outfit of my own—"

"Are you broke?"

"N—no! I wasn't yesterday. I am now." In a few sentences Pierce made known the facts of his recent loss, and pointed to Jim McCaskey's bandaged head.

When the elder brother had concluded, the Countess again addressed the meeting. "You men take it for granted that Phillips did the stealing because he needed grub," said she. "As a matter of fact he wasn't broke, he had a thousand dollars, and—"

"Say! Who hired you to argue this case?" It was Jim McCaskey speaking. He had edged his way forward and was scowling darkly at the woman. "What's the idea, anyhow? Are you stuck on this kid?"

The Countess Courteau eyed her interrogator coolly, her cheeks maintained their even coloring, her eyes were as icy blue as ever. It was plain that she was in no wise embarrassed by his insinuation.

Very quietly she said: "I'll tell you whether I am if you'll tell me who got his thousand dollars. Was it your brother?" Jim McCaskey recoiled; his face whitened. "Who hit you over the head?" the woman persisted. "Did he?"

"That's none of your business," Jim shouted. "I want to know what you're doing in this case. You say the kid was in Linderman last night. Well, I say—you're a—! How d'you know he was there? How d'you know he didn't steal that rice before he left, for that matter?"

"I know he was in Linderman because I was with him."

"With him? All night?" The speaker grinned insultingly.

"Yes, all night. I slept in the same tent with him and—"

"Now I've got your number," the younger McCaskey cried, in triumph.

"Bah!" The Countess shrugged unconcernedly. "As for the rice being stolen before he—"

"'Countess.' Ha!" Jim burst forth again. "Swell countess you are! The Dyea dance-halls are full of 'countesses' like you—counting per-

HE LUNGED FORWARD TO STAMP HIM BENEATH HIS HEELS, BUT STOUT
ARMS SEIZED HIM

centage checks. Boys, who are you going to believe? She slept all night—"

McCaskey got no further, for with a cry of rage Pierce Phillips set his muscles and landed upon him. It was a mighty blow and it found lodgment upon the side of its victim's face.

Jim McCaskey went down and his assailant, maddened completely by the feel of his enemy's flesh, lunged forward to stamp him beneath his heels. But stout arms seized him, bodies intervened, and he was hurled backward. A shout arose; there was a general scramble for the raised platform. There were yells of:

"Shame!"

"Hang on to him!"

"Stretch him up!"

"Dirty ingrate!"

Phillips fought with desperation; his struggles caused the structure to creak and to strain; men piled over it and joined in the fight. He was whining and sobbing in his fury.

Meanwhile ready hands had rescued Jim from the trampling feet and now held his limp body erect.

It was the clarion call of the Countess Courteau which first made itself heard above the din. She had climbed to the railing and was poised there with one arm outflung, a quivering finger leveled at Jim McCaskey's head.

"Look!" she cried. "Look, men—*at his head!* There's proof that he's been lying!" The victim of the assault had lost his cap in the scuffle, and

77

with it had gone the bandage. His head was bare now, and, oddly enough, it showed no matted hair, no cut, no bruise, no swelling. It was, in fact, a perfectly normal, healthy, well-preserved cranium.

Phillips ceased his struggles; he passed a shaking hand over his eyes to clear his vision; his captors released him and crowded closer to Jim McCaskey, who was now showing the first signs of returning consciousness.

"He told you he was held up—that his skull was cracked, didn't he?" The Countess threw back her head and laughed unrestrainedly. "My! But you men are fools! Now, then, who do you suppose got young Phillips' money? Use your wits, men."

There was a great craning of necks, a momentary hush, the while Jim McCaskey rolled his head loosely, opened his eyes, and stared wildly about.

The Countess bent down toward him, and now her cheeks had grown white, her blue eyes were flaming.

"Well, my man," she cried, in a shaking voice, "now you know what kind of a woman I am. 'Counting percentage checks,' eh?" She seemed upon the point of reaching out and throttling Jim with her long strong fingers. "Let's see you and your precious brother do a little counting. Count out a thousand dollars for this boy. Quick!"

It was 'Poleon Doret who searched the palsied victim. While other hands restrained the older brother he went through the younger one and, having done so, handed Pierce Phillips a bulky envelope addressed in the latter's handwriting.

"She's yours, eh?" 'Poleon inquired.

Phillips made a hasty examination, then nodded.

The Countess turned once more to the crowd. "I move that you apologize to Mr. Phillips. Are you game?" Her question met with a yell of approval. "Now, then, there's a new case on the docket, and the charge is highway robbery. Are you ready to vote a verdict?" Her face was set, her eyes still flashed.

"Guilty!" came with a roar.

"Very well. Hang the ruffians if you feel like it!"

She leaped down from her vantage-point, and without a word, without a glance behind her, set out along the Dyea trail.

CHAPTER V

"IOOKED kind of salty for a spell, didn't it?"
The grizzled leader of the posse, he who had
effected the capture of the thieves, was speaking
to Pierce. "Well, I'm due for a private apology.
I hope you cherish no hard feelings. Eh?"

"None whatever, sir. I'm only too glad to
get out whole and get my money back. It was
quite an experience." Already Phillips' mind
had ranged the events of the last crowded hour
into some sort of order; his fancy had tinged them
with a glamour already turning rosy with ro-
mance, and he told himself that his thrills had
been worth their price.

"Lucky that woman showed up. Who is she?"

Phillips shook his head. In his turn he inquired, "What are you going to do with the
McCaskeys?"

The elder man's face hardened. "I don't know.
This talk about hangin' makes me weary. I'd
hang 'em; I'd kick a bar'l out from under either
of 'em. I've done such things and I never had
any bad dreams."

But it was plain that the sentiment favoring
such extreme punishment had changed, for a sug-

gestion was made to flog the thieves and send them out of the country. This met with instant response. A motion was put to administer forty lashes and it was carried with a whoop.

Preparations to execute the sentence were immediately instituted. A scourge was prepared by wiring nine heavy leather thongs to a whip-handle, the platform was cleared, and a call was issued for a man to administer the punishment. Some delay ensued at this point, but finally a burly fellow volunteered, climbed to the stage, and removed his canvas coat.

Since the younger McCaskey appeared to be still somewhat dazed from the rough handling he had suffered, his brother was thrust forward. The latter was stripped to the waist, his wrists were firmly bound, then trussed up to one of the stout end-poles of the tent-frame which, skeleton-like, stood over the platform. This done, the committee fell back, and the wielder of the whip stepped forward.

The crowd had watched these grim proceedings intently; it became quite silent now. The hour was growing late, the day had been overcast, and a damp chill that searched the marrow was settling as the short afternoon drew to a close. The prisoner's naked body showed very white beneath his shock of coal-black hair; his flesh seemed tender and the onlookers stared at it in fascination.

Joe McCaskey was a man of nerve; he held himself erect; there was defiance in the gaze which

81

he leveled at the faces below him. But his brother·
Jim was not made of such stern stuff—he was the
meaner, the more cowardly of the pair—and these
methodical preparations, the certainty of his own
forthcoming ordeal, bred in him a desperate panic.
The sight of his brother's flesh bared to the bite
of the lash brought home to him the horrifying
significance of a flogging, and then, as if to em-
phasize that significance, the executioner gave his
cat-o'-nine-tails a practice swing. As the lashes
hissed through the air the victim at the post
stiffened rigidly, but his brother, outside the in-
closure, writhed in his tracks and uttered a faint
moan. Profiting by the inattention of his captors, Jim McCaskey summoned his strength and
with an effort born of desperation wrenched himself free. Hands grasped at him as he bolted,
bodies barred his way, but he bore them down;
before the meaning of the commotion had dawned
upon the crowd at large he had fought his way
out and was speeding down the street. But fleet-
footed men were at his heels, a roar of rage burst
from the mob, and in a body it took up the chase.
Down the stumpy, muddy trail went the pursuit,
and every command to halt spurred the fleeing
man to swifter flight. Cabin doors opened; people came running from their tents; some tried
to fling themselves in the way of the escaping
criminal; packers toiling up the trail heard the
approaching clamor, shook off their burdens and
endeavored to seize the figure that came bounding
ahead of it. But Jim dodged them all. Failing

in their attempt to intercept him, these new-
comers joined the chase, and the fugitive, once
the first frenzy of excitement had died in him,
heard their footsteps gaining on him. He was
stark mad by now; black terror throttled him.
Then some one fired a shot; that shot was followed by others; there came a scattered fusillade,
and with a mighty leap Jim McCaskey fell. He
collapsed in midair; he was dead when his pursuers reached him.

Mob spirit is a peculiar thing; its vagaries are
difficult to explain or to analyze. Some trivial
occurrence may completely destroy its temper,
or again merely serve to harden it and give it
edge. In this instance the escape, the flight, the
short, swift pursuit and its tragic ending, had the
effect, not of sobering the assembled citizens of
Sheep Camp, not of satisfying their long-slum-
bering rage, but of inflaming it, of intoxicating
them to a state of insane triumph. Like the Paris
mobs that followed shouting, in the wake of the
tumbrels bound for the guillotine, these men
came trooping back to the scene of execution, and
as they came they bellowed hoarsely and they
waved their arms.

Men react powerfully to environment; they
put on rough ways with rough clothes. Smooth
pavements, soap and hot water, safety-razors, are
strong civilizing agents, but a man begins to re-
vert in the time it takes his beard to grow. These
fellows had left the world they knew behind them;
they were in a world they knew not. Old stand-

ards had fallen, new standards had been reared, new values had attached to crime, therefore they demanded that the business in hand go on. Such was the spirit of the Chilkoot trail.

At the first stroke of the descending whip a howl went up—a merciless howl, a howl of fierce exultation. Joe McCaskey rocked forward upon the balls of his feet; his frame was racked by a spasm of agony; he strained at his thongs until his shoulder muscles swelled. The flesh of his back knotted and writhed; livid streaks leaped out upon it, then turned crimson and began to trickle blood.

"*One!*" roared the mob.

The wielder of the scourge swung his weapon again; again the leather strips wrapped around the victim's ribs and laid open their defenseless covering.

"*Two!*"

McCaskey lunged forward, then strained backward; the tent-frame creaked as he pulled at it. His head was drawn far back between his shoulders, his face was convulsed, and his gums were bared in a skyward grin. If he uttered any sound it was lost in the uproar.

"*Three!*"

It was a frightful punishment. The man's flesh was being stripped from his bones.

"*Four!*"

"*Five!*"

The count went on monotonously, for the fellow with the whip swung slowly, putting his whole strength behind every blow. When it had climbed to eight the prisoner's body was dripping with blood, his trousers-band was sodden with it. When it had reached ten he hung suspended by his wrists and only a fierce involuntary muscular reaction answered the caress of the nine lashes.

Forty stripes had been voted as the penalty, but 'Poleon Doret vaulted to the platform, seized the upraised whip, and tore it from the executioner's hand. He turned upon the crowd a countenance white with fury and disgust.

"Enough!" he shouted. "By Gar! You keel him next! If you mus' w'ip somebody, w'ip me; dis feller is mos' dead." He strode to the post and with a slash of his hunting-knife cut McCaskey down.

This action was greeted by an angry yell of protest; there was a rush toward the platform, but 'Poleon was joined by the leader of the posse, who scrambled through the press and ranged himself in opposition to the audience. The old man was likewise satiated with this torture; his face was wet with sweat; beneath his drooping gray mustache his teeth were set.

"Back up, you hyenas!" he cried, shrilly. "The show's over. The man took his medicine and he took it like a man. He's had enough."

"Gimme the whip. I'll finish the job," some one shouted.

The former speaker bent forward abristle with defiance.

"You try it!" he spat out. "You touch that whip, and by God, I'll kill you!" He lent point to this threat by drawing and cocking his six-shooter. "If you men ain't had enough blood for one day, I'll let a little more for you." His words ended in a torrent of profanity. "Climb aboard!" he shrilled. "Who's got the guts to try?"

Doret spoke to him shortly, "Dese men ain't goin' mak' no trouble, m'sieu'." With that he turned his back and, heedless of the clamor, began to minister to the bleeding man. He had provided himself with a bottle of lotion, doubtless some antiseptic snatched from the canvas drugstore down the street, and with this he wet a handkerchief; then he washed McCaskey's lacerated back. A member of the committee joined him in this work of mercy; soon others came to their assistance, and gradually the crowd began breaking up. Some one handed the sufferer a drink of whisky, which revived him considerably, and by the time he was ready to receive his upper garments he was to some extent master of himself.

Joe McCaskey accepted these attentions without a word of thanks, without a sign of gratitude. He appeared to be numbed, paralyzed, by the nervous shock he had undergone, and yet he was not paralyzed, for his eyes were intensely alive. They were wild, baleful; his roving glance was like poison to the men it fell upon.

"You're due to leave camp," he was told, "and

you're going to take the first boat from Dyea.
Is there anything you want to say. anything you
want to do, before you go?"

"I—want something to—eat," Joe answered,
hoarsely. "I'm hungry." These were the first
words he had uttered; they met with astonishment; nevertheless he was led to the nearest
restaurant. Surrounded by a silent, curious
group, he crouched over the board counter and
wolfed a ravenous meal. When he had finished
he rose, turned, and stared questioningly at the
circle of hostile faces; his eyes still glittered with
that basilisk glare of hatred and defiance. There
was something huge, disconcerting, about the man.
Not once had he appealed for mercy, not once
had he complained, not once had he asked about
his brother; he showed neither curiosity nor concern over Jim's fate, and now he betrayed the
utmost indifference to his own. He merely shifted
that venomous stare from one face to another as
if indelibly to photograph each and every one of
them upon his mind.

But the citizens of Sheep Camp were not done
with him yet. His hands were again bound, this
time behind him; a blanket roll was roped upon
his shoulders, upon his breast was hung a staring
placard which read:

"I am a thief! Spit on me and send me along."

Thus decorated, he met his crowning indignity.
Extending from the steps of the restaurant far
down the street twin rows of men had formed, and
this gauntlet Joe McCaskey was forced to run.

He bore this ordeal as he had borne the other. Men jeered at him, they flung handfuls of wet moss and mud at him, they spat upon him, some even struck him, bound as he was.

Sickened at the sight, Pierce Phillips witnessed the final chapter of this tragedy into which the winds of chance had blown him. For one instant only did his eyes meet those of his former tent-mate, but during that brief glance the latter made plain his undying hatred. McCaskey's gaze intensified, his upper lip drew back in a grimace similar to that which he had lifted to the sky when agony ran through his veins like fire; he seemed to concentrate the last ounce of his soul's energy in the sending of some wordless message. Hellish fury, a threat too baneful, too ominous, for expression dwelt in that stare; then a splatter of mire struck him in the face and blotted it out.

When the last jeer had died away, when the figure of Joe McCaskey had disappeared into the misty twilight, Phillips drew a deep breath. What a day this had been, what a tumult he had lived through, what an experience he had undergone! This was an adventure! He had lived, he had made an enemy. Life had come his way, and the consciousness of that fact caused him to tingle. This would be something to talk about; what would the folks back home say to this? And the Countess—that wonderful woman of ice and fire! That superwoman who could sway the minds of men, whose wit was quicker than light. Well, she had saved him, 'saved his good name, if not his neck, and his life was hers. Who was she? What mission brought her here? What hurry crowded on her heels? What idle chance had flung them into each other's arms? Or was it idle chance? Was there such a thing as chance, after all? Were not men's random fortunes all laid out in conformity with some obscure purpose to form a part of some intricate design? Dust he was, dust blown upon the breath of the North, as were these other human atoms which had been borne thither from the farthest quarters of the earth; but when that dust had settled would it not arrange itself into patterns mapped out at the hour of birth or long before? Somehow he believed that such would be the case.

As for the Countess, his way was hers, her way was his; he could not bear to think of losing her. She was big, she was great, she drew him by the spell of some strange magic.

The peppery old man who, with Doret's help, had defied the miners' meeting approached him to inquire:

"Say, why didn't old Tom come back with you from Linderman?"

"Old Tom?"

"Sure! Old Tom Linton. We're pardners. I'm Jerry Quirk."

"He was tired out."

"Tired!" Mr. Quirk snorted derisively. "What tired him? He can't tote enough grub to satisfy his own hunger. Me, I'm double-trippin'—relayin' our stuff to the Summit and breakin' my back at it. I can't make him understand we'd ought to keep the outfit together; he's got it scattered like a mad woman's hair. But old Tom's in the sere and yellow leaf: he's onnery. like all old men. I try to humor him, but—there's a limit." The speaker looked Pierce over shrewdly. "You said you was packin' for wages. Well, old Tom ain't any help to me. You look strong. Mebbe I could hire you."

Phillips shook his head. "I don't want work just now," said he. "I'm going to Dyea in the morning."

Jim McCaskey was buried where he had fallen, and there beside the trail, so that all who passed might read and ponder, the men of Sheep Camp raised a board with this inscription:

"Here lies the body of a thief."

CHAPTER VI

A CERTAIN romantic glamour attaches to all
new countries, but not every man is responsive to it. To the person who finds enjoyment,
preoccupation, in studying a ruin or in contemplating glories, triumphs, dramas long dead and
gone, old buildings, old cities, and old worlds
sound a resistless call. The past is peopled with
impressive figures, to be sure; it is a tapestry
into which are woven scenes of tremendous significance and events of the greatest moment, and
it is quite natural, therefore, that the majority
of people should experience greater fascination in
studying it than in painting new scenes upon a
naked canvas with colors of their own imagining.
To them new countries are crude, uninteresting.
But there is another type of mind which finds a
more absorbing spell in the contemplation of
things to come than of things long past; another
temperament to which the proven and the tried
possess a flat and tasteless flavor. They are restless, anticipative people; they are the ones who
blaze trails. To them great cities, established
order, the intricate structure of well-settled life,
are both monotonous and oppressive; they do

7   91

not thrive well thereunder. But put them out on the fringe of things, transplant them to wild soil, and the sap runs, they flower rankly.

To Pierce Phillips the new surroundings into which he had been projected were intensely stimulating; they excited him as he had never been excited, and each day he awoke to the sense of new adventures. Life, as he had known it, had always been good—and full, too, for that matter—and he had hugely enjoyed it; nevertheless, it had impressed upon him a sense of his own insignificance. He had been lost, submerged, in it. Here, on the threshold of a new world, he had begun to find himself, and the experience was delightful. By some magic he had been lifted to a common level with every other man, and no one had advantage over him. The momentous future was as much his as theirs and the God of Luck was in charge of things.

There was a fever in the very air he breathed, the food he ate, the water he drank. Life ran at a furious pace and it inspired in him supreme exhilaration to be swept along by it. Over all this new land was a purple haze of mystery—a sense of the Unknown right at hand. The Beyond was beckoning; it was as if great curtains had parted and he beheld vistas of tremendous promise. Keenest of all, perhaps, was his joy at discovering himself.

Appreciation of this miraculous rebirth was fullest when, at rare intervals, he came off the trail and back to Dyea, for then he renewed his touch with that other world, and the contrast became more evident.

Dyea throbbed nowadays beneath a mighty head of steam; it had grown surprisingly and it was intensely alive. Phillips never came back to it without an emotional thrill and a realization of great issues, great undertakings, in process of working out. The knowledge that he had a part in them aroused in him an intoxicating pleasure.

Dyea had become a metropolis of boards and canvas, of logs and corrugated iron. Stores had risen, there were hotels and lodging-houses, busy restaurants and busier saloons whence came the sounds of revelry by night and by day. It was a healthy revelry, by the way, like the boisterous hilarity of a robust boy. Dyea was just that— an overgrown, hilarious boy. There was nothing querulous or sickly about this child; it was strong, it was sturdy, it was rough; it romped with everybody and it grew out of its clothes overnight. Every house, every tent, in the town was crowded; supply never quite overtook demand.

Pack-animals were being imported, bridges were being built, the swamps were being hastily corduroyed; there was talk of a tramway up the side of the Chilkoot, but the gold rush increased daily, and, despite better means of transportation, the call for packers went unanswered and the price per pound stayed up. New tribes of Indians from down the coast had moved thither, babies and baggage, and they were growing rich. The stampede itself resembled the spring run of the silver salmon—it was equally mad, equally resistless. It was equally wasteful, too, for birds and beasts of prey fattened upon it and the outsetting current bore a burden of derelicts.

Values were extravagant; money ran like water; the town was wide open and it took toll from every new-comer. The ferment was kept active by a trickle of outgoing Klondikers, a considerable number of whom passed through on their way back to the States. These men had been educated to the liberal ways of the "inside" country and were prodigal spenders. The scent of the salt sea, the sight of new faces, the proximity of the open world, were like strong drink to them, hence they untied their mooseskin "pokes" and scattered the contents like sawdust. Their tales of the new El Dorado stimulated a similar recklessness among their hearers.

To a boy like Pierce Phillips, in whom the spirit of youth was a flaming torch, all this spelled glorious abandon, a supreme riot of Olympic emotions.

Precisely what reason he had for coming to town this morning he did not know; nevertheless, he was drawn seaward as by a mighty magnet. He told himself that ordinary gratitude demanded that he thank the Countess Courteau for her service to him, but as a matter of fact he was less interested in voicing his gratitude than in merely seeing her again. He was not sure but that she would resent his thanks; nevertheless, it was neces-

sary to seek her out, for already her image was
nebulous, and he could not piece together a satisfactory picture of her. She obsessed his thoughts,
but his intense desire to fix her indelibly therein
had defeated its purpose and had blurred the
photograph. Who was she? What was she?
Where was she going? What did she think of
him? The possibility that she might leave Dyea
before answering those questions spurred him into
a gait that devoured the miles.

But when he turned into the main street of the
town his haste vanished and a sudden embarrassment overtook him. What would he say to her,
now that he was here? How would he excuse
or explain his obvious pursuit? Would she see
through him? If so, what light would kindle in
those ice-blue eyes? The Countess was an unusual
woman. She knew men, she read them clearly,
and she knew how to freeze them in their tracks.
Pierce felt quite sure that she would guess his
motives, therefore he made up his mind to dis-
semble cunningly. He decided to assume a casual
air and to let chance arrange their actual meeting.
When he did encounter her, a quick smile of
pleased surprise on his part, a few simple words
of thanks, a manly statement that he was glad
she had not left before his duties permitted him
to look her up, and she would be completely deceived. Thereafter fate would decree how well or
how badly they got acquainted. Yes, that was
the way to go about it.

Having laid out this admirable program, he

immediately defied it by making a bee-line for the main hotel, a big board structure still in process of erection. His feet carried him thither in spite of himself. Like a homing-pigeon he went, and instinct guided him unerringly, for he found the Countess Courteau in the office.

She was dressed as on the day before, but by some magic she had managed to freshen and to brighten herself. In her hand she held her traveling-bag; she was speaking to the proprietor as Pierce stepped up behind her.

"Fifteen thousand dollars as it stands," he heard her say. "That's my price. I'll make you a present of the lumber. The *Queen* leaves in twenty minutes."

The proprietor began to argue, but she cut him short: "That's my last word. Three hundred per cent. on your money."

"But—"

"Think it over!" Her tone was cool, her words were crisp. "I take the lighter in ten minutes." She turned to find Phillips at her shoulder.

"Good morning!" Her face lit up with a smile; she extended her hand, and he seized it as a fish swallows a bait. He blushed redly.

"I'm late," he stammered. "I mean I—I hurried right in to tell you—"

"So they didn't hang you?"

"No! You were wonderful! I couldn't rest until I had told you how deeply grateful—"

"Nonsense!" The Countess shrugged her shoulders. "I'm glad you came before I left."

handle an oar, she called off the building crew and set them to new tasks, then she cleared the house of its guests. Rooms were invaded with peremptory orders to vacate; the steady help was put to undoing what they had already done, and soon the premises were in tumult. Such rooms as had been completed were dismantled even while the protesting occupants were yet gathering their belongings together. Beds were knocked down, bedding was moved out; windows, door-knobs, hinges, fixtures were removed; dishes, lamps, mirrors, glassware were assembled for packing.

Through all this din and clatter the Countess Courteau passed, spurring the wreckers on to speed. Yielding to Phillips' knowledge of transportation problems and limitations, she put him in general charge, and before he realized it he found that he was in reality her first lieutenant.

Toward evening a ship arrived and began to belch forth freight and passengers, whereupon there ensued a rush to find shelter.

Pierce was engaged in dismantling the office fixtures when a stranger entered and accosted him with the inquiry:

"Got any rooms?"

"No, sir. We're moving this hotel bodily to Dawson."

The new-comer surveyed the littered premises with some curiosity. He was a tall, gray-haired man, with a long, impassive face of peculiar ashen color. He had lost his left hand somewhere above the wrist and in place of it wore a metal hook. With this he gestured stiffly in the direction of a girl who had followed him into the building.

"She's got to have a bed," he declared. "I can get along somehow till my stuff is landed to-morrow." .

"I'm sorry," Pierce told him, "but the beds are all down and the windows are out. I'm afraid nobody could get much sleep here, for. we'll be at work all night."

"Any other hotels?"

"Some bunk-houses. But they're pretty full."

"Money no object, I suppose?" the one-armed man ventured

"Oh, none."

The stranger turned to his companion. "Looks like we'd have to sit up till our tents come off: I hope they've got chairs in this town."

"We can stay aboard the ship." The girl had a pleasant voice—she was, in fact, a pleasant sight to look upon, for her face was quiet and dignified, her eyes were level and gray, she wore a head of wavy chestnut hair combed neatly back beneath a trim hat.

Alaska, during the first rush, was a land of pretty women, owing to the fact that a large proportion of those who came North did so for the avowed purpose of trading upon that capital, but even in such company this girl was noticeable and Pierce Phillips regarded her with distinct approval.

"You can have my part of that," the man

THE WINDS OF CHANCE

told her, with a slight grimace. "This racket is music, to the bellow of those steers. And it smells better here. If I go aboard again I'll be hog-tied. Why, I'd rather sit up all night and deal casino to a mad Chinaman!"

"We'll manage somehow, dad." The girl turned to the door and her father followed her. He paused for a moment while he ran his eye up and down the busy street.

"Looks like old times, doesn't it, Letty?" Then he stepped out of sight.

When darkness came the wrecking crew worked on by the light of lamps, lanterns, and candles, for the inducement of double pay was potent.

Along about midnight Mr. Lucky Broad, the shell-man, picked his way through the bales and bundles and, recognizing Phillips, greeted him familiarly:

"Hello, kid! Where's her nibs, the corn-tassel Countess?"

"Gone to supper."

"Well, she sprung you, didn't she? Some gal! I knew you was all right, but them boys was certainly roily."

Pierce addressed the fellow frankly: "I'm obliged to you for taking my part. I hardly expected it."

"Why not? I got nothing against you. I got a sort of tenderness for guys like you—I hate to see 'em destroyed." Mr. Broad grinned widely and his former victim responded in like manner.

"I don't blame you," said the latter. "I was an awful knot-head, but you taught me a lesson."

"Pshaw!" The confidence-man shrugged his shoulders carelessly. "The best of 'em fall for the shells. I was up against it and had to get some rough money, but—it's a hard way to make a living. These pilgrims squawk so loud it isn't safe—you'd think their coin was soldered onto 'em. That's why I'm here. I understand her Grace is hiring men to go to Dawson."

"Yes."

"Well, take a flash at me." Mr. Broad stiffened his back, arched his chest, and revolved slowly upon his heels. "Pretty nifty, eh? What kind of men does she want?"

"Packers, boatmen—principally boatmen—fellows who can run white water."

The new applicant was undoubtedly in a happy and confident mood, for he rolled his eyes upward, exclaiming, devoutly: "I'm a gift from heaven! Born in a *batteau* and cradled on the waves—that's me!"

The Countess herself appeared out of the night at this moment and Pierce somewhat reluctantly introduced the sharper to her. "Here's an able seaman in search of a job," said he.

"Able seaman?" The woman raised her brows inquiringly.

"He said it." Mr. Broad nodded affirmatively. "I'm a jolly tar, a bo'sun's mate, a salt-horse wrangler. I just jumped a full-rigged ship—thimble-rigged!" He winked at Phillips and thrust his tongue into his cheek. "Here's my papers." From his shirt pocket he took a book of brown rice-papers and a sack of tobacco, then deftly fashioned a tiny cigarette.

"Roll one for me," said the Countess.

"Why, sure!" Mr. Broad obliged instantly and with a flourish.

"Are you really a boatman?" the woman inquired. "Don't stall, for I'll find you out." Pierce undertook to get her eye, but she was regarding Broad intently and did not see his signal.

"I'm all of that," the latter said, seriously.

"I'm going to move this outfit in small boats, two men to a boat, double crews through the cañon and in swift water. Can you get a good man to help you?"

"He's yours for the askin'—Kid Bridges. Ain't his name enough? He's a good packer, too; been packin' hay for two months. Pierce knows him." Again Mr. Broad winked meaningly at Phillips.

"Come and see me to-morrow," said the Countess.

Lucky nodded agreement to this arrangement. "Why don't you load the whole works on a scow?" he asked. "You'd save men and we could all be together—happy family stuff. That's what Kirby's going to do."

"Kirby?"

"Sam Kirby. 'One-armed' Kirby—you know. He got in to-day with a big liquor outfit. Him and his gal are down at the Ophir now, playing faro."

"No scow for mine," the Countess said, positively. "I know what I'm doing."

After the visitor had gone Pierce spoke his mind, albeit with some hesitancy. "That fellow is a gambler," said he, "and Kid Bridges is another. Bridges held my hand for a minute, the day I landed, and his little display of tenderness cost me one hundred and thirty-five dollars. Do you think you want to hire them?"

"Why not?" the Countess inquired. Then, with a smile, "They won't hold my hand, and they may be very good boatmen indeed." She dropped her cigarette, stepped upon it, then resumed her labors.

Phillips eyed the burnt-offering with disfavor. Until just now he had not known that his employer used tobacco, and the discovery came as a shock. He had been reared in a close home-circle, therefore he did not approve of women smoking; in particular he disapproved of the Countess, his Countess, smoking. After a moment of consideration, however, he asked himself what good reason there could be for his feeling. It was her own affair; why shouldn't a woman smoke if she felt like it? He was surprised at the unexpected liberality of his attitude. This country was indeed working a change in him; he was broadening rapidly. As a matter of fact, he assured himself, the Countess Courteau was an exceptional woman; she was quite different from the other members of her sex and the rules of decorum which obtained for them did not obtain for her. She was one in ten thousand, one in a million. Yes, and he was "her man."

While he was snatching a bit of midnight supper Pierce again heard the name of Kirby mentioned, and a reference to the big game in progress at the Ophir. Recalling Lucky Broad's words, he wondered if it were possible that Kirby and his girl were indeed the father and daughter who had applied at the Northern for shelter. It seemed incredible that a young woman of such apparent refinement could be a gambler's daughter, but if it were true she was not only the daughter of a "sporting man," but a very notorious one, judging from general comment. Prompted by curiosity, Pierce dropped in at the Ophir on his way back to work. He found the place crowded, as usual, but especially so at the rear, where the games were running. When he had edged his way close enough to command a view of the faro-table he discovered that Sam Kirby was, for a fact, the one-armed man he had met during the afternoon. He was seated, and close at his back was the gray-eyed, brown-haired girl with the pleasant voice. She was taking no active part in the game itself except to watch the wagers and the cases carefully. Now and then her father addressed a low-spoken word to her and she answered with a nod, a smile, or a shake of her head. She was quite at ease, quite at home; she was utterly oblivious to the close-packed ring of spectators encircling the table.

The sight amazed Phillips. He was shocked; he was mildly angered and mildly amused at the false impression this young woman had given. It seemed that his judgment of female types was exceedingly poor.

"Who is Mr. Kirby?" he inquired of his nearest neighbor.

"Big sport. He's rich—or he was; I heard he just lost a string of race-horses. He makes a fortune and he spends it overnight. He's on his way 'inside' now with a big saloon outfit. That's Letty, his girl."

Another man laughed under his breath, saying: "Old Sam won't bet a nickel unless she's with him. He's superstitious."

"I guess he has reason to be. She's his rudder," the first speaker explained.

Mr. Kirby rapped sharply upon the table with the steel hook that served as his left hand, then, when a waiter cleared a passageway through the crowd, he mutely invited the house employees to drink. The dealer declined, the lookout and the case-keeper ordered whisky, and Kirby signified by a nod that the same would do for him. But his daughter laid a hand upon his arm. He argued with her briefly, then he shrugged and changed his order.

"Make it a cigar," he said, witn a smile. "Boss's orders."

There was a ripple of laughter.

"Sam's a bad actor when he's drinking," one of Pierce's informants told him. "Letty keeps

108

him pretty straight, but once in a while he gets away. When he does—oh, *boy!*"

Long after he had returned to his tasks the memory of that still-faced girl in the foul, tobacco-laden atmosphere of the gambling-hall remained to bother Pierce Phillips; he could not get over his amazement and his annoyance at mistaking her for a—well, for a good girl.

Early in the morning, when he wearily ·went forth in quest of breakfast and a bed, he learned that the game at the Ophir was still going on.

"I want you to hire enough packers to take this stuff over in one trip—two at the most. Engage all you can. Offer any price." The Countess was speaking. She had snatched a few hours' sleep and was now back at the hotel as fresh as ever.

"You must take more rest," Pierce told her. "You'll wear yourself out at this rate."

She smiled brightly and shook her head, but he persisted. "Go back to sleep and let me attend to the work. I'm strong; nothing tires me."

"Nor me. I'll rest when we get to Dawson. Have those packers here day after to-morrow morning."

There were numerous freighters in Dyea, outfits with animals, too, some of them, but inquiry developed the fact that none were free to accept a contract of this size at such short notice, therefore Pierce went to the Indian village and asked for the chief. Failing to discover the old man, he began a tent-to-tent search, and while so engaged he stumbled upon Joe McCaskey.

The outcast was lying on a bed of boughs; his face was flushed and his eyes were bright with fever. Evidently, in avoiding the town he had sought shelter here and the natives had taken him in without question.

Overcoming his first impulse to quietly withdraw, Pierce bent down to the fellow and said, with genuine pity: "I'm sorry for you, Joe. Is there anything I can do?"

McCaskey stared up at him wildly; then a light of recognition kindled in his black eyes. It changed to that baleful gleam of hatred. His hair lay low upon his forehead and through it he glared. His face was covered with a smut of beard which made him even more repellent.

"I thought you were Jim," he croaked. "But Jim's—dead."

"You're sick. Can I help you? Do you want money or—"

"Jim's dead," the man repeated. "You killed him!"

"I? Nonsense. Don't talk—"

"You killed him. *You!*" McCaskey's unblinking stare became positively venomous; he showed his teeth in a frightful grin. "You killed him. But there's more of us. Plenty more. We'll get you." He appeared to derive a ferocious enjoyment from this threat, for he dwelt upon it. He began to curse his visitor so foully that Pierce

110

backed out of the tent and let the flap fall. It had been an unwelcome encounter; it left an unpleasant taste in his mouth.

As he went on in search of the village *shaman* he heard Joe muttering: "Jim's dead! Dead! Jim's dead!"

CHAPTER VII

SAM KIRBY'S outfit was one of the largest, one of the costliest, and one of the most complete that had ever been landed on the Dyea beach, for Kirby was a man who did things in a large way. He was a plunger; he had long since become case-hardened to risks and he knew how to weigh probabilities; hence the fact that he had staked his all upon one throw did not in the least disturb him. Many a time he had done the same and the dice had never failed to come out for him. Possessing a wide practical knowledge of new countries, he had shrewdly estimated the Klondike discovery at its true worth and had realized that the opportunity for a crowning triumph, a final clean-up, had come his way. This accounted for the energetic manner in which he had set about improving it.

Most men are successful in direct proportion to their ability to select and retain capable assistants. Fortune had favored Sam Kirby by presenting him with a daughter whose caution and good sense admirably supplemented his own best qualities, and he was doubly blessed in possessing the intense, nay, the ferocious, loyalty of one

Danny Royal, a dependable retainer who had graduated from various minor positions into a sort of castellan, an Admirable Crichton, a good left hand to replace that missing member which Kirby had lost during the white-hot climax of a certain celebrated feud—a feud, by the way, which had added a notch to the ivory handle of Sam's famous six-shooter. This Danny Royal was all things. He could take any shift in a gambling-house, he was an accomplished fixer, he had been a jockey and had handled the Kirby string of horses. He was a miner of sorts, too, having superintended the Rouletta Mine during its brief and prosperous history; as a trainer he was without a peer. He had made book on many tracks; he it was who had brought out the filly Rouletta, Sam Kirby's best-known thoroughbred, and "mopped up" with her. Both mine and mare Danny had named after Kirby's girl, and under Danny's management both had been quick producers. All in all, Royal was considered by those who knew him best as a master of many trades and a Jack of none. He was an irreligious man, but he possessed a code which he lived up to strictly; epitomized it ran as follows, "Sam Kirby's will be done!" He believed in but one god, and that Rouletta Kirby was his profit.

Equipped with the allegiance of such a man as Royal, together with several tons of high-proof spirits, a stock of case-goods and cigars, some gambling paraphernalia, and a moderate bank roll with which to furnish the same, old Sam felt safe in setting out for any country where gold was mined and where the trails were new.

Of course he took his daughter with him. Sooner than leave her behind he would have severed his remaining hand. Rouletta and Agnes, they constituted the foundation upon which the Kirby fortunes rested, they were the rocks to which Sam clung, they were his assets and his liabilities, his adjuncts and his adornments. Agnes was his gun.

Having seen his freight safely ashore, Kirby left Royal in charge of it, first impressing upon him certain comprehensive and explicit instructions; then he and Rouletta and Agnes went up the trail and over the Chilkoot. Somehow, between the three of them, they intended to have a scow built and ready when Danny landed the last pound of merchandise at Linderman.

Mr. Royal was an energetic little person. He began an immediate hunt for packers, only to discover that another outfit was ahead of his and that no men were immediately available. He was resourceful, he was in the habit of meeting and overcoming obstacles, hence this one did not greatly trouble him, once he became acquainted with the situation.

Two days and nights enabled the Countess Courteau to strip the Northern Hotel, to assemble the movable appurtenances thereto, and to pack them into boxes, bales, and bundles, none of which weighed more than one hundred pounds. This lapse of time likewise enabled the Indians

whom Pierce had hired to finish their contracts
and return to the coast. In spite of the appalling
amount of freight, Pierce believed he had enough
men to move it in two trips, and when the hour
came to start the Countess complimented him
upon his thorough preparations. As swiftly as
might be he formed his packers in line, weighed
their burdens, and sent them on their journey.
These preparations occasioned much confusion
and a considerable crowd assembled. Among the
onlookers was a bright-eyed, weazened little man
who attached himself to the chief and engaged
him in conversation.

When the last burden-bearer had departed the
Countess directed Lucky Broad and Kid Bridges
to stay in the hotel and stand guard over the
remainder of her goods.

"Take six-hour shifts," she told them. "I'll
hold you responsible for what's here."

"It's as safe as wheat," Broad assured her.

"I'll camp at the Scales with the stuff that has
gone forward, and Pierce will bring the Indians
back."

"D'you think you can ride herd on it?" Bridges
inquired. "I understand there's a lawless element at large."

The Countess smiled. "I'm sort of a lawless
element myself when I start," she said. Her
eyes twinkled as she measured Mr. Bridges' burly
proportions. "You're going to miss your alfalfa
bed before I get you to Linderman."

The Kid nodded seriously. "I know," said

he. "Serves me right for quittin' a profession for a trade, but I got to look over this Dawson place. They say it's soft pickin'. Lucky is taking his stock in trade along, all three of 'em, so maybe we'll tear off a penny or two on the way."

Pierce's pack consisted of a tent for the Countess, some bedding, and food; with this on his back he and his employer set out to overtake their train. This they accomplished a short distance below the first crossing of the river. Already the white packers, of whom there were perhaps a score, had drawn together; the Indians were following them in a long file. Having seen his companion safely across the stream, Pierce asked her, somewhat doubtfully:

"Do you think Broad and his partner are altogether trustworthy?"

"Nobody is that," she told him. "But they're at least intelligent. In this kind of a country I prefer an intelligent crook to an honest fool. Most people are honest or dishonest when and as they think it is to their advantage to be so. Those men want to get to Dawson, and they know the Police would never let them across the Line. I'm their only chance. They'll stand assay."

It was mid-forenoon when the Countess halted Pierce, who was a short distance ahead of her, saying: "Wait! Didn't you hear somebody calling us?"

They listened. They were about to move onward when there came a faint hallo, and far down the trail behind them they saw a figure approaching. After a moment of scrutiny Pierce declared:

"Why, it's Broad!"

"Something has happened!" The Countess stepped upon a fallen log and through her cupped palms sent forth an answering call. Mr. Broad waved his hat and broke into a run. He was wet with sweat, he was muddy and out of breath, when he finally overtook them.

"Whew!" he panted. "Thought I'd never run you down. Well, set yourselves."

"What's wrong?" demanded the woman.

"Plenty. You've been double-crossed, whipsawed. Your noble red men have quit you; they dumped your stuff at the river and made a deal at double rates to move Sam Kirby's freight. They're back in Dyea now, the whole works."

The Countess Courteau exploded with a man's oath. Her face was purple; her eyes were blazing.

"Danny Royal, Kirby's man, done it. Sam's gone on to Linderman to build a boat. I saw Danny curled up on the chief's ear while you were loading. After you'd gone him and the old pirate followed. Me 'n' Bridges never thought anything about it until by and by back came the whole party, empty. Danny trooped 'em down to the beach and begun packin' 'em. I know him, so I asked him what the devil. 'Hands off!' says he. 'Sam Kirby's got a rush order in ahead of yours, and these refreshments is going through by express. I've raised your ante. Money no object, understand? I'll boost the price again if

I have to, and keep on boosting it.' Then he warned me not to start anything or he'd tack two letters onto the front of my name. He'd do it, too. I took it on the run, and here I am."

"Sam Kirby, eh?" The Countess' flaming rage had given place to a cool, calculating anger.

Pierce protested violently. "I hired those Indians. We agreed on a price and everything was settled."

"Well, Danny unsettled it. They're workin' for him and he intends to keep 'em."

"What about our white packers?" the woman inquired of Broad.

"They must have crossed before Danny caught up, or he'd have had them, too. 'Money no object,' he said. I'm danged if I'd turn a trick like that."

"Where's our stuff?"

"At the Crossing."

The Countess turned back down the trail and Pierce followed her. "I'll settle this Royal," he declared, furiously.

"Danny's a bad boy," Lucky Broad warned, falling into step. "If old Sam told him to hold a buzz-saw in his lap he'd do it. Maybe there wouldn't be much left of Danny, but he'd of hugged it some while he lasted."

Little more was said during the swift return to the river. It was not a pleasant journey, for the trail was miserable, the mud was deep, and there was a steady upward flow of traffic which it was necessary to stem. There were occasional

118

interruptions to this stream, for here and there horses were down and a blockade had resulted. Behind it men lay propped against logs or tree-trunks, resting their tired frames and listening apathetically to the profanity of the horse-owners. Rarely did any one offer to lend a helping hand, for each man's task was equal to his strength. In one place a line of steers stood belly deep in the mire, waiting the command to plow forward.

Broken carts, abandoned vehicles of various patterns, lined the way; there were many swollen carcasses underfoot, and not infrequently pedestrians crossed mud-holes by stepping from one to another, holding their breaths and battling through swarms of flies. Much costly impedimenta strewed the roadside—each article a milestone of despair, a monument to failure. There were stoves, camp furniture, lumber, hardware, boat fittings. The wreckage and the wastage of the stampede were enormous, and every ounce, every dollar's worth of it, spoke mutely of blasted hopes. Now and then one saw piles of provisions, some of which had been entirely abandoned. The rains had ruined most of them.

When the Countess came to her freight she paused. "You said Royal was loading his men when you left?" She faced Broad inquiringly.

"Right!"

"Then he'll soon be along. We'll wait here." Of Phillips she asked, "Do you carry a gun?"

Pierce shook his head. "What are you going to do?" He could see that she was boiling inwardly, and although his own anger had increased at every moment during the return journey, her question caused him genuine apprehension.

Avoiding a direct answer, the woman said: "If Royal is with the Indians, you keep your eye on him. I want to talk to them."

"Don't inaugurate any violent measures," Mr. Broad cautioned, nervously. "Danny's a sudden sort of a murderer. Of course, if worse comes to worst, I'll stick, but—my rating in the community ain't A 1. There's a lot of narrow-minded church members would like to baptize me at high tide. As if that would get their money back!"

A suggestion of a smile crept to the Countess' lips and she said, "I knew you'd stick when I hired you." Then she seated herself upon a box.

Danny Royal did accompany his packers. He did so as a precaution against precisely such a *coup* as he himself had engineered, and in order to be doubly secure he brought the head Indian with him. The old tribesman had rebelled mildly, but Royal had been firm, and in consequence they were the first two to appear when the procession came out of the woods.

The chief halted at sight of Phillips, the man who had hired him and his people, but at a word from Royal he resumed his march. He averted his eyes, however, and he held his head low, showing that this encounter was not at all to his liking. Royal, on the contrary, carried off the meeting easily. He grinned at Lucky Broad and was about to pass on when the Countess Courteau rose to her feet and stepped into the trail.

"Just a minute!" she said. Of Royal's companion she sternly demanded, "What do you mean by this trick?"

The old redskin shot her a swift glance; then his face became expressionless and he gazed stolidly at the river.

"What do you mean?" the woman repeated, in a voice quivering with fury.

"Him people—" the chief began, but Royal spoke for him. Removing his hat, he made a stiff little bow, then said, courteously enough:

"I'm sorry to hold you up, ma'am, but—"

"You're not holding me up; I'm holding you up," the woman broke in. "What do you take me for, anyhow?" She stared at the white man so coldly, there was such authority and such fixity of purpose in her tone and her expression, that his manner changed.

"I'm on orders," said he. "There's no use to argue. I'd talk plainer to you if you was a man."

But she had turned her eyes to the chief again. "You lying scoundrel!" she cried, accusingly. "I made a straight deal with you and your people and I agreed to your price. I'm not going to let you throw me down!"

The wooden-faced object of her attack became inexplicably stupid; he strove for words. "Me no speak good," he muttered. "Me no savvy—"

"Perhaps you'll savvy this." As the Countess spoke she took from her pocket a short-barreled revolver, which she cocked and presented in a capable and determined manner so close to the old native's face that he staggered backward, fending off the attack. The woman followed him.

"Look here!" Danny Royal exploded. He made a movement with his right hand, but Pierce Phillips and Lucky Broad stepped close to him. The former said, shortly:

"If you make a move I'll brain you!"

"That's me," seconded Mr. Broad. "Lift a finger, Danny, and we go to the mat."

Royal regarded the two men searchingly. "D'you think I'll let you people stick me up?" he queried.

"You're stuck up!" the Countess declared, shortly. "Make sure of this—I'm not bluffing. I'll shoot. Here—you!" she called to one of the packers at the rear of the line who had turned and was making off. "Get back where you were and stay there." She emphasized this command with a wave of her weapon and the Indian obeyed with alacrity. "Now then, Mr. Royal, not one pound of Sam Kirby's freight will these people carry until mine is over the pass. I don't recognize you in this deal in any way. I made a bargain with the chief and I'll settle it with him. You keep out. If you don't, my men will attend to you."

It was surprising what a potent effect a firearm had upon the aged *shaman*. His mask fell off and his knowledge of the English language was magically refreshed. He began a perfectly intelligible protest against the promiscuous display of loaded weapons, particularly in crowded localities. He was a peaceful man, the head of a peaceful people, and violence of any sort was contrary to his and their code. "This was no way in which to settle a dispute—"

"You think not, eh? Well, it's my way," stormed the Countess. "I'll drop the first man who tries to pass. If you think I won't, try me. Go ahead, try me!" Mr. Royal undertook to say something more, but without turning her head the woman told Phillips, "Knock him down if he opens his mouth."

"*Will* I?" Pierce edged closer to his man, and in his face there was a hunger for combat which did not look promising to the object of his attentions.

Lucky Broad likewise discouraged the exjockey by saying, "If you call her hand, Danny, I'll bust you where you're biggest."

The Countess still held the muzzle of her revolver close to the chief's body. Now she said, peremptorily: "You're going to end this joke right now. Order their packs off, *quick!*"

This colloquy had been short, but, brief as the delay had been, it had afforded time for newcomers to arrive. Amazed at the sight of a raging woman holding an army of red men at bay, several "mushers" dropped their burdens and came running forward to learn the meaning of it. The Countess explained rapidly, whereupon one exclaimed:

"Go to it, sister!"

Another agreed heartily. "When you shoot, shoot low. We'll see you through."

"I don't need any assistance," she told them. "They'll keep their agreement or they'll lose their head man. Give the word, Chief."

The old redskin raised his voice in expostulation, but one of the late-comers broke in upon him:

"Aw, shut up, you robber! You're gettin' what you need."

"I'm going to count three," the woman said, inflexibly. Her face had grown very white; her eyes were shining dangerously. "At four I shoot. One! Two—!"

The wrinkled Indian gave a sign; his tribesmen began to divest themselves of their loads.

"Pile it all up beside the trail. Now get under my stuff and don't let's have any more nonsense. The old price goes and I sha'n't raise it a penny." Turning to Danny Royal, she told him: "You could have put this over on a man, but women haven't any sense. I haven't a bit. Every cent I own is tied up in this freight and it's going through on time. I think a lot of it, and if you try to delay it again I'm just foolish enough to blow a hole in this savage—and you, too. Yes, and a miners' meeting would cheer me for doing it."

There was a silence; then Mr. Royal inquired: "Are you waiting for me to speak? Well, all I've got to say is if the James boys had had a sister they'd of been at work yet. I don't know how to tackle a woman."

124

"Are you going to keep hands off?"

"Sure! I'm licked. You went about it in the right way. You got me tied."

"I don't know whether you're lying or not. But just to make sure I'm going to have Lucky walk back to town with you to see that you don't get turned around."

Danny removed his hat and made a sweeping bow; then he departed in company with his escort. The Indians took up those burdens which they had originally shouldered, and the march to the Chilkoot was resumed. Now, however, the Countess Courteau brought up the rear of the procession and immediately in advance of her walked the head man of the Dyea tribe.

CHAPTER VIII

IT was a still, clear morning, but autumn was in the air and a pale sun lacked the necessary heat to melt a skin of ice which, during the night, had covered stagnant pools. The damp moss which carpets northern forests was hoary with frost and it crackled underfoot. Winter was near and its unmistakable approach could be plainly felt.

A saw-pit had been rigged upon a sloping hillside—it consisted of four posts about six feet long upon which had been laid four stringers, like the sills of a house; up to this scaffold led a pair of inclined skids. Resting upon the stringers was a sizable spruce log which had been squared and marked with parallel chalk-lines and into which a whip-saw had eaten for several feet. Balanced upon this log was Tom Linton; in the sawdust directly under him stood Jerry Quirk. Mr. Linton glared downward, Mr. Quirk squinted fiercely upward. Mr. Linton showed his teeth in an ugly grin and his voice was hoarse with fury; Mr. Quirk's gray mustache bristled with rage, and anger had raised his conversational tone to a high pitch. Both men were perspiring, both were shaken to the core.

"*Don't shove!*" Mr. Quirk exclaimed, in shrill irritation. "How many times d'you want me to tell you not to shove? You bend the infernal thing."

"I never shoved," Linton said, thickly. "Maybe we'd do better if you'd quit hanging your weight on those handles every time I lift. If you've got to chin yourself, take a limb—or I'll build you a trapeze. You pull down, then lemme lift—"

Mr. Quirk danced with fury. "Chin myself? Shucks! You're petered out, that's what ails you. You 'ain't got the grit and you've throwed up your tail. Lift her clean—don't try to saw goin' up, the teeth ain't set that way. Lift, take a bite, then leggo. Lift, bite, leggo. Lift, bite—"

"Don't say that again!" shouted Linton. "I'm a patient man, but—" He swallowed hard, then with difficulty voiced a solemn, vibrant warning, "Don't say it again, that's all!"

Defiance instantly flamed in Jerry's watery eyes. "I'll say it if I want to!" he yelled. "I'll say anything I feel like sayin'! Some folks can't understand English; some folks have got lignum-vity heads and you have to tell 'em—"

"You couldn't tell me anything!"

"Sure! That's just the trouble with **you**— *nobody* can tell you anything!"

"I whip-sawed before you was born!"

Astonishment momentarily robbed Mr. Quirk of speech, then he broke out more indignantly than ever. "Why, you lyin' horse-thief, you never heard of a whip-saw till we bought our outfit. You was for tying one end to a limb and the other end to a root and then rubbin' the log up and down it."

"I never meant that. I was fooling and you know it. That's just like you, to—"

"Say, if you'd ever had holt of a whip-saw in all your useless life, the man on the other end of it would have belted you with the handle and buried you in the sawdust. I'd ought to, but I 'ain't got the heart!" The speaker spat on his hands and in a calmer, more business-like tone said: "Well, come on. Let's go. This is our last board."

Tom Linton checked an insulting remark that had just occurred to him. It had nothing whatever to do with the subject under dispute, but it would have goaded Jerry to insanity, therefore it clamored for expression and the temptation to hurl it forth was almost irresistible. Linton, however, prided himself upon his self-restraint, and accordingly he swallowed his words. He clicked his teeth, he gritted them—he would have enjoyed sinking them into his partner's throat, as a matter of fact—then he growled, "Let her whiz!"

In unison the men resumed their interrupted labors; slowly, rhythmically, their arms moved up and down, monotonously their aching backs bent and straightened, inch by inch the saw blade ate along the penciled line. It was killing work, for it called into play unused, under-developed muscles, yes, muscles which did not and never would or could exist. Each time Linton lifted the saw it grew heavier by the fraction of a pound. Whenever Quirk looked up to note progress his eyes were filled with stinging particles of sawdust. His was a tearful job: sawdust was in his hair, his beard, it had sifted down inside his neckband and it itched his moist body. It had worked into his underclothes and he could not escape it even at night in his bed. He had of late acquired the habit of repeating over and over, with a pertinacity intensely irritating to his partner, that he could taste sawdust in his food—a statement manifestly false and well calculated to offend a camp cook.

After they had sawed for a while Jerry cried: "Hey! She's runnin' out again." He accompanied this remark by an abrupt cessation of effort. As a result the saw stopped in its downward course and Tom's chin came into violent contact with the upper handle.

The man above uttered a cry of pain and fury; he clapped a hand to his face as if to catch and save his teeth.

Jerry giggled with a shameless lack of feeling. "Spit 'em out," he cackled. "They ain't no more good to you than a mouthful of popcorn." He was not really amused at his partner's mishap; on the contrary, he was more than a little concerned by it, but fatigue had rendered him absurdly hysterical, and the constant friction of mental, spiritual, and physical contact with Tom had fretted his soul as that sawdust inside his clothes had fretted his body. "He, he! Ho, ho!" he chortled. "You don't shove. Oh no! All the same, whenever I stop pullin' you butt your brains out."

"I didn't shove!" The ferocity of this denial was modified and muffled by reason of the fact that a greater part of the speaker's hand was inside his mouth and his fingers were taking stock of its contents.

"All right, you didn't shove. Have it your own way. I said she was runnin' out again. We ain't cuttin' wedges, we're cuttin' boat-seats."

"Well, why don't you pull straight? I can't follow a line with you skinning the cat on your end."

"My fault again, eh?" Mr. Quirk showed the whites of his eyes and his face grew purple. "Lemme tell you something, Tom. I've studied you, careful, as man and boy, for a matter of thirty years, but I never seen you in all your hideousness till this trip. I got you now, though; I got you all added up and subtracted and I'll tell you the answer. It's my opinion, backed by figgers, that you're a dam'—" He hesitated, then with a herculean effort he managed to gulp the remainder of his sentence. In a changed voice he said: "Oh, what's the use? I s'pose you've got feelin's. Come on, let's get through."

Linton peered down over the edge of the log. "It's your opinion I'm a what?" he inquired, with vicious calmness.

"Nothing. It's no use to tell you. Now then, lift, bite, leg— Why don't you lift?"

"I *am* lifting. Leggo your end!" Mr. Linton

tugged violently, but the saw came up slowly. It rose and fell several times, but with the same feeling of dead weight attached to it. Tom wiped the sweat out of his eyes and once again in a stormy voice he addressed his partner: "If you don't get off them handles I'll take a stick and knock you off. What you grinnin' at?"

"Why, she's stuck, that's all. Drive your wedge—" Jerry's words ended in an agonized yelp; he began to paw blindly. "You did that a-purpose."

"Did what?"

"Kicked sawdust in my eyes. I saw you!"

Mr. Linton's voice when he spoke held that same sinister note of restrained ferocity which had characterized it heretofore. "When I start kicking I won't kick sawdust into your eyes! I'll kick your eyes into that sawdust. That's what I'll do. I'll stomp 'em out like a pair of grapes."

"You try it! You try anything with me," Jerry chattered, in a simian frenzy. "You've got a bad reputation at home; you're a *malo hombre* —a side-winder, you are, and your bite is certain death. That's what they say. Well, ever see a Mexican hog eat a rattler? That's me—wild hog!"

"'*Wild* hog.' What's wild about you?" sneered the other. "You picked the right animal but the wrong variety. Any kind of a hog makes a bad partner."

For a time the work proceeded in silence, then the latter speaker resumed: "You said I was

131

a dam' something or other. What was it?"
The object of this inquiry maintained an offensive, nay an insulting, silence. "A what?" Linton persisted.

Quirk looked up through his mask of sawdust.
"If you're gettin' tired again why don't you say
so? I'll wait while you rest." He opened his eyes
in apparent astonishment, then he cried: "Hello!
Why, it's rainin'."

"It ain't raining," Tom declared.

"Must be—your face is wet." Once more the
speaker cackled shrilly in a manner intended to
be mirthful, but which was in reality insulting
beyond human endurance. "I never saw moisture on your brow, Tom, except when it rained
or when you set too close to a fire."

"What was it you wanted to call me and was
scared to?" Mr. Linton urged, venomously. "A
dam' what?"

"Oh, I forget the precise epithet I had in mind.
But a new one rises to my lips 'most every min-
ute. I think I aimed to call you a dam' old fool.
Something like that."

Slowly, carefully, Mr. Linton descended from
the scaffold, leaving the whip-saw in its place.
He was shaking with rage, with weakness, and
with fatigue.

"'Old'? *Me* old? I'm a fool, I admit, or I
wouldn't have lugged your loads and done your
work the way I have. But, you see, I'm strong
and vigorous and I felt sorry for a tottering wreck
like you—"

"'Lugged *my* loads'?" snorted the smaller man. "*Me* a wreck? My Gawd!"

"—I did your packing and your washing and your cooking, and mine, too, just because you was feeble and because I've got consideration for my seniors. I was raised that way. I honored your age, Jerry. I knew you was about all in, but I never *called* you old. I wouldn't hurt your feelings. What did you do? You set around on your bony hips and criticized and picked at me. But you've picked my last feather off and I'm plumb raw. Right here we split!"

Jerry Quirk staggered slightly and leaned against a post for support. His knees were wobbly; he, too, ached in every bone and muscle; he, too, had been goaded into an insane temper, but that which maddened him beyond expression was this unwarranted charge of incompetency.

"Split it is," he agreed. "That 'll take a load off my shoulders."

"We'll cut our grub fifty-fifty, then I'll hit you a clout with the traces and turn you a-loose."

Jerry was still dazed, for his world had come to an end, but he pretended to an extravagant joy and managed to chirp: "Good news—the first I've had since we went pardners. I'll sure kick up my heels. What'll we do with the boat?"

"Cut her in two."

"Right. We'll toss up for ends. We'll divide everything the same way, down to the skillet."

"Every blame' thing," Linton agreed.

Side by side they set off heavily through the woods.

Quarrels similar to this were of daily occurrence on the trail, but especially common were they here at Linderman, for of all the devices of the devil the one most trying to human patience is a whip-saw. It is a saying in the North that ·to know a man one must eat a sack of flour with him; it is also generally recognized that a partnership which survives the vexations of a saw-pit is time and weather proof—a predestined union more sacred and more perfect even than that of matrimony. Few indeed have stood the test.

It was in this loosening of sentimental ties, in the breach of friendships and the birth of bitter enmities, where lay the deepest tragedy of the Chilkoot and the Chilkat trails. Under ordinary, normal circumstances men of opposite temperaments may live with each other in harmony and die in mutual accord, but circumstances here were extraordinary, abnormal. Hardship, monotony, fatigue score the very soul; constant close association renders men absurdly petulant and childishly quarrelsome. Many are the heartaches charged against those early days and those early trails.

Of course there was much less internal friction in outfits like Kirby's or the Countess Courteau's, where the men worked under orders, but even there relations were often strained. Both Danny Royal and Pierce Phillips had had their troubles, their problems—nobody could escape them—but

134

on the whole they had held their men together
pretty well and had made fast progress, all things
considered. Royal had experience to draw upon,
while Phillips had none; nevertheless, the Countess was a good counselor and this brief training
in authority was of extreme value to the younger
man, who developed some of the qualities of
leadership. As a result of their frequent con-
ferences a frank, free intimacy had sprung up
between Pierce and his employer, an intimacy
both gratifying and disappointing to him. Just
how it affected the woman he could not tell. As
a matter of fact he made little effort to learn,
being for the moment too deeply concerned in
the great change that had come over him.

Pierce Phillips made no effort to deceive himself: he was in love, yes, desperately in love, and
his infatuation grew with every hour. It was his
first serious affair and quite naturally its newness
took his breath. He had heard of puppy love and
he scorned it, but this was not that kind, he told
himself; his was an epic adoration, a full-grown,
deathless man's affection such as comes to none
but the favored of the gods and then but once
in a lifetime. The reason was patent—it lay in
the fact that the object of his soul-consuming
worship was not an ordinary woman. No, the
Countess was cast in heroic mold and she inspired
love of a character to match her individuality;
she was one of those rare, flaming creatures the
like of whom illuminate the pages of history. She
was another Cleopatra, a regal, matchless creature.

To be sure, she was not at all the sort of woman he had expected to love, therefore he loved her the more; nor was she the sort he had chosen as his ideal. But it is this abandonment of old ideals and acceptance of new ones which marks development, which signalizes youth's evolution into maturity. She was a never-ending surprise to Pierce, and the fact that she remained a well of mystery, an unsounded deep that defied his attempts at exploration, excited his imagination and led him to clothe her with every admirable trait, in no few of which she was, of course, entirely lacking.

He was very boyish about this love of his. Lacking confidence to make known his feelings, he undertook to conceal them and believed he had succeeded. No doubt he had, so far as the men in his party were concerned—they were far too busy to give thought to affairs other than their own—but the woman had marked his very first surrender and now read him like an open page, from day to day. His blind, unreasoning loyalty, his complete acquiescence to her desires, his extravagant joy in doing her will, would have told her the truth even without the aid of those numerous little things which every woman understands. Now, oddly enough, the effect upon her was only a little less disturbing than upon him, for this first boy-love was a thing which no good woman could have treated lightly: its simplicity, its purity, its unselfishness were different to anything she had known—so different, for instance, to that affection which Count Courteau had bestowed upon her as to seem almost sacred—therefore she watched its growth with gratification not unmixed with apprehension. It was flattering and yet it gave her cause for some uneasiness.

As a matter of fact, Phillips was boyish only in this one regard; in other things he was very much of a man—more of a man than any one the Countess had met in a long time—and she derived unusual satisfaction from the mere privilege of depending upon him. This pleasure was so keen at times that she allowed her thoughts to take strange shape, and was stirred by yearnings, by impulses, by foolish fancies that reminded her of her girlhood days.

The boat-building had proceeded with such despatch, thanks largely to Phillips, that the time for departure was close at hand, and inasmuch as there still remained a reasonable margin of safety the Countess began to feel the first certainty of success. While she was not disposed to quarrel with such a happy state of affairs, nevertheless one thing continued to bother her: she could not understand why interference had failed to come from the Kirby crowd. She had expected it, for Sam Kirby had the name of being a hard, conscienceless man, and Danny Royal had given proof that he was not above resorting to desperate means to gain time. Why, therefore, they had made no effort to hire her men away from her, especially as men were almost unobtainable here at Linderman, was something that baffled her.

She had learned by bitter experience to put trust in no man, and this, coupled perhaps with the natural suspicion of her sex, combined to excite her liveliest curiosity and her deepest concern; she could not overcome the fear that this unspoken truce concealed some sinister design.

Feeling, this afternoon, a strong desire to see with her own eyes just what progress her rivals were making, she called Pierce away from his work and took him with her around the shore of the lake.

"Our last boat will be in the water to-morrow," he told her. "Kirby can't hold us up now, if he tries."

"I don't know," she said, doubtfully. "He is as short-handed as we are. I can't understand why he has left us alone so long."

Phillips laughed. "He probably knows it isn't safe to trifle with you."

The Countess shook her head. "I couldn't bluff him. He wouldn't care whether I'm a woman or not."

"Were you bluffing when you held up Royal? I didn't think so."

"I don't think so, either. There's no telling what I might have done—I have a furious temper."

"That's nothing to apologize for," the young man declared, warmly. "It's a sign of character, force. I hope I never have reason to feel it."

"You? How absurd! You've been perfectly dear. You couldn't be otherwise."

"Do you think so, really? I'm awfully glad."

138

The Countess was impelled to answer this boy's eagerness by telling him frankly just how well she thought of him, just how grateful she was for all that he had done, but she restrained herself.

"All the fellows have been splendid, especially those two gamblers," she said, coolly. After a moment she continued: "Don't stop when we get to Kirby's camp. I don't want him to think we're curious."

Neither father nor daughter was in evidence when the visitors arrived at their destination, but Danny Royal was superintending the final work upon a stout scow the seams of which were being calked and daubed with tar. Mast and sweeps were being rigged; Royal himself was painting a name on the stern.

At sight of the Countess the ex-horseman dropped his brush and thrust his hands aloft, exclaiming, "Don't shoot, ma'am!" His grin was friendly; there was no rancor in his voice. "How you gettin' along down at your house?" he inquired.

"Very well," the Countess told him.

"We'll get loaded to-morrow," said Pierce.

"Same here," Royal advised. "Better come to the launching. Ain't she a bear?" He gazed fondly at the bluff-bowed, ungainly barge. "I'm goin' to bust a bottle of wine on her nose when she wets her feet. First rainy-weather hack we ever had in the family. Her name's *Rouletta*."

"I hope she has a safe voyage."

10   139

Royal eyed the speaker meditatively. "This trip has got my goat," he acknowledged. "Water's all right when it's cracked up and put in a glass, but—it ain't meant to build roads with. I've heard a lot about this cañon and them White Horse Rapids. Are they bad?" When the Countess nodded, his weazened face darkened visibly. "Gimme a horse and I'm all right, but water scares me. Well, the *Rouletta's* good and strong and I'm goin' to christen her with a bottle of real champagne. If there's anything in good liquor and a good name she'll be a lucky ship."

When they were out of hearing the Countess Courteau repeated: "I don't understand it. They could have gained a week."

"We could, too, if we'd built one scow instead of those small boats,"⸴ Pierce declared.

"Kirby is used to taking chances; he can risk all his eggs in one basket if he wants to, but—not I." A moment later the speaker paused to stare at a curious sight. On the beach ahead of her stood a brand-new rowboat ready for launching. Near it was assembled an outfit of gear and provisions, divided into two equal piles. Two old men, armed each with a hand-saw, were silently at work upon the skiff. They were sawing it in two, exactly in the middle, and they did not look up until the Countess greeted them.

"Hello! Changing the model of your boat?" she inquired.

The partners straightened themselves stiffly and removed their caps.

"Yep!" said Quirk, avoiding his partner's eyes.

"Changing her model," Mr. Linton agreed, with a hangdog expression.

"But—why? What for?"

"We've split," Mr. Quirk explained. Then he heaved a sigh. "It's made a new man of me a'ready."

"My end will look all right when I get her boarded up," Linton vouchsafed, "but Old Jerry drew the hind quarters." His shoulders heaved in silent amusement.

"'Old' Jerry!" snapped the smaller man. "Where'd you get the 'old' at? I've acted like a feeble-minded idiot, I'll admit—bein' imposed on so regular—but that's over and I'm breathin' free. Wait till you shove off in that front end; it 'ain't got the beam and you'll upset. Ha!" He uttered a malicious bark. "You'll drownd!" Mr. Quirk turned indignant eyes upon the visitors. "The idea of *him* callin' *me* 'old.' Can you beat that?"

"Maybe I will drown," Linton agreed, "but drowning ain't so bad. It's better than being picked and pecked to death by a blunt-billed buzzard. I'd look on it as a kind of relief. Anyhow, you won't be there to see it; you'll be dead of rheumatism. I've got the tent."

"Huh! The stove's mine. I'll make out."

"Have you men quarreled after all these years?" the Countess made bold to inquire.

Jerry answered, and it was plain that all sentiment had been consumed in the fires of his present wrath. "I don't quarrel with a dam' old fool; I give him his way."

Linton's smoky eyes were blazing when he cried, furiously: "Cut that 'old' out, or I'll show you something. Your mind's gone—senile decay, they call it—but I'll—"

Quirk flung down his saw and advanced belligerently around the hull of the boat. He was bristling with the desire for combat.

"What 'll you show me?" he shrilly challenged. "You're bigger than me, but I'll cut you down: I'll—"

The Countess stepped between the two men, crying, impatiently:

"Don't be silly. You're worn out and irritable, both of you, and you're acting like perfect idiots. You'll have everybody laughing at you."

Jerry diverted his fury to this intermediary. "Is that so?" he mocked. "Well, let 'em laugh; it 'll do 'em good. You're a nice woman, but this ain't ladies' day at our club and we don't need no outside advice on how to run our party."

"Oh, very well!" The Countess shrugged and turned away, motioning Pierce to follow her. "Fight it out to suit yourselves."

Quirk muttered something about the insolence of strangers; then he picked up his saw. In silence the work was resumed, and later, when the boat had been divided, each man set about boarding up and calking the open end of his respective half. Neither of them was expert in the use of

142

carpenter's tools, therefore it was supper-time before they finished, and the result of their labor was nothing to be proud of. Each now possessed a craft that would float, no doubt, but which in few other respects resembled a boat; Linton's was a slim, square-ended wedge, while Quirk's was a blunt barge, fashioned on the fines of a watering-trough. They eyed the freaks with some dismay, but neither voiced the slightest regret nor acknowledged anything but supreme satisfaction.

Without a word they gathered up their tools and separated to prepare their evening meals. Linton entered his tent, now empty, cold, and cheerless; Quirk set up his stove in the open and rigged a clumsy shelter out of a small tarpaulin. Under this he spread his share of the bedding. Engaged in this, he realized that his two blankets promised to be woefully inadequate to the weather and he cocked an apprehensive eye heavenward. What he saw did not reassure him, for the evening sky was overcast and a cold, fitful wind blew from off the lake. There was no doubt about it, it looked like rain—or snow—perhaps a combination of both. Mr. Quirk felt a shiver of dread run through him, and his heart sank at the prospect of many nights like this to come. He derived some scanty comfort from the sight of old Tom puttering wearily around a camp-fire, the smoke from which followed him persistently, bringing tears to his smarting eyes and strangling complaints from his lungs.

143

"He's tryin' to burn green wood," Jerry said, aloud, "the old fool!"

A similar epithet was upon his former partner's tongue. Linton was saying to himself, "Old Jerry's enjoying life now, but wait till his fire goes out and it starts to rain."

He chuckled maliciously and then rehearsed a speech of curt refusal for use when Quirk came to the tent and begged shelter from the weather. There would be nothing doing, Tom made up his mind to that; he tried several insults under his breath, then he offered up a vindictive prayer for rain, hail, sleet, and snow. A howling Dakota blizzard, he decided, would exactly suit him. He was a bit rusty on prayers, but whatever his appeal may have lacked in polish it made up in earnestness, for never did petition carry aloft a greater weight of yearning than did his.

Tom fried his bacon in a stewpan, for the skillet had been divided with a cold chisel and neither half was of the slightest use to anybody. After he had eaten his pilot-bread, after he had drunk his cup of bitter tea and crept into bed, he was prompted to amend his prayer, for he discovered that two blankers were not going to be enough for him. Even the satisfaction of knowing that Jerry must feel the want even more keenly than did he failed to warm him sufficiently for thorough comfort. Tom was tired enough to swoon, but he refused to close his eyes before the rain came— what purpose was served by retributive justice unless a fellow stayed on the job to enjoy it?

Truth to say, this self-denial cost him little, for the night had brought a chill with it and the tent was damp. Linton became aware, ere long, that he couldn't go to sleep, no matter how he tried, so he rose and put on extra clothes. But even then he shivered, and thereafter, of course, his blankets served no purpose whatever. He and Old Jerry were accustomed to sleeping spoon fashion, and not only did Tom miss those other blankets, but also his ex-partner's bodily heat. He would have risen and rekindled his camp-fire had it not been for his reluctance to afford Quirk the gratification of knowing that he was uncomfortable. Some people were just malicious enough to enjoy a man's sufferings.

Well, if he were cold here in this snug shelter, Jerry must be about frozen under his flapping fly. Probably the old fool was too stubborn to whimper; no doubt he'd pretend to be enjoying himself, and would die sooner than acknowledge himself in the wrong. Jerry had courage, that way, but—this would serve him right, this would cure him. Linton was not a little disappointed when the rain continued to hold off.

CHAPTER IX

THE change in the weather had not escaped
Pierce Phillips' notice, and before going to
bed he stepped out of his tent to study the sky.
It was threatening. Recalling extravagant stories
of the violence attained by storms in this moun-
tain-lake country, he decided to make sure that
his boats and cargo were out of reach of any
possible danger, and so walked down to the shore.

A boisterous wind had roused Lake Linderman,
and out of the inky blackness came the sound of
its anger. As Pierce groped his way up to the
nearest skiff he was startled by receiving a sharp
challenge in the Countess Courteau's voice.

"Who is that?" she cried.

"It's I, Pierce," he answered, quickly. He discovered the woman finally, and, approaching
closer, he saw that she was sitting on a pile of
freight, her heels drawn up beneath her and her
arms clasped around her knees. "I came down to
make sure everything was snug. But what are
you doing here?"

She looked down into his upturned face and her
white teeth showed in a smile. "I came for the
same purpose. Now I'm waiting for the storm

to break. You can make out the clouds when your eyes grow accustomed—"

"It's too windy. You'll catch cold," he declared.

"Oh, I'm warm, and I love storms!" She stared out into the night, then added, "I'm a stormy creature."

Again he urged her to return to her tent, and in his voice was such genuine concern that she laid her hand upon his shoulder. It was a warm, impulsive gesture and it betrayed a grateful appreciation of his solicitude; it was the first familiarity she had ever permitted herself to indulge in, and when she spoke it was in an unusually intimate tone:

"You're a good friend, Pierce. I don't know what I'd do without you."

Phillips' surprise robbed him momentarily of speech. This woman possessed a hundred moods; a few hours before she had treated him with a cool indifference that was almost studied; now, without apparent reason, she had turned almost affectionate. Perhaps it was the night, or the solitude, that drew them together; whatever the reason, those first few words, that one impulsive gesture, assured Pierce that they were very close to each other, for the moment at least.

"I'm—glad," he said, finally. "I wish I were more— I wish—"

"What?" she queried, when he hesitated.

"I wish you *couldn't* do without me." It was out; he realized in a panic that his whole secret

147

was hers. With no faintest intention of speaking, even of hinting at the truth, he had blurted forth a full confession. She had caught him off guard, and, like a perfect ass, he had betrayed himself. What would she think? How would she take his audacity, his presumption? He was surprised to feel her fingers tighten briefly before her hand was withdrawn.

The Countess Courteau was not offended. Had it not been for that pressure upon his shoulder Phillips would have believed that his words had gone unheard, for she entirely ignored them.

"Night! Wind! Storm!" she said, in a queer, meditative tone. "They stir the blood, don't they? Not yours, perhaps, but mine. I was always restless. You see, I was born on the ocean —on the way over here. My father was a sailor; he was a stormy-weather man. At a time like this everything in me quickens, I'm aware of impulses I never feel at other times—desires I daren't yield to. It was on a stormy night that the Count proposed to me." She laughed shortly, bitterly. "I believed him. I'd believe anything —I'd do, I'd dare anything—when the winds are reckless." She turned abruptly to her listener and it seemed to him that her eyes were strangely luminous. "Have you ever felt that way?"

He shook his head.

"Lucky for you; it would be a man's undoing. Tell me, what am I? What do you make of me?" While the young man felt for an answer she ran on: "I'd like to know. What sort of woman do

148

you consider me? How have I impressed you? Speak plainly—no sentiment. You're a clean-minded, unsophisticated boy. I'm curious to hear—"

"I can't speak like a boy," he said, gravely, but with more than a hint of resentment in his tone, "for—I'm not a boy. Not any longer."

"Oh yes, you are! You're fresh and wholesome and honorable and— Well, only boys are that. What do I seem, to you?"

"You're a chameleon. There's nobody in the world quite like you. Why, at this minute you're different even to yourself. You — take my breath—"

"Do you consider me harsh, masculine—?"

"Oh no!"

"I'm glad of that. I'm not, really. I've had a hard experience and my eyes were opened early. I know poverty, disappointment, misery, everything unpleasant, but I'm smart and I know how to get ahead. I've never stood still. I've learned how to fight, too, for I've had to make my own way. Why, Pierce, you're the one man who ever did me an unselfish favor or a real, disinterested courtesy. Do you wonder that I want to know what kind of a creature you consider me?"

"Perhaps I'm not altogether unselfish," he told her, sullenly.

The Countess did not heed this remark; she did not seem to read the least significance into it. Her chin was upon her knees, her face was turned again to the darkness whence came the rising voice of stormy waters. The wind whipped a strand of her hair into Phillips' face.

"It is hard work fighting men—and women, too—and I'm awfully tired. Tired inside, you understand. One gets tired fighting alone—always alone. One has dreams of—well, dreams. It's a pity they never come true."

"What are some of them?" he inquired.

The woman, still under the spell of her hour, made as if to answer; then she stirred and raised her head. "This isn't a safe night to talk about them. I think I shall go to bed." She extended her hand to Phillips, but instead of taking it he reached forth and lifted her bodily down out of the wind. She gasped as she felt his strong hands under her arms; for a moment her face brushed his and her fragrant breath was warm against his cheek. Phillips lowered her gently, slowly, until her feet were on the ground, but even then his grasp lingered and he held her close to him.

They stood breast to breast for a moment and Pierce saw that in this woman's expression was neither fear nor resentment, but some strange emotion new-born of the night—an emotion which his act had started into life and which as yet she did not fully understand. Her eyes were wide and wondering; they remained fixed upon his, and that very fixity suggested a meaning so surprising, so significant, that he felt the world spin dizzily under him. She was astonished, yet expectant; she was stunned but ready. He experienced a fierce desire to hold her closer, closer,

150

to crush her in his arms, and although she resisted faintly, unconsciously she yielded; her inner being answered his without reserve. She did not turn her face away when his came closer, even when his lips covered hers.

After a long moment she surrendered wholly, she snuggled closer and bowed her head upon his shoulder. Her cheek against his was very cold from the wind and Pierce discovered that it was wet with tears.

"It has been a long fight," she sighed, in a voice that he could scarcely hear. "I didn't know how tired I was."

Phillips groped for words, but he could find nothing to say, his ordered thoughts having fled before this sudden gust of ardor as leaves are whirled away before a tempest. All he knew was that in his arms lay a woman he had knelt to, a worshipful goddess of snow and gold before whom he had abased himself, but who had turned to flesh at his first touch.

He kissed her again and again, warmly, tenderly, and yet with a ruthless fervor that grew after each caress, and she submitted passively, the while those tears stole down her cheeks. In reality she was neither passive nor passionless, for her body quivered and Phillips knew that his touch had set her afire; but rather she seemed to be exhausted and at the same time enthralled as by some dream from which she was loath to rouse herself.

After a while her hand rose to his face and

151

stroked it softly, then she drew herself away from him and with a wan smile upon her lips said:

"The wind has made a fool of me."

"No, no!" he cried, forcefully. "You asked me what I think of you— Well, now you know."

Still smiling, she shook her head slowly, then she told him, "Come! I hear the rain."

"But I want to talk to you. I have so much to say—"

"What is there to talk about to-night? Hark!" They could feel, rather than hear, the first warnings of the coming downpour, so hand in hand they walked up the gravelly beach and into the fringe of the forest where glowed the dull illumination from lamplit canvas walls. When they paused before the Countess' tent Pierce once more enfolded her in his arms and sheltered her from the boisterous breath of the night. His emotions were in a similar tumult, but as yet he could not voice them, he could merely stammer:

"You have never told me your name."

"Hilda."

"May I—call you that?"

She nodded. "Yes—when we are alone. Hilda Halberg, that was my name."

"Hilda! Hilda—Phillips." Pierce tried the sound curiously. The Countess drew back abruptly, with a shiver; then, in answer to his quick concern, said:

"I—I think I'm cold."

He undertook to clasp her closer, but she held him off, murmuring:

"Let it be Hilda Halberg for to-night. Let's not think of— Let's not think at all. Hilda— bride of the storm. There's a tempest in my blood, and who can think with a tempest raging?"

She raised her face and kissed him upon the lips, then, disengaging herself once more from his hungry arms, she stepped inside her shelter. The last he saw of her was her luminous smile framed against the black background; then she let the tent-fly fall.

As Phillips turned away big raindrops began to drum upon the near-by tent roofs, the spruce-tops overhead bent low, limbs threshed as the gusty night wind beat upon them. But he heard none of it, felt none of it, for in his ears rang the music of the spheres and on his face lingered the warmth of a woman's lips, the first love kiss that he had ever known.

Tom Linton roused himself from a chilly doze to find that the rain had come at last. It was a roaring night; his tent was bellied in by the force of the wind, and the raindrops beat upon it with the force of buckshot. Through the entrance slit, through the open stovepipe hole, the gale poured, bringing dampness with it and rendering the interior as draughty as a corn-crib. Rolling himself more tightly in his blankets, Linton addressed the darkness through chattering teeth.

"Darned old fool! This 'll teach him!"

He strained his ears for sounds of Jerry, but

could hear nothing above the slatting of wet canvas, the tattoo of drops, and the roar of wind in the tree-tops. After the first violence of the squall had passed he fancied he could hear his former partner stirring, so he arose and peered out into the night. At first he could see nothing, but in time he dimly made out Jerry struggling with his tarpaulin. Evidently the fly had blown down, or up, and its owner was restretching it. Linton grinned. That would drench the old dodo to the skin and he'd soon be around, begging shelter.

"But I won't let him in, not if he drowns," Tom muttered, harshly. He recalled one of Jerry's gibes at the saw-pit, a particularly unfeeling, nay, a downright venomous insult which had rankled steadily ever since. His former friend had seen fit to ridicule honest perspiration and to pretend to mistake it for raindrops. That remark had been utterly uncalled for and it had betrayed a wanton malice, a malevolent desire to wound; well, here was a chance to even the score. When Jerry came dripping to the tent door, Tom decided he would poke his head out into the deluge and then cry in evident astonishment: "Why, Jerry, you've been working, haven't you? You're all sweaty!" Mr. Linton giggled out loud. That would be a refinement of sarcasm; that would be a get-back of the finest. If Jerry insisted upon coming in out of the wet he'd tell him gruffly to get out of there and try the lake for a change.

But Mr. Quirk made no move in the direction of the tent; instead he built a fire in his stove and crouched over it, endeavoring vainly to shelter himself from the driving rain. Linton watched him with mingled impatience and resentment. Would the old fool never get enough? Jerry was the most unreasonable, the most tantalizing person in the world.

After a time Mr. Linton found that his teeth were chattering and that his frame had been smitten as by an ague; reluctantly he crept back into bed. He determined to buy, beg, borrow, or steal some more bedding on the morrow—early on the morrow in order to forestall Jerry. Jerry would have to find a tent somewhere, and inasmuch as there were none to be had here at Linderman, he would probably have to return to Dyea. That would delay him seriously—enough, perhaps, so that the jaws of winter would close down upon him. Through the drone of pattering drops there came the faint sound of a cough.

Mr. Linton sat up in bed. "Pneumonia!" he exclaimed. Well, Jerry was getting exactly what he deserved. He had called him, Tom, an "old fool," a "dam' old fool," to be precise. The epithet in itself meant nothing—it was in fact a fatuous and feeble term of abuse as compared to the opprobrious titles which he and Jerry were in the habit of exchanging—it was that abominable adjective which hurt. Jerry and he had called each other many names at times, they had exchanged numerous gibes and insults, but nothing like that hateful word "old" had ever passed between them until this fatal morning. Jerry

11   155

Quirk himself was old, the oldest man in the world, perhaps, but Tom had exercised an admirable regard for his partner's feelings and had never cast it up to him. Thus had his consideration been repaid. However, the poor fellow's race was about run, for he couldn't stand cold or exposure. Why, a wet foot sent him to bed. How, then, could a rickety ruin of his antiquity withstand the ravages of pneumonia—galloping pneumonia, at that?

Linton reflected that common decency would demand that he wait over a day or two and help bury the old man—people would expect that much of him. He'd do it. He'd speak kindly of the departed; he'd even erect a cross and write an epitaph upon it—a kindly, lying epitaph extolling the dead man's virtues, and omitting all mention of his faults.

Once more that hacking cough sounded, and the listener stirred uneasily. Jerry had some virtues—a few of the common, elemental sort—he was honest and he was brave, but, for that matter, so were most people. Yes, the old scoundrel had nerve enough. Linton recalled a certain day, long past, when he and Quirk had been sent out to round up some cattle-rustlers. Being the youngest deputies in the sheriff's office, the toughest jobs invariably fell to them. Those were the good, glad days, Tom reflected. Jerry had made a reputation on that trip and he had saved his companion's life—Linton flopped nervously in his bed at the memory. Why think of days dead and gone? Jerry was an altogether different man in those times. He neither criticized nor permitted others to criticize his team-mate, and, so far as that particular obligation went, Linton had repaid it with compound interest. If anything, the debt now lay on Jerry's side.

Tom tried to close the book of memory and to consider nothing whatever except the rankling present, but, now that his thoughts had begun to run backward, he could not head them off. He wished Jerry wouldn't cough; it was a distressing sound, and it disturbed his rest. Nevertheless, that hollow, hacking complaint continued and finally the listener arose, lit a lantern, put on a slicker and untied his tent flaps.

Jerry's stove was sizzling in the partial shelter of the canvas sheet; over it the owner crouched in an attitude of cheerless dejection.

"How you making out?" Tom inquired, gruffly. His voice was cold, his manner was both repellent and hostile.

"Who, me?" Jerry peered up from under his glistening sou'wester. "Oh, I'm doin' fine!"

Linton remained silent, ill at ease; water drained off his coat; his lantern flared smokily in the wind. After a time he cleared his throat and inquired:

"Wet?"

"Naw!"

There was a long pause, then the visitor inquired: "Are you lying?"

"Unh-hunh!"

Again silence claimed both men until Tom broke out, irritably: "Well, you aim to set here all night?"

"Sure! I ain't sleepy. I don't mind a little mist and I'm plenty warm." This cheerful assertion was belied by the miserable quaver in which it was voiced.

"Why don't you—er—run over to my tent?" Linton gasped and swallowed hard. The invitation was out, the damage was done. "There's lots of room."

Mr. Quirk spared his caller's further feelings by betraying no triumph whatever. Rather plaintively he declared: "I got *room* enough here. It ain't exactly room I need." Again he coughed.

"Here! Get a move on you, quick," Linton ordered, forcefully. "The idea of you setting around hatching out a lungful of pneumonia bugs! Git! I'll bring your bedding."

Mr. Quirk rose with alacrity. "Say! Let's take my stove over to your tent and warm her up. I bet you're cold?"

"N-no! I'm comfortable enough." The speaker's teeth played an accompaniment to this mendacious denial. "Of course I'm not sweating any, but—I s'pose the stove would cheer things up, eh? Rotten night, ain't it?"

"Worst I ever saw. Rotten country, for that matter."

"You said something," Mr. Linton chattered. He nodded his head with vigor.

It was wet work moving Jerry's belongings,

158

but the transfer was finally effected, the stove was set up and a new fire started. This done, Tom brought forth a bottle of whisky.

"Here," said he, "take a snifter. It'll do you good."

Jerry eyed the bottle with frank astonishment before he exclaimed: "Why, I didn't know you was a drinkin' man. You been hidin' a secret vice from me?"

"No. And I'm not a drinking man. I brought it along for—you. I—er—that cough of yours used to worry me, so—"

"Pshaw! I cough easy. You know that."

"You take a jolt and"—Linton flushed with embarrassment—"and I'll have one with you. I was lying just now; I'm colder 'n a frog's belly."

"Happy days," said Quirk, as he tipped the bottle.

"A long life and a wicked one!" Linton drank in his turn. "Now then, get out of those cold compresses. Here's some dry underclothes— thick, too. We'll double up those henskin blankets—for to-night—and I'll keep the fire a-going. I'll cure that cough if I sweat you as white as a washwoman's thumb."

"You'll do nothing of the sort," Jerry declared, as he removed his sodden garments and hung them up. "You'll crawl right into bed with me and we'll have a good sleep. You're near dead."

But Linton was by no means reassured; his tone was querulous when he cried: "Why didn't you come in before you caught cold? S'pose you

get sick on me now? But you won't. I won't
let you." In a panic of apprehension he dug out
his half of the contents of the medicine-kit and
began to paw through them. "Who got the
cough syrup, Jerry; you or me?" The speaker's
voice broke miserably.

Mr. Quirk laid a trembling hand upon his ex-
partner's shoulder; his voice, too, was shaky
when he said, "You're awful good to me, Tom."

The other shook off the grasp and undertook
to read the labels on the bottles, but they had
become unaccountably blurred and there was a
painful lump in his throat. It seemed to him that
Old Jerry's bare legs looked pitifully thin and
spidery and that his bony knees had a rheumatic
appearance.

"Hell! I treated you mighty mean," said he.
"But I 'most died when you—began to cough.
I thought sure—" Tom choked and shook his
gray head, then with the heel of his harsh palm
he wiped a drop of moisture from his cheek.
"Look at me—cryin'!" He tried to laugh and
failed.

Jerry, likewise, struggled with his tears.

"You—you dam' old fool!" he cried, affectionately.

Linton smiled with delight. "Give it to me,"
he urged. "Lam into me, Jerry. I deserve it.
Gosh! I was lonesome!"

A half-hour later the two friends were lying
side by side in their bed and the stove was glowing
comfortably. They had ceased shivering. Old

Jerry had "spooned" up close to old Tom and his bodily heat was grateful.

Linton eyed the fire with tender yearning. "That's a good stove you got."

"She's a corker, ain't she?" .

"I been thinking about trading you a half interest in my tent for a half interest in her."

"The trade's made." There was a moment of silence. "What d'you say we hòok up together —sort of go pardners for a while? I got a long outfit and a short boat. I'll put 'em in against yours. I bet we'd get along all right. I'm onnery, but I got good points."

Mr. Linton smiled dreamily. "It's a go. I need a good partner."

"I'll buy a new fryin'-pan out of my money. Mine got split, somehow."

Tom chuckled. "You darned old fool!" said he.

Jerry heaved a long sigh and snuggled closer; soon he began to snore. He snored in a low and confidential tone at first, but gradually the sound increased in volume and rose in pitch.

Linton listened to it with a thrill, and he assured himself that he had never heard music of such soul-satisfying sweetness as issued from the nostrils of his new partner.

CHAPTER X

TO the early Klondikers, Chilkoot Pass was a personality, a Presence at once sinister, cruel, and forbidding. So, too, only in greater measure, was Miles Cañon. The Chilkoot toyed with men, it wore them out, it stripped them of their strength and their manhood, it wrecked their courage and it broke their hearts. The cañon sucked them in and swallowed them. This cañon is nothing more nor less than a rift in a great basaltic barrier which lies athwart the river's course, the entrance to it being much like the door in a wall. Above it the waters are dammed and into it they pour as into a flume; down it they rage in swiftly increasing fury, for it is steeply pitched, and, although the gorge itself is not long, immediately below it are other turbulent stretches equally treacherous. It seems as if here, within the space of some four miles, Nature had exhausted her ingenuity in inventing terrors to frighten invaders, as if here she had combined every possible peril of river travel. The result of her labors is a series of cataclysms.

Immediately below Miles Cañon itself are the Squaw Rapids, where the torrent spills itself over

a confusion of boulders, bursting into foam and
gyrating in dizzy whirlpools, its surface broken
by explosions of spray or pitted by devouring
vortices resembling the oily mouths of marine
monsters. Below this, in turn, is the White
Horse, worst of all. Here the flood somersaults
over a tremendous reef, flinging on high a gleaming
curtain of spray. These rapids are well named,
for the tossing waves resemble nothing more than
runaway white horses with streaming manes and
tails.

These are by no means all the dangers that con-
fronted the first Yukon stampeders—there are
other troublesome waters below—for instance,
Rink Rapids, where the river boils and bubbles
like a kettle over an open fire, and Five Fingers,
so-called by reason of a row of knobby, knuckled
pinnacles that reach up like the stiff digits of a
drowning hand and split the stream into diver-
gent channels—but those three, Miles Cañon,
the Squaw, and White Horse, were the worst and
together they constituted a menace that tried
the courage of the bravest men.

In the cañon, where the waters are most nar-
rowly constricted, they heap themselves up into
a longitudinal ridge or bore, a comb perhaps four
feet higher than the general level. To ride this
crest and to avoid the destroying fangs that lie
in wait on either side is a feat that calls for nerve
and skill and endurance on the part of boatmen.
The whole four miles is a place of many voices,
a thundering place that numbs the senses and

destroys all hearing. Its tumult is heard afar and it covers the entire region like a blanket. The weight of that sound is oppressive.

Winter was at the heels of the Courteau party when it arrived at this point in its journey; it brought up the very tail of the autumn rush and the ice was close behind. The Countess and her companions had the uncomfortable feeling that they were inside the jaws of a trap which might be sprung at any moment, for already the hills were dusted with gray and white, creeks and rivulets were steadily dwindling and shelf ice was forming on the larger streams, the skies were low and overcast and there was a vicious tingle to the air. Delays had slowed them up, as, for instance, at Windy Arm, where a gale had held them in camp for several days; then, too, their boats were built of poorly seasoned lumber and in consequence were in need of frequent attention. Eventually, however, they came within hearing of a faint whisper, as of wind among pine branches, then of a muffled murmur that grew to a sullen diapason. The current quickened beneath them, the river-banks closed in, and finally beetling cliffs arose, between which was a cleft that swallowed the stream.

Just above the opening was a landing-place where boats lay gunwale to gunwale, and here the Courteau skiffs were grounded. A number of weather-beaten tents were stretched among the trees. Most of them were the homes of pilots, but others were occupied by voyagers who preferred to chance a winter's delay as the price of portaging their goods around rather than risk their all upon one throw of fortune. The great majority of the arrivals, however, were restowing their oufits, lashing them down and covering them preparatory to a dash through the shouting chasm. There was an atmosphere of excitement and apprehension about the place; every face was strained and expectant; fear lurked in many an eye.

On a tree near the landing were two placards. One bore a finger pointing up the steep trail to the top of the ridge, and it was marked:

"This way—two weeks."

The other pointed down directly into the throat of the roaring gorge. It read:

"This way—two minutes."

Pierce Phillips smiled as he perused these signs; then he turned up the trail, for in his soul was a consuming curiosity to see the place of which he had heard so much.

Near the top of the slope he met a familiar figure coming down—a tall, upstanding French-Canadian who gazed out at the world through friendly eyes.

'Poleon Doret recognized the new-comer and burst into a boisterous greeting.

"Wal, wal!" he cried. "You 'ain't live' to be hung yet, eh? Now you come lookin' for me, I bet."

"Yes. You're the very man I want to see."

"Good! I tak' you t'rough."

Phillips smiled frankly. "I'm not sure I want

165

to go through. I'm in charge of a big outfit and I'm looking for a pilot and a professional crew. I'm a perfect dub at this sort of thing."

'Poleon nodded. "Dere's no use risk it if you 'ain't got to, dat's fac'. I don' lost no boats yet, but—sometam's I bus' 'em up pretty bad." He grinned cheerily. "Dese new-comer get scare' easy an' forget to row, den dey say 'Poleon she's bum pilot. You seen de cañon yet?" When Pierce shook his head the speaker turned back and led the way out to the rim.

It was an impressive spectacle that Phillips beheld. Perhaps a hundred feet directly beneath him the river whirled and leaped; cross-currents boiled out from projecting irregularities in the walls; here and there the waters tumbled madly and flung wet arms aloft, while up out of the gorge came a mighty murmur, redoubled by the echoing cliffs. A log came plunging through and it moved with the speed of a torpedo. Phillips watched it, fascinated.

"Look! Dere's a boat!" 'Poleon cried. In between the basalt jaws appeared a skiff with two rowers, and a man in the stern. The latter was braced on wide-spread legs and he held his weight upon a steering-sweep. Down the boat came at a galloping gait, threshing over waves and flinging spray head-high; it bucked and it dove, it buried its nose and then lifted it, but the oarsman continued to maintain it on a steady course.

"Bravo!" Doret shouted, waving his cap. To Pierce he said: "Dat's good pilot an' he knows swif' water. But dere's lot of feller here who ain't so good. Dey tak' chance for beeg money. Wal, w'at you t'ink of her? She's dandy, eh?"

"It's an — inferno," Phillips acknowledged: "You earn all the money you get for running it."

"You don' care for 'im, w'at?"

"I do not. I don't mind taking a chance, but— what chance would a fellow have in there? Why, he'd never come up."

"Dat's right."

Phillips stared at his companion curiously. "You must need money pretty badly."

The giant shook his head in vigorous denial. "No! Money? Pouf! She come, she go. But, you see—plenty people drowned if somebody don' tak' dem t'rough, so—I stay. Dis winter I build myse'f nice cabin an' do li'l trappin'. Nex' summer I pilot again."

"Aren't you going to Dawson?" Pierce was incredulous; he could not understand this fellow.

Doret's expression changed; a fleeting sadness settled in his eyes. "I been dere," said he. "I ain't care much for seciu' beeg city. I'm lonesome feller." After a moment he exclaimed, more brightly: "Now we go. I see if I can hire crew to row your boats."

"How does she look to you?" Lucky Broad inquired, when Pierce and his companion appeared. He and Bridges had not taken the trouble to acquaint themselves with the cañon, but immediately upon landing had begun to stow away their freight and to lash a tarpaulin over it.

"Better go up and see for yourself," the young man suggested.

Lucky shook his head. "Not me," he declared. "I can hear all I want to. Listen to it! I got a long life ahead of me and I'm going to nurse it."

Kid Bridges was of like mind, for he said: "Sure! We was a coupla brave guys in Dyea, but what's the good of runnin' up to an undertaker and giving him your measurements? He'll get a tape-line on you soon enough."

"Then you don't intend to chance it?" Pierce inquired.

Broad scowled at the questioner. "Say! I wouldn't walk down that place if it was froze."

"Nor me," the other gambler seconded. "Not for a million dollars would I tease the embalmer that way. Not for a million. Would you, Lucky?"

Broad appeared to weigh the figures carefully; then he said, doubtfully: "I'm a cheap guy. I might risk it once—for five hundred thousand, cash. But that's rock bottom; I wouldn't take a nickel less."

Doret had been listening with some amusement; now he said, "You boys got wide pay-streak, eh?"

Bridges nodded without shame. "Wider 'n a swamp, and yeller 'n butter."

"Wal, I see w'at I can do." The pilot walked up the bank in search of a crew.

In the course of a half-hour he was back again and with him came the Countess Courteau. Calling Pierce aside, the woman said, swiftly: "We can't get a soul to help us; everybody's in a rush. We'll have to use our own men."

"Broad and Bridges are the best we have," he told her, "but they refuse."

"You're not afraid, are you?"

Now Pierce was afraid and he longed mightily to admit that he was, but he lacked the courage to do so. He smiled feebly and shrugged, whereupon the former speaker misread his apparent indifference and flashed him a smile.

"Forgive me," she said, in a low voice. "I know you're not." She hurried down to the water's edge and addressed the two gamblers in a business-like tone: "We've no time to lose. Which one of you wants to lead off with Doret and Pierce?"

The men exchanged glances. It was Broad who finally spoke. "We been figuring it would please us better to walk," he said, mildly.

"Suit yourselves," the Countess told them, coolly. "But it's a long walk from here to Dawson." She turned back to Pierce and said: "You've seen the cañon. There's nothing so terrible about it, is there?"

Phillips was conscious that 'Poleon Doret's eyes were dancing with laughter, and anger at his own weakness flared up in him. "Why, no!" he lied, bravely. "It will be a lot of fun."

Kid Bridges leveled a sour look at the speaker. "Some folks have got low ideas of entertainment," said he. "Some folks is absolutely depraved that way. You'd probably enjoy a broken arm—it would feel so good when it got well."

The Countess Courteau's lip was curled contemptuously when she said: "Listen! I'm not going to be held up. There's a chance, of course, but hundreds have gone through. I can pull an oar. Pierce and I will row the first boat."

Doret opened his lips to protest, but Broad obviated the necessity of speech by rising from his seat and announcing: "Deal the cards! I came in on no pair; I don't aim to be raised out ahead of the draw—not by a woman."

Mr. Bridges was both shocked and aggrieved by his companion's words. "You going to tackle it?" he asked, incredulously.

Lucky made a grimace of intense abhorrence in Pierce's direction. "Sure! I don't want to miss all this fun I hear about."

"When you get through, if you do, which you probably won't," Bridges told him, with a bleak and cheerless expression, "set a gill-net to catch me. I'll be down on the next trip."

"Good for you!" cried the Countess.

"It ain't good for me," the man exclaimed, angrily. "It's the worst thing in the world for me. I'm grand-standing and you know it. So's Lucky, but there wouldn't be any living with him if he pulled it off and I didn't."

Doret chuckled. To Pierce he said, in a low voice: "Plenty feller mak' fool of demse'f on dat woman. I know all 'bout it. But she 'ain't mak' fool of herse'f, you bet."

"How do you mean?" Pierce inquired, quickly.

'Poleon eyed him shrewdly. "Wal, tak' you. You're scare', ain't you? But you sooner die so long she don't know it. Plenty oder feller jus' lak' dat." He walked to the nearest skiff, removed his coat, and began to untie his boots.

Lucky Broad joined the pilot, then looked on uneasily at these preparations. "What's the idea?" he inquired. "Are you too hot?"

'Poleon grinned at him and nodded. Very reluctantly Broad stripped off his mackinaw, then seated himself and tugged at his footgear. He paused, after a moment, and addressed himself to Bridges.

"It's no use, Kid. I squawk!" he said.

"Beginning to weaken, eh?"

"Sure! I got a hole in my sock—look! Somebody 'll find me after I've been drowned a week or two, and what 'll they say?"

"Pshaw! You won't come up till you get to St. Michael's, and you'll be spoiled by that time." Kid Bridges tried to smile, but the result was a failure. "You'll be swelled up like a dead horse, and so 'll I. They won't know us apart."

When Pierce had likewise stripped down and taken his place at the oars, Broad grumbled: "The idea of calling me 'Lucky'! It ain't in the cards." He spat on his hands and settled himself in his seat, then cried, "Well, lead your ace!"

As the little craft moved out into the stream, Pierce Phillips noticed that the Kirby scow, which had run the Courteau boats a close race all

12

the way from Linderman, was just pulling into the bank. Lines had been passed ashore and, standing on the top of the cargo, he could make out the figure of Rouletta Kirby.

In spite of a strong steady stroke the rowboat seemed to move sluggishly; foam and debris bobbed alongside and progress appeared to be slow, but when the oarsmen lifted their eyes they discovered that the shores were running past with amazing swiftness. Even as they looked, those shores rose abruptly and closed in, there came a mounting roar, then the skiff was sucked in between high, rugged walls. Unseen hands reached forth and seized it, unseen forces laid hold of it and impelled it forward; it began to plunge and to wallow; spray flew and wave-crests climbed over the gunwales.

Above the tumult 'Poleon was urging his crew to greater efforts. "Pull hard!" he shouted. "Hi! Hi! Hi!" He swayed in unison to their straining bodies. "Mak' dose oar crack," he yelled. "By Gar, dat's goin' some!"

The fellow's teeth were gleaming, his face was alight with an exultant recklessness, he cast defiance at the approaching terrors. He was alert, watchful; under his hands the stout ash steering-oar bent like a bow; he flung his whole strength into the battle with the waters. Soon the roar increased until it drowned his shouts and forced him to pantomime his orders. The boat was galloping through a wild smother of ice-cold spray and the reverberating cliffs were streaming past

172

like the unrolling scenery on a painted canvas panorama.

It was a hellish place; it echoed to a demoniac din and it was a tremendous sensation to brave it, for the boat did not glide nor slip down the descent; it went in a succession of jarring leaps; it lurched and twisted; it rolled and plunged as if in a demented effort to unseat its passengers and scatter its cargo. To the occupants it seemed as if its joints were opening, as if the boards themselves were being wrenched loose from the ribs to which they were nailed. The men were drenched, of course, for they traveled in a cloud of spume; their feet were ankle-deep in cold water, and every new deluge caused them to gasp.

How long it lasted Pierce Phillips never knew; the experience was too terrific to be long lived. It was a nightmare, a hideous phantasmagoria of frightful sensations, a dissolving stereopticon of bleak, scudding walls, of hydrophobic boulders frothing madly as the flood crashed over them, of treacherous whirlpools, and of pursuing breakers that reached forth licking tongues of destruction. Then the river opened, the cliffs fell away, and the torrent spewed itself out into an expanse of whirlpools—a lake of gyrating funnels that warred with one another and threatened to twist the keel from under the boat.

'Poleon swung close in to the right bank, where an eddy raced up against the flood; some one flung a rope from the shore and drew the boat in.

"Wal! I never had no better crew," cried the

pilot. "W'at you t'ink of 'im, eh?" He smiled down at the white-lipped oarsmen, who leaned forward, panting and dripping.

"Is—that all of it?" Lucky Broad inquired, weakly.

"*Mais non!* Look! Dere's W'ite 'Orse." Doret indicated a wall of foam and spray farther down the river. Directly across the expanse of whirlpools stood a village named after the rapids. "You get plenty more bimeby."

"You're wrong. I got plenty right now," Broad declared.

"I'm glad the Countess didn't come," said Phillips.

When the men had wrung out their clothes and put on their boots they set out along the back trail over the bluffs.

Danny Royal was not an imaginative person. He possessed, to be sure, the superstitions of the average horseman and gambler, and he believed strongly in hunches, but he was not fanciful and he put no faith in dreams and portents. It bothered him exceedingly, therefore, to discover that he was weighed down by an unaccountable but extremely oppressive sense of apprehension. How or why it had come to obsess him he could not imagine, but for some reason Miles Cañon and the stormy waters below it had assumed terrible potentialities and he could not shake off the conviction that they were destined to prove his undoing. This feeling he had allowed to grow until

174

THE WINDS OF CHANCE

now a fatalistic apathy had settled upon him and his usual cheerfulness was replaced by a senseless irritability. He suffered explosions of temper quite as surprising to the Kirbys, father and daughter, as to himself. On the day of his arrival he was particularly ugly, wherefore Rouletta was impelled to remonstrate with him.

"What ails you, Danny?" she inquired. "You'll have our men quitting."

"I wish they would," he cried. "Boatmen! They don't know as much about boats as me and Sam."

"They do whatever they're told."

Royal acknowledged this fact ungraciously. "Trouble is we don't know what to tell 'em to do. All Sam knows is 'gee' and 'haw,' and I can't steer anything that don't wear a bridle. Why, if this river wasn't fenced in with trees we'd have taken the wrong road and been lost, long ago."

Rouletta nodded thoughtfully. "Father is just as afraid of water as you are. He won't admit it, but I can tell. It has gotten on his nerves and —I've had hard work to keep him from drinking."

"Say! Don't let him get started on *that!*" Danny exclaimed, earnestly. "That *would* be the last touch."

"Trust me. I—"

But Kirby himself appeared at that moment, having returned from a voyage of exploration. Said he: "There's a good town below. I had a chance to sell the outfit."

175

"Going to do it?" Danny could not conceal his eagerness.

The elder man shook his gray head. "Hardly. I'm no piker."

"I wish you and Danny would take the portage and trust the pilot to run the rapids," Rouletta said.

Kirby turned his expressionless face upon first one then the other of his companions. "Nervous?" he inquired of Royal.

The latter silently admitted that he was.

"Go ahead. You and Letty cross afoot—"

"And you?"

"Oh, I'm going to stick!"

"Father—" the girl began, but old Sam shook his head.

"No. This is my case bet, and I'm going to watch it."

Royal's weazened face puckered until it resembled more than ever a withered apple. "Then I'll stick, too," he declared. "I never laid down on you yet, Sam."

"How about you, Letty?"

The girl smiled. "Why, I wouldn't trust you boys out of my sight for a minute. Something would surely happen."

Kirby stooped and kissed his daughter's cheek. "You've always been our mascot, and you've always brought us luck. I'd go to hell in a paper suit if you were along. You're a game kid, too, and I want you to be like that, always. Be a thoroughbred. Don't weaken, no matter how

176

bad things break for you. This cargo of rum is worth the best claim in Dawson, and it 'll put us on our feet again. All I want is one more chance. Double and quit—that's us."

This was an extraordinarily long speech for "One-armed" Kirby; it showed that he was deeply in earnest.

"Double and quit?" breathed the girl. "Do you mean it, dad?"

He nodded: "I'm going to leave you heeled. I don't aim to take my eyes off this barge again till she's in Dawson."

Rouletta's face was transformed; there was a great gladness in her eyes—a gladness half obscured by tears. "Double and quit. Oh—I've dreamed of—quitting—so often! You've made me very happy, dad."

Royal, who knew this girl's dreams as well as he knew his own, felt a lump in his throat. He was a godless little man, but Rouletta Kirby's joys were holy things to him, her tears distressed him deeply, therefore he walked away to avoid the sight of them. Her slightest wish had been his law ever since she had mastered words enough to voice a request, and now he, too, was happy to learn that Sam Kirby was at last ready to mold his future in accordance with her desires. Letty had never liked their mode of life; she had accepted it under protest, and with the passing years her unspoken disapproval had assumed the proportions of a great reproach. She had never put that disapproval into words—she was far too loyal for that—but Danny had known. He knew her ambitions and her possibilities, and he had sufficient vision to realize something of the injustice she suffered at her father's hands. Sam loved his daughter as few parents love a child, but he was a strange man and he showed his affection in characteristic ways. It pleased Royal greatly to learn that the old man had awakened to the wrong he did, and that this adventure would serve to close the story, as all good stories close, with a happy ending.

In spite of these cheering thoughts, Danny was unable wholly to shake off his oppressive forebodings, and as he paused on the river-bank to stare with gloomy fascination at the jaws of the gorge they returned to plague him. The sound that issued out of that place was terrifying, the knowledge that it frightened him enraged the little man.

It was an unpropitious moment for any one to address Royal; therefore, when he heard himself spoken to, he whirled with a scowl upon his face. A tall French-Canadian, just back from the portage, was saying:

"M'sieu', I ain't good hand at mix in 'noder feller's bizneses, but—dat pilot you got she's no good."

Royal looked the stranger over from head to foot. "How d'you know?" he inquired, sharply.

"Biccause—I'm pilot myse'f."

"Oh, I see! You're one of the *good* ones." Danny's air was surly, his tone forbidding.

"Yes."

"Hate yourself, don't you? I s'pose you want his job. Is that it? No wonder—five hundred seeds for fifteen minutes' work. Soft graft, I call it." The speaker laughed unpleasantly. "Well, what does a *good* pilot charge?"

"Me?" The Canadian shrugged indifferently. "I charge you one t'ousan' dollar."

Royal's jaw dropped. "The devil you say!" he exclaimed.

"I don't want de job—your scow's no good—but I toss a coin wit' you. One t'ousan' dollar or—free trip."

"Nothing doing," snapped the ex-horseman.

"*Bien!* Now I give you li'l *ad*-vice. Hol' hard to de right in lower end dis cañon. Dere's beeg rock dere. Don't touch 'im or you goin' spin lak' top an' mebbe you go over W'ite 'Orse side-ways. Dat's goin' smash you, sure."

Royal broke out, peevishly: "Another hot tip, eh? Everybody's got some feed-box information—especially the ones you don't hire. Well, I ain't scared—"

"Oh yes, you are!" said the other man. "Every-body is scare' of dis place."

"Anyhow, I ain't scared a thousand dollars' worth. Takes a lot to scare me that much. I bet this place is as safe as a chapel and I bet our scow goes through with her tail up. Let her bump; she'll finish with me on her back and all her weights. I built her and I named her."

Danny watched the pilot as he swung down to the stony shore and rejoined Pierce Phillips; then he looked on in fascination while they removed their outer garments, stepped into a boat with Kid Bridges, and rowed away into the gorge.

"It's—got my goat!" muttered the little jockey.

CHAPTER XI

ALTHOUGH scows larger than the *Rouletta* had run Miles Cañon and the rapids below in safety, perhaps none more unwieldy had ever done so. Royal had built his barge stoutly, to be sure, but of other virtues the craft had none. When loaded she was so clumsy, so obstinate, so headstrong that it required unceasing effort to hold her on a course; as for rowing her, it was almost impossible. She took the first swooping rush into the cañon, strange to say, in very good form, and thereafter, by dint of herculean efforts, Royal and his three men managed to hold her head down-stream. Sweeping between the palisades, she galloped clumsily onward, wallowing like a hippopotamus. Her long pine sweeps, balanced and bored to receive thick thole-pins, rose and fell like the stiff legs of some fat, square-bodied spider; she reared her bluff bow; then she dove, shrouding herself in spray.

It was a journey to terrify experienced rivermen; doubly terrifying was it to Royal and Kirby, who knew nothing whatever of swift water and to whom its perils were magnified a thousandfold.

In spite of his apprehension, which by now had

quickened into panic, Danny rose to the occasion
with real credit. His face was like paper, his eyes
were wide and strained; nevertheless, he kept his
gaze fixed upon the pilot and strove to obey the
latter's directions implicitly. Now with all his
strength he heaved upon his sweep; now he
backed water violently; at no time did he trust
himself to look at the cliffs which were scudding
past, nor to contemplate the tortuous turns in the
gorge ahead. That would have been too much
for him. Even when his clumsy oar all but grazed
a bastion, or when a jagged promontory seemed
about to smash his craft, he refused to cease his
frantic labors or to more than lift his eyes. He
saw that Rouletta Kirby was very pale, and he
tried to shout a word of encouragement to her, but
his cry was thin and feeble, and it failed to pierce
the thunder of the waters. Danny hoped the girl
was not as frightened as he, nor as old Sam—the
little man would not have wished such a punishment upon his worst enemy.

Kirby, by reason of his disability, of course,
was prevented from lending any active help with
the boat and was forced to play a purely passive
part. That it was not to his liking any one could
have seen, for, once the moorings were slipped,
he did not open his lips; he merely stood beside
Rouletta, with the fingers of his right hand sunk
into her shoulder, his gray face grayer than ever.
Together they swayed as the deck beneath them
reeled and pitched.

"Look! We're nearly through!" the girl cried

in his ear, after what seemed an interminable time.

Kirby nodded. Ahead he could see the end of the cañon and what appeared to be freer water; out into this open space the torrent flung itself. The scow was riding the bore, that ridge of water upthrust by reason of the pressure from above; between it and the exit from the chute was a rapidly dwindling expanse of tossing waves. Kirby was greatly relieved, but he could not understand why those rollers at the mouth of the gorge should rear themselves so high and should foam so savagely.

The bluffs ended, the narrow throat vomited the river out, and the scow galloped from shadow into pale sunlight.

The owner of the outfit drew a deep breath, his clutching fingers relaxed their nervous hold. He saw that Danny was trying to make himself heard and he leaned forward to catch the fellow's words, when suddenly the impossible happened. The deck beneath his feet was jerked backward and he was flung to his knees. Simultaneously there came a crash, the sound of rending, splintering wood, and over the stern of the barge poured an icy deluge that all but swept father and daughter away. Rouletta screamed, then she called the name of Royal.

"Danny! Danny!" she cried, for both she and old Sam had seen a terrible thing.

The blade of Royal's sweep had been submerged at the instant of the collision and, as a

consequence, the force of that rushing current
had borne it forward, catapulting the man on the
other end overboard as cleanly, as easily as a
school-boy snaps a paper pellet from the end of a
pencil. Before their very eyes the Kirbys saw
their lieutenant, their lifelong friend and servitor,
picked up and hurled into the flood.

"Danny!" shrieked the girl. The voice of the
rapids had changed its tone now, for a cataract
was drumming upon the after-deck and there
was a crashing and a smashing as the piles of
boxes came tumbling down. The scow drove
higher upon the reef, its bow rose until it stood at
a sharp incline, and meanwhile wave after wave
cut like a broach over the stern, which steadily
sank deeper. Then the deck tilted drunkenly
and an avalanche of case-goods was spilled over
the side.

Sam Kirby found himself knee-deep in ice water;
a roller came curling down upon him, but with a
frantic clutch he laid hold of his daughter. He
sank the steel hook that did service as a left hand
into a pile of freight and hung on, battling to
maintain his footing. With a great jarring and
jolting the *Rouletta* rose from the deluge, hung
balanced for a moment or two, and then, relieved
of a portion of her cargo, righted herself and
swung broadside to the stream as if upon a pivot;
finally she was carried free. Onward she swept,
turning end for end, pounding, staggering, as other
rocks from below bit into her bottom.

The river was very low at this season, and the

Rouletta, riding deep because half filled, found obstacles she would otherwise have cleared. She was out of the crooked channel now and it was impossible to manage her, so in a crazy succession of loops and swoops she gyrated down toward that tossing mane of spray that marked the White Horse.

With eyes of terror Sam Kirby scanned the boiling expanse through which the barge was drifting, but nowhere could he catch sight of Danny Royal. He turned to shout to his pilot, only to discover that he also was missing and that the steering-sweep was smashed.

"God! *He's* gone!" cried the old man. It was true; that inundation succeeding the mishap had swept the after-deck clean, and now the scow was not only rudderless, but it lacked a man of experience to direct its course.

Rouletta Kirby was tugging at her father's arm. She lifted a white, horrified face to his and exclaimed: "Danny! I saw him—go!"

Her father's dead face was twitching; he nodded silently. Then he pointed at the cataract toward which they were being carried. He opened his lips to say something, but one of the crew came running back, shouting hoarsely and waving his arms.

"We're going over," the fellow clamored. "We'll all be drowned!"

Kirby felled him with a blow from his artificial hand; then, when the man scrambled to his feet, his employer ordered:

"Get busy! Do what you can!"

For himself, he took Royal's sweep and struggled with it. But he was woefully ignorant of how to apply his strength and had only the faintest idea what he ought to do.

Meanwhile the thunder of the White Horse steadily increased.

Having brought the last of the Courteau boats through the cañon, 'Poleon Doret piloted the little flotilla across to the town of White Horse and there collected his money, while Pierce Phillips and the other men pitched camp.

The labor of making things comfortable for the night did not prevent Lucky Broad from discussing at some length the exciting incidents of the afternoon.

"I hope her Highness got an eyeful of me shooting the chutes," said he, "for that's my farewell trip—positively my last appearance in any water act."

"Mighty decent of you and the Kid to volunteer," Pierce told him.

"It sure was," the other agreed. "Takes a coupla daredevils like him and me to pull that kind of a bonehead play."

Mr. Bridges, who was within hearing distance, shrugged with an assumption of careless indifference. "It takes more 'n a little lather to scare me," he boasted. "I'm a divin' Venus and I ate it up!"

"You—liar!" Lucky cried. "Why, every quill

on your head was standing up and you look five years older 'n you did this morning! You heard the undertaker shaking out your shroud all the way down—you know you did. I never seen a man as scared as you was!" When Bridges accepted the accusation with a grin, the speaker ran on, in a less resentful tone: "I don't mind saying it hardened my arteries some. It made me think of all my sins and follies; I remembered all the bets I'd overlooked. Recollect that pioneer we laid for four hundred at Dyea?"

The Kid nodded. "Sure! I remember him easy. He squawked so loud you gave him back half of it."

"And all the time he had a thousand sewed in his shirt! Wasted opportunities like that lay heavy on a man when he hears the angels tuning up and smells the calla-lilies."

Bridges agreed in all seriousness, and went on to say: "Lucky, if I gotta get out of this country the way I got into it I'm going to let you bury me in Dawson. Look at them rapids ahead of us! Why, the guy that laid out this river was off his nut!"

"You're talking sense. We'll stick till they build a railroad up to us or else we'll let 'em pin a pair of soft-pine overcoats on the two of us. The idea of us calling ourselves wiseacres and doing circus stunts like this! We're suckers! We'll be working in the mines next. I bet I'll see you poulticed onto a pick-handle before we get out."

13   187

"Not me! I've raised my last blister, and if ever I get another callous it 'll be from layin' abed. Safe and sane, that's me. I—"

Bridges' words were cut short by an exclamation from Doret, who had approached, in company with the Countess Courteau.

"Hallo!" the French Canadian broke in. "Dere comes dat beeg barge."

Out from the lower end of the gorge the Kirby craft had emerged; it was plunging along with explosions of white foam from beneath its bow and with its sweeps rising and falling rhythmically. To Doret's companions it seemed that the scow had come through handily enough and was in little further danger, but 'Poleon, for some reason or other, had blazed into excitement. Down the bank he leaped; then he raised his voice and sent forth a loud cry. It was wasted effort, for it failed to carry. Nevertheless, the warning note in his voice brought his hearers running after him.

"What's the matter?" Pierce inquired.

The pilot paid no heed; he began waving his cap in long sweeps, cursing meanwhile in a patois which the others could not understand.

Even while they stared at the *Rouletta* she drove head on into an expanse of tumbling breakers, then—the onlookers could not believe their eyes—she stopped dead still, as if she had come to the end of a steel cable or as if she had collided with an invisible wall. Instantly her entire after part was smothered in white. Slowly her bow

188

rose out of the chaos until perhaps ten feet of her bottom was exposed, then she assumed a list.

The Countess uttered a strangled exclamation. "Oh—h! Did you see? There's a man overboard!"

Her eyes were quick, but others, too, had beheld a dark bundle picked up by some mysterious agency and flung end over end into the waves.

The *Rouletta's* deck-load was dissolving; a moment or two and she turned completely around, then drifted free.

"Why—they brought the *girl* along!" cried the Countess, in growing dismay. "Sam Kirby should have had better sense. He ought to be hung—"

From the tents and boats along the bank, from the village above, people were assembling hurriedly, a babel of oaths, of shouts arose.

'Poleon found his recent employer plucking at his sleeve.

"There's a woman out there—Kirby's girl," she was crying. "Can't you do something?"

"Wait!" He flung off her grasp and watched intently.

Soon the helpless scow was abreast of the encampment, and in spite of the frantic efforts of her crew to propel her shoreward she drifted momentarily closer to the cataract below. Manifestly it was impossible to row out and intercept the derelict before she took the plunge, and so, helpless in this extremity, the audience began to stream down over the rounded boulders which formed the margin of the river. On the opposite bank another crowd was keeping pace with the wreck. As they ran, these people shouted at one another and gesticulated wildly. Their faces were white, their words were meaningless, for it was a spectacle tense with imminent disaster that they beheld; it turned them sick with apprehension.

Immediately above White Horse the current gathers itself for the final plunge, and although, at the last moment, the *Rouletta* seemed about to straighten herself out and take the rapids head on, some malign influence checked her swing and she lunged over quarteringly to the torrent.

A roar issued from the throats of the beholders; the craft reappeared, and then, a moment later, was half hidden again in the smother. It could be seen that she was completely awash and that those galloping white-maned horses were charging over her. She was buffeted about as by battering-rams; the remainder of her cargo was being rapidly torn from her deck. Soon another shout arose, for human figures could be seen still clinging to her.

Onward the scow went, until once again she fetched up on a reef or a rock which the low stage of the river had brought close to the surface; there she hung.

'Poleon Doret had gone into action ere this. Having satisfied himself that some of the *Rouletta's* crew remained alive, he cast loose the painter of the nearest skiff and called to Phillips, who was standing close by:

"Come on! We goin' get dose people!"

Now Pierce had had enough rough water for one day; it seemed to him that there must be other men in this crowd better qualified by training than he to undertake this rescue. But no one stepped forward, and so he obeyed Doret's order. As he slipped out of his coat and kicked off his boots, he reflected, with a sinking feeling of disappointment, that his emotions were not by any means such as a really courageous man would experience. He was completely lacking in enthusiasm for this enterprise, for it struck him as risky, nay, foolhardy, insane, to take a boat over that cataract in an attempt to snatch human beings out from the very midst of those threshing breakers. It seemed more than likely that all hands would be drowned in the undertaking, and he could not summon the reckless abandon necessary to face that likelihood with anything except the frankest apprehension. He was surprised at himself, for he had imagined that when his moment came, if ever it did, that he, Phillips, would prove to be a rather exceptional person; instead he discovered that he was something of a coward. The unexpectedness of this discovery astonished the young man. Being deeply and thoroughly frightened, it was nothing less than the abhorrence at allowing that fright to become known which stiffened his determination. In his own sight he dwindled to very small proportions; then came the realization that Doret was having difficulty in securing volunteers to go with them, and he was considerably heartened at finding he was not greatly different from the rest of these people.

"Who's goin' he'p us?" the Frenchman was shouting. "Come now, you stout fellers. Dere's lady on dat scow. 'Ain't nobody got nerve?"

It was a tribute to the manhood of the North that after a brief hesitation several men offered themselves. At the last moment, however, Broad and Bridges elbowed the others aside, saying: "Here, you! That's our boat and we know how she handles."

Into the skiff they piled and hurriedly stripped down; then, in obedience to Doret's command, they settled themselves at the forward oars, leaving Pierce to set the stroke.

'Poleon stood braced in the stern, like a gondolier, and when willing hands had shot the boat out into the current he leaned his weight upon the after oars; beneath his and Pierce's efforts the ash blades bent. Out into the hurrying flood the four men sent their craft; then, with a mighty heave, the pilot swung its bow down-stream and helped to drive it directly at the throat of the cataract.

There came a breath-taking plunge during which the rescuing skiff and its crew were hidden from the view of those on shore; out into sight they lunged again and, in a cloud of spray, went galloping through the stampeding waves. At risk of capsizing they turned around and, battling furiously against the current, were swept down, stern first, upon the stranded barge. Doret's face was turned back over his shoulder, he was measuring distance, gauging with practised eye the whims and vagaries of the tumbling torrent; when he flung himself upon the oars Pierce Phillips felt his own strength completely dwarfed by that of the big pilot. 'Poleon's hands inclosed his in a viselike grasp; he wielded the sweeps as if they were reeds, and with them he wielded Phillips.

Two people only were left upon the *Rouletta*, that sidewise plunge having carried the crew away. Once again Sam Kirby's artificial hand had proved its usefulness, and without its aid it is doubtful if either he or his daughter could have withstood the deluge. For a second time he had sunk that sharp steel hook into the solid wood and had managed, by virtue of that advantage, to save himself and his girl. Both of them were half drowned; they were well-nigh frozen, too; now, however, finding themselves in temporary security, Kirby had broached one of the few remaining cases of bottled goods. As the rowboat came close its occupants saw him press a drink upon his daughter, then gulp one for himself.

It was impossible either to lay the skiff alongside the wreck with any degree of care or to hold her there; as a matter of fact, the two hulls collided with a crash, Kid Bridges' oar snapped off short and the side of the lighter boat was smashed in. Water poured over the rescuers. For an instant it seemed that they were doomed, but, clawing fiercely at whatever they could lay hands upon, they checked their progress long enough for the castaways to obey Doret's shout of command. The girl flung herself into Pierce's arms; her father followed, landing in a heap amidships. Even as they jumped the skiff was torn away and hurried onward by the flood.

Sam Kirby raised himself to his knees and turned his ashen face to Rouletta.

"Hurt you any, kid?" he inquired.

The girl shook her head. She was very white, her teeth were chattering, her wet dress clung tightly to her figure.

Staring fixedly at the retreating barge the old man cried: "All gone! All gone!" Then, bracing himself with his good hand, he brandished his steel hook at the rapids and heaped curses upon them.

A half-mile below the wreck 'Poleon Doret brought his crippled skiff into an eddy, and there the crowd, which had kept pace with it down the river-bank, lent willing assistance in effecting a landing.

As Kirby stepped ashore he shook hands with the men who had jeopardized their lives for him and his daughter; in a cheerless, colorless voice he said, "It looks to me like you boys had a drink coming." From his coat pocket he drew a bottle of whisky; with a blow of that artificial hand he struck off its neck and then proffered it to Doret. "Drink hearty!" said he. "It's all that's left of a good outfit!"

CHAPTER XII

A CHILLY twilight had fallen by the time the castaways arrived at the encampment above the rapids. Kirby and his daughter were shaking from the cold. The Countess Courteau hurried on ahead to start a fire in her tent, and thither she insisted upon taking Rouletta, while her men attended to the father's comfort.

On the way up there had been considerable speculation among those who knew Sam Kirby best, for none of them had ever seen the old fellow in quite such a frame of mind as now. His misfortune had crushed him; he appeared to be numbed by the realization of his overwhelming loss; gone entirely was that gambler's nonchalance for which he was famous. The winning or the losing of large sums of money had never deeply stirred the old sporting-man; the turn of a card, the swift tattoo of horses' hoofs, often had meant far more to him in dollars and cents than the destruction of that barge-load of liquor; he had seen sizable fortunes come and go without a sign of emotion, and yet to-night he was utterly unnerved.

With a man of less physical courage such an

ordeal as he had undergone might well have excused a nervous collapse, but Kirby had no nerves; he had, times without number, proved himself to be a man of steel, and so it greatly puzzled his friends to see him shaken and broken.

He referred often to Danny Royal's fate, speaking in a dazed and disbelieving manner, but through that daze ran lightning-bolts of blind, ferocious rage—rage at the river, rage at this hostile, sinister country and at the curse it had put upon him. Over and over, through blue lips and chattering teeth, he reviled the rapids; more than once he lifted the broken-necked bottle to his lips. Of thanksgiving, of gratitude at his own and his daughter's deliverance, he appeared to have none, at least for the time being.

Rouletta's condition was pitiable enough, but she was concerned less with it than with her father's extraordinary behavior, and when the Countess undertook to procure for her dry clothing she protested:

"Please don't trouble. I'll warm up a bit; then I must go back to dad."

"My dear, you're chilled through—you'll die in those wet things," the older woman told her.

Miss Kirby shook her head and, in a queer, strained, apprehensive voice, said: "You don't understand. He's had a drink; if he gets started—" She shivered wretchedly and hid her white face in her hands, then moaned: "Oh, what a day! Danny's gone! I saw him drown—"

"There, there!" The Countess comforted her

as best she could. "You've had a terrible experience, but you mustn't think of it just yet. Now let me help you."

Finding that the girl's fingers were stiff and useless, the Countess removed the wet skirt and jacket, wrung them out, and hung them up. Then she produced some dry undergarments, but Miss Kirby refused to put them on.

"You'll need what few things you have," said she, "and—I'll soon warm up. There's no telling what dad will do. I must keep an eye on him."

"You give yourself too much concern. He's chilled through and it's natural that he should take a drink. My men will give him something dry to wear, and meanwhile—"

Rouletta interrupted with a shake of her head, but the Countess gently persisted:

"Don't take your misfortune too hard. The loss of your outfit means nothing compared with your safety. It was a great tragedy, of course, but you and your father were saved. You still have him and he has you."

"Danny knew what was coming," said the girl, and tears welled into her eyes, then slowly overflowed down her white cheeks. "But he faced it. He was game. He was a good man at heart. He had his faults, of course, but he loved dad and he loved me; why, he used to carry me out to see the horses before I could walk; he was my friend, my playmate, my pal. He'd have done murder for me!" Through her tears Rouletta looked up. "It's hard for you to believe that I know, after what he did to you, but—you know how men are on the trail. Nothing matters. He was angry when you outwitted him, and so was father, for that matter, but I told them it served us right and I forbade them to molest you further."

"You did that? Then it's you I have to thank." The Countess smiled gravely. "I could never understand why I came off so easily."

"I'm glad I made them behave. You've more than repaid—" Rouletta paused, she strained her ears to catch the sound of voices from the neighboring tents. "I don't hear father," said she. "I wonder if he could have gone?"

"Perhaps the men have put him to bed—"

But Miss Kirby would not accept this explanation. "I'm afraid—" Again she listened apprehensively. "Once he gets a taste of liquor there's no handling him; he's terrible. Even Danny couldn't do anything with him; sometimes even I have failed." Hurriedly she took down her sodden skirt and made as if to draw it on.

"Oh, child, you *mustn't!* You simply must *not* go out this way. Wait here. I'll find him for you and make sure he's all right."

The half-clad girl smiled miserably. "Thank you," said she. But when the Countess had stepped out into the night she finished dressing herself. Her clothing, of course, was as wet as ever, for the warmth of the tent in these few moments had not even heated it through; nevertheless, her apprehension was so keen that she was conscious of little bodily discomfort.

198

"You were right," the Countess announced when she returned. "He slipped into some borrowed clothes and went up-town. He told the boys he couldn't sit still. But you mustn't follow—at least in that dress—"

"Did he—drink any more?"

"I'm afraid he did."

Heedless of the elder woman's restraining hands, Rouletta Kirby made for the tent opening. "Please don't stop me," she implored. "There's no time to lose and—I'll dry out in time."

"Let me go for you."

"No, no!"

"Then may I go along?"

Again the girl shook her head. "I can handle him better alone. He's a strange man, a terrible man, when he's this way. I—hope I'm not too late."

Rouletta's wet skirts slatted about her ankles as she ran; it was a windy, chilly night, and, in spite of the fact that it was a steep climb to the top of the low bluff, she was chilled to the bone when she came panting into the sprawling cluster of habitations that formed the temporary town of White Horse. Tents were scattered over a dim, stumpy clearing, lights shone through trees that were still standing, a meandering trail led past a straggling row of canvas-topped structures, and from one of these issued the wavering, metallic notes of a phonograph, advertising the place as a house of entertainment.

Sam Kirby was at the bar when his daughter

discovered him, and her first searching look brought dismay to the girl. Pushing her way through the crowd, she said, quietly:

"Father!"

"Hello!" he exclaimed, in surprise. "What are you doing here?"

"I want to speak to you."

"Now, Letty," he protested, when sne had drawn him aside, "haven't you been through enough for one day? Run back to the Countess' camp where I left you."

"Don't drink any more," she implored. with an agony of dread in her face.

Kirby's bleak countenance set itself in stony lines. "I've got to," said he. "I'm cold—frozen to the quick. I need something to warm me up."

Letty could smell the whisky on his breath, she could see a new light in his eyes and already she sensed rather than observed a subtle change in his demeanor.

"Oh, dad!" she quavered; then she bowed her head weakly upon his arm and her shoulders shook.

Kirby laid a gentle hand upon her, then exclaimed, in surprise: "Why, kid, you're still wet! Got those same clothes on, haven't you?" He raised his voice to the men he had just left. "Want to see the gamest girl in the world? Well, here she is. You saw how she took her medicine to-day? Now listen to this: she's wet through, but she came looking for her old dad—afraid he'd get into trouble!"

Disregarding the crowd and the appreciative murmur her father's praise evoked, Rouletta begged, in a low, earnest voice: "Please, dear, come away. Please—you know why. Come away—won't you—for my sake?"

Kirby stirred uneasily. "I tell you I'm cold," he muttered, but stopped short, staring. "Yes, and I see Danny. I see him as he went overboard. Drowned! I'll never get him out of my sight. I can't seem to understand that he's gone, but—everything's gone, for that matter. Everything!"

"Oh no, dad. Why, you're here and I'm here! We've been broke before."

Kirby smiled again, but cheerlessly. "Oh, we ain't exactly broke; I've got the bank-roll on me and it 'll pull us through. We've had bad luck for a year or two, but it's bound to change. You cheer up—and come over to the stove. What you need is to warm up while I get you a little drink."

Rouletta gazed up into the gray face above her. "Dad, look at me." She took his hand. "Haven't we had enough trouble for one day?"

The gambler was irritated at this persistence and he showed it. "Don't be foolish," he cried, shortly. "I know what I need and I know what I can stand. These men are friends of mine, and you needn't be uneasy. Now, kid, you let me find a place for you to spend the night."

"Not until you're ready to go along."

"All right, stick around for a little while. I won't be long." Old Sam drew a bench up beside

201

the stove and seated the girl upon it. "I'm all broke up and I've just got to keep moving," he explained, more feelingly. Then he returned to the bar.

Realizing that he was completely out of hand and that further argument was futile, Rouletta Kirby settled herself to wait. In spite of her misery, it never occurred to her to abandon her father to his own devices, even for an hour—she knew him too well to run that risk. But her very bones were frozen and she shivered wretchedly as she held her shoes up to the stove. Although the fire began slowly to dry her outer garments, the clothes next to her flesh remained cold and clammy. Even so, their chill was as nothing to the icy dread that paralyzed the very core of her being.

Pierce Phillips told himself that this had been a wonderful day—an epoch-making day—for him. Lately he had been conscious that the North was working a change in him, but the precise extent of that change, even the direction it was taking, had not been altogether clear; now, however, he thought he understood.

He had been quite right, that first hour in Dyea, when he told himself that Life lay just ahead of him—just over the Chilkoot. Such, indeed, had proved to be the case. Yes, and it had welcomed him with open arms; it had ushered him into a new and wondrous world. His hands had fallen to men's tasks, experience had come to him by leaps and bounds. In a rush he had emerged from groping boyhood into full maturity; physically, mentally, morally, he had grown strong and broad and brown. Having abandoned himself to the tides of circumstance, he had been swept into a new existence where Adventure had rubbed shoulders with him, where Love had smiled into his eyes. Danger had tested his mettle, too, and to-day the final climax had come. What roused his deepest satisfaction now was the knowledge that he had met that climax with credit. To-night it seemed to him that he had reached full manhood, and in the first flush of realization he assured himself that he could no longer drift with the aimless current of events, but must begin to shape affairs to his own ends.

More than once of late he had pondered a certain thought, and now, having arrived at a decision, he determined to act upon it. Ever since that stormy evening at Linderman his infatuation for Hilda had increased, but, owing to circumstances, he had been thwarted in enjoying its full delights. During the daylight hours of their trip, as matter of fact, the two had never been alone together even for a quarter of an hour; they had scarcely had a word in confidence, and in cousequence he had been forced to derive what comfort he could from a chance look, a smile, some inflection of her voice. Even at night, after camp was pitched, it had been little better, for the thin walls of her canvas shelter afforded little privacy, and, being mindful of appearances, he had never permitted himself to be alone with her very long at a time—only long enough, in fact, to make sure that his happiness was not all a dream. A vibrant protestation now and then, a secret kiss or two, a few stolen moments of delirium, that was as far as his love-affair had progressed. Not yet had he and Hilda arrived at a definite understanding; never had they thoroughly talked out the subject that engrossed them both, never had they found either time or opportunity in which to do more than sigh and whisper and hold hands, and as a result the woman remained almost as much of a mystery to Pierce as she had been at the moment of her first surrender.

It was an intolerable situation, and so, under the spell of his buoyant spirits, he determined to make an end of it once for all.

The Countess recognized his step when he came to her tent and she spoke to him. Mistaking her greeting for permission to enter, he untied the strings and stepped inside, only to find her unprepared for his reception. She had made her shelter snug, a lively fire was burning, the place was fragrant of pine boughs, and a few deft feminine touches here and there had transformed it into a boudoir. Hilda had removed her jacket and waist and was occupied in combing her hair, but at Pierce's unexpected entrance she hurriedly gathered the golden shower about her bare shoulders and voiced a protest at his intrusion. He stood smiling down at her and refused to withdraw.

Never had Phillips seen such an alluring picture. Now that her hair was undone, its length and its profusion surprised him, for it completely mantled her, and through it the snowy whiteness of her bare arms, folded protectingly across her rounded breasts, was dazzling. The sight put him in a conquering mood; he strode forward, lifted her into his embrace, then smothered her gasping protest with his lips. For a long moment they stood thus. Finally the woman freed herself, then chided him breathlessly, but the fragrance of her hair had gone to his brain; he continued to hold her tight, meanwhile burying his face in the golden cascade.

Roughly, masterfully, he rained kisses upon her. He devoured her with his caresses, and the heat of his ardor melted her resistance until, finally, she surrendered, abandoning herself wholly to his passion.

When, after a time, she flung back her head and pushed him away, her face, her neck, her shoulders were suffused with a coral pinkness and her eyes were misty.

"You must be careful!" she whispered in a tone that was less of a remonstrance than an invitation. "Remember, we're making shadowgraphs for our neighbors. That's the worst of a tent at night— one silhouettes one's very thoughts."

"Then put out the light," he muttered, thickly; but she slipped away, and her moist lips mocked him in silent laughter.

"The idea! What in the world has come

over you? Why, you're the most impetuous boy—"

"Boy!" Pierce grimaced his dislike of the word. "Don't be motherly; don't treat me as if I had rompers on. You're positively maddening to-night. I never saw you like this. Why, your hair"—he ran his hands through that silken shower once more and pressed it to his face—"it's glorious!"

The Countess slipped into a combing-jacket; then she seated herself on the springy couch of pine branches over which her fur robe was spread, and deftly caught up her long runaway tresses, securing them in place with a few mysterious twists and expert manipulations.

"Boy, indeed!" he scoffed, flinging himself down beside her. "That's over with, long ago."

"Oh, I don't feel motherly," she asserted, still suffused with that telltale flush. "Not in the way you mean. But you'll always be a boy to me— and to every other woman who learns to care for you."

"Every other woman?" Pierce's eyes opened. "What a queer speech. There aren't going to be any *other* women." He looked on while she lighted a cigarette, then after a moment he inquired, "What do you mean?"

She answered him with another question. "Do you think I'm the only woman who will love you?"

"Why—I haven't given it any thought! What's the difference, as long as you're the only one *I* care for? And I do love you, I worship—"

"But there *will* be others," she persisted. "There are bound to be. You're that kind."

"Really?"

The Countess nodded her head with emphasis. "I can read men; I can see the color of their souls. You have the call."

"What call?" Pierce was puzzled.

"The—well, the sex-call, the sex appeal."

"Indeed? Am I supposed to feel flattered at that?"

"By no means; you're not a cad. Men who possess that attraction are spoiled sooner or later. You don't realize that you have it, and that's what makes you so nice, but—I felt it from the first, and when you feel it you'll probably become spoiled, too, like the others." This amused Phillips, but the woman was in sober earnest. "I mean what I say. You're the kind who cause women to make fools of themselves—old or young, married or single. When a girl has it—she's lost."

"I'm not sure I understand. At any rate, **you** haven't made a fool of yourself."

"No?" The Countess smiled vaguely, questioningly. She opened her lips to say more, but changed her mind and in an altered tone declared, "My dear boy, if you understood fully what I'm driving at you'd be insufferable." Laying her warm hand over his, she continued: "You resent what you call my 'motherly way,' but if I were sixteen and you were forty it would be just the same. Women who are afflicted with that sex

THE WINDS OF CHANCE

appeal become men's playthings; the man who possesses it always remains a 'boy' to the woman who loves him—a bad boy, a dangerous boy, perhaps, but a boy, nevertheless. She may, and probably will, adore him fiercely, passionately, jealously, but at the same time she will hover him as a hen hovers her chick. He will be both son and lover to her."

He had' listened closely, but now he stirred uneasily. "I don't follow you," he said. "And it isn't exactly pleasant for a fellow to be told that he's a baby Don Juan, to be called a male vampire in knee-pants—especially by the woman he's going to marry." Disregarding her attempt to speak, he went on: "What you said about other women—the way you said it—sounded almost as if—well, as if you expected there would be such, and didn't greatly care. You didn't mean it that way, I hope. You do care, don't you, dear? You do love me?" The face Phillips turned upon the Countess Courteau was earnest, worried.

Her fingers tightened over his hand. When she spoke there was a certain listlessness, a certain fatigue in her tone. "Do you need to ask that after—what happened just now? Of course I care. I care altogether too much. That's the whole trouble. You see, the thing has run away with me, Pierce; it has carried me off my feet, and—that's precisely the point I'm trying to make."

He slipped an arm about her waist and drew

208

her close. "I knew it wasn't merely an animal appeal that stirred you. I knew it was something bigger and more lasting than that."

"Even yet you don't understand," she declared. "The two may go together and—" But without allowing her to finish he said, vibrantly:

"Whatever it is, you seem to find it an obstacle, an objection. Why struggle against the inevitable? You *are* struggling—I've seen you fighting something ever since that first night when truth came to us out of the storm. But, Hilda dear, I adore you. You're the most wonderful creature in the world! You're a goddess! I feel unworthy to touch the hem of your garments, but I know that you are mine! Nothing else matters. Think of the miracle, the wonder of it! It's like a beautiful dream. I've had doubts about myself, and that's why I've let matters drift. You see, I was a sort of unknown quantity, but now I know that I've found myself. To-day I went through hell and—I came out a man. I'm going to play a man's part right along after this." He urged her eagerly. "We've a hard trip ahead of us before we reach Dawson; winter may overtake us and delay us. We can't continue in this way. Why wait any longer?"

"You mean—?" the woman inquired, faintly.

"I mean this—marry me here, to-morrow."

"No, no! Please—" The Countess freed herself from Pierce's embrace.

"Why not? Are you afraid of me?" She shook her head silently.

"Then why not to-morrow instead of next month? Are you afraid of yourself?"

"No, I'm afraid of—what I must tell you."

Phillips' eyes were dim with desire, he was ablaze with yearning; in a voice that shook he said: "Don't tell me anything. I won't hear it!" Then, after a brief struggle with himself, he continued, more evenly: "That ought to prove to you that I've grown up. I couldn't have said it three months ago, but I've stepped out of—of the nursery into a world of big things and big people, and I want you. I dare say you've lived —a woman like you must have had many experiences, many obstacles to overcome; but— I might not understand what they were even if you told me, for I'm pretty green. Anyhow, I'm sure you're good. I wouldn't believe you if you told me you weren't. It's no credit to me that I haven't confessions of my own to make, for I'm like other men and it merely so happens that I've had no chance to—soil myself. The credit is due to circumstance."

"Everything is due to circumstance," the woman said. "Our lives are haphazard affairs; we're blown by chance—"

"We'll take a new start to-morrow and bury the past, whatever it is."

"You make it absolutely necessary for me to speak," the Countess told him. Her tone again had a touch of weariness in it, but Pierce did not see this. "I knew I'd have to, sooner or later, but it was nice to drift and to dream—oh, it was

210

pleasant—so I bit down on my tongue and I listened to nothing but the song in my heart." She favored Pierce with that shadowy, luminous smile he had come to know. "It was a clean, sweet song and it meant a great deal to me." When he undertook to caress her she drew away, then sat forward with her heels tucked close into the pine boughs, her chin upon her knees. It was her favorite attitude of meditation; wrapped thus in the embrace of her own arms, she appeared to gain the strength and the determination necessary to go on.

"I'm not a weak woman," she began, staring at the naked candle-flame which gave light to the tent. "It wasn't weakness that impelled me to marry a man I didn't love; it was the determination to get ahead and the ambition to make something worth while out of myself—a form of selfishness, perhaps, but I tell you all women are selfish. Anyhow, he seemed to promise better things and to open a way whereby I could make something out of my life. Instead of that he opened my eyes and showed me the world as it is, not as I had imagined it to be. He was—no good. You may think I was unhappy over that, but I wasn't. Really, he didn't mean much to me. What did grieve me, though, was the death of my illusions. He was mercenary—the fault of his training, I dare say—but he had that man-call I spoke about. It's really a woman-call. He was weak, worthless, full of faults, mean in small things, but he had an attraction and it was impossible to resist mothering him. Other women felt it and yielded to it, so finally we went our separate ways. I've seen nothing of him for some time now, but he keeps in touch with me and—I've sent him a good deal of money. When he learns that I have prospered in a big way he'll undoubtedly turn up again."

Pierce weighed the significance of these words; then he smiled. "Dear, it's all the more reason why we should be married at once. I'd dare him to annoy you then."

"My boy, don't you understand? I can't marry you, being still married to him."

Phillips recoiled; his face whitened. Dismay, reproach, a shocked surprise were in the look he turned upon his companion.

"Still married!" he gasped. "Oh—Hilda!"

She nodded and lowered her eyes. "I supposed you knew—until I got to telling you, and then it was too late."

Pierce rose; his lips now were as colorless as his cheeks. "I'm surprised, hurt," he managed to say. "How should I know? Why, this is wretched—rotten! People will say that I've got in a mess with a married woman. That's what it looks like, too." His voice broke huskily. "How could you do it, when I meant my love to be clean, honorable? How could you let me put myself, and you, in such a position?"

"You see!" The woman continued to avoid his eye. "You haven't grown up. You haven't the least understanding."

"I understand this much," he cried, hotly, "that you've led me to make something worse than a cad of myself. Look here! There are certain things which no decent fellow goes in for —certain things he despises in other men—and that's one of them." He turned as if to leave, then he halted at the tent door and battled with himself. After a moment, during which the Countess Courteau watched him fixedly, he whirled, crying:

"Well, the damage is done. I love you. I can't go along without you. Divorce that man. I'll wait."

"I'm not sure I have legal grounds for a divorce. I'm not sure that I care to put the matter to a test—as yet."

"*What?*" Pierce gazed at her, trying to understand. "Say that over again!"

"You think you've found yourself, but—have you? I know men pretty well and I think I know you. You've changed—yes, tremendously —but what of a year, two years from now? You've barely tasted life and this is your first intoxication."

"Do you love me, or do you not?" he demanded.

"I love you as you are now. I may hate you as you will be to-morrow. I've had my growth; I've been through what you're just beginning— we can't change together."

"Then will you promise to marry me afterward?"

213

The Countess shook her head. "It's a promise that would hold only me. Why ask it?"

"You're thinking of no one but yourself," he protested, furiously. "Think of me. I've given you all I have, all that's best and finest in me. I shall never love another woman—"

"Not in quite the way you love me, perhaps, but the peach ripens even after its bloom has been rubbed off. You *have* given me what is best and finest, your first love, and I shall cherish it."

"Will you marry me?" he cried, hoarsely. She made a silent refusal.

"Then I can put but one interpretation upon your actions."

"Don't be too hasty in your judgment. Can't you see? I was weak. I was tired. Then you came, like a draught of wine, and—I lost my head. But I've regained it. I dreamed my dream, but it's daylight now and I'm awake. I know that you believe me a heartless, selfish woman. Maybe I am, but I've tried to think for you, and to act on that good impulse. I tell you I would have been quite incapable of it before I knew you. A day, a month, a year of happiness! Most women of my age and experience would snatch at it, but I'm looking farther ahead than that. I can't afford another mistake. Life fits me, but you—why, you're bursting your seams."

"You've puzzled me with a lot of words," the young man said, with ever-growing resentment, "but what do they all amount to? You amused yourself with me and ' ready enough to

ou re

continue so long as I pour my devotion at your
feet. Well, I won't do it. If you loved me
truly you wouldn't refuse to marry me. Isn't
that so? True love isn't afraid, it doesn't quibble
and temporize and split hairs the way you do.
No, it steps out boldly and follows the light.
You've had your fun, you've—broken my heart."
Phillips' voice shook and he swallowed hard.
"I'm through; I'm done. I shall never love
another woman as I love you, but if what you
said about that sex-call is true, I—I'll play the
game as you played it." He turned blindly and
with lowered head plunged out of the tent into
the night.

The Countess listened to the sounds of his de-
parting footsteps; then, when they had ceased,
she rose wearily and flung out her arms. There
was a real and poignant distress in her eyes.

"Boy! Boy!" she whispered. "It was sweet,
but—there had to be an end."

For a long time she stood staring at nothing;
then she roused herself with a shiver, refilled the
stove, and seated herself again, dropping her chin
upon her knees as she did instinctively when in
deep thought.

"If only I were sure," she kept repeating to
herself. "But he has the call and—I'm too old."

CHAPTER XIII

ROULETTA KIRBY could not manage to get
warm. The longer she sat beside the stove the
colder she became. This was not strange, for the
room was draughty, people were constantly coming
in and going out, and when the door was opened
the wind caused the canvas walls of the saloon to
bulge and its roof to slap upon the rafters. The
patrons were warmly clad in mackinaw, flannel,
and fur. To them the place was comfortable
enough, but to the girl who sat swathed in sodden
undergarments it was like a refrigerator. More
than once she regretted her heedless refusal of
the Countess Courteau's offer of a change; several times, in fact, she was upon the point of
returning to claim it, but she shrank from facing
that wintry wind, so low had her vitality fallen.
Then, too, she reasoned that it would be no easy
task to find the Countess at this hour of the night,
for the beach was lined with a mile of tents, all
more or less alike. She pictured the search, herself groping her way from one to another, and
mumbling excuses to surprised occupants. No,
it was better to stay here beside the fire until
her clothes dried out.

She would have reminded her father of her discomfort and claimed his assistance only for the certainty that he would send her off to bed, which was precisely what she sought to prevent. Her presence irritated him; nevertheless, she knew that his safety lay in her remaining. Sam Kirby sober was in many ways the best of fathers; he was generous, he was gentle, he was considerate. Sam Kirby drunk was another man entirely— a thoughtless, wilful, cruel man, subject to vagaries of temper that were as mysterious to the girl who knew him so well as they were dangerous to friend and foe alike. He was drunk now, or in that peculiar condition that passed with him for drunkenness. Intoxication in his case was less a condition of body than a frame of mind, and it required no considerable amount of liquor to work the change. Whisky, even in small quantities, served to suspend certain of his mental functions; it paralyzed one lobe of his brain, as it were, while it aroused other faculties to a preternatural activity and awoke sleeping devils in him. The more he drank the more violent became his destructive mood, the more firmly rooted became his tendencies and proclivities for evil. The girl well knew that this was an hour when he needed careful watching and when to leave him unguarded, even temporarily, meant disaster. Rouletta clenched her chattering teeth and tried to ignore the chills that raced up and down her body.

White Horse, at this time, was purely a makeshift camp, hence it had no facilities for gambling.

The saloons themselves were little more than liquor caches which had been opened overnight for the purpose of reaping quick profits; therefore such games of chance as went on were for the most part between professional gamblers who happened to be passing through and who chose to amuse themselves in that way.

After perhaps an hour, during which a considerable crowd had come and gone, Sam Kirby broke away from the group with which he had been drinking and made for the door. As he passed Rouletta he paused to say:

"I'm going to drift around a bit, kid, and see if I can't stir up a little game."

"Where are we going to put up for the night?" his daughter inquired.

"I don't know yet; it's early. Want to turn in?"

Rouletta shook her head.

"I'll find a place somewhere. Now you stick here where it's nice and warm. I'll be back by and by."

With sinking heart the girl watched him go. After a moment she rose and followed him out into the night. She was surprised to discover that the mud under foot had frozen and that the north wind bore a burden of fine, hard snow particles. Keeping well out of sight, she stumbled to another saloon door, and then, after shivering wretchedly outside for a while, she stole in and crept up behind the stove.

She was very miserable indeed by this time,

and as the evening wore slowly on her misery increased. After a while her father began shaking dice with some strangers, and the size of their wagers drew an audience of interested bystanders.

Rouletta realized that she should not have exposed herself anew to the cold, for now her sensations had become vaguely alarming. She could not even begin to get warm, except now and then when a burning fever replaced her chill; she felt weak and ill inside; the fingers she pressed to her aching temples were like icicles. Eventually —she had lost all track of time—her condition became intolerable and she decided to risk her father's displeasure by interrupting him and demanding that he secure for both of them a lodging-place at once.

There were several bank-notes of large denomination on the plank bar-top and Sam Kirby was watching a cast of dice when his daughter approached; therefore he did not see her. Nor did he turn his head when she laid a hand upon his arm.

Now women, especially pretty women, were common enough sights in Alaskan drinking-places. So it was not strange that Rouletta's presence had occasioned neither comment nor curiosity. More than once during the last hour or two men had spoken to her with easy familiarity, but they had taken no offense when she had turned her back. It was quite natural, therefore, that the fellow with whom Kirby was gambling should interpret her effort to claim attention as an attempt

15

to interrupt the game, and that he should misread the meaning of her imploring look. There being considerable money at stake, he frowned down at her, then with an impatient gesture he brushed her aside.

"None of that, sister!" he warned her. "You get out of here."

Sam Kirby was in the midst of a discussion with the proprietor, across the bar, and because there was a deal of noise in the place he did not hear his daughter's low-spoken protest.

"Oh, I mean it!" The former speaker scowled at Rouletta. "You dolls make me sick, grabbing at every nickel you see. Beat it, now! There's plenty of young suckers for you to trim. If you can't respect an old man with gray hair, why—" The rest of his remark caused the girl's eyes to widen and the chattering voices to fall silent.

Sam Kirby turned, the dice-box poised in his right hand.

"Eh? What's that?" he queried, vaguely.

"I'm talking to this pink-faced gold-digger—"

"Father!" Rouletta exclaimed.

"I'm just telling her—"

The fellow repeated his remark, whereupon understanding came to Kirby and his expression slowly altered. Surprise, incredulity, gave place to rage; his eyes began to blaze.

"You said that to—*her?*" he gasped, in amazement. "To *my kid?*" There was a moment of tense silence during which the speaker appeared to be numbed by the insult, then, "By God!"

220

Sam placed the dice-box carefully upon the bar. His movement was deliberate, but he kept his flaming gaze fixed upon the object of his wrath, and into his lean, ashen countenance came such demoniac fury as to appal those who saw it.

Rouletta uttered a faint moan and flung herself at her father; with a strength born of terror she clung to his right wrist. In this she was successful, despite old Sam's effort to shake her off, but she could not imprison both his arms. Kirby stepped forward, dragging the girl with him; he raised that wicked artificial left hand and brought it sweeping downward, and for a second time that day the steel shaft met flesh and bone. His victim spun upon his heels, then, with outflung arms and an expression of shocked amazement still upon his face, he crashed backward to the floor.

Kirby strode to him; before other hands could come to Rouletta's assistance and bear him out of reach he twice buried his heavy hobnailed boot in the prostrate figure. He presented a terrible exhibition of animal ferocity, for he was growling oaths deep in his throat and in his eyes was the light of murder. He fought for liberty with which to finish his task, and those who restrained him found that somehow he had managed to draw an ivory-handled six-shooter from some place of concealment. Nor could they wrench the weapon away from him.

"He insulted my kid—my girl Letty!" Kirby muttered, hoarsely.

When the fallen man had been lifted to his feet

and hurried out of the saloon old Sam tried his best to follow, but his captors held him fast. They pleaded with him, they argued, they pacified him as well as they could. It was a long time, however, before they dared trust him alone with Rouletta, and even then they turned watchful eyes in his direction.

"I didn't want anything to happen." The girl spoke listlessly.

Kirby began to rumble again, but she interrupted him. "It wasn't the man's fault. It was a perfectly natural mistake on his part, and I've learned to expect such things. I—I'm sick, dad. You must find a place for me, quick."

Sam agreed readily enough. The biting cold of the wind met them at the door. Rouletta, summoning what strength she could, trudged along at his side. It did not take them long to canvass the town and to discover that there were no lodgings to be had. Rouletta halted finally, explaining through teeth that chattered:

"I—I'm frozen! Take me back where there's a stove—back to the saloon—anywhere. Only do it quickly."

"Pshaw! It isn't cold," Kirby protested, mildly.

The nature of this remark showed more plainly than anything he had said or done during the evening that the speaker was not himself. It signified such a dreadful change in him, it marked so surely the extent of his metamorphosis, that Rouletta's tears came.

"Looks like we'd have to make the best of it and stay awake till morning," the father went on, dully.

"No, no! I'm too sick," the girl sobbed, "and too cold. Leave me where I can keep warm; then go find the Countess and—ask her to put me up."

Returning to their starting-point, Kirby saw to his daughter's comfort. as best he could, after which he wandered out into the night once more. His intentions were good, but he was not a little out of patience with Letty and still very angry with the man who had affronted her; rage at the insult glowed within his disordered brain and he determined, before he had gone very far, that his first duty was to right that wrong. Probably the miscreant was somewhere around, or, if not, he would soon make his appearance. Sam decided to postpone his errand long enough to look through the other drinking-places and to settle the score.

No one, on seeing him thus, would have suspected that he was drunk; he walked straight, his tongue was obedient, and he was master of his physical powers to a deceptive degree; only in his abnormally alert and feverish eyes was there a sign that his brain was completely crazed.

Rouletta waited for a long while, and steadily her condition grew worse. She became lightheaded, and frequently lost herself in a sort of painful doze. She did not really sleep, however, for her eyes were open and staring; her wits wandered away on nightmare journeys, returning

223

only when the pains became keener. Her fever was high now; she was nauseated, listless; her chest ached and her breathing troubled her when she was conscious enough to think. Her surroundings became unreal, too, the faces that appeared and disappeared before her were the faces of dream figures.

Unmindful of his daughter's need, heedless of the passage of time, Sam Kirby loitered about the saloons and waited patiently for the coming of a certain man. After a time he bought some chips and sat in a poker game, but he paid less attention to the spots on his cards than to the door through which men came and went. These latter he eyed with the unblinking stare of a serpent.

Pierce Phillips' life was ruined. He was sure of it. Precisely what constituted a ruined life, just how much such a one differed from a successful life, he had only the vaguest idea, but his own, at the moment, was tasteless, spoiled. Dire consequences were bound to follow such a tragedy as this, so he told himself, and he looked forward with gloomy satisfaction to their realization; whatever they should prove to be, however terrible the fate that was to overtake him, the guilt, the responsibility therefor, lay entirely upon the heartless woman who had worked the evil, and he earnestly hoped they would be brought home to her.

Yes, the Countess Courteau was heartless,

wicked, cruel. Her unsuspected selfishness, her lack of genuine sentiment, her cool, calculating caution, were shocking. Pierce had utterly misread her at first; that was plain.

That he was really hurt, deeply distressed, sorely aggrieved, was true enough, for his love—infatuation, if you will—was perfectly genuine and exceedingly vital. Nothing is more real, more vital, than a normal boy's first infatuation, unless it be the first infatuation of a girl; precisely wherein it differs from the riper, less demonstrative affection that comes with later years and wider experience is not altogether plain. Certainly it is more spontaneous, more poignant; certainly it has in it equal possibilities for good or evil. How deep or how disfiguring the scar it leaves depends entirely upon the healing process. But, for that matter, the same applies to every heart affair.

Had Phillips been older and wiser he would not have yielded so readily to despair; experience would have taught him that a woman's "No" is not a refusal; wisdom would have told him that the absolute does not exist. But, being neither experienced nor wise, he mistook the downfall of his castle for the wreck of the universe, and it never occurred to him that he could salvage something, or, if need be, rebuild upon the same foundations.

What he could neither forget nor forgive at this moment was the fact that Hilda had not only led him to sacrifice his honor, or its appearance, but also that when he had managed to reconcile himself to that wrong she had lacked the courage to meet him half-way. There were but two explanations of her action: either she was weak and cowardly or else she did not love him. Neither afforded much consolation.

In choosing a course of conduct no man is strong enough to divorce himself entirely from his desires, to follow the light of pure reason, for memories, impulses, yearnings are bound to bring confusion. Although Pierce told himself that he must renounce this woman—that he had renounced her—nevertheless he recalled with·a thrill the touch of her bare arms and the perfume of her streaming golden hair as he had buried his face in it, and the keenness of those memories caused him to cry out. The sex-call had been stronger than he had realized; therefore, to his present grief was added an inescapable, almost irresistible feeling of physical distress—a frenzy of balked desire—which caused him to waver irresolutely, confusing the issue dreadfully.

For a long time he wandered through the night, fighting his animal and his spiritual longings, battling with irresolution, striving to reconcile himself to the crash that had overwhelmed him. More than once he was upon the point of rushing back to the woman and pouring out the full tide of his passion in a desperate attempt to sweep away her doubts and her apprehensions. What if she should refuse to respond? He would merely succeed in making himself ridiculous and in sac-

rificing what little appearance of dignity he retained. Thus pride prevented, uncertainty paralyzed him.

Some women, it seemed to him, not bad in
themselves, were born to work evil, and evidently
Hilda was one of them. She had done her task
well in this instance, for she had thoroughly
blasted his life! He would pretend to forget,
but nevertheless he would see to it that she was
undeceived, and that the injury she had done him
remained an ever-present reproach to her. That
would be his revenge. Real forgetfulness, of
course, was out of the question. How could he
assume such an attitude? As he pondered the
question he remembered that there were artificial
aids to oblivion. Ruined men invariably took to
drink. Why shouldn't he attempt to drown his
sorrows? After all, might there not be real and
actual relief in liquor? After consideration he
decided to try it.

From a tent saloon near by came the sounds
of singing and of laughter, and thither he turned
his steps. When he entered the place a lively
scene greeted him. Somehow or other a small
portable organ had been secured, and at this a
bearded fellow in a mackinaw coat was seated.
He was playing a spirited accompaniment for
two women, sisters, evidently, who sang with the
loud abandon of professional "coon shouters."
Other women were present, and Phillips recognized them as members of that theatrical troupe
he had seen at Sheep Camp—as those "actresses"

to whom Tom Linton had referred with such elaborate sarcasm. All of them, it appeared, were out for a good time, and in consequence White Horse was being treated to a free concert.

The song ended in a burst of laughter and applause, the men at the bar pounded with their glasses, and there was a general exodus in that direction. One of the sisters flung herself enthusiastically upon the volunteer organist and dragged him with her. There was much hilarity and a general atmosphere of license and unrestraint.

Phillips looked on moodily; he frowned, his lip curled. All the world was happy, it seemed, while he nursed a broken heart. Well, that was in accord with the scheme of things—life was a mad, topsy-turvy affair at best, and there was nothing stable about any part of it. He felt very grim, very desperate, very much abused and very much outside of all this merriment.

Men were playing cards at the rear of the saloon, and among the number was Sam Kirby. The old gambler showed no signs of his trying experience of the afternoon; in fact, it appeared to have been banished utterly from his mind. He was drinking, and even while Pierce looked on he rapped sharply with his iron hand to call the bartender's attention. Meanwhile he scanned intently the faces of all new-comers.

When the crowd had surged back to the organ Pierce found a place at the bar and called for a drink of whisky—the first he had ever ordered. This was the end he told himself.

He poured the glass nearly full, then he gulped the liquor down. It tasted much as it smelled, hence he derived little enjoyment from the experience. As he stripped a bill from his sizable roll of bank-notes the bartender eyed him curiously and seemed upon the point of speaking, but Pierce turned his shoulder.

After perhaps five minutes the young man acknowledged a vague disappointment; if this was intoxication there was mighty little satisfaction in it, he decided, and no forgetfulness whatever. He was growing dizzy, to be sure, but aside from that and from the fact that his eyesight was somewhat uncertain he could feel no unusual effect. Perhaps he expected too much; perhaps, also, he had drunk too sparingly. Again. he called for the bottle, again he filled his glass, again he carelessly displayed his handful of paper currency.

Engaged thus, he heard a voice close to his ear; it said:

"Hello, man!"

Pierce turned to discover that a girl was leaning with elbows upon the plank counter at his side and looking at him. Her chin was supported upon her clasped fingers; she was staring into his face.

She eyed him silently for a moment, during which he returned her unsmiling gaze. She dropped her eyes to the whisky-glass, then raised them again to his.

"Can you take a drink like that and not feel it?" she inquired.

"No. I want to feel it; that's why I take it," he said, gruffly.

"What's the idea?"

"Idea? Well, it's my own idea—my own business."

The girl took no offense; she maintained her curious observation of him; she appeared genuinely interested in acquainting herself with a man who could master such a phenomenal quantity of liquor. There was mystification in her tone when she said:

"But—I saw you come in alone. And now you're drinking alone."

"Is that a reproach? I beg your pardon." Pierce swept her a mocking bow. "What will you have?"

Without removing her chin from its resting-place, the stranger shook her head shortly, so he downed his beverage as before. The girl watched him interestedly as he paid for it.

"That's more money than I've seen in a month," said she. "I wouldn't be so free and easy with it, if I were you."

"No? Why not?"

She merely shrugged, and continued to study him with that same disconcerting intentness—she reminded him of a frank and curious child.

Pierce noticed now that she was a very pretty girl, and quite appropriately dressed, under the circumstances. She wore a boy's suit, with a short skirt over her knickerbockers, and, since she was slim, the garments added to her appearance of immaturity. Her face was oval in outline, and it was of a perfectly uniform olive tint; her eyes were large and black and velvety, their lashes were long, their lids were faintly smudged with a shadowy under-coloring that magnified their size and intensified their brilliance. Her hair was almost black, nevertheless it was of fine texture; a few unruly strands had escaped from beneath her fur cap and they clouded her brow and temples. At first sight she appeared to be foreign, and of that smoky type commonly associated with the Russian idea of beauty, but she was not foreign, not Russian; nor were her features predominantly racial.

"What's your name?" she asked, suddenly.

Pierce told her. "And yours?" he inquired.

"Laure."

"Laure what?"

"Just Laure—for the present."

"Humph! You're one of this—theatrical company, I presume." He indicated the singers across the room.

"Yes. Morris Best hired us to work in his place at Dawson."

"I remember your outfit at Sheep Camp. Best was nearly crazy—"

"He's crazier now than ever." Laure smiled for the first time and her face lit up with mischief. "Poor Morris! We lead him around by his big nose. He's deathly afraid he'll lose us, and we know it, so we make his life miserable."

She turned serious abruptly, and with a candor quite startling said, "I like you."

"Indeed!" Pierce was nonplussed.

The girl nodded. "You looked good to me when you came in. Are you going to Dawson?"

"Of course. Everybody is going to Dawson."

"I suppose you have partners?"

"No!" Pierce's face darkened. "I'm alone— very much alone." He undertook to speak in a hollow, hopeless tone.

"Big outfit?"

"None at all. But I have enough money for my needs and—I'll probably hook up with somebody." Now there was a brave but cheerless resignation in his words.

Laure pondered for a moment; even more carefully than before she studied her companion. That the result satisfied her she made plain by saying:

"Morris wants men. I can get him to hire you. Would you like to hook up with us?"

"I don't know. It doesn't much matter. Will you have something to drink now?"

"Why should I? They don't give any percentage here. Wait! I'll see Morris and tell you what he says." Leaving Pierce, the speaker hurried to a harassed little man of Hebraic countenance who was engaged in the difficult task of chaperoning this unruly aggregation of talent. To him she said:

"I've found a man for you, Morris."

"Man?"

"To go to Dawson with us. That tall, good-looking fellow at the bar."

Mr. Best was bewildered. "What ails you?" he queried. "I don't want any men, and you know it."

"You want this fellow, and you're going to hire him."

"Am I? What makes you think so?"

"Because it's—him or me," Laure said, calmly.

Mr. Best was both surprised and angered at this cool announcement. "You mean, I s'pose, that you'll quit," he said, belligerently.

"I mean that very thing. The man has money—"

Best's anger disappeared as if by magic; his tone became apologetic. "Oh! Why didn't you say so? If he'll pay enough, and if you want him, why, of course—"

Laure interrupted with an unexpected dash of temper. "He isn't going to pay you anything: you're going to pay him—top wages, too. Understand?"

The unhappy recipient of this ultimatum raised his hands in a gesture of despair. "Himmel! There's no understanding you girls! There's no getting along with you, either. What's on your mind, eh? Are you after him or his coin?"

"I—don't know." Laure was gazing at Phillips with a peculiar expression. "I'm not sure. Maybe I'm after both. Will you be good and hire him, or—"

"Oh, you've got me!" Best declared, with frank

resentment. "If you want him, I s'pose I'll have to get him for you, but"—he muttered an oath under his breath—"you'll ruin me. Oy! Oy! I'll be glad when you're all in Dawson and at work."

After some further talk the manager approached Phillips and made himself known. "Laure tells me you want to join our troupe," he began.

"I'll see that he pays you well," the girl urged. "Come on."

Phillips' thoughts were not quite clear, but, even so, the situation struck him as grotesquely amusing. "I'm no song-and-dance man," he said, with a smile. "What would you expect me to do? Play a mandolin?"

"I don't know exactly," Best replied. "Maybe you could help me ride herd on these Bernhardts." He ran a hand through his thin black hair, thinner now by half than when he left the States. "If you could do that, why—you could save my reason."

"He wants you to be a Simon Legree," Laure explained.

The manager seconded this statement by a nod of his head. "Sure! Crack the whip over 'em. Keep 'em in line. Don't let 'em get married. I thought I was wise to hire good-lookers, but—I was crazy. They smile and they make eyes and the men fight for 'em. They steal 'em away. I've had a dozen battles and every time I've been licked. Already four of my girls are gone. If I lose four more I can't open; I'll be ruined. Oy! Such a country! Every day a new love-affair; every day more trouble—"

Laure threw back her dark head and laughed in mischievous delight. "It's a fact," she told Pierce. "The best Best gets is the worst of it. He's not our manager, he's our slave; we have lots of fun with him." Stepping closer to the young man, she slipped her arm within his and, looking up into his face, said, in a low voice: "I knew I could fix it, for I always have my way. Will you go?" When he hesitated she repeated: "Will you go with me or—shall I go with you?"

Phillips started. His brain was fogged and he had difficulty in focusing his gaze upon the eager, upturned face of the girl; nevertheless, he appreciated the significance of this audacious inquiry and there came to him the memory of his recent conversation with the Countess Courteau. "Why do you say that?" he queried, after a moment. "Why do you want me to go?"

Laure's eyes searched his; there was an odd light in them, and a peculiar intensity which he dimly felt but scarcely understood. "I don't know," she confessed. She was no longer smiling, and, although her gaze remained hypnotically fixed upon his, she seemed to be searching her own soul. "I don't know," she said again, "but you have a—call."

In spite of this young woman's charms, and they were numerous enough, Phillips was not strongly drawn to her; resentment, anger, his rankling sense of injury, all these left no room for other emotions. That she was interested in him he still had sense enough to perceive; her amazing proposal, her unmistakable air of proprietorship, showed that much, and in consequence a sort of malicious triumph arose within him. Here, right at hand, was an agency of forgetfulness, more potent by far than the one to which he had first turned. Dangerous? Yes. But his life was ruined. What difference, then, whether oblivion came from alcohol or from the drug of the poppy? Deliberately he shut his ears to inner warnings; he raised his head defiantly.

"I'll go," said he.

"We leave at daylight," Best told him.

CHAPTER XIV

WITH 'Poleon Doret to be busy was to be contented, and these were busy times for him. His daily routine, with trap and gun, had made of him an early riser and had bred in him a habit of greeting the sun with a song. It was no hardship for him, therefore, to cook his breakfast by candle-light, especially now that the days were growing short. On the morning after his rescue of Sam Kirby and his daughter 'Poleon washed his dishes and cut his wood; then, finding that there was still an hour to spare before the light would be sufficient to run Miles Cañon, he lit his pipe and strolled up to the village. The ground was now white, for considerable snow had fallen during the night; the day promised to be extremely short and uncomfortable. 'Poleon, however, was impervious to weather of any sort; his good humor was not dampened in the least.

Even at this hour the saloons were well patronized, for not only was the camp astir, but also the usual stale crowd of all-night loiterers was not yet sufficiently intoxicated to go to bed. As 'Poleon neared the first resort, the door opened and a woman emerged. She was silhouetted briefly

237

against the illumination from within, and the pilot was surprised to recognize her as Rouletta Kirby. He was upon the point of speaking to her when she collided blindly with a man who had preceded him by a step or two.

The fellow held the girl for an instant and helped her to regain her equilibrium, exclaiming, with a laugh: "Say! What's the matter with you, sister? Can't you see where you're going?" When Rouletta made no response the man continued in an even friendlier tone, "Well, I can see; my eyesight's good, and it tells me you're about the best-looking dame I've run into to-night." Still laughing, he bent his head as if to catch the girl's answer. "Eh? I don't get you. Who d'you say you're looking for?"

'Poleon was frankly puzzled. He resented this man's tone of easy familiarity and, about to interfere, he was restrained by Rouletta's apparent indifference. What ailed the girl? It was too dark to make out her face, but her voice, oddly changed and unnatural, gave him cause for wonderment. Could it be—'Poleon's half-formed question was answered by the stranger who cried, in mock reproach: "Naughty! Naughty! You've had a little too much, that's what's the matter with you. Why, you need a guardeen." Taking Rouletta by the shoulders, the speaker turned her about so that the dim half-light that filtered through the canvas wall of the tent saloon shone full upon her face.

'Poleon saw now that the girl was indeed not

herself; there was a childish, vacuous expression upon her face; she appeared to be dazed and to comprehend little of what the man was saying. This was proved by her blank acceptance of his next insinuating words: "Say, it's lucky I stumbled on to you. I been up all night and so have you. S'pose we get better acquainted. What?".

Rouletta offered no objection to this proposal; the fellow slipped an arm about her and led her away, meanwhile pouring a confidential murmur into her ear. They had proceeded but a few steps when 'Poleon Doret strode out of the gloom and laid a heavy hand upon the man.

"My frien'," he demanded, brusquely, "w'ere you takin' dis lady?"

"Eh?" The fellow wheeled sharply. "What's the idea? What is she to you?"

"She ain't not'in' to me. But I seen you plenty tams an'—you ain't no good."

Rouletta spoke intelligibly for the first time: "I've no place to go—no place to sleep. I'm very —tired."

"There you've got it," the girl's self-appointed protector grinned. "Well, I happen to have room for her in my tent." As Doret's fingers sank deeper into his flesh the man's anger rose; he undertook to shake off the unwelcome grasp. "You leggo! You mind your own business—"

"Dis goin' be my biznesse," 'Poleon announced. "Dere's somet'ing fonny 'bout dis—"

"Don't get funny with me. I got as much right to her as you have—"

239

'Poleon jerked the man off his feet, then flung
him aside as if he were unclean. His voice was
hoarse with disgust when he cried:

"Get out! Beat it! By Gar! You ain't fit for
touch decent gal. You spik wit' her again, I tear
you in two piece!"

Turning to Rouletta he said, "Mam'selle, you
lookin' for your papa, eh?"

Miss Kirby was clasping and unclasping her
fingers, her face was strained, her response came
in a mutter so low that 'Poleon barely caught it:

"Danny's gone—gone— Dad, he's— No use
fighting it— It's the drink—and there's nothing
I can do."

It was 'Poleon's turn to take the girl by the
shoulders and wheel her about for a better look at
her face. A moment later he led her back into the
saloon. She was so oddly obedient, so docile, so
unquestioning, that he realized something was
greatly amiss. He laid his hand against her flushed
cheek and found it to be burning hot, whereupon
he hastily consulted the nearest bystanders. They
agreed with him that the girl was indeed ill—more
than that, she was half delirious.

"*Sacré!* W'at's she doin' roun' a saloon lak dis?"
he indignantly demanded. "How come she's
gettin' up biffore daylight, eh?"

It was the bartender who made plain the facts:
"She ain't been to bed at all, Frenchy. She's been
up all night, ridin' herd on old Sam Kirby. He's
drinkin', understand? He tried to get some place
for her to stay, along about midnight, but there

240

wasn't any. She's been settin' there alongside of
the stove for the last few hours and I been sort of
keepin' an eye on her for Sam's sake."

Doret breathed an oath. "Dat's nice fader she's
got! I wish I let 'im drown."

"Oh, he ain't exactly to blame. He's on a bender
—like to of killed a feller in here. Somebody'd
ought to take care of this girl till he sobers up."

During this conference Rouletta stood quivering, her face a blank, completely indifferent to her
surroundings. 'Poleon made her sit down, and but
for her ceaseless whispering she might have been
in a trance.

Doret's indignation mounted as the situation
became plain to him.

"Fine t'ing!" he angrily declared. "W'at for
you fellers leave dis seeck gal settin' up, eh? Me,
I come jus' in tam for catch a loafer makin' off
wit' her." Again he swore savagely. "Dere's
some feller ain't wort' killin'. Wal, I got good
warm camp; I tak' her dere, den I fin' dis fader."

"Sam won't be no good to you. What she needs
is a doctor, and she needs him quick," the bartender averred.

"*Eh bien!* I fin' him, too! Mam'selle"—'Poleon
turned to the girl—"you're bad seeck, dat's fac'.
You care for stop in my tent?" The girl stared up
at him blankly, uncomprehendingly; then, drawn
doubtless by the genuine concern in his troubled
gaze, she raised her hand and placed it in his. She
left it there, the small fingers curling about his
big thumb like those of a child. "Poor li'l bird!"

241

The woodsman's brow puckered, a moisture gathered in his eyes. "Dis is hell, for sure. Come, den, *ma petite*, I fin' a nes' for you." He raised her to her feet; then, removing his heavy woolen coat, he placed it about her frail shoulders. When she was snugly buttoned inside of it he led her out into the dim gray dawn; she went with him obediently.

As they breasted the swirling snowflakes Doret told himself that, pending Sam Kirby's return to sanity, this sick girl needed a woman's care quite as much as a doctor's; naturally his thoughts turned to the Countess Courteau. Of all the women in White Horse, the Countess alone was qualified to assume charge of an innocent child like this, and he determined to call upon her as soon as he had summoned medical assistance.

When, without protest, Rouletta followed him into his snug living-quarters, Doret thought again of the ruffian from whom he had rescued her and again he breathed a malediction. The more fully he became aware of the girl's utter helplessness the angrier he grew, and the more criminal appeared her father's conduct. White Horse made no pretense at morality; it was but a relay station, a breathing-point where the mad rush to the Klondike paused; there was neither law nor order here; the women who passed through were, for the most part, shameless creatures; the majority of the men were unruly, unresponsive to anything except an appeal to their animal appetites. Sympathy, consideration, chivalry had all but vanished

242

in the heat of the great stampede. That Sam
Kirby should have abandoned his daughter to such
as these was incredible, criminal. Mere intoxication did not excuse it, and 'Poleou vowed he would
give the old man a piece of his mind at the first
opportunity.

His tent was still warm; a few sticks of dry
spruce caused the little stove to grow red; he
helped Rouletta to lie down upon his bed, then he
drew his blankets over her.

"You stay here li'l while, eh?" He rested a
comforting hand upon her shoulder. "'Poleon
goin' find your papa now. Bimeby you goin' feel
better."

He was not sure that she understood him, for
she continued to mutter under her breath and began to roll her head as if in pain. Then he summoned all the persuasiveness he could. "Dere
now, you're safe in 'Poleon's house; he mak' you
well dam' queeck."

A good many people were stirring when the
pilot climbed once more to the stumpy clearing
where the village stood, and whomsoever he met
he questioned regarding Sam Kirby; it did not
take him long to discover the latter's whereabouts.
But 'Poleon's delay, brief as it had been, bore
tragic consequences. Had he been a moment or
two earlier he might have averted a catastrophe
of far-reaching effect, one that had a bearing upon
many lives.

The Gold Belt Saloon had enjoyed a profitable
all-night patronage; less than an hour previously

243

Morris Best had rounded up the last of his gay song-birds and put an end to their carnival. The poker game, however, was still in progress at the big round table. Already numerous early risers were hurrying in to fortify themselves against the raw day just breaking, and among these last-named, by some evil whim of fate, chanced to be the man for whom Sam Kirby had so patiently waited. The fellow had not come seeking trouble —no one who knew the one-armed gambler's reputation sought trouble with him—but, learning that Kirby was still awake and in a dangerous mood, he had entered the Gold Belt determined to protect himself in case of eventualities.

Doret was but a few seconds behind the man, but those few seconds were fateful. As the pilot stepped into the saloon he beheld a sight that was enough to freeze him motionless. The big kerosene lamps, swung from the rafter braces above, shed over the interior a peculiar sickly radiance, yellowed now by reason of the pale morning light outside. Beneath one of the lamps a tableau was set. Sam Kirby and the man he had struck the night before were facing each other in the center of the room, and Doret heard the gambler cry:

"I've been laying for you!"

Kirby's usually impassive face was a sight; it was fearfully contorted; it was the countenance of a maniac. His words were loud and uncannily distinct, and the sound of them had brought a breathless hush over the place. At the moment of Doret's entrance the occupants of the saloon seemed petrified; they stood rooted in their tracks as if the anger in that menacing voice had halted them in mid-action. 'Poleon, too, turned cold, for it seemed to him that he had opened the door upon a roomful of wax figures posed in theatric postures. Then in the flash of an eye the scene dissolved into action, swift and terrifying.

What happened was so unexpected, it came with such a lack of warning, that few of the witnesses, even though they beheld every move, were able later to agree fully upon details. Whether Kirby actually fired the first shot, or whether his attempt to do so spurred his antagonist to lightning quickness, was long a matter of dispute. In a flash the room became a place of deafening echoes. Shouts of protest, yells of fright, the crash of overturning furniture, the stamp of fleeing feet mingled with the loud explosion of gunshots— pandemonium.

Fortunately the troupe of women who had been here earlier were gone and the tent was by no means crowded. Even so, there were enough men present to raise a mighty turmoil. Some of them took shelter behind the bar, others behind the stove and the tables; some bolted headlong for the door; still others hurled themselves bodily against the canvas walls and ripped their way out.

The duel was over almost as quickly as it had begun. Sam Kirby's opponent reeled backward and fetched up against the bar; above the din his hoarse voice rose:

"He started it! You saw him! Tried to kill me!"

He waved a smoking pistol-barrel at the gambler, who had sunk to his knees. Even while he was shouting out his plea for justification Kirby slid forward upon his face and the fingers of his outstretched hand slowly unloosed themselves from his gun.

It had been a shocking, a sickening affair; the effect of it had been intensified by reason of its unexpectedness, and now, although it was over, excitement gathered fury. Men burst forth from their places of concealment and made for the open air; the structure vomited its occupants out into the snow.

'Poleon Doret had been swept aside, then borne backward ahead of that stampede, and at length found himself wedged into a corner. He heard the victor repeating: "You saw him. Tried to kill me!" The speaker turned a blanched face and glaring eyes upon those witnesses who still remained. "He's Sam Kirby. I had to get him or he'd have got me." He pressed a hand to his side, then raised it; it was smeared with blood. In blank stupefaction the man stared at this phenomenon.

Doret was the first to reach that motionless figure sprawled face down upon the floor; it was he who lifted the gray head and spoke Kirby's name. A swift examination was enough to make quite sure that the old man was beyond all help. Outside, curiosity had done its work and the human tide was setting back into the wrecked saloon. When 'Poleon rose with the body in his arms he was surrounded by a clamorous crowd. Through it he bore the limp figure to the cloth-covered card-table, and there, among the scattered emblems of Sam Kirby's calling, 'Poleon deposited his burden. By those cards and those celluloid disks the old gambler had made his living; grim fitness was in the fact that they should carpet his bier.

When 'Poleon Doret had forced his way by main strength out of the Gold Belt Saloon, he removed his cap and, turning his face to the wind, he breathed deeply of the cool, clean air. His brow was moist; he let the snowflakes fall upon it the while he shut his eyes and strove to think. Engaged thus, he heard Lucky Broad address him.

With the speaker was Kid Bridges; that they had come thither on the run was plain, for they were panting.

"What's this about Kirby?" Lucky gasped.

"We heard he's just been croaked!" the Kid exclaimed.

'Poleon nodded. "I seen it all. He had it comin' to him," and with a gesture he seemed to brush a hideous picture from before his eyes.

"Old Sam! *Dead!*"

Broad, it seemed, was incredulous. He undertook to bore his way into the crowd that was pressing through the saloon door, but Doret seized him.

"Wait!" cried the latter. "Dat ain't all; dat ain't de worst."

"Sayl. Where's Letty?" Bridges inquired. "Was she with him when it happened? Does she know—"

"Dat's w'at I'm goin' tell you." In a few words 'Poleon made known the girl's condition, how he had happened to encounter her, and how he had been looking for her father when the tragedy occurred. His listeners showed their amazement and their concern.

"Gosh! That's tough!" It was Broad speaking. "Me 'n' the Kid had struck camp and was on our way down to fix up our boat when we heard about the killin'. We couldn't believe it, for Sam—"

"Seems like it was a waste of effort to save that outfit," Bridges broke in. "Sam dead and Letty dyin'—all in this length of time! She's a good kid; she's goin' to feel awful. Who's goin' to break the news to her?"

"I don' know." 'Poleon frowned in deep perplexity. "Dere's doctor in dere now," he nodded toward the Gold Belt. "I'm goin' tak' him to her, but she mus' have woman for tak' care of her. Mebbe Madame la Comtesse—"

"Why, the Countess is gone! She left at daylight. Me 'n' the Kid are to follow as soon as we get our skiff fixed."

"Gone?"

"Sure!"

"*Sacré!* De one decent woman in dis place. Wall" 'Poleon shrugged. "Dose dance-hall gal' is got good heart—"

"Hell! They pulled out ahead of our gang.

Best ran his boats through the White Horse late yesterday and he was off before it was light. I know, because Phillips told me. He's joined out with 'em—blew in early and got his war-bag. He left the Countess flat."

Doret was dumfounded at this news and he showed his dismay.

"But—dere's no more women here!" he stammered. "Dat young lady she's seeck; she mus' be nurse'. By Gar! Who's goin' do it, eh?"

The three of them were anxiously discussing the matter when they were joined by the doctor to whom 'Poleon had referred. "I've done all there is to do here," the physician announced. "Now about Kirby's daughter. You say she's delirious?" The pilot nodded. He told of Rouletta's drenching on the afternoon previous and of the state in which he had just found her. "Jove! Pneumonia, most likely. It sounds serious, and I'm afraid I can't do much. You see I'm all ready to go, but— of course I'll do what I can."

"Who's goin' nurse her?" 'Poleon demanded for a second time. "Dere ain't no women in dis place."

The physician shook his head. "Who indeed? It's a wretched situation! If she's as ill as you seem to think, why, we'll have to do the best we can, I suppose. She probably won't last long. Come!" Together he and the French Canadian hurried away.

CHAPTER XV

IT was afternoon when Lucky Broad and Kid Bridges came to 'Poleon Doret's tent and called its owner outside.

"We're hitched up and ready to say 'gid-dap,' but we came back to see how Letty's getting along," the former explained.

'Poleon shook his head doubtfully; his face was grave. "She's bad seeck."

"Does she know about old Sam?"

"She ain't know not'in'. She's crazee altogether. Poor li'l gal, she's jus' lak baby. I'm scare' as hell."

The confidence-men stared at each other silently; then they stared at Doret. "What we goin' to do about it?" the Kid inquired, finally.

'Poleou was at a loss for an answer; he made no secret of his anxiety. "De doctor say she mus' stay right here—"

"*Here?*"

"He say if she get cold once more—pouf! She die lak dat! Plenty fire, plenty blanket, medicine every hour, dat's all. I'm prayin' for come along some woman—any kin' of woman at all—I don' care if she's squaw."

"There ain't any skirts back of us. Best's out-fit was the last to leave Linderman. There won't be any more till after the freeze-up."

"*Eh bien!* Den I 's pose I do de bes' I can. She's poor seeck gal m'beeg, cold countree wit' no frien's, no money—"

"No money?" Broad was startled. "Why, Sam was 'fat'! He had a bank-roll—"

"He lose five t'onsan' dollar' playin' card las' night. Less 'n eighty dollar' dey lef' him. Eighty dollar' an'—dis." From the pocket of his macki-naw 'Poleon drew Kirby's revolver, that famous single-action six-shooter, the elaborate ivory grip of which was notched in several places. Broad and his partner eyed the weapon with intense interest.

"That's Agnes, all right!" the former declared. "And that's where old Sam kept his books." He ran his thumb-nail over the significant file-marks on the handle. "Looks like an alligator had bit it."

Bridges was even more deeply impressed by the announcement of Kirby's losses than was his part-ner. "Sam must of been easy pickin', drunk like that. He was a gamblin' fool when he was right, but I s'pose he couldn't think of nothin' except fresh meat for Agnes. Letty had him tagged proper, and I bet she'd of saved him if she hadn't of gone off her nut. D'you think she's got a chance?"

"For get well?" 'Poleon shrugged his wide shoulders. "De doctor say it's goin' be hard pull. He's goin' stay so long he can, den—wal, mebbe 'noder doctor come along. I hope so."

"If she does win out, then what?" Broad inquired.

'Poleon considered the question. "I s'pose I tak' her back to Dyea an' send her home. I got some dog."

Lucky studied the speaker curiously; there was a peculiar hostile gleam in his small, colorless eyes. "Medicine every hour, and a steady fire, you say. You don't figger to get much sleep, do you?"

"*Non.* No. But me, I'm strong feller; I can sleep hangin' up by de ear if I got to."

"What's the big idea?"

"Eh?" Doret was frankly puzzled. "W'at you mean, 'beeg idea'?"

"What d'you expect to get out of all this?"

"*M'sieu'!*" The French Canadian's face flushed, he raised his head and met the gaze of the two men. There was an air of dignity about him as he said: "Dere's plenty t'ing in dis worl' we don' get pay' for. You didn't 'spect no pay yesterday when you run de W'ite 'Orse for save dis gal an' her papa, did you? No. Wal, I'm woodsman, river-man; I ain't dam' stampeder. Dis is my countree, we're frien's together long tam; I love it an' it loves me. I love de birds and hanimals, an' dey're frien's wit' me also. 'Bout spring-tam, w'en de grub she's short, de Canada jays dey come to visit me, an' I feed dem; sometam' I fin' dere's groun-squirrel's nest onder my tent, an' mebbe mister squirrel creep out of his hole, t'inkin' summer is come. Dat feller he's hongry; he steal my food an' he set 'longside my stove for eat him.

252

You t'ink I hurt dose he'pless li'l t'ing? You s'pose I mak' dem pay for w'at dey eat?"

'Poleon was soaring as only his free soul could soar; he indicated the tent at his back, whence issued the sound of Rouletta Kirby's ceaseless murmurings.

"Dis gal—she's tiny snowbird wit' broken wing. *Bien!* I fix her wing de bes' I can. I mak' her well an' I teach her to fly again. Dat's all." Broad and Bridges had listened attentively, their faces impassive. Lucky was the first to speak.

"Letty's a good girl, y'understand. She's different to these others—"

'Poleon interrupted with a gesture of impatience. "It ain't mak' no difference if she's good or bad. She's seeck."

"Me 'n' the Kid have done some heavy thinkin', an' we'd about decided to get a high stool and take turns lookin' out Letty's game, just to see that her bets went as they laid, but I got a hunch you're a square guy. What *d'you* think, Kid?"

Mr. Bridges nodded his head slowly. "I got the same hunch. The point is this," he explained. "We can't very well throw the Countess—we got some of her outfit—and, anyhow, we'd be about as handy around an invalid as a coupla cub bears. I think we'll bow out. But, Frenchy"—the gambler spoke with intense earnestness—"if ever we hear a kick from that gal we'll—we'll foller you like a track. Won't we, Lucky?"

"We'll foller him to hell!" Mr. Broad feelingly declared.

253

Gravely, ceremoniously, the callers shook hands with Doret, then they returned whence they had come. They went their way; Rouletta's delirium continued; 'Poleon's problem increased daily; meanwhile, however, the life of the North did not slacken a single pulse-beat.

Never since their earliest associations had Tom Linton and Jerry Quirk found themselves in such absolute accord, in such complete harmony of understanding, as during the days that immediately followed their reconciliation. Each man undertook to outdo the other in politeness; each man forced himself to be considerate, and strove at whatever expense to himself to lighten the other's burdens; all of their relations were characterized by an elaborate, an almost mid-Victorian courtesy. A friendly rivalry in self-sacrifice existed between them; they quarreled good-naturedly over the dish-washing, that disgusting rite which tries the patience of every grown man; when there was wood to be cut they battled with each other for the ax.

But there is a limit to politeness; unfailing sunshine grows tedious, and so does a monotonous exercise of magnanimity.

While it had been an easy matter to cut their rowboat in two, the process of splicing it together again had required patience and ingenuity, and it had resulted in delay. By the time they arrived at Miles Cañon, therefore, the season was far advanced and both men, without knowing it, were in a condition of mind to welcome any sort of a squall that would serve to freshen the unbearably stagnant atmosphere of amiability in which they were slowly suffocating.

Here for the first time the results of their quarrel arose to embarrass them; they could find no pilot who would risk his life in a craft so badly put together as theirs. After repeated discouragements the partners took counsel with each other; reluctantly they agreed that they were up against it.

"Seems like I've about ruined us," Mr. Quirk acknowledged, ruefully.

"You? Why, Jerry, it was my fault we cut the old ship in two," Mr. Linton declared.

The former speaker remonstrated, gently. "Now, Tom, it's just like you to take the blame, but it was my doin's; I instigated that fratricidal strife."

Sweetly but firmly Linton differed with his partner. "It ain't often that you're wrong, Jerry, old boy—it ain't more than once or twice in a lifetime—but you're wrong now. I'm the guilty wretch and I'd ought to hang for it. My rotten temper—"

"Pshaw! You got one of the nicest dispositions I ever see—in a man. You're sweeter 'n a persimmon. I pecked at you till your core was exposed. I'm a thorn in the flesh, Tom, and folks wouldn't criticize you none for doin' away with me."

"You're 'way off. I climbed you with my spurs—"

"Now, Tom!" Sadly Mr. Quirk wagged his

255

gray head. "I don't often argue with anybody, especially with you, but the damnable idea of dividin' our spoils originated in my evil mind and I'm goin' to pay the penalty. I'll ride this white-pine outlaw through by myself. You ear him down till I get both feet in the stirrups, then turn him a-loose; I'll finish settin' up and I won't pull leather."

"How you talk! Boats ain't like horses; it'll take a good oarsman to navigate these rapids—"

"Well?" Quirk looked up quickly. "I'm a good oarsman." There was a momentary pause. "Ain't I?"

Mr. Linton hastily remedied his slip of the tongue. "You're a bear!" he asserted, with feeling. "I don't know as I ever saw a better boatman than you, for your weight and experience, but— there's a few things about boats that you never had the chance to pick up, you being sort of a cactus and alkali sailor. For instance, when you want a boat to go 'gee' you have to pull on the 'off' oar. It's plumb opposite to the way you steer a horse."

"Sure! Didn't I figger that out for the both of us? We 'most had a runaway till I doped it out."

Now this was a plain perversion of fact, for it was Tom who had made the discovery. Mr. Linton was about to so state the matter when he reflected that doubtless Jerry's intentions were honest and that his failing memory was to blame for the misstatement. It was annoying to be

256

robbed of the credit for an important discovery, of course, but Tom swallowed his resentment.

"The point is this," he said, with a resumption of geniality. "You'd get all wet in them rapids, Jerry, and—you know what that means. I'd rather take a chance on drowning myself than to nurse you through another bad cold."

It was a perfectly sincere speech—an indirect expression of deep concern that reflected no little credit upon the speaker's generosity. Tom was exasperated, therefore, when Jerry, by some characteristic process of crooked reasoning, managed to misinterpret it. Plaintively the latter said:

"I s'pose I *am* a handicap to you, Tom. You're mighty consid'rate of my feelin's, not to throw it up to me any oftener than you do."

"I don't throw it up to you none. I never did. No, Jerry, I'll row the boat. You go overland and keep your feet dry."

"A lot of good that would do." Mr. Quirk spoke morosely. "I'd starve to death walkin' around if you lost the grub."

This struck Tom Linton as a very narrow, a very selfish way of looking at the matter. He had taken no such view of Jerry's offer; he had thought less about the grub than about his partner's safety. It was an inconsiderate and unfeeling remark. After a moment he said:·

"You know I don't throw things up to you, Jerry. I ain't that kind." Mr. Quirk stirred uneasily. "You didn't mean to say that, did you?"

What Jerry would have answered is uncertain,

for his attention at the moment was attracted by a stranger who strode down the bank and now accosted him and his partner jointly.

"*Bon jour, m'sieu's!*" said the new-comer. "I'm lookin' for buy some lemon'. You got some, no?"

Mr. Quirk spoke irritably. "Sure. We've got a few, but they ain't for sale."

The stranger—Quirk remembered him as the Frenchman, Doret, whom he had seen at Sheep Camp—smiled confidently.

"Oh yes! Everyt'ing is for sale if you pay 'nough for him," said he.

Now this fellow had broken the thread of a conversation into which a vague undertone of acrimony was creeping—a conversation that gave every indication of developing into an agreeable and soul-satisfying difference of opinion, if not even into a loud and free-spoken argument of the old familiar sort. To have the promise of an invigorating quarrel frustrated by an idiotic diversion concerning lemons caused both old men to turn their pent-up exasperation upon the speaker.

"We've got use for our lemons and we're going to keep them," said Tom. "We're lemon-eaters—full of acid—that's us."

"We wouldn't give lemon aid to nobody." Jerry grinned in malicious enjoyment of his own wit.

"You got how many?" 'Poleon persisted.

"Oh, 'bout enough! Mebbe a dozen or two."

"I buy 'em. Dere's poor seeck lady—"
258

Tom cut in brusquely. "You won't buy anything here. Don't tell us your troubles. We've got enough of our own, and poverty ain't among the number."

"W'at trouble you got, eh? Me, I'm de trouble man. Mebbe I fix 'em."

Sourly the partners explained their difficulty. When 'Poleon understood he smiled again, more widely.

"Good! I mak' bargain wit' you, queeck. Me, I'm pilot of de bes' an' I tak' your boat t'rough for dose lemon'."

The elderly men sat up; they exchanged startled glances.

"D'you mean it?"

"I'm goin' have dose lemon'."

"Can't you buy any in the saloons?"

"No. Wal, w'at you say?"

Tom inquired of his partner, "Reckon you can get along without 'em, Jerry?"

"Why, I been savin' 'em for you."

"Then it's a go!"

"One t'ing you do for me, eh?" 'Poleon hesitated momentarily. "It's goin' tak' tam for fin' dam' fool to he'p me row dat bateau, but—I fin' him. Mebbe you set up wit' li'l seeck gal while I'm gone. What?" In a few words he made known the condition of affairs at his camp, and the old men agreed readily enough. With undisguised relief they clambered stiffly out of their boat and followed the French Canadian up the trail. As they toiled up the slope 'Poleon explained:

"De doctor he's go to Dawson, an' t'ree day dis gal been layin' seeck—crazee in de head. Every hour medicine, all de tam fire in de stove! *Sapré!* I'm half 'sleep."

"We'll set up with her as long as you want," Tom volunteered. "Being a family man myself, I'm a regular nurse."

"Me, too," Jerry exclaimed. "I never had no family, but I allus been handy around hosses, and hosses is the same as people, only bigger—"

Mr. Linton stifled a laugh at this remark. "That 'll show you!" said he. "You leave it to me, Jerry."

"Well, ain't they?"

"No."

"They are, too."

"Plumb different."

The argument waxed hot; it had reached its height when 'Poleon laid a finger upon his lips, commanding silence. On tiptoe he led the two men into his tent. When he had issued instructions and left in search of a boatman the partners seated themselves awkwardly, their caps in their hands. Curiously, apprehensively, they studied the fever-flushed face of the delirious girl.

"Purty, ain't she?" Jerry whispered.

Tom nodded. "She's sick, all right, too," he said in a similar tone; then, after a moment: "I've been thinking about them lemons. We're getting about a hundred dollars a dozen for 'em. Kind of a rotten trick, under the circumstances. I'm sorry you put it up to that feller the way you did."

Mr. Quirk stiffened, his eyes widened in astonishment.

"Me? I didn't put it up to him. You done it. They're your lemons."

"How d'you figure they're mine?".

"You bought 'em, didn't you?"

"I *paid* for 'em, if that's what you mean, but I bought 'em for you, same as I bought that liquor. You've et most of 'em, and you've drank most of the whisky. You needed it worse than I did, Jerry, and I've always considered—"

Now any reference, any reflection upon his physical limitations, however remote or indirect, aroused Jerry's instant ire. "At it again, ain't you?" he cried, testily. "I s'pose you'll forget about that whisky in four or five years. I hope so—"

"'Sh-h!" Tom made a gesture commanding silence, for Jerry had unconsciously raised his voice. "What ails you?" he inquired, sweetly.

"Nothin' ails me," Jerry muttered under his breath. "That's the trouble. You're allus talkin' like it did—like I had one foot in the grave and was gaspin' my last. I'm hard as a hickory-nut. I could throw you down and set on you."

Mr. Linton opened his bearded lips, then closed them again; he withdrew behind an air of wounded dignity. This, he reflected, was his reward for days of kindness, for weeks of uncomplaining sacrifice. Jerry was the most unreasonable, the most difficult person he had ever met; the more one did for him the crankier he became. There was no gratitude in the man, his skin wouldn't hold it. Take the matter of their tent, for instance: how would the old fellow have managed if he, Tom, had not, out of pure compassion, taken pity on him and rescued him from the rain back there at Linderman? Had Jerry remembered that act of kindness? He had not. On the contrary, he had assumed, and maintained, an attitude of indulgence that was in itself an offense— yes, more than an offense. Tom tried to center his mind upon his partner's virtues, but it was a difficult task, for honesty compelled him to admit that Jerry assayed mighty low when you analyzed him with care. Mr. Linton gave up the effort finally with a shake of his head.

"What you wigwaggin' about?" Jerry inquired, curiously. Tom made no answer. After a moment the former speaker whispered, meditatively: "*I'd* have *give* him the lemons if he'd asked *me* for 'em. Sick people need lemons."

"Sometimes they do and sometimes they don't," Mr. Linton whispered, shortly.

"Lemons is acid, and acid cuts phlegm."

"Lemons ain't acid; they're alkali."

This statement excited a derisive snort from Mr. Quirk. "Alkali! My God! Ever taste alkali?" Jerry had an irritating way of asserting himself in regard to matters of which he knew less than nothing; his was the scornful certainty of abysmal ignorance.

"Did you ever give lemons to sick folks?" Tom inquired, in his turn.

"Sure! Thousands."

Now this was such an outrageous exaggeration that Linton was impelled to exclaim:

"*Rats!* You never *saw* a thousand sick folks."

"I didn't say so. I said I'd given thousands of lemons—"

"Oh!" Tom filled his pipe and lit it, whereupon his partner breathed a sibilant warning:

"Put out that smudge! D'you aim to strangle the girl?"

With a guilty start the offender quenched the fire with his thumb.

"The idea of lightin' sheep-dip in a sick-room!" Mr. Quirk went on. With his cap he fanned violently at the fumes.

"You don't have to blow her out of bed," Tom growled. Clumsily he drew the blankets closer beneath the sick girl's chin, but in so doing he again excited his companion's opposition.

"Here!" Jerry protested. "She's burnin' up with fever. You blanket 'em when they've got chills." Gently he removed the covers from Rouletta's throat.

Linton showed his contempt for this ridiculous assertion by silently pulling the bedding higher and snugly tucking it in. Jerry promptly elbowed him aside and pulled it lower. Tom made an angry gesture, and for a third time adjusted the covers to suit himself, whereupon Jerry immediately changed them to accord with his ideas.

Aggressively, violently, but without words this

263

time, the partners argued the matter. They were glaring at each other, they had almost come to blows when, with a start, Jerry looked at his watch. Swiftly he possessed himself of the medicine-glass and spoon; to Tom he whispered:

"Quick! Lift her up."

Linton refused. "Don't you know. *anything?*" he queried. "Never move a sick person, unless you have to. Give it to her as she lays."

"How you goin' to feed medicine out of a spoon to anybody layin' down?" the other demanded.

"Easy!" Tom took the glass and the teaspoon; together the two men bent over the bed.

But Linton's hands were shaky; when he pressed the spoon to Rouletta's lips he spilled its contents. The girl rolled her head restlessly.

"Pshaw! She moved."

"She never moved," Jerry contradicted. "You missed her." From his nostrils issued that annoying, that insulting, snort of derision which so sorely tried his partner's patience. "You had a fair shot at her, layin' down, Tom, and you never touched her."

"Maybe I'd have had better luck if you hadn't jiggled me."

"Hell! Who jiggled—?"

"'Sh—h!" Once more Mr. Quirk had spoken aloud. "If you've got to holler, go down by the rapids."

After several clumsy attempts both men agreed that their patient had doubtless received the equivalent of a full dose of medicine, so Tom replaced the glass and spoon. "I'm a little out of practice," he explained.

"I thought you done fine." Jerry spoke with what seemed to be genuine commendation. "You got it into her nose every time."

Tom exploded with wrath and it was Jerry's turn to command silence.

"Why don't you hire a hall?" the latter inquired. "Or mebbe I better tree a 'coon for you so you can bark as loud as you want to. Family man! Huh!" Linton bristled aggressively, but the whisperer continued:

"One head of children don't make a family any more 'n one head of heifers makes a herd."

Tom paled; he showed his teeth beneath his gray mustache. Leaning forward, he thrust his quivering bearded face close to the hateful countenance opposite him. "D'you mean to call my daughter a heifer?" he demanded, in restrained fury.

"Keep them whiskers to yourself," Jerry snapped. "You can't pick a row with me, Tom; I don't quarrel with nobody. I didn't call your daughter a heifer, and you know I didn't. No doubt she would of made a fine woman if she'd of grown up, but— Say! I bet I know why you lost her. I bet you poured so much medicine in her crib that she drownded." Jerry giggled at this thought.

"That ain't funny," the other rumbled. "If I thought you meant to call a member of my family a heifer—."

"You've called your wife worse 'n that. I've heard you."

"I meant everything I said. She was an old catamount and—"

"Prob'bly she was a fine woman." Jerry had a discourteous habit of interrupting. "No wonder she walked out and left you flat—she was human. No doubt she had a fine character to start with. So did I, for that matter, but there's a limit to human endurance."

"You don't have to put up with me any longer than you want to," Linton stormed, under his breath. "We can get a divorce easy. All it takes is a saw."

"You made that crack once before, and I called your bluff!" Jerry's angry face was now outthrust; only with difficulty did he maintain a tone inaudible to the sick girl. "Out of pity I helped you up and handed you back your crutches. But this time I'll let you lay where you fall. A hundred dollars a dozen for lemons! For a poor little sick girl! You 'ain't got the bowels of a shark!"

"It was your proposition!"

"It wasn't!"

"It was!"

"Some folks lie faster 'n a goat can gallop."

"Meaning me?"

"Who else would I mean?"

"Why don't you *call* me a liar and be done with it?"

"I do. It ain't news to anybody but you!"

Having safely landed his craft below the rapids, 'Poleon Doret hurried back to his tent to find the partners sitting knee to knee, face to face, and hurling whispered incoherencies at each other. Both men were in a poisonous mood, both were ripe for violence. They overflowed with wrath. They were glaring; they shook their fists; they were racked with fury; insult followed abuse; and the sounds that issued from their throats were like the rustlings of a corn-field in an autumn gale. Nor did inquiry elicit a sensible explanation from either.

"Heifer, eh? Drowned my own child, did I?" Tom ground his teeth in a ferocious manner.

"Don't file your tusks for me," Jerry chattered; "file the saw. We're goin' to need it."

"You men goin' cut dat boat in two again?" 'Poleon inquired, with astonishment.

"Sure. And everything we've got."

It was Linton who spoke; there was a light of triumph in his eyes, his face was ablaze with an unholy satisfaction. "We've been drawing lots for twenty minutes, and this time—*I got the stove!*"

18

CHAPTER XVI

ONCE again Tom and Jerry's skiff had been halved, once again its owners smarted under the memory of insults unwarranted, of gibes that no apology could atone for. This time it had been old Jerry who cooked his supper over an open fire and old Tom who stretched the tarpaulin over his stove. Neither spoke; both were sulky, avoiding each other's eye; there was an air of bitter, implacable hostility.

Into this atmosphere of constraint came 'Poleon Doret, and, had it not been for his own anxieties, he would have derived much amusement from the situation. As it was, however, he was quite blind to it, showing nothing save his own deep feeling of concern.

"*M'sieu's*," he began, hurriedly, "dat gal she's gettin' more seeck. I'm scare' she's goin' die tonight. Mebbe you set up wit' me, eh?"

Tom quickly volunteered: "Why, sure! I'm a family man. I—"

"Family man!" Jerry snorted, derisively. "He had one head, mister, and he lost it inside of a month. I'm a better nurse than him."

"*Bien!* I tak' you both," said 'Poleon.

But Jerry emphatically declined the invitation. "Cut me out if you aim to make it three-handed— I'd Jim the deck, sure. No, I'll set around and watch my grub-pile."

Tom addressed himself to 'Poleon, but his words were for his late partner.

"That settles me," said he. "I'll have to stick close to home, for there's people I wouldn't trust near a loose outfit."

This was, of course, a gratuitous affront. It was fathered in malice; it had its intended effect. Old Jerry hopped as if springs in his rheumatic legs had suddenly let go; he uttered a shrill war-whoop—a wordless battle-cry in which rage and indignation were blended.

"If a certain old buzzard-bait sets up with you, Frenchy, count your spoons, that's all. I know him. A hundred dollars a dozen for lemons! He'd rob a child's bank. He'd steal milk out of a sick baby's bottle."

The pilot frowned. "Dis ain't no tam for callin' names," said he. "To-night dat gal goin' die or —she's goin' begin get well. Me, I'm mos' dead now. Mebbe you fellers forget yourse'f li'l while an' he'p me out."

Tom stirred uneasily. With apparent firmness he undertook to evade the issue, but in his eyes was an expression of uncertainty. Jerry, too, was less obdurate than he had pretended. After some further argument he avoided a weak surrender by muttering:

"All right. Take *him* along, so I'll know my

grub's safe, and I'll help you out. I'm a good hand
with hosses, and hosses are like humans, only bigger. They got more sense and more affection, too.
They know when they're well off. Now if a hoss
gets down you got to get him up and walk him
around. My idea about this girl—"

Mr. Linton groaned loudly, then to 'Poleon he
cried: "Lead the way. You watch the girl and
I'll watch this vet'rinary."

That was an anxious and a trying night for the
three men. They were unskilled in the care of the
sick; nevertheless, they realized that the girl's
illness had reached its crisis and that, once the
crisis had passed, she would be more than likely
to recover. Hour after hour they sat beside her,
administering her medicine regularly, maintaining
an even temperature in the tent, and striving, as
best they could, to ease her suffering. This done,
they could only watch and wait, putting what
trust they had in her youth and her vitality. Their
sense of helplessness oppressed the men heavily;
their concern increased as the hours dragged along
and the life within the girl flared up to a blaze or
flickered down to a mere spark.

Doret was in a pitiable state, on the verge of
exhaustion, for his vigil had been long and faithful;
it was a nightmare period of suspense for him.
Occasionally he dozed, but only to start into
wakefulness and to experience apprehensions
keener than before. The man was beside himself,
and his anxiety had its effect upon Tom and

Jerry. Their compassion increased when they learned how Sam Kirby had been taken off and how Rouletta had been brought to this desperate pass. The story of her devotion, her sacrifice, roused their deepest pity, and in the heat of that emotion they grew soft.

This mellowing process was not sudden; no spirit of forgiveness was apparent in either of the pair. Far from it. Both remained sullen, unrelenting; both maintained the same icy front. They continued to ignore each other's presence and they exchanged speech only with Doret. Nevertheless, their sympathy had been stirred and a subtle change had come over them.

This change was most noticeable in Linton. As the night wore on distressing memories, memories he considered long dead and gone, arose to harass him. It was true that he had been unhappily married, but time had cured the sting of that experience, or so he had believed. He discovered now that such was not the case; certain incidents of those forgotten days recurred with poignant effect. He had experienced the dawn of a father's love, a father's pride; he lost himself in a melancholy consideration of what might have been had not that dawn been darkened. How different, how full, how satisfying, if— As he looked down upon the fair, fever-flushed face of this girl he felt an unaccustomed heartache, a throbbing pity and a yearning tenderness. The hand with which he stroked the hair back from her brow and rearranged her pillow was as gentle as a woman's.

Jerry, too, altered in his peculiar way. As the hours lengthened, his wrinkled face became less vinegary, between his eyes there appeared a deepening frown of apprehension. More than once he opened his lips to ask Tom's opinion of how the fight progressed, but managed in time to restrain himself. Finally he could maintain silence no longer, so he spoke to Doret:

"Mister! It looks to me like she ain't doin' well."

'Poleon rose from his position beside the stove; he bent over the sick-bed and touched Rouletta's brow with his great hand. In a low voice he addressed her:

"*Ma sœur! Ma petite sœur!* It's 'Poleon spik to you."

Rouletta's eyes remained vacant, her ceaseless whispering continued and the man straightened himself, turning upon his elderly companions. Alarm was in his face; his voice shook.

"*M'sieu's!* W'at shall we do? Queeck! Tell me."

But Tom and Jerry were helpless, hopeless. Doret stared at them; his hands came slowly together over his breast, his groping fingers interlocked; he closed his eyes, and for a moment he stood swaying. Then he spoke again as a man speaks who suffers mortal anguish. "She mus' not die! She—mus' not die! I tell you somet'ing now: dis li'l gal she's come to mean whole lot for me. At firs' I'm sorry, de same lak you feel. Sure! But bimeby I get to know her, for she talk, talk—all tam she talk, lak crazee person, an' I learn to know her soul, her life. Her soul is w'ite,

272

m'sieu's, it's w'ite an' beautiful; her life—I fit 'im together in little piece, lak broken dish. Some piece I never fin', but I save 'nough to mak' picture here and dere. Sometam I smile an' listen to her; more tam' I cry. She mak' de tears splash on my hand.

"Wal, I begin talk back to her. I sing her li'l song, I tell her story, I cool her face, I give her medicine, an' den she sleep. I sit an' watch her—how many day an' night I watch her I don' know. Sometam I sleep li'l bit, but when she stir an' moan I spik to her an' sing again until—she know my voice."

'Poleon paused; the old men watched his working face.

"*M'sieu's*," he went on, "I'm lonely man. I got no frien's, no family; I live in dreams. Dat's all I got in dis whole worl'—jus' dreams. One dream is dis, dat some day I'm going find somet'ing to love, somet'ing dat will love me. De hanimals I tame dey run away; de birds I mak' play wit' dey fly south when de winter come. I say, 'Doret, dis gal she's poor, she's frien'less, she's alone. She's very seeck, but you goin' mak' her well. She ain't goin' run away. She ain't goin' fly off lak dem birds. No. She's goin' love you lak a broder, an' mebbe she's goin' let you stay close by.' *Dieu!* Dat's fine dream, eh? It mak' me sing inside; it mak' me warm an' glad. I w'isper in her ear, '*Ma sœur! Ma petite sœur!* It's your beeg broder 'Poleon dat spik. He's goin' mak' you well,' an' every tam she onderstan'. But now—"

A sob choked the speaker; he opened his tight-shut eyes and stared miserably at the two old men. "I call to her an' she don' hear. W'at I'm goin' do, eh?"

Neither Linton nor Quirk made reply. 'Poleon leaned forward; fiercely he inquired:

"Which one of you feller' is de bes' man? Which one is go to church de mos'?"

Tom and Jerry exchanged glances. It was the latter who spoke:

"Tom—this gentleman—knows more about churches than I do. He was married in one."

Mr. Linton nodded. "But that was thirty years ago, so I ain't what you'd call a regular attendant. I used to carry my religion in my wife's name, when I had a wife."

"You can pray?"

Tom shook his head doubtfully. "I'd be sure to make a mess of it."

Doret sank to a seat; he lowered his head upon his hands. "Me, too," he confessed. "Every hour I mak' prayer in my heart, but—I can't spik him out."

"If I was a good talker I'd take a crack at it," Jerry ventured, "but—I'd have to be alone."

Doret's lips had begun to move; his companions knew that he was voicing a silent appeal, so they lowered their eyes. For some moments the only sound in the tent was the muttering of the delirious girl.

Linton spoke finally; his voice was low, it was husky with emotion: "I've been getting acquainted with myself to-night—first time in a long while. Things look different than they did. What's the good of fighting, what's the use of hurrying and trampling on each other when this is the end? Gold! It won't buy anything worth having. You're right, Doret; somebody to love and to care for, somebody that cares for you, that's all there is in the game. I had dreams, too, when I was a lot younger, but they didn't last. It's bad for a man to quit dreaming; he gets mean and selfish and onnery. Take me—I ain't worth skinning. I had a kid—little girl—I used to tote her around in my arms. Funny how it makes you feel to tote a baby that belongs to you; seems like all you've got is wrapped up in it; you live two lives. My daughter didn't stay long. I just got started loving her when she went away. She was—awful nice."

The speaker blinked, for his eyes were smarting. "I feel, somehow, as if she was here to-night—as if this girl was her and I was her daddy. She might have looked something like this young lady if she had lived. She would have made a big difference in me."

Tom felt a hand seek his. It was a bony, big-knuckled hand not at all like 'Poleon Doret's. When it gave his fingers a strong, firm, friendly pressure his throat contracted painfully. He raised his eyes, but they were blurred; he could distinguish nothing except that Jerry Quirk had sidled closer and that their shoulders all but touched.

Now Jerry, for all of his crabbedness, was a sentimentalist; he also was blind, and his voice was equally husky when he spoke:

"I'd of been her daddy, too, wouldn't I, Tom? We'd of shared her, fifty-fifty. I've been mean to you, but I'd of treated *her* all right. If you'll forgive me for the things I've said to you maybe the Lord will forgive me for a lot of other things. Anyhow, I'm goin' to do a little rough prayin' for this kid. I'm goin' to ask Him to give her a chance."

Mr. Quirk did pray, and if he made a bad job of it, as he more than suspected, neither of his earthly hearers noticed the fact, for his words were honest, earnest. When he had finished Tom Linton's arm was around his shoulders; side by side the old men sat for a long time. Their heads were bowed; they kept their eyes upon Rouletta Kirby's face. Doret stood over them, motionless and intense; they could hear him sigh and they could sense his suffering. When the girl's pain caused her to cry out weakly, he knelt and whispered words of comfort to her.

Thus the night wore on.

The change came an hour or two before dawn and the three men watched it with their hearts in their throats. Mutely they questioned one another, deriving deep comfort from each confirmatory nod and gesture, but for some time they dared not voice their growing hope. Rouletta's fever was breaking, they felt sure; she breathed more deeply, more easily, and she coughed less. Her discomfort lessened, too, and finally, when the

E BY SIDE THE OLD MEN SAT. . . . DORET STOOD OVER THEM
MOTIONLESS AND INTENSE

candle-light grew feeble before the signs of coming day, she fell asleep. Later the men rose and stole out of the tent into the cold.

Doret was broken. He was limp, almost lifeless; there were deep lines about his eyes, but, nevertheless, they sparkled.

"She's goin' get well," he said, uncertainly. "I'm goin' teach dat li'l bird to fly again."

The partners nodded.

"Sure as shootin'," Jerry declared.

"Right-o!" Linton agreed. "Now then"—he spoke in an energetic, purposeful tone—"I'm going to put Jerry to bed while I nail that infernal boat together again."

"Not much, you ain't!" Jerry exclaimed. "You know I couldn't sleep a wink without you, Tom. What's more, I'll never try."

Arm in arm the two partners set off down the river-bank. 'Poleon smiled after them. When they were out of sight he turned his face up to the brightening sky and said, aloud:

"*Bon Dieu,* I t'ank you for my sister's life."

Pierce Phillips awoke from a cramped and troubled slumber to find himself lying upon a pile of baggage in the stern of a skiff. For a moment he remained dazed; then he was surprised to hear the monotonous creak of oars and to feel that he was in motion. A fur robe had been thrown over him; it was powdered with snowflakes, but it had kept him warm. He sat up to discover Laure facing him.

"Hello!" said he. "You here?"

The girl smiled wearily. "Where did you think I'd be? Have a good sleep?"

He shrugged and nodded, and, turning his eyes shoreward, saw that the forest was flowing slowly past. The boat in which he found himself was stowed full of impedimenta; forward of Laure a man was rowing listlessly, and on the seat beyond him were two female figures bundled to the ears in heavy wraps. They were the 'coon-shouting sisters whose song had drawn Pierce into the Gold Belt Saloon the evening before. In the distance were several other boats.

"You feel tough, I'll bet." Laure's voice was sympathetic.

After a moment of consideration Pierce shook his head. "No," said he. "I feel fine—except that I'm hungry. I could eat a log-chain."

"No headache?"

"None. Why?"

Laure's brown eyes widened in admiration and astonishment. "Jimminy! You're a hound for punishment. You must have oak ribs. Were you weaned on rum?"

"I never took a drink until last night. I'm a rank amateur."

"Really!" The girl studied him with renewed interest. "What set you off?"

Pierce made no answer. His face seemed fixed in a frown. His was a tragic past; he could not bear to think of it, much less could he speak of it. Noting that the oarsman appeared to be weary,

278

Pierce volunteered to relieve him, an offer which was quickly accepted. As he seated himself and prepared to fall to work Laure advised him:

"Better count your money and see if it's all there."

He did as directed. "It's all here," he assured her.

She flashed him a smile, then crept into the place he had vacated and drew up the robe snugly. Pierce wondered why she eyed him with that peculiar intentness. Not until she had fallen asleep did he suspect with a guilty start that the robe was hers and that she had patiently waited for him to finish his sleep while she herself was drooping with fatigue. This suspicion gave him a disagreeable shock; he began to give some thought to the nature of his new surroundings. They were of a sort to warrant consideration; for a long time he rowed mechanically, a frown upon his brow.

In the first place, he was amazed to find how bravely he bore the anguish of a breaking heart, and how little he desired to do away with himself. The world, strangely enough, still remained a pleasant place, and already the fret for new adventure was stirring in him. He was not happy—thoughts of Hilda awoke real pain, and his sense of injury burned him like a brand— nevertheless, he could not make himself feel so utterly hopeless, so blackly despondent as the circumstances plainly warranted. He was, on the whole, agreeably surprised at his powers of resistance and of recuperation, both physical and emotional. For instance, he should by all means experience a wretched reaction from his inebriety; as a matter of fact, he had never felt better in his life; his head was clear, he was ravenously hungry. Then, too, he was not altogether hopeless; it seemed quite probable that he and Hilda would again meet, in which event there was no telling what might happen. Evidently liquor agreed with him; in his case it was not only an anodyne, but also a stimulus, spurring him to optimistic thought and independent action. Yes, whisky roused a fellow's manhood. It must be so, otherwise he would never have summoned the strength to snap those chains which bound him to the Countess Courteau, or the reckless courage to embark upon an enterprise so foreign to his tastes and to his training as this one.

His memory of the later incidents of the night before was somewhat indistinct, as was his recollection of the scene when he had served his notice upon the Countess. Of this much he felt certain, however, he had done the right thing in freeing himself from a situation that reflected discredit upon his manhood. Whether he had acted wisely by casting in his lot with Morris Best's outfit was another matter altogether. He was quite sure he had not acted wisely, but there is a satisfaction at certain times in doing what we know to be the wrong thing.

Pierce was no fool; even his limited experience in the North had taught him a good deal about the character of dance-hall women and of the men who handled them; he was in no wise deceived, therefore, by the respectability with which the word "theatrical" cloaked this troupe of wanderers; it gave him a feeling of extreme self-consciousness to find himself associated with such folk; he felt decidedly out of place.

What would his people think? And the Countess Courteau?· Well, it would teach her that a man's heart was not a football; that a man's love was not to be juggled with. He had made a gesture of splendid recklessness; he would take the consequences.

In justice to the young man, be it said he had ample cause for resentment, and whatever of childishness he displayed was but natural, for true balance of character is the result of experience, and as yet he had barely tasted life.

As for the girl Laure, she awoke no real interest in him, now that he saw her in the light of day; he included her in his general, vague contempt for all women of her type. There was, in fact, a certain contamination in her touch. True, she was a little different from the other members of the party—greatly different from Pierce's preconceived ideas of the "other sort"—but not sufficiently different to matter. It is the privilege of arrogant youth to render stern and conclusive judgment.

. Best waved his party toward the shore shortly before dusk. A landing-place was selected, tents, bedding, and paraphernalia were unloaded; then, while the women looked on, the boatmen began

pitching camp. The work had not gone far before
Phillips recognized extreme inefficiency in it. Confusion grew, progress was slow, Best became more
and more excited. Irritated at the general inepti-
tude, Pierce finally took hold of things and in a
short time had made all snug for the night.

Lights were glowing in the tents when he found
his way through the gloom to the landing in
search of his own belongings. Seated on the gunwale of a skiff he discovered Laure.

"I've been watching you," she said. "You're
a handy man."

He nodded. "Is this the way Best usually
makes camp?"

"Sure. Only it usually takes him much longer.
I'll bet he's glad he hired you."

Pierce murmured something.

"Are you glad he did?"

"Why, yes—of course."

"What do you think of the other girls?"

"I haven't paid much attention to them," he
told her, frankly.

There was a moment's pause; then Laure said:
"Don't!"

"Eh?"

"I say, don't!"

Phillips shrugged. In a world-weary, cynical
tone he asserted, "Women don't interest me."

"What ails you to-day?" Laure inquired, curiously.

"Nothing. I'm not much of a ladies' man, that's
all."

"Yes, you are. Anyhow, you were last night."

"I was all tuned up, then," he explained. "That's not my normal pitch."

"Don't you like me as well as you did?"

"Why—certainly."

"Is there another woman?"   '

"'Another'?" Pierce straightened himself. "There's not even one. What difference would it make if there were?"

"Oh, none." Laure's teeth flashed through the gloom. "I was just curious. Curiosity killed a cat, didn't it? Will you help me up the bank?"

Pierce took the speaker's arm; together they climbed the gravelly incline toward the illumination from the cook fire. In the edge of the shadows Laure halted and her hand slipped down over Pierce's.

"Remember!" she said, meaningly. "Don't— or you'll hear from me."

19

CHAPTER XVII

LAURE had no cause to repeat her admonition, for, in the days that followed, Pierce Phillips maintained toward the women members of the party an admirable attitude of aloofness. He was not rude, neither was he discourteous; he merely isolated himself from them and discouraged their somewhat timid advances toward friendship. This doubtless would have met with Laure's whole-hearted approval had he not treated her in precisely the same way. She had at first assumed a somewhat triumphant air of proprietorship toward him, but this quickly gave way to something entirely different. They began to know each other, to be sure; for hours upon end they were together, which could have resulted in nothing less than a thorough acquaintance; notwithstanding this, there lurked behind Phillips' friendly interest an emotional apathy that piqued the girl and put her on her mettle. She hid her chagrin under an assumption of carelessness, but furtively she studied him, for every hour he bulked bigger to her. He exercised a pronounced effect upon her; his voice, his laughter, brought a light and a sparkle to her eyes; she could not rest when he was out of her sight. His appeal, unconscious on his part, struck to the very core of her being. To discover that she lacked a similar appeal for him roused the girl to desperation; she lay awake nights, trying to puzzle out the reason, for this was a new experience to her. Recalling their meeting and the incidents of that first night at White Horse, she realized that here was a baffling secret and that she did not possess the key to it.

One night the truth came home to her. Best had made camp later than usual, and as a result had selected a particularly bad spot for it—a brushy flat running back from a high, overhanging bank beneath which ran a swirling eddy.

The tents were up, a big camp-fire was blazing brightly, when Pierce Phillips, burdened with a huge armful of spruce boughs and blinded by the illumination, stepped too close to the river's rim and felt the soil beneath him crumble away. Down he plunged, amid an avalanche of earth and gravel; the last sound he heard before the icy waters received him was Laure's affrighted scream. An instant later he had seized a "sweeper," to which he clung until help arrived. He was wet to the skin, of course; his teeth were chattering by the time he had regained the camp-fire. Of the entire party, Laure alone had no comment to make upon the accident. She stood motionless, leaning for support against a tent-pole, her face hidden in her hands. Best's song-birds were noisily twittering about Pierce; Best himself was congratulating the young man upon his ability to swim, when Laure spoke, sharply, imperiously:

"Somebody find his dry things, quickly. And you, Morris, get your whisky."

While one of the men ran for Pierce's duffle-bag, Best came hurrying with a bottle which he proffered to Pierce. The latter refused it, asserting that he was quite all right; but Laure exclaimed:

"Drink! Take a good one, then go into our tent and change as fast as you can."

"Sure!" the manager urged. "Don't be afraid of good liquor. There isn't much left. Drink it all."

A short time later, when Pierce reappeared, clad in dry garments, he felt none the worse for his mishap, but when he undertook to aid in the preparations for the night he suspected that he had taken his employer's orders too literally, for his brain was whirling. Soon he discovered that his movements were awkward and his hands uncertain, and when his camp-mates began to joke he desisted with a laughing confession that he had imbibed too much.

Laure drew him out of hearing, then inquired. anxiously, "Are you all right again?"

"Sure! I feel great."

"I—I thought I'd die when I saw you disappear." She shuddered and hid her face in her hands for a second time. It was quite dark where they stood; they were sheltered from observation.

"Served me right," he declared. "Next time I'll look where—" He halted in amazement. "Why, Laure, I believe you're crying!"

She lifted her face and nodded. "I'm frightened yet." She laid trembling, exploratory hands upon him, as if to reassure herself of his safety. "Pierce! Pierce!" she exclaimed, brokenly.

Suddenly Phillips discovered that this girl's concern affected him deeply, for it was genuine—it was not in the least put on. All at once she seemed very near to him, very much a part of himself. His head was spinning now and something within him had quickened magically. There was a new note in his voice when he undertook to reassure his companion. At his first word Laure looked up, startled; into her dark eyes, still misty with tears, there flamed a light of wonder and of gladness. She swayed closer; she took the lapels of his coat between her gloved fingers and drew his head down to hers; then she kissed him full upon the lips. Slowly, resolutely, his arms encircled her.

On the following morning Laure asked Morris Best for a bottle of whisky. The evenings were growing cold and some of the girls needed a stimulant while camp was being pitched, she explained. The bottle she gave to Pierce, with a request to stow it in his baggage for safekeeping, and that night when they landed, cramped and chilly, she prevailed upon him to open it and to drink. The experiment worked. Laure began to understand that when Pierce Phillips' blood flowed warmly, when he was artificially exhilarated, then he saw her with the eyes of a lover. It was not a flattering discovery, but the girl contented herself, for by

287

now she was desperate enough to snatch at straws. Thenceforth she counted upon strong drink as her ally.

The closing scenes of the great autumn stampede to Dawson were picturesque, for the rushing river was crowded with boats all racing with one another. 'Neath lowering skies, past ghostly shores seen dimly through a tenuous curtain of sifting snowflakes, swept these craft; they went by ones and by twos, in groups and in flotillas; hourly the swirling current bore them along, and as the miles grew steadily less the spirits of the crews mounted. Loud laughter, songs, yells of greeting and encouragement, ran back and forth; a triumphant joyfulness, a Jovian mirth, animated these men of brawn, for they had met the North and they had bested her. Restraint had dropped away by now, and they reveled in a new-found freedom. There was license in the air, for Adventure was afoot and the Unknown beckoned.

Urged on by oar and sweep, propelled by favoring breezes, the Argonauts pressed forward exultantly. At night their roaring camp-fires winked at one another like beacon lights along some friendly channel. Unrolling before them was an endless panorama of spruce and birch and cottonwood, of high hills white with snow, of unexplored valleys dark with promise. As the Yukon increased in volume it became muddy, singing a low, hissing song, as if the falling particles of snow melted on its surface and turned to steam.

Out of all the traffic that flowed past the dance-hall party, among all the boats they overhauled and left behind, Pierce Phillips nowhere recognized the Countess Courteau's outfit. Whether she was ahead or whether they had outdistanced her he did not know and inquiry rewarded him with no hint.

During this journey a significant change gradually came over the young man. Familiarity, a certain intimacy with his companions, taught him much, and in time he forgot to look upon them as pariahs. Best, for instance, proved to be an irritable but good-hearted little Hebrew; he developed a genuine fondness for Pierce, which he took every occasion to show, and Pierce grew to like him. The girls, too, opened their hearts and made him feel their friendship. For the most part they were warm, impulsive creatures, and Pierce was amazed to discover how little they differed from the girls he had known at home. Among their faults he discovered unusual traits of character; there was not a little kindliness, generosity, and of course much cheerfulness. They were free-handed with what they had; they were ready with a smile, a word of encouragement or of sympathy; they were absurdly grateful, too, for the smallest favor or the least act of kindness. Moreover, they behaved themselves extremely well.

They were an education to Phillips; he acknowledged that he had gravely misjudged them, and he began to suspect that they had taught him something of charity.

As for Laure, he knew her very well by now and she knew him—even better. This knowledge had come to them not without cost—wisdom is never cheap—but precisely what each of them had paid or was destined to pay for their better understanding of each other they had not the slightest idea. One thing the girl by this time had made sure of, *viz.*, when Pierce was his natural self he felt her appeal only faintly. On the other hand, the moment he was not his natural self, the moment his pitch was raised, he saw allurements in her, and at such times they met on common ground. She made the most of this fact.

Dawson City burst into view of the party without warning, and no El Dorado could have looked more promising. Rounding a bend of the river, they beheld a city of logs and canvas sprawled between the stream and a curving mountain-side. The day was still and clear, hence vertical pencil-markings of blue smoke hung over the roofs; against the white background squat dwellings stood out distinctly, like diminutive dolls' houses. Upon closer approach the river shore was seen to be lined with scows and rowboats; a stern-wheeled river steamer lay moored abreast of the town. Above it a valley broke through from the north, out of which poured a flood of clear, dark water. It was the valley of the Klondike, magic word.

The journey was ended. Best's boats were unloaded, his men had been paid off, and now his troupe had scattered, seeking lodgings. As in a dream Pierce Phillips joined the drifting current of humanity that flowed through the long, front streets and eddied about the entrances of amusement-places. He asked himself if he were indeed awake, if, after all, this was his Ultima Thule? Already the labor, the hardship, the adventure of the trip seemed imaginary; even the town itself was unreal. Dawson was both a disappointment and a satisfaction to Pierce. It was not what he had expected and it by no means filled the splendid picture he had painted in his fancy. Crude, raw, unfinished, small, it was little more than Dyea magnified. But in enterprise it was tremendous; hence it pleased and it thrilled the youth. He breathed its breath, he drank the wine of its intoxication, he walked upon air with his head in the clouds.

Pierce longed for some one to whom he could confide his feeling of triumph, but nowhere did he recognize a face. Finally he strolled into one of the larger saloons and gambling-houses, and was contentedly eying the scene when he felt a gaze fixed upon him. He turned his head, opened his lips to speak, then stiffened in his tracks. He could not credit his senses, for there, lounging at ease against the bar, his face distorted into an evil grin, stood Joe McCaskey!

Pierce blinked; he found that his jaw had dropped in amazement. McCaskey enjoyed the sensation he had created; he leered at his former camp-mate, and in his expression was, a hint of that same venom he had displayed when he had run the gauntlet at Sheep Camp after his flogging. He broke the spell of Pierce's amazement and proved himself to be indeed a reality by uttering a greeting.

Pierce was inclined to ignore the salutation, but curiosity got the better of him and he answered:

"Well! This is a surprise. Do you own a pair of seven-league boots or—what?"

McCaskey bared his teeth further. In triumph he said: "Thought you'd lost me, didn't you? But I fooled you—fooled all of you. I jumped out to the States and caught the last boat for St. Michael, made connections there with the last up-river packet, and—here I am. I don't quit; I'm a finisher."

Pierce noted the emphasis with which Joe's last words were delivered, but as yet his curiosity was unsatisfied. He wondered if the fellow was sufficiently calloused to disregard his humiliating experience or if he proposed in some way to conceal it. Certainly he had not evaded recognition, nor had he made the slightest attempt to alter his appearance. From his bold insouciance it seemed evident that he was totally indifferent as to who recognized him. Either the man possessed moral courage of the extremest sort or else an unbelievable effrontery.

As for Pierce, he was deeply resentful of Joe's false accusation—the memory of that was ineradicable—nevertheless, in view of the outcome of that cowardly attempt, he had no desire for further revenge. It seemed to him that the fellow had been sufficiently punished for his misdeed; in fact, he could have found it easy to feel sorry for him had it not been for the ill-concealed malice in Joe's present tone and attitude.

He was upon the point of answering Joe's indirect threat with a warning, when his attention was attracted to a short, thick-set, nervous man at his elbow. The latter had edged close and was staring curiously at him. He spoke now, saying:

"So you're Phillips, eh?"

It was Joe who replied: "Sure. This is him."

There was no need of an introduction. Pierce recognized the stranger as another McCaskey, for the family likeness was stamped upon his features. During an awkward moment the two men eyed each other, and Joe McCaskey appeared to gloat as their glances clashed.

"This is Frank," the latter explained, with a malicious grin. "He and Jim was pals. And, say! Here's another guy you ought to meet." He laid a hand upon still a second stranger, a man leaning across the bar in conversation with a white-aproned attendant. "Count, here's that fellow I told you about."

The man addressed turned, exposing a handsome, smiling blond face ornamented with a well-cared-for mustache. "I beg pardon?" he exclaimed, vacuously.

"Meet Phillips. He can give you some dope on your wife." Joe chuckled. Phillips flushed; then he paled; his face hardened.

"Ah! To be sure." Count Courteau bowed,

but he did not extend his hand. "Phillips! Yes, yes. I remember. You will understand that I'm distracted for news of Hilda. She is with you, perhaps?"

"I left her employ at White Horse. If she's not here, she'll probably arrive soon."

"Excellent; I shall surprise her."

Pierce spoke dryly. "I'm afraid it won't be so much of a surprise as you think. She rather expects you." With a short nod and with what pretense of carelessness he could assume he moved on toward the rear of the building, whence came the sounds of music and the voice of a dance-hall caller.

For some time he looked on blindly at the whirling figures. Joe McCaskey here! And Count Courteau! What an astonishing coincidence! And yet there was really nothing so remarkable about it; doubtless the same ship had brought them north, in which event they could not well have avoided a meeting. Pierce remembered Hilda's prophecy that her indigent husband would turn up, like a bad penny. His presence was agitating—for that matter, so was the presence of Joe McCaskey's brother Frank, as yet an unknown quantity. That he was an enemy was certain; together, he and Joe made an evil team, and Pierce was at a loss just how to meet them.

Later, when he strolled out of the saloon, he saw the three men still at the bar; their heads were together; they were talking earnestly.

CHAPTER XVIII

ROULETTA KIRBY was awakened by the sound of chopping; in the still, frosty morning the blows of the ax rang out loudly. For a moment she lay staring upward at the sloping tent-roof over her bed, studying with sleepy interest the frost-fringe formed by her breath during the night. This fringe was of intricate design; it resembled tatters of filmy lace and certain fragments of it hung down at least a foot, a warning that the day was to be extremely cold. But Rouletta needed no proof of that fact beyond the evidence of her nose, the tip of which was like ice and so stiff that she could barely wrinkle it. She covered it now with a warm palm and manipulated it gently, solicitously.

There was a damp, unpleasant rime of hoar-frost standing on the edge of her fur robe, and this she gingerly turned back. Cautiously she freed one arm, then raised herself upon her elbow. Reaching up, she struck the taut canvas roof a sharp blow; then with a squeak, like the cry of a frightened marmot, she dodged under cover just in time to avoid the frosty shower.

The chopping abruptly ceased. 'Poleon's voice

greeted her gaily: "*Bon jour, ma sœur!* By golly! You gettin' be de mos' lazy gal! I 'spect you sleep all day only I mak' beeg noise."

"Good morning!" Rouletta's voice was muffled. As if repeating a lesson, she ran on: "Yes, I feel fine. I had a dandy sleep; didn't cough and my lungs don't hurt. And no bad dreams. So I want to get up. There! I'm well."

"You hongry, too, I bet, eh?"

"Oh, I'm dying. And my nose—it won't work."

Doret shouted his laughter. "You wait. I mak' fire queeck an' cook de breakfas', den—you' nose goin' work all right. I got beeg s'prise for dat li'l nose to-day."

The top of Rouletta's head, her eyes, then her mouth, came cautiously out from hiding.

"What is it, 'Poleon? Something to eat?"

"*Sapre!* What I tol' you? Every minute 'eat, eat'! You' worse dan barmy of Swede'. I ain't goin' tol' you what is dis s'prise—bimeby you smell him cookin'."

"*Moose meat!*" Rouletta cried.

"No!" 'Poleon vigorously resumed his labor; every stroke of the ax was accompanied by a loud "Huh!" "I tol' you not'in'!" he declared; then after a moment he voiced one word, "Caribou!"

Again Rouletta uttered a famished cry.

Soon the tent strings were drawn and the axman pushed through the door, his arms full of dry spruce wood. He stood smiling down at the face framed snugly in the fox fur; then he dropped his burden and knelt before the stove. In a moment there came a promising crackle, followed quickly by an agreeable flutter which grew into a roar as the stove began to draw.

"*Caribou!*" Rouletta's eyes were bright with curiosity and an emotion far more material. "Where in the world—?"

"Some hinjun hunter mak' beeg kill. I got more s'prise as dat, too. By golly! Dis goin' be regular Chris'mas for you."

Rouletta stirred. There was stubborn defiance in her tone when she said: "I'm going to get up and I'm—going—outdoors—clothes or no clothes. I'll wrap the robe around me and play I'm a squaw." She checked 'Poleon's protest. "Oh, I'm perfectly well, and the clothes I have are thick enough."

"Look out you don' froze yourse'f. Dat pretty dress you got is give you chillsblain in Haugust." The speaker blew upon his fingers and sat back upon his heels, his eyes twinkling, his brown face wreathed in smiles.

"Then I can do it? You'll let me try?" Rouletta was all eagerness.

"We'll talk 'bout dat bimeby. First t'ing we goin' have beeg potlatch, lak Siwash weddin'."

"Goody! Now run away while I get up."

But the man shook his head. "Don' be soch hurry. Dis tent warm slow. Las' night de reever is froze solid so far you look. Pretty queeck people come."

"Do you think they'll have extra clothes—something warm that I can wear?"

297

"Sure! I fix all dat." Still smiling, 'Poleon
rose and went stooping out of the tent, tying the
flaps behind him. A few rods distant was another
shelter which he had pitched for himself; in front
of it, on a pole provision-cache, were two quarters
of frozen caribou meat, and seated comfortably
in the snow beneath, eyes fixed upon the prize,
were several "husky" dogs of unusual size. At
'Poleon's appearance they began to caper and to
fawn upon him.

"Ho, you ole t'iefs!" he cried, sternly. "You
lak steal dose meat, I bet! Wal, I eat you 'live."
Stretching on tiptoe, he removed one of the quarters and bore it into his tent. The dogs gathered
just outside the door; cautiously they nosed the
canvas aside; and as 'Poleon set to work with
hatchet and hunting-knife their bright eyes followed his every move.

"Non!" he exclaimed, with a ferocious frown.
"You don't get so much as li'l smell. You t'ink
ma sœur goin' hongry to feed loafer' lak you?"
Bushy gray tails began to stir, the heads came
farther forward, there was a most unmannerly
licking of chops. "By Gar! You sound lak'
miner-man eatin' soup. W'at for you 'spect nice
grub? You don' work none." 'Poleon removed a
layer of fat, divided it, and tossed a portion to
each animal. The morsels vanished with a single
gulp, with one wolfish click of sharp white teeth.
"No, I give you not'in'."

For no reason whatever the speaker broke into
loud laughter; then, to further relieve his bubbling

joyousness, he began to hum a song. As he worked his song grew louder, until its words were audible to the girl in the next tent.

> *"Oh, la voix du beau Nord qui m'appelle,*
> *Pour bénir avec lui le jour,*
> *Et désormais toute peine cruelle*
> *Fuira devant mon chant d'amour.*
> *D'amour, d'amour."*

> ("Oh, the voice of the North is a-calling me,
> To join in the praise of the day,
> So whatever the fate that's befalling me,
> I'll sing every sorrow away. Away, away.")

The Yukon stove was red-hot now, and Rouletta Kirby's tent was warm. She seated herself before a homely little dresser fashioned from two candle-boxes, and began to arrange her hair. Curiously she examined the comb and brush. They were, or had been, 'Poleon's; so was the pocket-mirror hanging by a safety-pin to the canvas wall above. Rouletta recalled with a smile the flourish of pride with which he had presented to her this ludicrous bureau and its fittings. Was there ever such a fellow as this Doret? Was there ever a heart so big, so kind? A stranger, it seemed to the girl that she had known him always. There had been days—days interminable—when he had seemed to be some dream figure; an indistinct, unreal being at once familiar and unfamiliar, friendly and for-bidding; then other days during which he had gradually assumed substance and actuality and during which she had come to know him. Follow-

20   299

ing her return to sanity, Rouletta had experienced periods of uncertainty and of terror, then hours of embarrassment the mere memory of which caused her to shrink and to hide her head. Those were times of which, even yet, she could not bear to think. Hers had been a slow recovery and a painful, nay a tragic, awakening, but, as she had gained the strength and the ability to understand and to suffer, 'Poleon, with a tact and a thoughtfulness unexpected in one of his sort, had dropped the character of nurse and assumed the rôle of friend and protector. That had been Rouletta's most difficult ordeal, the most trying time for both of them, in fact; not one man in ten thousand could have carried off such an awkward situation at a cost so low to a woman's feelings. It was, of course, the very awkwardness of that situation, together with 'Poleon's calm, courageous method of facing it, that had given his patient the strength to meet him half-way and that had made her convalescence anything less than a torture.

And the manner in which he had allowed her to learn all the truth about herself—bit by bit as her resistance grew—his sympathy, his repression, his support! He had to know just how far to go; he had spared her every possible heartache, he had never permitted her to suffer a moment of trepidation as to herself. No. Her first conscious feeling, now that she recalled it, had been one of implicit, unreasoning faith in him. That confidence had increased with every hour; dismay, despair, the wish to die had given place to resignation, then to hope, and now to a brave self-confidence. Rouletta knew that her deliverance had been miraculous and that this man, this total stranger, out of the goodness of his heart, had given her back her life. She never ceased pondering over it.

She was now sitting motionless, comb and brush in hand, when 'Poleon came into the tent for a second time and aroused her from her abstraction. She hastily completed her toilette, and was sitting curled up on her bed when the aroma of boiling coffee and the sound of frying steak brought her to her feet. With a noisy clatter she enthusiastically arranged the breakfast dishes.

"How wonderful it is to have an appetite in the morning!" said she; then: "This is the last time you're going to cook. You may chop the wood and build the fires, but I shall attend to the rest. I'm quite able."

"*Bien!*" The pilot smiled his agreement. "Everybody mus' work to be happy—even dose dog. W'at you t'ink? Dey loaf so long dey begin fight, jus' lak' people." He chuckled. "Pretty queeck we hitch her up de sled an' go fly to Dyea. You goin' henjoy dat, *ma sœur*. Mebbe we meet dose cheechako' comin' in an' dey holler: 'Hallo, Frenchy! How's t'ing' in Dawson?' an' we say: 'Pouf! We don' care 'bout Dawson; we goin' home.'".

"Home!" Rouletta paused momentarily in her task.

"Sure! Now—*voilà!* Breakfas' she's serve in de

baggage-car." With a flourish he poured the coffee, saying, "Let's see if you so hongry lak you pretend, or if I'm goin' keep you in bed some more."

Rouletta's appetite was all—yes, more—than she had declared it to be. The liberality with which she helped herself to oatmeal, her lavish use of the sugar - spoon, and her determined attack upon the can of "Carnation" satisfied any lingering doubts in Doret's mind. Her predatory interest in the appetizing contents of the frying-pan—she eyed it with the greedy hopefulness of a healthy urchin—also was eloquent of a complete recovery and brought a thrill of pride to her benefactor.

"Gosh! I mak' bad nurse for hospital," he grinned. "You eat him out of house an' lot." He finished his meal, then looked on until Rouletta leaned back with regretful satisfaction; thereupon he broke out:

"Wal, I got more s'prise for you."

"You—you can't surprise a toad, and—I feel just like one. Isn't food good?"

Now Rouletta had learned much about this big woodsman's peculiarities; among other things she had discovered that he took extravagant delight in his so-called "s'prises." They were many and varied, now a titbit to tempt her palate, or again a native doll which needed a complete outfit of moccasins, cap, and parka, and which he insisted he had met on the trail, very numb from the cold; again a pair of rabbit-fur sleeping-socks for herself.

That crude dresser, which he had completed without her suspecting him, was another. Always he was making or doing something to amuse or to occupy her attention, and, although his gifts were poor, sometimes absurdly simple, he had, nevertheless, the power of investing them with importance. Being vitally interested in all things, big or little, he stimulated others to share in that interest. Life was an enjoyable game, inanimate objects talked to him, every enterprise was tinted imaginary colors, and he delighted in pretense—welcome traits to Rouletta, whose childhood had been starved.

"What is my new s'prise?" she queried. But, without answering, 'Poleon rose and left the tent; he was back a moment later with a bundle in his hands. This bundle he unrolled, displaying a fine fur parka, the hood of which was fringed with a deep fox-tail facing, the skirt and sleeves of an elaborate checker-board pattern of multicolored skins. Gay squirrel-tail streamers depended from its shoulders as further ornamentation. Altogether it was a splendid specimen of Indian needlework and Rouletta gasped with delight.

"How *wonderful!*" she cried. "Is—it for me?"

The pilot nodded. "Sure t'ing. De purtiest one ever I see. But look!" He called her attention to a beaver cap, a pair of beaded moose-hide mittens, and a pair of small fur boots that went with the larger garments—altogether a complete outfit for winter travel. "I buy him from dose hinjun hunter. Put him on, queeck."

303

Rouletta slipped into the parka; she donned cap and mittens; and 'Poleon was in raptures.

"By golly! Dat's beautiful!" he declared. "Now you' fix for sure. No matter how col' she come, your li'l toes goin' be warm, you don' froze your nose—"

"You're good and true—and—" Rouletta faltered, then added, fervently, "I shall always thank God for knowing you."

Now above all things Doret dreaded his "sister's" serious moods or any expression of her gratitude; he waved her words aside with an airy gesture and began in a hearty tone:

"We don't stop dis place no longer. To-morrow we start for Dyea. W'at you t'ink of dat, eh? Pretty queeck you be home." When his hearer displayed no great animation at the prospect he exclaimed, in perplexity: "You fonny gal. Ain't you care?"

"I have no home," she gravely told him.

"But your people—dey goin' be glad for see you?"

"I have no people, either. You see, we lived a queer life, father and I. I was all he had, outside of poor Danny Royal, and he—was all I had. Home was where we happened to be. He sold everything to come North; he cut all ties and risked everything on a single throw. That was his way, our way—all or nothing. I've been thinking lately; I've asked myself what he would have wished me to do, and—I've made up my mind."

"So?" 'Poleon was puzzled.

"I'm not going 'outside.' I'm going to Dawson. 'Be a thoroughbred. Don't weaken.' That's what he always said. Sam Kirby followed the frontier and he made his money there. Well, I'm his girl, his blood is in me. I'm going through."

'Poleon's brow was furrowed in deep thought; it cleared slowly. "Dawson she's bad city, but you're brave li'l gal and—badness is here," he tapped his chest with a huge forefinger. "So long de heart she's pure, not'in' goin' touch you." He nodded in better agreement with Rouletta's decision. "Mebbe so you're right. For me, I'm glad, very glad, for I t'ink my bird is goin' spread her wing' an' fly away south lak all de res', but now— *bien!* I'm satisfy! We go to Dawson."

"Your work is here," the girl protested. "I can't take you away from it."

"Fonny t'ing 'bout work," 'Poleon said, with a grin. "Plenty tam I try to run away from him, but always he catch up wit' me."

"You're a poor man. I can't let you sacrifice too much."

"Poor?" The pilot opened his eyes in amazement. "*Mon Dieu!* I'm reech feller. Anybody is reech so long he's well an' happy. Mebbe I sell my claim."

"Your claim? Have you a claim? At Dawson?"

The man nodded indifferently. "I stake him las' winter. He's pretty claim to look at—plenty snow, nice tree for cabin, dry wood, everyt'ing but gold. Mebbe I sell him for beeg price."

"Why doesn't it have any gold?" Rouletta was genuinely curious.

"Why? Biccause I stake him," 'Poleon laughed heartily. "Dose claim I stake dey never has so much gold you can see wit' your eye. Not one, an' I stake t'ousan'. Me, I hear dose man talk 'bout million dollar; I'm drinkin' heavy so I t'ink I be millionaire, too. But bimeby I'm sober ag'in an' my money she's gone. I'm res'less feller; I don' stop long no place."

"What makes you think it's a poor claim?"

'Poleon shrugged. "All my claim is poor. Me, I'm onlucky. Mebbe so I don' care enough for bein' reech. W'at I'll do wit' pile of money, eh? Drink him up? Gamble? Dat's fun for while. Every spring I sell my fur an' have beeg tam; two weeks I'm drunk, but—dat's plenty. Any feller dat's drunk more 'n two weeks is bum. No!" He shook his head and exposed his white teeth in a flashing smile. "I'm cut off for poor man. I mak' beeg soccess of dat."

Rouletta studied the speaker silently for a moment. "I know." She nodded her complete understanding of his type. "Well, I'm not going to let you do that any more."

"I don' hurt nobody," he protested. "I sing plenty song an' fight li'l bit. A man mus' got some fun."

"Won't you promise—for my sake?"

'Poleon gave in after some hesitation; reluctantly he agreed. "*Eh bien!* Mos' anyt'ing I promise for you, *ma sœur*. But—she's goin' be

THE WINDS OF CHANCE

mighty poor trip for me. S'pose mebbe I forget dose promise?"

"I sha'n't let you. I've seen too much drinking —gambling. I'll hold you to your pledge."

Again the man smiled; there was a light of warm affection in his eyes. "By Gar! It's nice t'ing to have sister w'at care for you. When we goin' start for Dawson, eh?"

"To-morrow."

CHAPTER XIX

EVERY new and prosperous mining-camp has an Arabian Nights atmosphere, characteristic, peculiar, indescribable. Especially noticeable was this atmosphere in the early Arctic camps, made up as they were of men who knew little about mining, rather less about frontier ways, and next to nothing about the country in which they found themselves. These men had built fabulous hopes, they dwelt in illusion, they put faith in the thinnest of shadows. Now the most practical miner is not a conservative person; he is erratic, credulous, and extravagant; reasonless optimism is at once his blessing and his curse. Nevertheless, the "old-timers" of the Yukon were moderate indeed as compared with the adventurous holiday-seekers who swarmed in upon their tracks. Being none too well balanced themselves, it was only natural that the exuberance of these new arrivals should prove infectious and that a sort of general auto-intoxication should result. That is precisely what happened at Dawson. Men lost all caution, all common sense; they lived in a land of rosy imaginings; hard-bought lessons of experience were forgotten; reality disappeared; fancy took wing and left fact behind; expectations were capitalized and no exaggeration was too wild to challenge acceptance. It became a City of Frenzy.

It was all very fine for an ardent youth like Pierce Phillips; it set him ablaze, stirring a fever in his blood. Having won thus far, he made the natural mistake of believing that the race was his; so he wasted little time in the town, but very soon took to the hills, there to make his fortune and be done with it.

Here came his awakening. Away from the delirium of the camp, in contact with cold reality, he began to learn something of the serious, practical business of gold-mining. Before he had been long on the creeks he found that it was no child's play to wrest treasure from the frozen bosom of a hostile wilderness, and that, no matter how rich or how plentiful the treasure, Mother Earth guarded her secrets jealously. He began to realize that the obstacles he had so blithely overcome in getting to the Klondike were as nothing to those in the way of his further success. Of a sudden his triumphal progress slowed down and he came to a pause; he began to mark time.

There was work in plenty to be had, but, like most of the new-comers, he was not satisfied to take fixed wages. They seemed paltry indeed compared with the drunken figures that were on every lip. In the presence of the uncertain he could not content himself with a sure thing. Nevertheless, he was soon forced to the necessity of resorting to it, for through the fog of his mis-

apprehensions, beneath the obscurity of his ignorance, he began to discover the true outline of
things and to understand that his ideas were
impractical.

To begin with, every foot of ground in the proven
districts was taken, and even when he pushed
out far afield he found that the whole country was
plastered with locations: rivers, creeks and tribu-
taries, benches and hillsides, had been staked.
For many miles in every direction blazed trees and
pencil notices greeted him—he found them in
places where it seemed no foot but his had ever
trod. In Dawson the Gold Commissioner's office
was besieged by daily crowds of claimants; it
would have taken years of work on the part of a
hundred thousand men to even prospect the
ground already recorded on the books.

Back and forth Phillips came and went, he
made trips with pack and hand-sled, he slept out in
spruce forests, in prospectors' tents, in new cabins
the sweaty green logs of which were still dripping,
and when he had finished he was poorer by a good
many dollars and richer only in the possession of a
few recorder's receipts, the value of which he had
already begun to doubt.

Disappointed he was, but not discouraged. It
was all too new and exciting for that. Every visit
to Bonanza or El Dorado inspired him. It would
have inspired a wooden man. For miles those
valleys were smoky from the sinking fires, and
their clean white carpets were spotted with piles
of raw red dirt. By day they echoed to blows of

axes, the crash of falling trees, the plaint of windlasses, the cries of freighters; by night they became vast caldrons filled with flickering fires; tremendous vats, the vapors from which were illuminated by hidden furnaces. One would have thought that here gold was being made, not sought —that this was a region of volcanic hot springs where every fissure and vent-hole spouted steam. It was a strange, a marvelous sight; it stirred the imagination to know that underfoot, locked in the flinty depths of the frozen gravel, was wealth unmeasured and unearned, rich hoards of yellow gold that yesterday were ownerless.

A month of stampeding dulled the keen edge of Pierce's enthusiasm, so he took a breathing-spell in which to get his bearings.

The Yukon had closed and the human flotsam and jetsam it had borne thither was settling. Pierce could feel a metamorphic agency at work in the town; already new habits of life were crystallizing among its citizens; and beneath its whirlpool surface new forms were in the making. It alarmed him to realize that as yet his own affairs were in suspense, and he argued, with all the hot impatience of youth, that it was high time he came to rest. Opportunities were on every side of him, but he knew not where or how to lay hold of them to his best advantage. More than ever he felt himself to be the toy of circumstance, more than ever he feared the fallibility of his judgment and the consequences of a mistake. He was in a mood both dissatisfied and irresolute when he

311

encountered his two trail friends, Tom Linton
and Jerry Quirk. Pierce had seen them last at
Linderman, engaged in prosecuting a stampeders'
divorce; he was surprised to find them reunited.

"I never dreamed you'd get through," he told
them, when greetings had passed. "Did you come
in one boat or in two?"

Jerry grinned. "We sawed up that outlaw four
times. We'd have split her end to end finally,
only we run out of pitch to cork her up."

"That boat was about worn out with our bick-
erings," Tom declared. "She ain't over half the
length she was—all the rest is sawdust. If the
nail-holes in her was laid end to end they'd reach
to Forty Mile. We were the last outfit in, as it
was, and we'd of missed a landing if a feller hadn't
run out on the shore ice and roped us. First town
I ever entered on the end of a lariat. Hope I don't
leave it the same way."

"Guess who drug us in," Jerry urged.

"I've no idea," said Pierce.

"Big Lars Anderson."

"Big Lars of El Dorado?"

"He's the party. He was just drunk enough to
risk breakin' through. When he found who we was
—well, he gave us the town; he made us a present
of Dawson and all points north, together with
the lands, premises, privileges, and hereditaments
appurtenant thereto. I still got a kind of a hang-
over headache and have to take soda after my
meals."

"Lars was a sheepman when we knew him,"

Tom explained. "Jerry and I purloined him from some prominent cow-gentlemen who had him all decorated up ready to hang, and he hasn't forgotten it. He got everybody full the night we landed, and wound up by buying all the fresh eggs in camp. Forty dozen. We had 'em fried. He's a prince with his money."

"He owns more property tnan anybody," said Pierce.

"Right! And he gave us a 'lay.'"

Phillips' eyes opened. "A lay? On El Dorado?" he queried, in frank amazement.

"No. Hunker. He says it's a good creek. We're lookin' for a pardner."

"What kind of a partner?"

It was Linton who answered. "Well, some nice, easy-going, hard-working young feller. Jerry and I are pretty old to wind a windlass, but we can work underground where it's warm."

"'Easy-goin',' that's the word," Jerry nodded. "Tom and me get along with each other like an order of buckwheat cakes, but we're set in our ways and we don't want anybody to come between us."

"How would I do?" Pierce inquired, with a smile.

Tom answered promptly. "If your name was put to a vote I know one of us that wouldn't blackball you."

"Sure!" cried his partner. "The ballot-box would look like a settin' of pigeon eggs. Think it over and let us know. We're leavin' to-morrow."

A lease on Hunker Creek sounded good to

Phillips. Big Lars Anderson had been one of the
first arrivals from Circle City; already he was
rated a millionaire, for luck had smiled upon him;
his name was one to conjure with. Pierce was
about to accept the offer made when Jerry said:

"Who d'you s'pose got the lay below ours?
That feller McCaskey and his brother."

"McCaskey!"

"He's an old pal of Anderson's."

"Does Big Lars know he's a thief?"

Jerry shrugged. "Lars ain't the kind that lis-
tens to scandal and we ain't the kind that carries
it."

Pierce meditated briefly; then he said, slowly,
"If your lay turns out good so will McCaskey's."
His frown deepened. "Well, if there's a law of
compensation, if there's such a thing as retributive
justice—you have a bad piece of ground."

"But there ain't any such thing," Tom quickly
asserted. "Anyhow, it don't work in mining-
camps. If it did the saloons would be reading-
rooms and the gamblers would take in washing.
Look at the lucky men in this camp—bums, most
of 'em. George Carmack was a squaw-man, and
he made the strike."

Pierce felt no fear of Joe McCaskey, only dislike
and a desire to avoid further contact with him.
The prospect of a long winter in close proximity to
a proven scoundrel was repugnant. Balanced
against this was the magic of Big Lars' name. It
was a problem; again indecision rose to trouble
him.

"I'll think it over," he said, finally.

Farther down the street Phillips' attention was arrested by an announcement of the opening of the Rialto Saloon and Theater, Miller & Best, proprietors. Challenged by the name of his former employer and drawn by the sounds of merriment from within, Pierce entered. He had seen little of Laure since his arrival; he had all but banished her from his thoughts, in fact; but he determined now to look her up.

The Rialto was the newest and the most pretentious of Dawson's amusement palaces. It comprised a drinking-place with a spacious gambling-room adjoining. In the rear of the latter was the theater, a huge log annex especially designed as the home of Bacchus and Terpsichore.

The front room was crowded; through an archway leading to the gambling-hall came the noise of many voices, and over all the strains of an orchestra at the rear. Ben Miller, a famous sporting character, was busy weighing gold dust at the massive scales near the door when Pierce entered.

The theater, too, was packed. Here a second bar was doing a thriving business, and every chair on the floor, every box in the balcony overhanging three sides of it, was occupied. Waiters were scurrying up and down the wide stairway; the general hubbub was punctuated by the sound of exploding corks as the Klondike spendthrifts advertised their prosperity in a hilarious contest of prodigality.

All Dawson had turned out for the opening, and

Pierce recognized several of the El Dorado kings, among them Big Lars Anderson.

These new-born magnates were as thriftless as locusts, and in the midst of their bacchanalian revels Pierce felt very poor, very obscure. Here was the roisterous spirit of the Northland at full play; it irked the young man intensely to feel that he could afford no part in it. Laure was not long in discovering him. She sped to him with the swiftness of a swallow; breathlessly she inquired:

"Where have you been so long? Why didn't you let me know you were back?"

"I just got in. I've been everywhere." He smiled down at her, and she clutched the lapel of his coat, then drew him out of the crowd. "I dropped in to see how you were getting along."

"Well, what do you think of the place?"

"Why, it looks as if you'd all get rich in a night."

"And you? Have you done anything for yourself?"

Pierce shook his head; in a few words he recounted his goings and his comings, his efforts and his failures. Laure followed the recital with swift, birdlike nods of understanding; her dark eyes were warm with sympathy.

"You're going at it the wrong way," she asserted when he had finished. "You have brains; make them work. Look at Best, look at Miller, his new partner; they know better than to mine. Mining is a fool's game. Play a sure thing, Pierce. Stay here in town and live like a human being; here's where the money will be made."

"Do you think I *want* to go flying over hill and dale, like a tumbleweed? I haven't had warm feet in a week and I weep salt tears when I see a bed. But I'm no Crœsus; I've got to hustle. I think I've landed something finally." He told of Tom and Jerry's offer, but failed to impress his listener.

"If you go out to Hunker Creek I'll scarcely ever see you," said she. "That's the first objection. I've nearly died these last three weeks. But there are other objections. You couldn't get along with those old men. Why, they can't get along with each other! Then there's Joe McCaskey to think of. Why run into trouble?"

"I've thought of all that. But Big Lars is on the crest of his wave; he has the Midas touch; everything he lays his hands on turns to gold. He believes in Hunker—"

"I'll find out if he does," Laure said, quickly. "He's drinking. He'll tell me anything. Wait!" With a flashing smile she was off.

She returned with an air of triumph. "You'll learn to listen to me," she declared. "He says Hunker is low grade. That's why he lets lays on it instead of working it himself. Lars is a fox."

"He said that?"

"The best there is in it is wages. Those were his very words. Would you put up with Linton and Quirk and the two McCaskeys for wages? Of course not. I've something better fixed up for you." Without explaining, she led Pierce to the bar, where Morris Best was standing.

Best was genuinely glad to see his former employee; he warmly shook Pierce's hand.

"I've got 'em going, haven't I?" he chuckled.

Laure broke out, imperiously: "Loosen up, Morris, and let's all have a drink on the house. You can afford it."

"Sure!" With a happy grin the proprietor ordered a quart bottle of wine. "I can afford more than that for a friend. We put it over, didn't we, kid?" He linked arms with Pierce and leaned upon him. "Oy! Such trouble we had with these girls, eh? But we got 'em here, and now I got Dawson going. I'll be one of these Rockyfeller magnets, believe me."

Pierce had not tasted liquor since his last farewell to Laure. Three weeks of hard work in the open air had effected a chemical change in his make-up, a purification of his tissues, and as a result Best's liquor mounted quickly to his head and warmed his blood. When he had emptied his glass Laure saw that it was promptly refilled.

"So you've cut out the stampeding," Morris continued. "Good! You've got sense. Let the rough-necks do it. This here Front Street is the best pay-streak in the Klondike and it won't pinch out. Why? Because every miner empties his poke into it." The speaker nodded, and leaned more intimately against Phillips. "They bring in their Bonanza dust and their El Dorado nuggets and salt our sluices. That's the system. It's simpler as falling down a log. What?"

"Come to the good news," Laure urged.

"This little woman hates you, don't she?" Best winked. "Just like she hates her right eye. You got her going, kid. Well, you can start work to-morrow."

"Start work? Where?" Pierce was bewildered.

"Miller's looking for a gold-weigher. We'll put you out in the saloon proper."

"'Saloon proper'?" Pierce shook his head in good-natured refusal. "I dare say it's the fault of my bringing-up, but—I don't think there's any such thing. I'm an outdoor person. I'm one of the rough-necks who salts your sluice-boxes. I think I'd better stick to the hills. It's mighty nice of you, though, and I'm much obliged."

"Are you going to take that other offer?" Laure inquired. When Pierce hesitated she laid hold of his other arm. "I won't let you go," she cried. "I want you here—"

"Nonsense!" he protested. "I can't do anything for you. I have nothing—"

"Have I ever asked you for anything?" she blazed at him. "I can take care of myself, but—I want you. I sha'n't let you go."

"Better think it over," Best declared. "We need a good man."

"Yes!" Laure clung to Pierce's hand. "Don't be in a hurry. Anyhow, stay and dance with me while we talk about it. We've never had a dance together. Please!"

The proprietor of the theater was in a genial mood. "Stick around," he seconded. "Your credit is good and it won't worry me none if you

never take up your tabs. Laure has got the right
idea; play 'em safe and sure, and let the other feller
do the work. Now we'll have another bottle."

The three of them were still standing at the bar
when the curtain fell on the last vaudeville act
and the audience swarmed out into the gambling-
room of the main saloon. Hastily, noisily, the
chairs were removed from the dance floor, then
the orchestra began a spirited two-step and a
raucous-voiced caller broke into loud exhortations.
In a twinkling the room had refilled, this time
with whirling couples.

Laure raised her arms, she swayed forward into
Pierce's embrace, and they melted into the throng.
The girl could dance; she seemed to float in ca-
dence with the music; she became one with her
partner and answered his every impulse. Never
before had she seemed so utterly and so completely
to embody the spirit of pleasure; she was ardent,
alive, she pulsated with enjoyment; her breath
was warm, her dark, fragrant hair brushed Phillips' cheek; her olive face was slightly flushed;
and her eyes, uplifted to his, were glowing. They
voiced adoration, abandon, surrender.

The music ended with a crash; a shout, a storm
of applause followed; then the dancers swarmed
to the bar, bearing Pierce and his companion with
them. Laure was panting. She clung fiercely,
jealously, to Phillips' arm.

"Dance with me again. Again! I never knew
what it was—" She trembled with a vibrant
ecstasy.

Drinks were set before them. The girl spurned hers, but absent-mindedly pocketed the pasteboard check that went with it. While yet Pierce's throat was warm from the spirits there began the opening measures of a languorous waltz and the crowd swept into motion again. There was no refusing the invitation of that music.

Later in the evening Phillips found Tom and Jerry; his color was deeper than usual, his eyes were unnaturally bright.

"I'm obliged to you," he told them, "but I've taken a job as weigher with Miller & Best. Good luck, and—I hope you strike it rich."

When he had gone Tom shook his head. His face was clouded with regret and, too, with a vague expression of surprise.

"Too bad," he said. "I didn't think he was that kind."

"Sure!" Jerry agreed. "I thought he'd make good."

CHAPTER XX

MORRIS BEST'S new partner was a square
gambler, so called. People there were who
sneered at this description and considered it a
contradiction as absurd as a square circle or an
elliptical cube. An elementary knowledge of the
principles of geometry and of the retail liquor business proved the non-existence of such a thing as a
straight crook, so they maintained. But be that
as it may, Ben Miller certainly differed from the
usual run of sporting-men, and he professed peculiar ideas regarding the conduct of his trade.
Those ideas were almost puritanical in their
nature. Proprietorship of recreation centers similar to the Rialto had bred in Mr. Miller a profound
distrust of women as a sex and of his own ability
successfully to deal with them; in consequence,
he refused to tolerate their presence in his immediate vicinity. That they were valuable, nay,
necessary, ingredients in the success of an enterprise such as the present one he well knew—
Miller was, above all, a business man—but in
making his deal with Best he had insisted positively that none of the latter's song-birds were ever
to enter the front saloon. That room, Miller
maintained, was to be his own, and he proposed

to exercise dominion over it. As for the gambling-hall, that of necessity was neutral territory and he reluctantly consented to permit the girls to patronize it so long as they behaved themselves. For his part, he yielded all responsibility over the theater, and what went on therein, to Best. He agreed to stay out of it.

This division of power worked admirably, and Miller's prohibitions were scrupulously observed. He was angered, therefore, when, one morning, his rule was broken. At the moment he was engaged in weighing, checking up, and sacking his previous night's receipts, he looked up with a frown when a woman's—a girl's—voice interrupted him.

"Are you Ben Miller?" the trespasser inquired.

Miller nodded shortly. He could be colder than a frog when he chose.

"I'm looking for work," explained the visitor.

"You got the wrong door," he told her. "You want the dance-hall. We don't allow women in here."

"So I understand."

Miller's frown deepened. "Well, then, beat it! Saloons are masculine gender and—"

"I'm not a dance-hall girl, I'm a dealer," the other broke in.

"You're a—*what?*" Ben's jaw dropped; he stared curiously at the speaker. She was pretty, very pretty, in a still, dignified way; she had a fine, intelligent face and she possessed a poise, a carriage, that challenged attention.

"A dealer? What the deuce can you deal?" he managed to ask.

"Anything—the bank, the wheel, the tub, the cage—"

Disapproval returned to the man's countenance; there was an admonitory sternness to his voice when he said: "It ain't very nice to see a kid like you in a place like this. I don't know where you learned that wise talk, but—cut it out. Go home and behave yourself, sister. If you're broke, I'll stake you; so'll anybody, for that matter."

His visitor stirred impatiently. "Let's stick to business. I don't want a loan. I'm a dealer and I want work."

Morris Best bustled out of the adjoining room at the moment, and, noting a feminine figure in this forbidden territory, he exclaimed:

"Hey, miss! Theater's in the rear."

Miller summoned him with a backward jerk of his head. "Morris, this kid's looking for a job— as dealer," said he.

"*Dealer?*" Best halted abruptly. "That's funny."

"What is funny about it?" demanded the girl. "My father was a gambler. I'm Rouletta Kirby."

"Are you Sam Kirby's girl?" Miller inquired. When Rouletta nodded he removed his hat, then he extended his hand. "Shake," said he. "Now I've got you. You've had a hard time, haven't you? We heard about Sam and we thought you was dead. Step in here and set down." He motioned to the tiny little office which was curtained off from general view.

Rouletta declined with a smile. "I really want work as a dealer. That's the only thing I can do well. I came here first because you have a good reputation."

"Kirby's kid don't have to deal nothing. She's good for any kind of a stake on his name."

"Dad would be glad to hear that. He was a —great man. He ran straight." Rouletta's eyes had become misty at Miller's indirect tribute to her father; nevertheless, she summoned a smile and went on: "He never borrowed, and neither will I. If you can't put me to work I'll try somewhere else."

"How did you get down from White Horse?" Miller inquired, curiously.

"'Polcou Doret brought me."

"I know Doret. He's aces."

"Can you really deal?" Best broke in.

"Come. I'll prove that I can." Rouletta started for the gambling-room and the two men followed. Best spoke to his partner in a low voice:

"Say, Ben, if she can make a half-way bluff at it she'll be a big card. Think of the play she'll get."

But Miller was dubious. "She's nothing but a kid," he protested. "A dealer has got to have experience, and, besides, she ain't the kind that belongs in a dump. Somebody'd get fresh and— I'd have to bust him."

There was little activity around the tables at this hour of the day; the occupants of the gambling-room were, for the most part, house employees who were waiting for business to begin. The majority of these employees were gathered about the faro layout, where the cards were being run in a perfunctory manner to an accompaniment of gossip and reminiscence. The sight of Ben Miller in company with a girl evoked some wonder. This wonder increased to amazement when Miller ordered the dealer out of his seat; it became open-mouthed when the girl took his place, then broke a new deck of cards, deftly shuffled them, and slipped them into the box. At this procedure the languid lookout, who had been comfortably resting upon his spine, uncurled his legs, hoisted himself into an attitude of attention, and leaned forward with a startled expression upon his face.

The gamblers crowded closer, exchanging expectant glances; Ben Miller and Morris Best helped themselves to chips and began to play. These were queer doings; the case-hardened onlookers prepared to enjoy a mildly entertaining treat. Soon grins began to appear; the men murmured, they nudged one another, they slapped one another on the back, for what they saw astonished and delighted them. The girl dealt swiftly, surely; she handled the paraphernalia of the faro-table with the careless familiarity of long practice; but stranger still, she maintained a poise, a certain reserve and feminine dignity which were totally incongruous.

When, during a pause, she absent-mindedly shuffled a stack of chips, the Mocha Kid permitted his feelings to get the better of him.

"Hang me for a horse-thief!" he snickered. "Will you look at that?" Now the Mocha Kid was a ribald character, profanity was a part of him, and blasphemy embellished his casual speech. The mildness of his exclamation showed that he was deeply moved. He continued in the same admiring undertone: "I seen a dame once that could deal a bank, but she couldn't pay and take. This gal can size up a stack with her eyes shut!"

Nothing could have more deeply intrigued the attention of these men than the sight of a modest, quiet, well-behaved young woman exhibiting all the technic of a finished faro-dealer. It was contrary to their experience, to their ideas of fitness. Mastery of the gaming-table requires years of practice to acquire, and not one of these professionals but was as proud of his own dexterity as a fine pianist; to behold a mere girl possessed of all the knacks and tricks and mannerisms of the craft excited their keenest risibilities. In order the more thoroughly to test her skill several of them bought stacks of chips and began to play in earnest; they played their bets open, they coppered, they split, they strung them, and at the finish they called the turn. Rouletta paid and took; she measured stacks of counters with unerring facility, she overlooked no bets. She ran out the cards, upset the box, and began to reshuffle the cards.

"Well, I'm a son of a gun!" declared the look-out. He doubled up in breathless merriment, he rocked back and forth in his chair, he stamped his feet. A shout of laughter issued from the others.

Ben Miller closed the cases with a crash. "You'll do," he announced. "If there's anything you don't know I can't teach it to you." Then to the bystanders he said: "This is Sam Kirby's girl. She wants work, and if I thought you coyotes knew how to treat a lady I'd put her on."

"Say!" The Mocha Kid scowled darkly at his employer. "What kinda guys do you take us for? What makes you think we don't know—"

He was interrupted by an angry outburst, by a chorus of resentful protests, the indignant tone of which seemed to satisfy Miller. The latter shrugged his shoulders and rose. Rouletta stirred as if to follow suit, but eager hands stayed her, eager voices urged her to remain.

"Run 'em again, miss," begged Tommy Ryan, the roulette-dealer. Mr. Ryan was a pale-faced person whose addiction to harmful drugs was notorious; his extreme pallor and his nervous lack of repose had gained for him the title of "Snowbird." Tommy's hollow eyes were glowing, his colorless lips were parted in an engaging smile. "Please run 'em once more. I 'ain't had so much fun since my wife eloped with a drummer in El Paso."

Rouletta agreed readily enough, and her admiring audience crowded closer. Their interest was magnetic, their absorption and their amusement

328

were communicated to some new-comers who had dropped in. Before the girl had dealt half the cards these bona-fide customers had found seats around the table and were likewise playing. They, too, enjoyed the novel experience, and the vehemence with which they insisted that Rouletta retain her office proved beyond question the success of Miller's experiment.

It was not yet midday, nevertheless the news spread quickly that a girl was dealing bank at the Rialto, and soon other curious visitors arrived. Among them was Big Lars Anderson. Lars did not often gamble, but when he did he made a considerable business of it and the sporting fraternity took him seriously. Anything in the nature of an innovation tickled the big magnate immensely, and to evidence his interest in this one he purchased a stack of chips. Ere long he had lost several hundred dollars. He sent for Miller, finally, and made a good-natured complaint that the game was too slow for him.

"Shall I raise the limit?" the proprietor asked of Rouletta. The girl shrugged indifferently, whereupon the Mocha Kid and the Snowbird embraced each other and exchanged admiring profanities in smothered tones.

Big Lars stubbornly backed his luck, but the bank continued to win, and meanwhile new arrivals dropped in. Two, three hours the play went on, by which time all Dawson knew that a big game was running and that a girl was in the dealer's chair. Few of the visitors got close enough to verify the intelligence without receiving a *sotto voce* warning that rough talk was taboo—Miller's ungodly clan saw to that—and on the whole the warning was respected. Only once was it disregarded; then a heavy loser breathed a thoughtless oath. Disapproval was marked, punishment was condign; the lookout leisurely descended from his eyrie and floored the offender with a blow from his fist.

When the resulting disturbance had quieted down the defender of decorum announced with inflexible firmness, but with a total lack of heat:

"Gents, this is a sort of gospel game, and it's got a certain tone which we're going to maintain. The limit is off, except on cussing, but it's mighty low on that. Them of you that are indisposed to swallow your cud of regrets will have it knocked out of you."

"Good!" shouted Big Lars. He pounded the table with the flat of his huge palm. "By Jingo! I'll make that unanimous. If anybody has to cuss let him take ten paces to the rear and cuss the stove."

It was well along in the afternoon when Rouletta Kirby pushed back her chair and rose. She was very white; she passed an uncertain hand over her face, then groped blindly at the table for support. At these signs of distress a chorus of alarm arose.

"It's nothing," she smiled. "I'm just—hungry. I've been pretty ill and I'm not very strong yet."

Lars Anderson was dumfounded, appalled. "Hungry? My God!" To his companions he shouted: "D'you hear that, boys? She's starved out!"

The boys had heard; already they had begun to scramble. Some ran for the lunch-counter in the adjoining room, others dashed out to the nearest restaurants. The Snowbird so far forgot his responsibilities as to abandon the roulette-wheel and leave its bank-roll unguarded while he scurried to the bar and demanded a drink, a tray of assorted drinks, fit for a fainting lady. He came flying back, yelling, "Gangway!" and, scattering the crowd ahead of him, he offered brandy, whisky, crème de menthe, hootch, absinthe and bitters to Rouletta, all of which she declined. He was still arguing the medicinal value of these beverages when the swinging doors from the street burst open and in rushed the Mocha Kid, a pie in each hand. Other eatables and drinkables appeared as by magic, the faro-table was soon spread with the fruits of a half-dozen hasty and hysterical forays.

Rouletta stared at the apprehensive faces about her, and what she read therein caused her lips to quiver and her voice to break when she tried to express her thanks.

"Gosh! Don't cry!" begged the Mocha Kid. With a counterfeit assumption of juvenile hilarity he exclaimed: "Oh, look at the pretty pies! They got little Christmas-trees on their lids, 'ain't they? Um-yum! Rich and juicy! I stuck up

the baker and stole his whole stock, but I slipped
and spilled 'em F. O. B.—flat on the boardwalk."

Rouletta laughed. "Let's end the game and
all have lunch," she suggested, and her invitation
was accepted.

Big Lars spoke up with his mouth full of pastry:
"We don't allow anybody to go hungry in this
camp," said he. "We're all your friends, miss,
and if there's anything you want and can't afford,
charge it to me."

Rouletta stopped to speak with Miller, on her
way out. "Do I get the position?" she inquired.

"Say! You know you get it!" he told her.
"You go on at eight and come off at midnight."

"What is the pay?"

"I pay my dealers an ounce a shift, but—you
can write your own ticket. How is two ounces?"

"I'll take regular wages," Rouletta smiled.

Miller nodded his approval of this attitude;
then his face clouded. "I've been wondering how
you're going to protect your bank-roll. Things
won't always be like they were to-day. I s'pose
I'll have to put a man on—"

"I'll protect it," the girl asserted. "Agnes and
I will do that."

The proprietor was interested. "Agnes? Holy
Moses! Is there two of you? Have you got a
sister? Who's Agnes?" .

"She's an old friend of my father's."

Miller shrugged. "Bring her along if you want
to," he said, doubtfully, "but those old dames
are trouble-makers."

"Yes, Agnes is all of that, but"—Rouletta's eyes were dancing—"she minds her own business and she'll guard the bank-roll."

Lucky Broad and Kid Bridges had found employment at the Rialto soon after it opened. As they passed the gold-scales on their way to work Pierce Phillips halted them.

"I've some good news for you, Lucky," he announced. "You've lost your job."

"Who, me?" Broad was incredulous.

"Miller has hired a new faro-dealer, and you don't go on until midnight." Briefly Pierce retold the story that had come to his ears when he reported for duty that evening.

Broad and Bridges listened without comment, but they exchanged glances. They put their heads together and began a low-pitched conversation. They were still murmuring when Rouletta appeared, in company with 'Poleon Doret.

'Poleon's face lighted at sight of the two gamblers. He strode forward, crying: "Hallo! I'm glad for see you some more." To the girl he said: "You 'member dese feller'. Dey he'p save you in de rapids."

Rouletta impulsively extended her hands. "Of course! Could I forget?" She saw Pierce Phillips behind the scales and nodded to him. "Why, we're all here, aren't we? I'm so glad. Everywhere I go I meet friends."

Lucky and the Kid inquired respectfully regarding her health, her journey down the river, her reasons for being here; then when they had drawn her aside the former interrupted her flow of explanations to say:

"Listen, Letty. We got just one real question to ask and we'd like a straight answer. Have you got any kick against this Frenchman?"

"Any kick of any kind?" queried Bridges. "We're your friends; you can tip us off."

The sudden change in the tone of their voices caused the girl to start and to stare at them. She saw that both men were in sober earnest; the reason behind their solicitude she apprehended.

She laid a hand upon the arm of each. Her eyes were very bright when she began: "'Poleon told me how you came to his tent that morning after—you know, and he told me what you said. Well, it wasn't necessary. He's the dearest thing that ever lived!"

"Why'd he put you to work in a place like this?" Bridges roughly demanded.

"He didn't. He begged me not to try it. He offered me all he has—his last dollar. He—"

Swiftly, earnestly, Rouletta told how the big woodsman had cared for her; how tenderly, faithfully, he had nursed her back to health and strength; how he had cast all his plans to the winds in order to bring her down the river. "He's the best, the kindest, the most generous man I ever knew," she concluded. "His heart is clean and—his soul is full of music."

"'Stá bueno!" cried Lucky Broad, in genuine

334

relief. "We had a hunch he was right, but—you can't always trust those Asiatic races."

Ben Miller appeared and warmly greeted his new employee. "Rested up, eh? Well, it's going to be a big night. Where's Agnes—the other one? Has she got cold feet?"

"No, just a cold nose. Here she is." From a small bag on her arm Rouletta drew Sam Kirby's six-shooter. "Agnes was my father's friend. Nobody ever ran out on her."

Miller blinked, he uttered a feeble exclamation, then he burst into a mighty laugh. He was still shaking, his face was purple, there were tears of mirth in his eyes, when he followed Broad, Bridges, and Rouletta into the gambling-room.

There were several players at the faro-table when the girl took her place. Removing her gloves, she stowed them away in her bag. From this bag she extracted the heavy Colt's revolver, then opened the drawer before her and laid it inside. She breathed upon her fingers, rubbing the circulation back into them, and began to shuffle the cards. Slipping them into the box, the girl settled herself in her chair and looked up into a circle of grinning faces. Before her level gaze eyes that had been focused queerly upon her fell. The case-keeper's lips were twitching, but he bit down upon them. Gravely he said:.

"Well, boys, let's go!"

CHAPTER XXI

IN taking charge of a sick girl, a helpless, hopeless stranger, 'Poleon Doret had assumed a responsibility far greater than he had anticipated,
and that responsibility had grown heavier every
day. Having, at last, successfully discharged it,
he breathed freely, his first relaxation in a long
time; he rejoiced in the consciousness of a difficult
duty well performed. So far as he could see there
was nothing at all extraordinary, nothing in the
least improper, about Rouletta's engagement at
the Rialto. Any suggestion of impropriety, in
fact, would have greatly surprised him, for saloons
and gambling-halls filled a recognized place in
the every-day social life of the Northland. Customs were free, standards were liberal in the early
days; no one, 'Poleon least of all, would have
dreamed that they were destined to change in a
night. Had he been told that soon the country
would be dry, and gambling-games and dance-halls
be prohibited by law, he would have considered
the idea too utterly fantastic for belief; the mere
contemplation of such a dreary prospect would
have proved extremely dispiriting. He—and the
other pioneers of his kind—would have been

tempted immediately to pack up and move on to some freer locality where a man could retain his personal liberty and pursue his happiness in a manner as noisy, as intemperate, and as undignified as suited his individual taste.

In justice to the saloons, be it said, they were more than mere drinking-places; they were the pivots about which revolved the business life of the North country. They were meeting-places, social centers, marts of trade; looked upon as evidences of enterprise and general prosperity, they were considered desirable assets to any community. Everybody patronized them; the men who ran them were, on the whole, as reputable as the men engaged in other pursuits. No particular stigma attached either to the places themselves or to the people connected with them.

These gold-camps had a very simple code. Work of any sort was praiseworthy and honorable, idleness or unproductivity was reprehensible. Mining, storekeeping, liquor-selling, gambling, steamboating, all were occupations which men followed as necessity or convenience prompted. A citizen gained repute by the manner in which he deported himself, not by reason of the nature of the commodity in which he dealt. Such, at least, was the attitude of the "old-timers."

Rouletta's instant success, the fact that she had fallen among friends, delighted a woodsman like 'Poleon, and, now that he was his own master again, he straightway surrendered himself to the selfish enjoyment of his surroundings. His nature and his training prescribed the limits of those pleasures; they were quite as simple as his everyday habits of life; he danced, he gambled, and he drank.

To-night he did all three, in the reverse order. To him Dawson was a dream city; its lights were dazzling, its music heavenly, its games of chance enticing, and its liquor was the finest, the smoothest, the most inspiriting his tongue had ever tested. Old friends were everywhere, and new ones, too, for that matter. Among them were alluring women who smiled and sparkled. Each place 'Poleon entered was the home of carnival.

By midnight he was gloriously drunk. Ere daylight came he had sung himself hoarse, he had danced two holes in his moccasins, and had conducted three fist-fights to a satisfactory if not a successful conclusion. It had been a celebration that was to live in his memory. He strode blindly off to bed, shouting his complete satisfaction with himself and with the world, retired without undressing, and then sang himself to sleep, regardless of the protests of the other lodgers.

"Say! That Frenchman is a riot," Kid Bridges declared while he and Lucky Broad were at breakfast. "He's old General Rough-houser, and he set an altogether new mark in disorderly conduct last night. Letty 'most cried about it."

"Yeah? Those yokels are all alike—one drink and they declare a dividend." Lucky was only mildly concerned. "I s'pose the vultures picked him clean."

"Nothin' like it," Bridges shook his head. "He gnawed 'em naked, then done a war-dance with their feathers in his hat. He left 'em bruised an' bleedin'."

For a time the two friends ate in silence, then Broad mused, aloud: "Letty 'most cried, eh? Say, I wonder what she really thinks of him?"

"I don't know. Miller told me she was all broke up, and I was goin' to take her home and see if I could fathom her true feelin's, but—Phillips beat me to it."

"Phillips! He'll have to throw out the life-line if Laure gets onto that. She'll take to Letty just like a lone timber-wolf."

"Looks like she'd been kiddin' us, don't it? She calls him her 'brother' and he says she's his masseur—you heard him, didn't you?" There was another pause. "What's a masseur, anyhow?"

"A masseur," said Mr. Broad, "is one of those women in a barber-shop that fixes your finger-nails. Yes, I heard him, and I'm here to say that I didn't like the sound of it. I don't yet. He may mean all right, but—them foreigners have got queer ideas about their women. Letty's a swell kid and she's got a swell job. What's more, she's got a wise gang riding herd on her. It's just like she was in a church—no danger, no annoyance, nothing. If Doret figures to start a barber-shop with her for his masseur, why, we'll have to lay him low with one of his own razors."

Mr. Bridges nodded his complete approval of this suggestion. "Right-o! I'll bust a mirror with him myself. Them barber-shops is no place for good girls."

Broad and Bridges pondered the matter during the day, and that evening they confided their apprehensions to their fellow-workers. The other Rialto employees agreed that things did not look right, and after a consultation it was decided to keep a watch upon the girl. This was done. Prompted by their pride in her, and a genuinely unselfish interest in her future, the boys made guarded attempts to discover the true state of her feelings for the French Canadian, but they learned little. Every indirect inquiry was met with a tribute to 'Poleon's character so frank, so extravagant, as to completely baffle them. Some of the investigators declared that Rouletta was madly in love with him; others were equally positive that this extreme frankness in itself proved that she was not. All agreed, however, that 'Poleon was not in love with her—he was altogether too enthusiastic over her growing popularity for a lover. Had the gamblers been thoroughly assured of her desires in the matter, doubtless they would have made some desperate effort to marry 'Poleon to her, regardless of his wishes—they were men who believed in direct action—but under the circumstances they could only watch and wait until the uncertainty was cleared up.

Meanwhile, as 'Poleon continued his celebration, Rouletta grew more and more miserable; at last he sobered up sufficiently to realize he was hurting her. He was frankly puzzled at this; he met her reproaches with careless good-nature, brushing aside the remonstrances of Lucky Broad and his fellows by declaring that he was having the time of his life, and arguing that he injured nobody. In the end the girl prevailed upon him to stop drinking, and then bound him to further sobriety by means of a sacred pledge. When, perhaps a week later, he disappeared into the hills Rouletta and her corps of self-appointed guardians breathed easier.

But the boys did not relax their watchfulness; Rouletta was their charge and they took good care of her. None of the Rialto's patrons, for instance, was permitted to follow up his first acquaintance with "the lady dealer." Some member of the clan was always on hand to frown down such an attempt. Broad or Bridges usually brought her to work and took her home, the Snowbird and the Mocha Kid made it a practice to take her to supper, and when she received invitations from other sources one or the other of them firmly declined, in her name, and treated the would-be host with such malevolent suspicion that the invitation was never repeated. Far from taking offense at this espionage, Rouletta rather enjoyed it; she grew to like these ruffians, and that liking became mutual. Soon most of them took her into their confidence with a completeness that threatened to embarrass her, as, for instance, when they discussed in her hearing incidents in their colorful lives that the Mounted Police would

341

have given much to know. The Mocha Kid, in particular, was addicted to reminiscence of an incriminating sort, and he totally ignored Rouletta's protests at sharing the secrets of his guilty past. As for the Snowbird, he was fond of telling her fairy-stories. They were queer fairy-stories, all beginning in the same way:

"Once upon a time there was a beautiful Princess and her name was Rouletta."

All the familiar characters figured in these narratives, the Wicked Witch, the Cruel King, the Handsome Prince; there were other characters, too, such as the Wise Guy, the Farmer's Son, the Boob Detective, the Tough Mary Ann and the Stony-hearted Jailer.

The Snowbird possessed a fertile fancy but it ran in crooked channels; although he launched his stories according to Grimm, he sailed them through seas of crime, of violence, and of bloodshed too realistic to be the product of pure imagination. The adventures of the beautiful Princess Rouletta were blood-curdling in the extreme, and the doings of her criminal associates were unmistakably autobiographic. Naturally Rouletta never felt free to repeat these stories, but it was not long before she began to look forward with avid interest to her nightly entertainment.

Inasmuch as Pierce Phillips went off shift at the same time as did Rouletta, they met frequently, and more than once he acted as her escort. He offered such a marked contrast to the other employees of the Rialto, his treatment of her was at such total variance with theirs, that he interested her in an altogether different way. His was an engaging personality, but just why she grew so fond of him she could not tell; he was neither especially witty and accomplished nor did he lay himself out to be unusually agreeable. He was quiet and reserved; nevertheless, he had the knack of making friends quickly. Rouletta had known men like Broad and Bridges and the Mocha Kid all her life, but Pierce was of a type quite new and diverting. She speculated considerably regarding him.

Their acquaintance, while interesting, had not progressed much beyond that point when Rouletta experienced a disagreeable shock. She had strolled into the theater one evening and was watching the performance when Laure accosted her. As Rouletta had not come into close contact with any of the dance-hall crowd, she was surprised at the tone this girl assumed.

"Hello! Looking for new conquests?" Laure began.

Miss Kirby shook her head in vague denial, but the speaker eyed her with open hostility and there was an unmistakable sneer behind her next words:

"What's the matter? Have you trimmed all the leading citizens?"

"I've finished my work, if that's what you mean."

"Now you're going to try your hand at box-rustling, eh?"

Rouletta's expression altered; she regarded her inquisitor more intently. "You know I'm not," said she. "What are you driving at?"

"Well, why don't you? Are you too good?"

"Yes." The visitor spoke coldly. She turned away, but Laure stepped close and cried, in a low, angry voice:

"Oh no, you're not! You've fooled the men, but you can't fool us girls. I've got your number. I know your game."

"My game? Then why don't you take a shift in the gambling-room? Why work in here?"

"You understand me," the other persisted. "Too good for the dance-hall, eh? Too good to associate with us girls; too good to live like us! *You* stop at the Courteau House, the *respectable* hotel! Bah! Miller fell for you, but—you'd better let well enough alone."

"That's precisely what I do. If there were a better hotel than the Courteau House I'd stop there. But there isn't. Now, then, suppose you tell me what really ails you."

Laure's dusky eyes were blazing, her voice was hoarse when she answered:

"All right. I'll tell you. I want you to mind your own business. Yes, and I'm going to see that you do. You can't go home alone, can you? Afraid of the dark, I suppose, or afraid some man will speak to you. My goodness! The airs you put on—*you!* Sam Kirby's girl, the daughter of a gambler, a—"

"Leave my father out of this!" There was

344

something of Sam Kirby's force in this sharp command, something of his cold, forbidding anger in his daughter's face. "He's my religion, so you'd better lay off of him. Speak out. Where did I tread on your toes?"

"Well, you tread on them every time you stop at the gold-scales, if you want to know. I have a religion, too, and it's locked up in the cashier's cage."

There was a pause; the girls appraised each other with mutual dislike.

"You mean Mr. Phillips?"

"I do. See that you call him 'Mister,' and learn to walk home alone."

"Don't order me. I can't take orders."

Laure was beside herself at this defiance. She grew blind with rage, so much so that she did not notice Phillips himself; he had approached within hearing distance. "You've got the boss; he's crazy about you, but Pierce is mine—"

"What's that?" It was Phillips who spoke. "What are you saying about me?" Both girls started. Laure turned upon him furiously.

"I'm serving notice on this faro-dealer, that's all. But it goes for you, too—"

Phillips' eyes opened, his face whitened with an emotion neither girl had before seen. To Rouletta he said, quietly:

"The other boys are busy, so I came to take you home."

Laure cried, wildly, hysterically: "Don't do it! I warn you!"

"Are you ready to go?"

"All ready," Rouletta agreed. Together they left the theater.

Nothing was said as the two trod the snow-banked streets; not until they halted at the door of the Courteau House did Rouletta speak; then she said:

"I wouldn't have let you do this, only—I have a temper."

"So have I," Pierce said, shortly. "It's humiliating to own up."

"I was wrong. I have no right to hurt that girl's feelings."

"Right?" He laughed angrily. "She had no right to make a scene."

"Why not? She's fighting for her own, isn't she? She's honest about it, at least." Noting Pierce's expression of surprise, Rouletta went on: "You expect me to be shocked, but I'm not, for I've known the truth in a general way. You think I'm going to preach. Well, I'm not going to do that, either. I've lived a queer life; I've seen women like Laure—in fact, I was raised among them—and nothing they do surprises me very much. But I've learned a good many lessons around saloons and gambling-places. One is this: never cheat. Father taught me that. He gave everybody a square deal, including himself. It's a good thing to think about—a square deal all around, even to yourself."

"That sounds like an allopathic sermon of some sort," said Pierce, "but I can't see just how

346

it applies to me. However, I'll think it over.
You're a brick, Miss Kirby, and I'm sorry if you
had an unpleasant moment." He took Rouletta's
hand and held it while he stared at her with a
frank, contemplative gaze. "You're an unusual
person, and you're about the nicest girl I've met.
I want you to like me."

As he walked back down-town Pierce pondered
Rouletta's words, "a square deal all around, even
to yourself." They were a trifle puzzling. Whom
had he cheated? Surely not Laure. From the
very first he had protested his lack of serious interest in her, and their subsequent relations were
entirely the result of her unceasing efforts to ap-
propriate him to herself. He had resisted, she
had persisted. Nor could he see that he had
cheated—in other words, injured—himself. This
was a liberal country; its code was free and it took
little account of a man's private conduct. Nobody seriously blamed him for his affair with
Laure; he had lost no standing by reason of it.
It was only a part of the big adventure, a passing
phase of his development, an experience such as
came to every man. Since it had left no mark
upon him, and had not seriously affected Laure,
the score was even. He dismissed Rouletta's
words as of little consequence. In order, however, to prevent any further unpleasant scenes he
determined to put Laure in her place, once for all.

Rouletta went to her room, vaguely disturbed
at her own emotions. She could still feel the
touch of Phillips' hand, she could still feel his

gaze fixed earnestly, meditatively, upon hers, and she was amazed to discover the importance he had assumed in her thoughts. Importance, that was the word. He was a very real, a very interesting, person, and there was some inexplicable attraction about him that offset his faults and his failings, however grave. For one thing, he was not an automaton, like the other men; he was a living, breathing problem, and he absorbed Rouletta's attention.

She was sitting on the edge of her bed, staring at the wall, when the Countess Courteau knocked at her door and entered. The women had become good friends; frequently the elder one stopped to gossip. The Countess flung herself into a chair, rolled and lit a cigarette, then said:

"Well, I see you and Agnes saved the bank-roll again."

Rouletta nodded. "Agnes is an awful bluff. I never load her. But of course nobody knows that."

"You're a queer youngster. I've never known a girl quite like you. Everybody is talking about you."

"Indeed? Not the nice people?"

"Nice people?" The Countess lifted her brows. "You mean those at the Barracks and up on the hill? Yes, they're talking about you, too."

"I can imagine what they say." Rouletta drew her brows together in a frown. "No doubt they think I'm just like the dance-hall girls. I've seen a few of them—at a distance. They avoid me as if I had measles."

"Naturally. Do you care?"

"Certainly I care. I'd like to be one of them, not a—a specimen. Wouldn't you?"

"Um-m, perhaps. I dare say I could be one of them if it weren't for Courteau. People forget things quickly in a new country."

"Why did you take him back? I'm sure you don't care for him."

"Not in the least. He's the sort of man you can't love or hate; he's a nine-spot. Just the same, he protects me and—I can't help being sorry for him."

Rouletta smiled. "Fancy you needing protection and him giving—"

"You don't understand. He protects me from myself. I mean it. I'm as unruly as the average woman and I make a fool of myself on the slightest provocation. Henri is a loafer, a good-for-nothing, to be sure, but, nevertheless, I have resumed his support. It was easier than refusing it. I help broken miners. I feed hungry dogs. Why shouldn't I clothe and feed a helpless husband? It's a perfectly feminine, illogical thing to do."

"Other people don't share your opinion of him. He can be very agreeable. very charming, when he tries."

"Of course. That's his stock in trade; that's his excuse for being. Women are crazy about him, as you probably know, but—give me a man the men like." There was a pause. "So you don't enjoy the thing you're doing?"

"I hate it! I hate the whole atmosphere—the whole underworld. It's—unhealthy, stifling."

"What has happened?"

Slowly, hesitatingly, Rouletta told of her encounter with Laure. The Countess listened silently.

"It was an unpleasant shock," the girl concluded, "for it brought me back to my surroundings. It lifted the curtain and showed me what's really going on. It's a pity. Pierce Phillips is entangled with that creature, for he's a nice chap and he's got it in him to do big things. But it wasn't much use my trying to tell him that he was cheating himself. I don't think he understood. I feel almost—well, motherly toward him."

Hilda nodded gravely. "Of course you do. He has it."

"Has it? What?"

"The call—the appeal—the same thing that lets Henri get by."

"Oh, he's nothing like the Count!" Rouletta protested, quickly.

The elder woman did not argue the point. "Pierce has more character than Henri, but a man can lose even that in a gambling-house. I was very fond of him—fonder than I knew. Yes, it's a fact. I'm jealous of Laure, jealous of you—"

"*Jealous?* Of *me?* You're joking!"

"Of course. Don't take me seriously. Nevertheless, I mean it." The Countess smiled queerly and rose to her feet. "It's improper for a married woman to joke about such things, even a woman married to a no-good count, isn't it? And it's foolish, too. Well, I'm going to do something even more foolish—I'm going to give you some advice. Cut out that young man. He hasn't found himself yet; he's running wild. He's light in ballast and he's rudderless. If he straightens out he'll make some woman very happy; otherwise —he'll create a good deal of havoc. Believe me, I know what I'm talking about, for I collided with Henri and—look at the result!"

CHAPTER XXII

PIERCE PHILLIPS possessed the average
young American's capacities for good or evil.
Had he fallen among healthy surroundings upon
his arrival at Dawson, in all probability he would
have experienced a healthy growth. But, blown
by the winds of chance, he took root where he
dropped—in the low grounds. Since he possessed
the youthful power of quick and vigorous adapta-
tion, he assumed a color to match his environment. Of necessity this alteration was gradual;
nevertheless, it was real; without knowing it he
suffered a steady deterioration of moral fiber and
a progressive change in ideals.

His new life was easy; hours at the Rialto were
short and the pay was high. Inasmuch as the
place was a playground where cares were forgotten,
there was a wholly artificial atmosphere of gaiety
and improvidence about it. When patrons won
at the gambling-games, they promptly squandered
their winnings at the bar and in the theater;
when they lost, they cheerfully ignored their ill-
fortune. Even the gamblers themselves shared
this recklessness, this prodigality; they made
much money; nevertheless, they were usually

broke. Most of them drank quite as freely as did the customers.

This was not a temperance country. Although alcohol was not considered a food, it was none the less regarded as a prime essential of comfort and well-being. It was inevitable, therefore, that Pierce Phillips, a youth in his growing age, should adopt a good deal the same habits, as well as the same spirit and outlook, as the people with whom he came in daily contact.

Vice is erroneously considered hideous; it is supposed to have a visage so repulsive that the simplest stranger will shudder at sight of it and turn of his own accord to more attractive Virtue. If that were only true! More often than not it is the former that wears a smile and masquerades in agreeable forms, while the latter repels. This is true of the complex life of the city, where a man has landmarks and guide-posts of conduct to go by, and it is equally true of the less complicated life of the far frontier where he must blaze his own trail. Along with the strength and vigor and independence derived from the great outdoors, there comes also a freedom of individual conduct, an impatience at irksome restraints, that frequently offsets any benefits that accrue from such an environment.

So it was in Pierce's case. He realized, subconsciously, that he was changing, had changed; on the whole, he was glad of it. It filled him with contemptuous amusement, for instance, to look back upon his old puritanical ideas. They seemed now very narrow, very immature, very impractical, and he was gratified at his broader vision. The most significant alteration, however, entirely escaped his notice. That alteration was one of outlook rather than of inlook. Bit by bit he had come to regard the general crowd—the miners, merchants, townspeople—as outsiders, and himself as an insider—one of the wise, clever, ease-loving class which subsisted without toil and for whom a freer code of morals existed. Those outsiders were stupid, hard-working; they were somehow inferior. He and his kind were of a higher, more advanced order of intelligence; moreover, they were bound together by the ties of a common purpose and understanding and therefore enjoyed privileges denied their less efficient brethren.

If jackals were able to reason, doubtless they would justify their existence and prove their superiority to the common herd by some such fatuous argument.

Pierce's complacency received its first jolt when he discovered that he had lost caste in the eyes of the better sort of people—people such as he had been accustomed to associate with at home. This discovery came as the result of a chance meeting with a stranger, and, but for it, he probably would have remained unaware of the truth, for his newly made friends had treated him with consideration and nothing had occurred to disturb his complacency. He had acquired a speaking acquaintance with many of the best citizens, including the Mounted Police and even the higher Dominion officials, all of whom came to the Rialto. These men professed a genuine liking for him, and, inasmuch as his time was pretty full and there was plenty of amusement close at hand, he had never stopped to think that the side of Dawson life which he saw was merely the under side—that a real social community was forming, with real homes on the back streets, where already women of the better sort were living. Oblivious of these facts, it never occurred to Pierce to wonder why these men did not ask him to their cabins or why he did not meet their families.

He had long since become a night-hawk, mainly through a growing fondness for gambling, and he had arrived at the point where daylight impressed him as an artificial and unsatisfactory method of illumination. Recently, too, he had been drinking more than was good for him, and he awoke finally to the unwelcome realization that he was badly in need of fresh air and outdoor exercise.

After numerous half-hearted attempts, he arose one day about noon; then, having eaten a tasteless breakfast and strengthened his languid determination by a stiff glass of "hootch," he strolled out of town, taking the first random trail that offered itself. It was a wood trail, leading nowhere in particular, a fact which precisely suited his resentful mood. His blood moved sluggishly, he was short of breath, the cold was bitter. Before long he decided that walking was a profitless and stultifying occupation, a pastime for idiots

355

and solitaire-players; nevertheless, he continued in the hope of deriving some benefit, however indirect or remote.

It was a still afternoon. A silvery brightness beyond the mountain crests far to the southward showed where the low winter sun was sweeping past on its flat arc. The sky to the north was empty, colorless. There had been no wind for some time, and now the firs sagged beneath burdens of white; even the bare birch branches carried evenly balanced inch-deep layers of snow. Underfoot, the earth was smothered in a feathery shroud as light, as clean as the purest swan's-down, and into it Pierce's moccasins sank to the ankles. He walked as silently as a ghost. Through this queer, breathless hush the sounds of chopping, of distant voices, of an occasional dog barking followed him as he went deeper into the woods.

Time was when merely to be out in the forest on such a day would have pleased him, but gone entirely was that pleasure, and in its place there came now an irritation at the physical discomfort it entailed. He soon began to perspire freely, too freely; nevertheless, there was no glow to his body; he could think only of easy-chairs and warm stoves. He wondered what ailed him. Nothing could be more abhorrent than this, he told himself. Health was a valuable thing, no doubt, and he agreed that no price was too high to pay for it—no price, perhaps, except dull, uninteresting exercise of this sort. He was upon the point of turning back when the trail suddenly broke out into a natural clearing and he saw something which challenged his attention.

To the left of the path rose a steep bank, and beyond that the bare, sloping mountain-side. In the shelter of the bank the snow had drifted deep, but, oddly enough, its placid surface was churned up, as if from an explosion or some desperate conflict that had been lately waged. It had been tossed up and thrown down. What caused him to stare was the fact that no footprints were discernible—nothing except queer, wavering parallel streaks that led downward from the snowy turmoil to the level ground below. They resembled the tracks of some oddly fashioned sled.

Pierce halted, and with bent head was studying the phenomenon, when close above him he heard the rush of a swiftly approaching body; he looked up just in time to behold an apparition utterly unexpected, utterly astounding. Swooping directly down upon him with incredible velocity was what seemed at first glance to be a bird-woman, a valkyr out of the pages of Norse mythology. Wingless she was, yet she came like the wind, and at the very instant Pierce raised his eyes she took the air almost over his head—quite as if he had startled her into an upward flight. Upon her feet was a pair of long, Norwegian skees, and upon these she had scudded down the mountainside; where the bank dropped away she had leaped, and now, like a meteor, she soared into space. This amazing creature was clad in a blue-and-white toboggan suit, short skirt, sweater jacket, and knitted cap. As she hung outlined against the wintry sky Pierce caught a snap-shot glimpse of a fair, flushed, youthful face set in a ludicrous expression of open-mouthed dismay at sight of him. He heard, too, a high-pitched cry, half of warning, half of fright; the next instant there was a mighty upheaval of snow, an explosion of feathery white, as the human projectile landed, then a blur of blue-and-white stripes as it went rolling down the declivity.

"Good Lord!" Pierce cried, aghast; then he sped after the apparition. Only for the evidence of that undignified tumble, he would have doubted the reality of this flying Venus and considered her some creature of his imagination. There she lay, however, a thing of flesh and blood, ·bruised, broken, helpless; apprehensively he pictured himself staggering back to town with her in his arms.

He halted, speechless, when the girl sat up, shook the snow out of her hair, gingerly felt one elbow, then the other, and finally burst into a peal of ringing laughter. The face she lifted to his, now that it wore a normal expression, was wholly charming; it was, in fact, about the freshest, the cleanest, the healthiest and the frankest countenance he had ever looked into.

"Glory be!" he stammered. "I thought you were—completely spoiled."

"I'm badly twisted," the girl managed to gasp, "but I guess I'm all here. Oh! What a bump!"

"You scared me. I never dreamed—I didn't hear a thing until— Well, I looked up and there

358

you were. The sky was full of you. Gee! I thought I'd lost my mind. Are you quite sure you're all right?"

"Oh, I'll be black and blue again, but I'm used to that. That's the funniest one I've had, the very funniest. Why don't you laugh?"

"I'm—too rattled, I suppose. I'm not accustomed to flying girls. Never had them rain down on me out of the heavens."

The girl's face grew sober. "You're entirely to blame," she cried, angrily. "I was getting it beautifully until you showed up. You popped right out of the ground. What are you doing in the Queen's Park, anyhow? You've no business at the royal sports."

"I didn't mean to trespass."

"I think I'll call the guards."

"Call the court physician and make sure—"

"Pshaw! I'm not hurt." Ignoring his extended hand, she scrambled to her feet and brushed herself again. Evidently the queenly anger was short-lived, for she was beaming again, and in a tone that was boyishly intimate she explained:

"I'd made three dandy jumps and was going higher each time, but the sight of you upset me. Think of being upset by a perfectly strange man. Shows lack of social training, doesn't it? It's a wonder I didn't break a skee."

Pierce glanced apprehensively at the bluff overhead. "Hadn't we better move out of the way?" he inquired. "If the royal family comes dropping

in, we'll be ironed out like a couple of handker-
chiefs. I don't want to feel the divine right of the
king, or his left, either."

"There isn't any king—nor any royal family.
I'm just the Queen of Pretend."

"You're skee-jumping, alone? Is that what you
mean?"

The girl nodded.

"Isn't that a dangerous way to amuse yourself? I thought skees were—tricky."

"Have you ever ridden them?" the girl inquired, quickly.

"Never."

"You don't know what fun is. Here—" The
speaker stooped and detached her feet from the
straps. "Just have a go at it." Pierce protested,
but she insisted in a business-like way. "They're
long ones—too long for me. They'll just suit
you."

"Really, I don't care to—"

"Oh yes, you do. You must."

"You'll be sorry," Pierce solemnly warned her.
"When my feet glance off and leave me sticking
up in the snow to starve, you'll— Say! I can
think of a lot of things I want to do, but I don't
seem to find skee-jumping on the list."

"You needn't jump right away." Determination was in the girl's tone; there was a dancing
light of malice in her eyes. "You can practise a
bit. Remember, you laughed at me."

"Nothing of the sort. I was amazed, not
amused. I thought I'd flushed a very magnificent

360

pheasant with blue-and-white stripes, and I was afraid it was going to fly away before I got a good look at it. Now, then—" He slowly finished buckling the runners to his feet and looked up interrogatively. "What are your Majesty's orders?"

"Walk around. Slide down the hill."

"What on?"

The girl smothered a laugh and waved him away. She looked on while he set off with more or less caution. When he managed to maintain an upright position despite the antics of his skees her face expressed genuine disappointment.

"It's not so hard as I thought it would be," he soon announced, triumphantly. "A little awkward at first, but—" he cast an eye up at the bank. "You never know what you can do until you try."

"You've been skeeing before," she accused him, reproachfully.

"Never."

"Then you pick it up wonderfully. Try a jump."

Her mocking invitation spurred him to make the effort, so he removed the skees and waded a short distance up the hill. When he had secured his feet in position for a second time he called down:

"I'm going to let go and trust to Providence. Look out."

"The same to you," she cried. "You're wonderful, but—men can do anything, can't they?"

There was nothing graceful, nothing of the free

abandon of the practised skee-runner in Pierce's attitude; he crouched apelike, with his muscles set to maintain an equilibrium, and this much he succeeded in doing—until he reached the jumping-off place. At that point, however, gravity, which he had successfully defied, wreaked vengeance upon him; it suddenly reached forth and made him its vindictive toy. He pawed, he fought, he appeared to be climbing an invisible rope. With a mighty flop he landed flat upon his back, uttering a loud and dismayed grunt as his breath left him. When he had dug himself out he found that the girl, too, was breathless. She was rocking in silent ecstasy, she hugged herself gleefully, and there were tears in her eyes.

"I'm—so—sorry!" she exclaimed, in a thin, small voice. "Did you—trip over something?"

The young man grinned. "Not at all. I was afraid of a sprained ankle, so I hit on my head. We meet on common ground, as it were."

Once again he climbed the grade, once again he skidded downward, once again he went sprawling. Nor were his subsequent attempts more successful. After a final ignominious failure he sat where he had fetched up and ruefully took stock of the damage he had done himself. Seriously he announced:

"I was mistaken. Women are entitled to vote —they're entitled to anything. I've learned something else, too—Mr. Newton's interesting little theory is all wrong; falling bodies travel sixteen miles, not sixteen feet, the first second."

The girl demanded her skees, and, without
rising, Pierce surrendered them; then he looked
on admiringly while she attached them to her
feet and went zigzagging up the hill to a point
much higher than the one from which he had
dared to venture. She made a very pretty picture, he acknowledged, for she was vivid with
youth and color. She was lithe and strong and
confident, too; she was vibrant with the healthy
vigor of the out-of-doors.

She descended with a terrific rush, and this
time she took the air with grace and certainty.
She cleared a very respectable distance and
ricocheted safely down the landing-slope.

Pierce applauded her with enthusiasm. "Beautiful! My sincere congratulations, O Bounding
Fawn!"

"That's the best I've done," she crowed.
"You put me on my mettle. Now you try it
again."

Pierce did try again; he tried manfully, but
with a humiliating lack of success. He was
puffing and blowing, his face was wet with perspiration, he had lost all count of time, when his
companion finally announced it was time for her
to be going.

"You're not very fit, are you?" said she.

Pierce colored uncomfortably. "Not very,"
he confessed. He was relieved when she did not
ask the reason for his lack of fitness. Just why
he experienced such relief he hardly knew, but
suddenly he felt no great pride in himself nor in

the life that had brought him to such a state of flabbiness. Nor did he care to have this girl know who or what he was. Plainly she was one of those "nice people" at whom Laure and the other denizens of the Rialto were wont to sneer with open contempt; probably that was why he had never chanced to meet her. He felt cheated because they had not met, for she was the sort of girl he had known at home, the sort who believed in things and in whom he believed. Despite all his recently acquired wisdom, in this short hour she had made him over into a boy again, and somehow or other the experience was agreeable. Never had he seen a girl so cool, so candid, so refreshingly unconscious and unaffected as this one. She was as limpid as a pool of glacier water; her placidity, he imagined, had never been stirred, and in that fact lay much of her fascination.

With her skees slung over her shoulder, the girl strode along beside Phillips, talking freely on various topics, but with no disposition to chatter. Her mind was alert, inquisitive, and yet she had that thoughtful gravity of youth, wisdom coming to life. That Pierce had made a good impression upon her she implied at parting by voicing a sincere hope that they would meet again very soon.

"Perhaps I'll see you at the next dance," she suggested.

"Dance!" The word struck Pierce unpleasantly.

"Saturday night, at the Barracks."

"I'd love to come," he declared.

"Do. They're loads of fun. All the nice people go."

With a nod and a smile she was gone, leaving him to realize that he did not even know her name. Well, that was of no moment; Dawson was a small place, and—Saturday was not far off. He had heard about those official parties at the Barracks and he made up his mind to secure an invitation sufficiently formal to permit him to attend the very next one.

His opportunity came that night when one of the younger Mounted Police officers paused to exchange greetings with him. Lieutenant Rock was a familiar figure on the streets of Dawson and on the trails near by, a tall, upstanding Canadian with a record for unfailing good humor and relentless efficiency. He nodded at Pierce's casual reference to the coming dance at Headquarters.

"Great sport," said he. "It's about the only chance we fellows have to play."

When no invitation to share in the treat was forthcoming Pierce told of meeting a most attractive girl that afternoon, and, having obtained his hearer's interest, he described the youthful goddess of the snows with more than necessary enthusiasm. He became aware of a peculiar expression upon Rock's face.

"Yes. I know her well," the latter said, quietly. "D'you mean to say she invited you to the ball?"

"It wasn't exactly an invitation—"

"Oh! I see. Well"—Rock shook his head positively—"there's nothing doing, old man. It isn't your kind of a party. Understand?"

"I—don't understand," Pierce confessed in genuine surprise.

The officer eyed him with a cool, disconcerting directness. "We draw the lines pretty close—have to in a camp like this. No offense, I trust." With a smile and a careless wave of the hand he moved on, leaving Pierce to stare after him until he was swallowed up by the crowd in the gambling-room.

A blow in the face would not have amazed Pierce Phillips more, nor would it have more greatly angered him. So, he was ostracized! These men who treated him with such apparent good-fellowship really despised him; in their eyes he was a renegade; they considered him unfit to know their women. It was incredible!

This was the first deliberate slight the young man had ever received. His face burned, his pride withered under it; he would have bitten out his tongue rather than subject himself to such a rebuff. Who was Rock? How dared he? Rock knew the girl, oh yes! But he refused to mention her name—as if that name would be sullied by his, Pierce's, use of it. That hurt most of all; that was the bitterest pill. Society! Caste! On the Arctic Circle! It was to laugh!

But Phillips could not laugh. He could more easily have cried, or cursed, or raved; even to

366

pretend to laugh off such an affront was impossible. It required no more than this show of opposition to fan the embers of his flickering desire into full flame, and, now that he was forbidden to meet that flying goddess, it seemed to him that he must do so at whatever cost. He'd go to that dance, he decided, in spite of Rock; he'd go unbidden; he'd force his way in if needs be.

This sudden ardor died, however, as quickly as it had been born, leaving him cold with apprehension. What would happen if he took the bit in his teeth? Rock knew about Laure—those detestable redcoats knew pretty much everything that went on beneath the surface of Dawson life—and if Pierce ran counter to the fellow's warning he would probably speak out. Rock was just that sort. His methods were direct and forceful. What then? Pierce cringed inwardly at the contemplation. That snow-girl was so clean, so decent, so radically different from all that Laure stood for, that he shrank from associating them together even in his thoughts.

Well, he was paying the fiddler, and the price was high. Even here on the fringe of the frontier society exacted penalty for the breach of its conventions. Pierce's rebellion at this discovery, his resentment at the whole situation, prevented him from properly taking the lesson to heart. The issue was clouded, too, by a wholly natural effort at self-justification. The more he tried this latter, however, the angrier he became and the more humiliating seemed his situation.

He was in no mood to calmly withstand another shock, especially when that shock was administered by Joe McCaskey, of all persons; nevertheless, it came close upon the heels of Rock's insult.

Pierce had not seen either brother since their departure for Hunker Creek, therefore Joe's black visage leering through the window of the cashier's cage was an unwelcome surprise.

"Hello, Phillips! How are you making it?" the man inquired.

"All right."

Despite this gruffness, Joe's grin widened. There was nothing of pleasure at the meeting, nor of friendliness behind it, however. On the contrary, it masked both malice and triumph, as was plain when he asked:

"Did you hear about our strike?"

"What strike?"

"Why, it's all over town! Frank and I hit pay in our first shaft—three feet of twenty-cent dirt."

"Really?" Pierce could not restrain a movement of surprise.

Joe nodded and chuckled, meanwhile keeping his malignant gaze focused upon the younger man's face. "It's big. We came to town to buy grub and a dog-team and to hire a crew of hands. We've got credit at the A. C. Company up to fifty thousand dollars."

There was a brief pause which Pierce broke by inquiring, as casually as he could:

"Did Tom and Jerry have any luck?"

"Sure thing! They've hit it, the same as us.

You tossed off a home-stake, kid. Don't believe it, eh? Well, here's the proof—coarse gold from Hunker." With an ostentatious flourish the speaker flung down a half-filled poke, together with a bar check. "Cash me in, and don't let any of it stick to your fingers."

Pierce was impelled to hurl the gold sack at Joe's head, but he restrained himself. His hands were shaky, however, and when he untied the thongs he was mortified at spilling some of the precious yellow particles. Mortification changed to anger when the owner cried, sharply:

"Hey! Got cashier's ague, have you? Just cut out the sleight-of-hand!"

Pierce smothered a retort; silently he brushed the dust back into the blower and set the weights upon his scales. But McCaskey ran on with an insulting attempt at banter:

"I'm onto you short-weighers. Take your bit out of the drunks; I'm sober."

When Pierce had retied the sack and returned it he looked up and into Joe's face. His own was white, his eyes were blazing.

"Don't pull any more comedy here," he said, quietly. "That short-weight joke doesn't go at the Rialto."

"Oh, it don't? *Joke!*" McCaskey snorted. "I s'pose it's a joke to spill dust—when you can't get away with it. Well, I've spotted a lot of crooked cashiers in this town."

"No doubt. It takes a thief to catch a thief."

McCaskey started. His sneer vanished.

"Thief! Say—" he blustered, angrily. "D'you mean—" The clash, brief as it had been, had excited attention. Noting the fact that an audience was gathering, the speaker lowered his voice and, thrusting his black, scowling countenance closer to the cage opening, he said: "You needn't remind me of anything. I've got a good memory. Damn' good!" After a moment he turned his back and moved away.

When Pierce went off shift he looked up Lars Anderson and received confirmation of the Hunker strike. Lars was in a boisterous mood and eager to share his triumph.

"I knew that was a rich piece of ground," he chuckled, "and I knew I was handing those boys a good thing. But a fellow owes something to his friends, doesn't he?"

"I thought you said it was low grade?"

"Low grade!" Big Lars threw back his head and laughed loudly. "I never said nothing of the kind. Me knock my own ground? Why, I'd have banked my life on Hunker!"

Here was luck, Pierce told himself. A fortune had been handed him on a silver platter, and he had shoved it aside. He was sick with regret; he was furious with himself for his lack of wisdom; he hated Laure for the deception she had practised upon him. The waste he had made of this opportunity bred in him a feeling of desperation.

Toward the close of the show Laure found him braced against the bar; the face he turned upon her was cold, repellent. When she urged him to take her to supper he shook his head.

"What's the matter?" she inquired.

"Big Lars never told you Hunker was low grade," he declared.

The girl flushed; she tossed her dark head defiantly. "Well, what of it?"

"Simply this—Tom and Jerry and the McCaskeys have struck rich pay."

"Indeed?"

"You lied to me."

Laure's lips parted slowly in a smile. "What did you expect? What would any girl do?" She laid a caressing hand upon his arm. "I don't care how much they make or how poor you are—"

Pierce disengaged her grasp. "I care!" he cried, roughly. "I've lost my big chance. They've made their piles and I'm—well, look at me."

"You blame me?"

He stared at her for a moment. "What's the difference whether I blame you or myself? I'm through. I've been through for some time, but—this is curtain."

"Pierce!"

Impatiently he flung her off and strode out of the theater.

Laure was staring blindly after him when Joe McCaskey spoke to her. "Have a dance?" he inquired.

She undertook to answer, but her lips refused to frame any words; silently she shook her head.

"What's the idea? A lovers' quarrel?" McCas-

371

key eyed her curiously, then he chuckled mirthlessly. "You can come clean with me. I don't like
him any better than you do."

"Mind your own business," stormed the girl
in a sudden fury.

"That's what I'm doing, and minding it good.
I've got a lot of business—with that rat." Joe's
sinister black eyes held Laure's in spite of her
effort to avoid them; it was plain that he wished
to say more, but hesitated. "Maybe it would
pay us to get acquainted," he finally suggested.
"Frank and me and the Count are having a bottle
of wine upstairs. Better join us."

"I will," said Laure, after a moment. Together they mounted the stairs to the gallery
above.

CHAPTER XXIII

"WAL, w'at I tol' you?" 'Poleon Doret exclaimed, cheerfully. "Me, I'm cut off for poor man. If one dose El Dorado millionaire' give me his pay-dump, all de gold disappear biffore I get him in de sluice-box. Some people is born Jonah." Despite this melancholy announcement 'Poleon was far from depressed. On the contrary, he beamed like a boy and his eyes were sparkling with the joy of again beholding his "sister."

He had returned from the hills late this evening and now he had come to fetch Rouletta from her work. This was his first opportunity for a word with her alone.

The girl was not unmoved by his tale of blighted expectations; she refused, nevertheless, to accept it as conclusive. "Nonsense!" she said, briskly. "You know very well you haven't prospected your claim for what it's worth. You haven't had time."

"I don' got to prospec' him," 'Poleon asserted. "Dat's good t'ing 'bout dat claim. Some Swede fellers above me cross-cut de whole dam' creek an' don' fin' so much as one color. *Sapré!* Dat's

373

fonny creek. She 'ain't got no gravel." The
speaker threw back his head and laughed heartily.
"It's fac'! I 'scover de only creek on all de
Yukon wit'out gravel. Muck! Twenty feet of
solid frozen muck! It's lucky I stake on soch
bum place, eh? S'pose all winter I dig an' don'
fin' 'im out?"

For a moment Rouletta remained silent; then
she said, wearily:

"Everything is all wrong, all upside down, isn't
it? The McCaskeys struck pay; so did Tom and
Jerry. But you—why, in all your years in this
country you've never found anything. Where's
the justice—"

"No, no! I fin' somet'ing more better as dem
feller. I fin' a sister; I fin' you. By Gar! I
don't trade you for t'ousan' pay-streak!" Lowering his voice, 'Poleon said, earnestly, "I don' know
how much I love you, *ma sœur*, until I go 'way
and t'ink 'bout it."

Rouletta smiled mistily and touched the big
fellow's hand, whereupon he continued:

"All dese year I look in de mos' likely spot for
gold, an' don' fin' him. Wal, I mak' change. I
don' look in no more creek-bottom; I'm goin' hit
de high spot!"

Reproachfully the girl exclaimed, "You promised me to cut that out."

With a grin the woodsman reassured her: "No,
no! I mean I'm goin' dig on top de mountains."

"Not—really? Why, 'Poleon, gold is heavy!
It sinks. It's deep down in the creek-beds."

374

"It sink, sure 'nough," he nodded, "but where it sink from, eh? I don' lak livin' in low place, anyhow—you don' see not'in'. Me, I mus' have good view."

"What are you driving at?"

"I tell you: long tam ago I know old miner. He's forever talk 'bout high bars, old reever-bed, an' soch t'ing. We call him 'High Bar.' He mak' fonny story 'bout reever dat used to was on top de mountain. By golly! I laugh at him! But w'at you t'ink? I'm crossin' dose hill 'bove El Dorado an' I see place where dose miner is shoot dry timber down into de gulch. Dose log have dug up de snow an' I fin'—what?" Impressively the speaker whispered one word, "*Gravel!*"

Much to his disappointment, Rouletta remained impassive in the face of this startling announcement. Vaguely she inquired: "What of it? There's gravel everywhere. What you want is gold—"

"*Mon Dieu!*" 'Poleon lifted his hands in despair. "You're worse as cheechako. Where gravel is dere you fin' gold, ain't you?"

"Why—not always."

With a shrug. the woodsman agreed. "Of course, not always, but—"

"On top of a hill?"

"De tip top."

"How perfectly absurd! How could gold run uphill?"

"I don' know," the other confessed. "But, for

dat matter, how she run downhill? She 'ain't
got no legs. I s'pose de book hexplain it somehow. Wall I stake two claim—one for you, one
for me. It's dandy place for cabin! You look
forty mile from dat spot. Mak' you feel jus'
lak bird on top of high tree. Dere's plenty dry
wood, too, an' down below is de Forks—nice
town wit' saloon an' eatin'-place. You can hear
de choppin' an' de win'lass creakin' and smell
de smoke. It's fine place for singin' songs up
dere."

"'Poleon!" Rouletta tried to look her sternest.
"You're a great, overgrown boy. You can't stick
to anything. You're merely lonesome and you
want to get in where the people are."

"Lonesome! Don' I live lak bear when I'm
trappin'? Some winter I don' see nobody in de
least."

"Probably I made a mistake in bringing you
down here to Dawson," the girl continued, meditatively. "You were doing well up the river, and
you were happy. Here you spend your money;
you gamble, you drink—the town is spoiling you
just as it is spoiling the others."

"Um-m! Mebbe so," the man confessed.
"Never I felt lak I do lately. If I don' come
in town to-day I swell up an' bus'. I'm full of
t'ing' I can't say."

"Go to work somewhere."

"For wages? Me?" Doret shook his head
positively. "I try him once—cookin' for gang of
rough-neck'—but I mak' joke an' I'm fire'. Dem
376

feller kick 'bout my grub an' it mak' me mad, so one day I sharpen all de table-knife. I put keen edge on dem—lak razor." The speaker showed his white teeth in a flashing smile. "Dat's meanes' trick ever I play. *Sapré!* Dem feller cut deir mouth so fast dey mos' die of bleedin'. No, I ain't hired man for nobody. I mus' be free."

"Very well," Rouletta sighed, resignedly, "I won't scold you, for—I'm too glad to see you." Affectionately she squeezed his arm, whereupon he beamed again in the frankest delight. "Now, then, we'll have supper and you can take me home."

The Rialto was crowded with its usual midnight throng; there was the hubbub of loud voices and the ebb and flow of laughter. From midway of the gambling-hall rose the noisy exhortations of some amateur gamester who was breathing upon his dice and pleading earnestly, feelingly, with "Little Joe"; from the theater issued the strains of a sentimental ballad. As Rouletta and her companion edged their way toward the lunch-counter in the next room they were intercepted by the Snowbird, whose nightly labors had also ended.

"All aboard for the big eats," the latter announced. "Mocha's buttoned up in a stud game where he dassen't turn his head to spit. He's good for all night, but I'm on the job."

"I'm having supper with 'Poleon," Rouletta told him.

The Snowbird paused in dismay. "Say! You can't run out on a pal," he protested. "You got to O. K. my vittles or they won't harmonize."

"But 'Poleon has just come in from the creeks and we've a lot to talk about."

"Won't it keep? I never seen talk spoil overnight." When Rouletta smilingly shook her head Mr. Ryan dangled a tempting bait before her. "I got a swell fairy-story for you. I bet you'd eat it up. It's like this: Once upon a time there was a beautiful Princess named Rouletta and she lived in an old castle all covered with ivy. It was smothered up in them vines till you'd vamp right by and never see it. Along came a busted Prince who had been spendin' his vacation and some perfectly good ten-dollar bills in the next county that you could scarcely tell from the real thing. He was takin' it afoot, on account of the jailer's daughter, who had slipped him a file along with his laundry, but she hadn't thought to put in any lunch. See? Well, it's a story of how this here hungry Prince et the greens off of the castle and discovered the sleepin' Princess. It's a knockout. I bet you'd like it."

"I'm sure I would," Rouletta agreed. "Save it for to-morrow night."

The Snowbird was reluctant in yielding; he eyed 'Poleon darkly, and there was both resentment and suspicion in his somber glance when he finally turned away.

Not until Rouletta and her companion were perched upon their high stools at the oilcloth-

covered lunch-counter did the latter speak; then
he inquired, with a frown:

"Tell me, is any dese feller mak' love on you,
ma sœur?"

"Why, no! They're perfectly splendid, like
you. Why the terrible black look?"

"Gamblers! Sure-t'ing guys! Boosters! Bah!
Better dey lef' you alone, dat's all. You're nice
gal; too nice for dem feller."

Rouletta smiled mirthlessly; there was an expression in her eyes that the woodsman had never
seen. "'Too nice!' That's almost funny when
you think about it. What sort of men would make
love to me, if not gamblers, fellows like Ryan?"

'Poleon breathed an exclamation of astonishment at this assertion. "W'at you sayin'?" he
cried. "If dat loafer mak' fresh talk wit' you I
—pull him in two piece wit' dese fingers. Dere's
plenty good man. I—you—" He paused uncertainly; then his tone changed to one of appeal.
"You won't marry wit' nobody, eh? Promise me
dat."

"That's an easy promise, under the circumstances."

"*Bien!* I never t'ink 'bout you gettin' married. By gosh! dat's fierce t'ing, for sure! W'at
I'll do if—" 'Poleon shook his massive shoulders
as if to rid himself of such unwelcome speculations.

"No danger!"

Rouletta's crooked smile did not go unnoticed.
'Poleon studied her face intently; then he inquired:

25   379

"W'at ail' you, li'l sister?"

"Why—nothing."

"Oh yes! I got eye lak fox. You seeck?"

"The idea!" Miss Kirby pulled herself together, but there was such genuine concern in her companion's face that her chin quivered. She felt the need of saying something diverting; then abruptly she turned away.

'Poleon's big hand closed over hers; in a voice too low for any but her ears he said: "Somet'ing is kill de song in your heart, *ma petite.* I give my life for mak' you happy. Sometam you care for tell me, mebbe I can he'p li'l bit."

The girl suddenly bowed her head; her struggling tears overflowed reluctantly; in a weary, heartsick murmur she confessed:

"I'm the most miserable girl in the world. I'm so—unhappy."

Some instinct of delicacy prompted the woodsman to refrain from speaking. In the same listless monotone Rouletta continued:

"I've always been a lucky gambler, but—the cards have turned against me. I've been playing my own stakes and I've lost."

"You been playing de bank?" he queried, in some bewilderment.

"No, a gambler never plays his own game. He always bucks the other fellow's. I've been playing—hearts."

'Poleon's grasp upon her hand tightened. "I see," he said. "Wal, bad luck is boun' to change."

In Rouletta's eyes, when she looked up, was a

380

vision of some glory far beyond the woodsman's sight. Her lips had parted, her tears had dried. "I wonder—" she breathed. "Father's luck always turned. 'Don't weaken; be a thoroughbred!' That's what he used to tell me. He'd be ashamed of me now, wouldn't he? I've told you my troubles, 'Poleon, because you're all I have left. Forgive me, please, big brother."

"Forgive? *Mon Dieu!*" said he.

Their midnight meal was set out; to them it was tasteless, and neither one made more than a silent pretense of eating it. They were absorbed in their own thoughts when the sound of high voices, a commotion of some sort at the front of the saloon, attracted their attention. Rouletta's ears were the first to catch it; she turned, then uttered a breathless exclamation. The next instant she had slid down from her perch and was hurrying away. 'Poleon strode after her; he was at her back when she paused on the outskirts of a group which had assembled near the cashier's cage.

Pierce Phillips had left his post behind the scales; he, Count Courteau, and Ben Miller, the proprietor, were arguing hotly. Rock, the Police lieutenant, was listening to first one then another. The Count was deeply intoxicated; nevertheless, he managed to carry himself with something of an air, and at the moment he was making himself heard with considerable vehemence.

"I have been drinking, to be sure," he acknowledged, "but am I drunk? No. Damnation! There is the evidence." In his hand he was holding a small gold-sack, and this he shook defiantly under the officer's nose. "Do you call that eight hundred dollars? I ask you. Weigh it! Weigh it!"

Rock took the little leather bag in his fingers; then he agreed. "It's a lot short of eight hundred, for a fact, but—"

In a strong voice Phillips cried: "I don't know what he had. That's all there was in the sack when he paid his check."

The Count lurched forward, his face purple with indignation. "For shame!" he cried. "You thought I was blind. You thought I was like these other—cattle. But I know to a dollar—" He turned to the crowd. "Here! I will prove what I say. McCaskey, bear me out."

With a show of some reluctance Frank, the younger and the smaller of the two brothers, nodded to the Police lieutenant. "He's giving you the straight goods. He had eight hundred and something on him when he went up to the cage."

Rock eyed the speaker sharply. "How do you know?" said he.

"Joe and I was with him for the last hour and a half. Ain't that right, Joe?" Joe verified this statement. "Understand, this ain't any of our doings. We don't want to mix up in it, but the Count had a thousand dollars, that much I'll swear to. He lost about a hundred and forty up the street and he bought two rounds of drinks afterward. I ain't quick at figures—"

Pierce uttered a threatening cry. He moved toward the speaker, but Rock laid a hand on his arm and in a tone of authority exclaimed: "None of that, Phillips. I'll do all the fighting."

Ben Miller, who likewise had bestirred himself to forestall violence, now spoke up. "I'm not boosting for the house," said he, "but I want more proof than this kind of chatter. Pierce has been weighing here since last fall, and nobody ever saw him go south with a color. If he split this poke he must have the stuff on him. Let Rock search you, Pierce."

Phillips agreed readily enough to this suggestion, and assisted the officer's search of his pockets, a procedure which yielded nothing.

"Dat boy's no t'ief," 'Poleon whispered to Rouletta. "M'sieu' le Comte has been frisk' by somebody." The girl did not answer. She was intently watching the little drama before her.

During the search Miller forced his way out of the ring of spectators, unlocked the gate of the cashier's cage, and passed inside. "We keep our takin's in one pile, and I'll lay a little eight to five that they'll balance up with the checks to a pennyweight," said he. "Just wait till I add up the figgers and weigh—" He paused; he stooped; then he rose with something he had picked up from the floor beneath his feet.

"What have you got, Ben?" It was Rock speaking.

"Dam' if I know! There it is." The proprietor

shoved a clean, new moose-skin gold-sack through the wicket.

Rock examined the bag, then he lifted an inquiring gaze to Pierce Phillips. There was a general craning of necks, a shifting of feet, a rustle of whispers.

"Ah!" mockingly exclaimed Courteau. "I was dreaming, eh? To be sure!" He laughed disagreeably.

"Is this 'house' money?" inquired the redcoat.

Miller shook his head in some bewilderment. "We don't keep two kitties. I'll weigh it and see if it adds up with the Count's—"

'Oh, it will add up!" Phillips declared, his face even whiter than before. "It's a plant, so of course it will add up."

Defiantly he met the glances that were fixed upon him. As his eyes roved over the faces turned upon him he became conscious for the first time of 'Poleon's and Rouletta's presence, also that Laure had somehow appeared upon the scene. The latter was watching him with a peculiar expression of hostility frozen upon her features; her dark eyes were glowing, she was sneering faintly. Of all the bystanders, perhaps the two McCaskeys seemed the least inclined to take part in the affair. Both brothers, in fact, appeared desirous of effacing themselves as effectively as possible.

But Courteau's indignation grew, and in a burst of excitement he disclaimed the guilt implied in Pierce's words. "So! You plead in-

384

nocence! You imply that I robbed myself, eh? Well, how did I place the gold yonder? I ask you? Am I a magician?" He waved his arms wildly, then in a tone of malevolence he cried: "This is not the first time you have been accused of theft. I have heard that story about Sheep Camp."

"Sheep Camp, yes!" Phillips' eyes ignored the speaker; his gaze flew to Joe McCaskey's face and to him he directed his next words: "The whole thing is plain enough to me. You tried something like this once before, Joe, and failed. I suppose your back is well enough now for the rest of those forty lashes. Well, you'll get 'em—"

The Count came promptly to the rescue of his friend. "Ho! Again you lay your guilt upon others. Those miners at Sheep Camp let you off easy. Well, a pretty woman can do much with a miners' meeting, but here there will be no devoted lady to the rescue—no skirt to hide behind, for—"

Courteau got no further. Ignoring Rock's previous admonition, Pierce knocked the fellow down with a swift, clean blow. He would have followed up his attack only for the lieutenant, who grappled with him.

"Here! Do you want me to put you in irons?"

Courteau raised himself with difficulty; he groped for the bar and supported himself dizzily thereon, snarling from the pain. With his free hand he felt his cheek where Pierce's knuckles had found lodgment; then, as a fuller realization of the indignity his privileged person had suffered came home to him, he burst into a torrent of frenzied abuse.

"Shut up!" the officer growled, unsympathetically. "I know as much about that trial at Sheep Camp as you do, and if Phillips hadn't floored you I would. That's how you stand with me. You, too!" he shot at the McCaskeys. "Let me warn you if this is a frame-up you'll all go on the woodpile for the winter. D'you hear me? Of course, if you want to press this charge I'll make the arrest, but I'll just take you three fellows along so you can do some swearing before the colonel, where it 'll go on the records."

"Arrest? But certainly!" screamed the Count. "The fellow is a thief, a pig. He struck me. *Me!* You saw him. I—"

"Sure, I saw him!" the officer grinned. "I was afraid he'd miss you. Stop yelling and come along." With a nod that included the McCaskeys as well as the titled speaker he linked arms with Pierce Phillips and led the way out into the night.

"W'at fool biznesse!" Doret indignantly exclaimed. "Dat boy is hones' as church."

He looked down at the sound of Rouletta's voice; then he started. The girl's face was strained and white and miserable; her hands were clasped over her bosom; she was staring horrified at the door through which Phillips had been taken. She swayed as if about to fall. 'Poleon half dragged, half carried her out into the street;

386

with his arm about her waist he helped her toward her hotel.

The walk was a silent one, for Rouletta was in a state bordering upon collapse; gradually she regained control of herself and stumbled along beside him.

"They're three to one," she said, finally. "Oh, 'Poleon! They'll swear it on him. The Police are strict; they'll give him five years. I heard the colonel say so."

"Dere's been good deal of short - weighin', but—" Doret shook his head. "Nobody goin' believe Courteau. And McCaskey is dam' t'ief."

"If—only I—could help him. You'll go to him, 'Poleon, won't you? Promise."

Silently the Canadian assented. They had reached the door of the hotel before he spoke again; then he said slowly, quietly:

"You been playin' 'hearts' wit' *him, ma sœur?* You—you love him? Yes?"

"Oh—yes!" The confession came in a miserable gasp.

"*Bien!* I never s'pect biffore. Wal, dat's all right."

"The Police are swift and merciless," Rouletta persisted, fearfully. "They hate the Front Street crowd; they'd like to make an example."

"Go in your li'l bed an' sleep," he told her, gently. "Dis t'ing is comin' out all right. 'Poleon fix it, sure; he's dandy fixer."

For some time after the door had closed upon Rouletta the big fellow stood with bent head, staring at the snow beneath his feet. The cheer, the sympathy, had left his face; the smile had vanished from his lips; his features were set and stony. With an effort he shook himself, then murmured:

"Poor li'l bird! Wal, I s'pose now I got to bus' dat jail!"

CHAPTER XXIV

ALTHOUGH 'Poleon had spoken with confidence, he found, upon arriving at Police Headquarters, that the situation was by no means as simple as it had appeared, and that something more than a mere word regarding Phillips' character would be required to offset the very definite accusation against him. Courteau, he learned, had pressed his charge with vigor, and although the two McCaskeys had maintained their outward show of reluctance at being dragged into the affair, they had, nevertheless, substantiated his statements with a thoroughness and a detail that hinted more than a little at vindictiveness. Pierce, of course, had denied his guilt, but his total inability to explain how the gold-dust in dispute came to be concealed in the cashier's cage, to which no one but he had access, had left the Police no alternative except to hold him. By the time 'Poleon arrived Pierce had been locked up for the night.

Drawing Rock aside, Doret put in an earnest plea for his young friend. The lieutenant answered him with some impatience:

"I admit it looks fishy, but what is there to

do? The colonel likes Pierce, as we all do, but
—he had no choice."

"It's dirty frame-up."

"I imagine he believes so. And yet—how the
deuce did that sack get where it was? I was
standing alongside the McCaskeys when Courteau went up to pay his check, and I'm sure they
had no part in it."

"M'sieu' le Comte is sore," 'Poleon asserted.
"Me, I savvy plenty. Wal, how we goin' get
dat boy from out of jail, eh? By Gar! I bet I
don' sleep none if I'm lock up."

"Get bail for him."

'Poleon was frankly puzzled at this suggestion,
but when its nature had been explained his face
lit up.

"Ho! Dat's nice arrangements, for sure.
Come! I fix it now."

"Have you got enough money?"

"I got 'bout t'irty dollar, but dat ain't mak'
no differ. I go to workin' somewhere. Me, I'm
good for anyt'ing."

"That won't do," Rock smiled. "You don't
understand." Laboriously he made more plain
the mysteries of court procedure, whereupon his
hearer expressed the frankest astonishment.

"_Sacré!_" the latter exclaimed. "What for you
say two, t'ree _t'ousan'_ dollar? Courteau 'ain't
lose but six hundred, an' he's got it back. No!
I'm t'inkin' you Policemans is got good sense,
but I lak better a miners' meetin'. Us 'sourdough' mak' better law as dem feller at Ottawa."

"Morris Best was willing to go his bail," Rock informed him, "but Miller wouldn't allow it. Ben is sore at having the Rialto implicated—there's been so much short-weighing going on. Understand?"

'Poleon wagged his head in bewilderment. "I don' savvy dis new kin' of law you feller is bring in de country. S'pose I say, '*M'sieu' Jodge*, I know dis boy long tam; he don' steal dat gold.' De Jodge he say, 'Doret, how much money you got? T'ousand dollar?' I say, 'Sure! I got 'bout t'ousand dollar.' Den he tell me, 'Wal, dat ain't 'nough. Mebbe so you better gimme two t'ousan' dollar biffore I b'lieve you.' *Bien!* I go down-town an' win 'noder t'ousan' on de high card, or mebbe so I stick up some feller, den I come back and *m'sieu' le jodge* he say: 'Dat's fine! Now we let Phillips go home. He don' steal not'in'.' W'at I t'ink of dem proceedin's? Eh? I t'ink de jodge is dam' grafter!"

Rock laughed heartily. "Don't let Colonel Cavendish hear you," he cautioned. "Seriously now, he'd let Pierce go if he could; he told me so. He'll undoubtedly allow him the freedom of the Barracks, so he'll really be on parole until his trial."

. "Trial? You goin' try him again?" The woodsman could make little of the affair. "If you try him two tam, dose crook is mak' t'ief of Pierce for sure. One trial is plenty. I s'pose mebbe I better kill dem feller off an' settle dis t'ing."

"Don't talk like that," Rock told him. "I'm not saying they don't need killing, but—nobody gets away with that stuff nowadays."

"No?" 'Poleon was interested and a trifle defiant. "For why? You never catch me, *M'sieu'*. Nobody is able for doin' dat. I'm good traveler."

Rock eyed the stalwart speaker meditatively. "I'd hate to take your trail, that's a fact, but I'd have to do it. However, that would be a poor way to help Pierce. If he's really innocent, Courteau will have a hard job to convict him. I suggest that you let matters rest as they are for a day or so. We'll treat the kid all right."

On the way to her room Rouletta met the Countess Courteau, and in a few words made known the facts of Pierce's arrest. The elder woman listened in astonishment.

"Arrested? For theft? Absurd! Who made the charge?"

"Count Courteau."

"*Courteau?* Where did he get a thousand dollars?" The speaker's face was set in an expression of utter incredulity.

"I don't know. It's all too wretched, too terrible—" Rouletta's voice broke; she hid her face in her hands. For a moment there was silence; then the elder woman exclaimed, harshly, peremptorily:

"Tell me everything. Quick! There's a reason why I must know all about it."

Drawing Rouletta into her room, she forced her into a chair, then stood over her while the latter repeated the story in greater detail.

"So! That's it!" the Countess cried, at last. "The McCaskeys backed him up. Of course! And he referred to Sheep Camp—to me. He's the sort to do a thing like that. God! What a dog!" After a time she went on: "I'm sorry Pierce struck him; he'll never get over that and it will make it harder—much harder."

"You think it can be straightened out?" Rouletta's face was strained; her eyes searched the former speaker's face eagerly.

"It's *got* to be straightened out. It would be monstrous to allow—" The Countess shook her head, then, with a mirthless smile, exclaimed: "But what a situation! Henri, of all persons! It's pleasant for me, isn't it? Well, somebody planted that poke—probably one of the McCaskeys. They'd like to railroad the boy. Joe is as vindictive as an Indian and he blames Pierce and me for his brother's death."

In desperation Rouletta cried: "I'll pay the Count back his money—I'll double it."

"*His* money?" sneered the woman. "He hasn't a cent, except what I give him. That was McCaskey's dust." She stared at the apprehensive figure crouched upon the edge of the chair, and slowly her expression softened. In a gentler tone she said, "I see you didn't take my advice; you didn't heed my warning."

"Who ever heeds a warning like yours?"

"Does Pierce know that you—feel this way about him?"

Rouletta sighed wearily. "I didn't know myself, although I more than half suspected. I didn't permit myself to think, it made me so unhappy."

"It ought to satisfy me somewhat to learn that he doesn't care for you, but—somehow it doesn't. He didn't care for me, either. But I cared for him. I love him now, just as you love him— better, probably. Oh, why conceal it? I've spent a good many black hours thinking about it and trying to fight it. Mind you, it wasn't his fault; it was just fate. There are some fellows who go smiling and singing along through life— clean, decent fellows, too—attending to their own affairs in a perfectly proper manner, but leaving a trail of havoc behind them. It isn't so true of women—they're usually flirts—their smiles don't last and the echo of their songs dies out. He's perfectly impossible for me. I wouldn't marry him if I were free and if he asked me. But that has nothing whatever to do with the case."

"I had no idea!" Rouletta said. "I suppose there's no hope for me, either. I'm not his kind. He's told me about his life, his people. I wouldn't fit in."

"It isn't that—people are adaptable, they make themselves fit, for a while at least—it's a question of identities. As much a matter of family histories as anything else. You're his antithesis in every respect and—like should mate with like. Now then, about this other trouble. I must work in my own way, and I see but one. I'll have to pay high, but—" 'The speaker lifted her shoulders as if a cold wind had chilled her. "I've paid high, up to date, and I suppose I shall to the end. Meanwhile, if you can get him out of jail, do so by all means. I can't. I daren't even try."

When, at a late hour, Count Henri Courteau entered the establishment that bore his name he was both surprised and angered to find his wife still awake. The guests of the hotel were asleep, the place was quiet, but the Countess was reading in an easy-chair beside the office stove. She was in négligée, her feet were resting upon the stove fender. She turned her head to say:

"Well, Henri, you look better than I thought you would."

The Count passed a caressing hand over his swollen cheek and his discolored left eye. "You heard about the fight, eh?" he inquired, thickly.

"Yes—if you'd call it that."

Courteau grimaced, but there was a ring of triumph and of satisfaction in his voice when he cried:

"Well, what do you think of that fellow? It was like him, wasn't it, after I had caught him red-handed?"

"To punch you? Quite like him," agreed the woman.

"Pig! To strike a defenseless man. Without warning, too. It shows his breeding. And now" —the speaker sneered openly—"I suppose you will bail him out."

"Indeed! Why should I?"

"Oh, don't pretend innocence!" the Count stormed. "Don't act so unconcerned. What's your game, anyhow? Whatever it is, that fellow will cut cord-wood for the rest of the winter where the whole of Dawson can see him and say, 'Behold the lover of the Countess Courteau!'"

"There's some mistake. He isn't a thief."

"No?" The husband swayed a few steps closer, his face working disagreeably. "Already it is proved. He is exposed, ruined. Bah! He made of me a laughing-stock. Well, he shall suffer! A born thief, that's what he is. What have you to say?"

"Why—nothing. I hoped it was a mistake, that's all."

"You *hoped!* To be sure!" sneered the speaker. "Well, what are you going to do about it?" When his wife said nothing the man muttered, in some astonishment: "I didn't expect you to take it so quietly. I was prepared for a scene. What ails you?"

Hilda laid down her book. She turned to face her accuser. "Why should I make a scene?" she asked. "I've had nothing to do with Phillips since we parted company at White Horse. I've scarcely spoken to him, and you know it."

"You don't deny there was something between you?"

The woman shrugged non-committally, her lips parted in a faint, cheerless smile. "I deny nothing. I admit nothing."

Although Courteau's brain was fogged, he ex-

396

perienced a growing surprise at the self-possession with which his wife had taken this blow which he had aimed as much at her as at Pierce Phillips; he studied her intently, a mingling of suspicion, of anger, and of admiration in his uncertain gaze. He saw, for one thing, that his effort to reach her had failed and that she remained completely the mistress of herself. She reclined at ease in her comfortable chair, quite unstirred by his derision, his jubilation. He became aware, also, of the fact that she presented an extremely attractive picture, for the soft white fur of the loose robe she wore exposed an alluring glimpse of snowy throat and bosom; one wide sleeve had fallen back, showing a smoothly rounded arm; her silken ankles, lifted to the cozy warmth of the stove, were small and trim; her feet were shod in neat high-heeled slippers. The Count admired neatly shod ladies.

"You're a very smart-looking woman," he cried, with some reluctance. "You're beautiful, Hilda. I don't blame the young fool for falling. But you're too old, too wise—"

Hilda nodded. "You've said it. Too old and too wise. If I'd been as young and as silly as when I met you—who knows? He's a handsome boy."

Again the husband's anger blazed up.

"But I'm not young and silly," his wife interrupted.

"Just the same, you played me a rotten trick," the Count exploded. "And I don't forget. As

for him"—he swore savagely—"he'll learn that
it's not safe to humiliate me, to rob me of any
woman—wife or mistress. You've never told
me the half; I've had to guess. But I'm patient,
I know how to wait and to use my eyes and my
ears. Then to strike me! Perdition! I'll follow this through, never fear."

"How did you get a thousand dollars, Henri?"
the wife inquired, curiously.

Courteau's gaze shifted. "What difference? I
won it on a turn at the North Star; it was given
to me; I found it. Anyhow, I had it. It was a
good night for me; yes, a very good night. I had
my revenge and I showed my friends that I'm a
man to be reckoned with."

In a tone unexpectedly humble the woman
said: "I had no idea you cared very much what
I did or how I carried on. After all, it was your
own fault."

"Mine?" The Count laughed in derision and
astonishment.

"Exactly! If you had taken the trouble to
show me that you cared—well, things might have
been different. However—" The Countess rose,
and with another change of voice and manner
said: "Come along. Let's do something for
your eye."

The Count stared at her in bewilderment, then
he turned away, crying: "Bah! I want no help."
At the door he paused to jeer once more. "Pierce
Phillips! A common thief, a despicable creature
who robs the very man he had most deeply in-

jured. I've exposed him to the law and to public scorn. Sleep on that, my dear. Dream on it." With a chuckle he traced an uncertain course to the stairs, mounted them to his room, and slammed his door behind him.

He had undressed and flung himself into bed, but he had not yet fallen asleep when the door reopened and his wife entered, bearing in her hand a steaming pitcher of hot water. This she deposited; into it she dipped a folded towel.

"I'm sorry you're disfigured, Henri," she told him, quietly.

Despite his surly protests, she bathed and soothed his swollen features until he dropped asleep, after which she stole out and down to her room on the floor below. There, however, she paused, staring back up the empty stairway, a look of deepest loathing upon her face. Slowly, carefully, she wiped her hands as if they were unclean; her lips curled into a mirthless smile; then she passed into her chamber and turned the key behind her.

Rock had spoken truly in assuring 'Poleon that Pierce Phillips' lot would be made as easy for him as possible. That is what happened. No one at the Barracks appeared to take much stock in Courteau's charge, and even Colonel Cavendish, the commandant, took the trouble to send for him early the next morning and to ask for the whole story in detail. When Pierce had given it the officer nodded. "It looks very much like a spite case. I couldn't imagine your doing such a thing, my boy."

"It is a spite case, nothing else."

"Courteau is a rotter, and your affair with his wife explains his animosity."

"It wasn't exactly an 'affair,' sir." Pierce colored slightly as he went on to explain. "You see, I was perfectly honest. I didn't know there was a count, and when I learned there was I up stakes and ended it. She was the first woman who ever—. Well, sir, I admired her tremendously. She—impressed me wonderfully."

"No doubt," the colonel smiled. "She's an impressive person. Are you still fond of her?"

"Not in the same way."

"What about this girl Laure?"

This time Pierce flushed uncomfortably. "I've no excuses to offer there, sir—no explanations. We—just drifted together. It was a long trip and the Yukon does that sort of thing. Force of circumstance as much as anything, I presume. I've been trying to break away, but—" he shrugged.

"You've been a pretty foolish lad." Pierce remained silent at this accusation, and the colonel went on: "However, I didn't bring you here to lecture you. The Royal Mounted have other things to think about than young wasters who throw themselves away. After all, it's a free-and-easy country and if you want to play ducks and drakes it's your own business. I merely want you to realize that you've put yourself in a bad light and that you don't come into court with clean hands."

"I understand. I put in a wakeful night thinking about it. It's the first time in a long while that I've done any serious thinking."

"Well, don't be discouraged. A little thinking will benefit you. Now then, I'm going to put Rock at work on your case, and meanwhile you may have the liberty of the Barracks. You're a gentleman, and I trust you to act as one."

Pierce was only too grateful for this courtesy, and to realize that he retained the respect of this middle-aged, soldierly officer, whom he had long admired, filled him with deep relief. He gave his promise readily enough.

Later in the day Broad and Bridges came in to see him, and their indignation at the outrage, their positive assertion that it was nothing less than a deliberate conspiracy, and so considered among the Front Street resorts, immensely cheered him.

"You remember the holler I let up when them Sheep-Campers wanted to hang McCaskey?" Broad inquired. "It was my mistake. His ear and a hemp knot would go together like rheumatism and liniment."

Bridges agreed. "Funny, us three bein' tillicums, ain't it?" he mused. "Especially after the way we dredged you. We didn't need your loose change, but—there it was, so we took it."

"You'd of done better if you'd turned on the hollow of your foot that day and romped right

401

back to the old farm," Broad asserted. "You'd never of doubled up with the McCaskeys and you'd still be the blushing yokel you was."

"Yes, you're a different kid, now." Both gamblers, it seemed, were in the melancholy mood for moralizing. "Why, we was talkin' to Rouletta about you this morning. She's all bereaved up over this thing; she sent us here to cheer you. You was clean as an apple, then—and easier to pick—now you're just a common bar-fly, the same as us. Laure done it. She's the baby vampire that made a bum of you."

"You're not very flattering." Phillips smiled faintly.

"Oh, I'm sort of repeatin' what Letty said. She put me to thinkin'. She's quite a noisy little missionary when she gets started."

"Missionary!" Broad exclaimed, in disdain. "I don't like the word. Them birds is about as useful as a hip pocket in an undershirt. Why, missionaries don't do no real, lasting good outside of Indian villages! Us sure-thing guys are the best missionaries that ever struck this country. Look at the good we done around Dyea and Skagway. Them gospel-bringers never touched it. We met the suckers on the edge of the Frozen North and we turned 'em back by the score. Them three walnut husks done more good than the Ten Commandments. Yes, sir, a set of cheatin' tools will save more strayed lambs than a ship-load of Testaments."

"Letty figgers that somebody tossed that gold-sack over the top of the cage after you follered the Count out."

"Impossible," Pierce declared.

"I got an idea." It was Broad speaking again. "The mere contemplation of physical violence unmans that Frog. He'd about as soon have a beatin' as have a leg cut off with a case-knife. S'pose me and the Kid lure him to some lonely spot—some good yellin'-place—and set upon him with a coupla pick-handles. We'll make him confess or we'll maim and meller him till he backs out through his bootlegs. What d'yon say?"

Pierce shook his head. "Something must be done, but I doubt if that's it. It's tough to be—disgraced, to have a thing like this hanging over you. I wouldn't mind it half so much if I were up for murder or arson or any man's-sized crime. Anything except *stealing!*"

"A mere matter of choice," the former speaker lightly declared. "We got boys around the Rialto that has tried 'em all. They don't notice no particular difference."

For some time the three friends discussed the situation, then, when his visitors rose to go, Pierce accompanied them to the limits of the Barracks premises and there stood looking after them, realizing with a fresh pang that he was a prisoner. It was an unfortunate predicament, he reflected, and quite as unpleasant as the one which had brought him into conflict with the angry men of Sheep Camp. That had been an experience fraught with peril, but his present plight was little better, it seemed to him, for already he felt the weight of the Dominion over him, already he fancied himself enmeshed in a discouraging tangle of red tape. There was no adventurous thrill to this affair, nothing but an odious feeling of shame and disgrace which he could not shake off.

He was staring morosely at the ground between his feet when he heard a voice that caused him to start. There, facing him with a light of pleasure in her blue eyes, was the girl of the skees.

"Hello!" said she. She extended her hand, and her mitten closed over Pierce's fingers with a firm clasp. "I'm awfully glad to see you again, Mr—" She hesitated, then with a smile confessed, "Do you know, you're my only pupil and yet I've never heard your name."

"Phillips," said he.

"You don't deserve to be remembered at all, for you didn't come to the dance. And after you had promised, too."

"I couldn't come," he assured her, truthfully enough.

"I looked for you. I was quite hurt when you failed to appear. Then I thought perhaps you expected something more formal than a mere verbal invitation, and in that way I managed to save my vanity. If I'd known who you were or how to find you I'd have had my father send you a note. If it wasn't that, I'm glad. Well, there's another dance this week and I'll expect you."

"I—I'm not dancing," he stammered. "Not at the Barracks, anyhow."

404

The girl was puzzled; therefore Pierce summoned his courage and explained, with as brave an attempt at lightness as he could afford: "You see before you a victim of unhappy circumstance, a person to be shunned. I'm worse than a case of smallpox. I don't think you should be seen talking to me."

"What are you driving at?"

"I'm getting up the spiritual momentum necessary to tell you that I'm a thief! Truly. Anyhow, three choice gentlemen are so sure of it that they went to the trouble of perjuring themselves and having me arrested—"

"Arrested? *You?*"

"Exactly. And the evidence is very strong. I almost think I must be guilty."

"Are you?"

Pierce shook his head.

"Of course you're not. I remember, now—something father said at breakfast, but I paid no attention. You fought with that good-looking French count, didn't you?"

"Thank you for reminding me of the one cheerful feature connected with the entire affair. Yes, I raised my hand to him in anger—and let it fall, but Lieutenant Rock spoiled the whole party."

"Tell me everything, please."

Pierce was more than willing to oblige, and he began his recital at the time of his first meeting with Joe McCaskey on the beach at Dyea. While he talked the girl listened with that peculiar open-eyed meditative gravity he had noted upon their

405

former meeting. When he had finished she cried, breathlessly:

"Why, it's as exciting as a book!"

"You think so? I don't. If I were only a clever book character I'd execute sóme dramatic coup and confound my enemies—book people always do. But my mind is a blank, my ingenuity is at a complete standstill. I feel perfectly foolish and impotent. To save me, I can't understand how that gold got where it was, for the cashier's cage is made of wire and the door has a spring-lock. I heard it snap back of me when I followed the Count outside. I had an insane idea that his nose would stretch if I pulled it and I believe yet it would. Well, I've spent one night in the dungeon and I'm not cut out to enjoy that mode of life. All I can think about is the Prisoner of Chillon and the Man in the Iron Mask and other distressing instances of the law's injustice. I feel as if I'd grown a gray beard in the last twelve hours. Do I look much older than when we met?"

The girl shook her head. "It's tremendously dramatic. Think what a story it will make when it's over and when you look back on it."

"Do you feel that way, too?" Pierce inquired, curiously. "As if everything is an adventure? I used to. I used to stand outside of myself and look on, but now—I'm on the inside, looking out. I suppose it's the effect of the gray beard. Experience comes fast in this country. To one thing I've made up my mind, however; when I get out of this scrape, if I ever do, I'm going

THE WINDS OF CHANCE

away up into the hills where the wind can blow me clean, and stay there."

"It's a perfect shame!" the girl said, indignantly. "I shall tell father to fix it. He fixes everything I ask him to. He's wonderful, as you probably know."

"Inasmuch as I haven't the faintest idea who he is—"

"Why, he's Colonel Cavendish! I'm Josephine Cavendish. I thought everybody knew me."

Pierce could not restrain a start of surprise. Very humbly he inquired:

"Now that you understand who I am and what I'm charged with, do you want to—know me; be friends with me?"

"We *are* friends," Miss Cavendish warmly declared. "That's not something that may happen; it has happened. I'm peculiar about such matters; I have my own way of looking at them. And now that we're friends we're going' to be friends throughout and I'm going to help you. Come along and meet mother."

"I—don't know how far my parole extends," Pierce ventured, doubtfully.

"Nonsense! There's only one authority around here. Father thinks he's it, but he isn't. I am. You're my prisoner now. Give me your word you won't try to escape—"

"Escape!" Pierce smiled broadly. "I don't much care if I never get out. Prisons aren't half as bad as they're pictured."

"Then come!"

CHAPTER XXV

"YOU really must do something for this boy Pierce Phillips." Mrs. Cavendish spoke with decision.

The newspaper which the colonel was reading was barely six weeks old, therefore he was deeply engrossed in it, and he looked up somewhat absent-mindedly.

"Yes, yes. Of course, my dear," he murmured. "What does he want now?"

"Why, he wants his liberty! He wants this absurd charge against him dismissed! It's a shame to hold a boy of his character, his breeding, on the mere word of a man like Count Courteau."

Colonel Cavendish smiled quizzically. "You, too, eh?" said he.

"What do you mean by that?"

"Why, you're the fourth woman who has appealed to me since his arrest. I dare say I'll hear from others. I never saw a fellow who had the female vote so solidly behind him. I'm beginning to regard him as a sort of domestic menace."

"You surely don't believe him guilty?"

When her husband refused to commit himself Mrs. Cavendish exclaimed, "Rubbish!"

"First Josephine came to me," the colonel observed. "She was deeply indignant and considerably disappointed in me as a man and a father when I refused to quash the entire proceedings and apologize, on behalf of the Dominion Government, for the injury to the lad's feelings. She was actually peeved. What ails her I don't know. Then the Countess Courteau dropped in, and so did that 'lady dealer' from the Rialto. Now you take up his defense." The speaker paused thoughtfully for an instant. "It's bad enough to have the fellow hanging around our quarters at all hours, but Josephine actually suggested that we have him *dine* with us!"

"I know. She spoke of it to me. But he isn't 'hanging around at all hours.' Josephine is interested in his case, just as I am, because—"

"My dear! He's a weigher in a saloon, a gambling-house employee. D'you think it wise to raise such a dust about him? I like the boy myself—can't help liking him—but you understand what he's been doing? He's been cutting up; going the pace. I never knew you to countenance a fellow—"

"I never saw a boy toward whom I felt so—motherly," Mrs. Cavendish said, with some irrelevance. "I don't like wild young men any better than you do, but—he isn't a thief, of that I'm sure."

"Look here." Colonel Cavendish laid down his paper, and there was more gravity than usual in his tone. "I haven't told you everything, but it's evidently time I did. Phillips was mixed up with bad associates, the very worst in town—"

"So he told me."

"He couldn't have told you what I'm about to. He had a most unfortunate affair with a dance-hall girl—one that reflects no credit upon him. He was on the straight path to ruin and going at a gallop, drinking, gambling—everything."

"All the more reason for trying to save him. Remember, you were pretty wild yourself."

"Wait! I don't say he's guilty of this charge; I want to believe him innocent—I'd like to help prove it. For that very reason it occurred to me that Laure—she's the dance-hall girl—might throw some light on the matter, so I put Rock to work on her. Well, his report wasn't pleasant. The girl talked, but what she said didn't help Phillips. She confessed that he'd been stealing right along and giving her the money."

Mrs. Cavendish was shocked, incredulous. After a moment, however, she shook her head positively and exclaimed, "I don't believe a word of it."

"She's going to swear to it."

"Her oath would be no better than her word—"

"Good Lord!" the colonel cried, testily. "Has this young imp completely hypnotized you women? The Kirby girl is frightened to death, and the Countess—well, she told me herself that her husband's jealousy was at the bottom of the whole thing. Laure, in spite of what she said to Rock, is behaving like a mad person. I dropped in at the Rialto this evening and she asked me what was the worst Pierce could expect. I made it strong, purposely, and I thought she'd faint. No, it's a nasty affair, all through. And, by Jove! to cap the climax, you and Josephine take part in it! I flatter myself that I'm democratic, but— have him here to dine! Gad! That's playing democracy pretty strong."

"It isn't fair to imply that he's nothing more than a ladies' man. They're detestable. The men like Phillips, too."

"True," Cavendish admitted. "He has the God-given faculty of making friends, and for that alone I can forgive him almost anything. It's a wonderful faculty—better than being born lucky or rich or handsome. I'm fond of him, but I've favored him all I can. If I thought Josephine were seriously interested in him—well, I wouldn't feel so friendly." The speaker laughed shortly. "No. The man who claims that girl's attention must be clean through and through. He must stand the acid test."

When his wife silently approved this sentiment the colonel picked up his paper and resumed his reading.

Pierce's friends were indeed uniformly indignant, and without exception they maintained their faith in his innocence; most of them, in fact, actually applied themselves to the task of clearing him of Courteau's charge. But of the

latter the one who applied herself the most
thoughtfully, the most seriously, was the Countess
Courteau. Having reasoned that she herself was
indirectly responsible for his plight, she set about
aiding him in a thoroughly feminine and indirect
manner. It was an unpleasant undertaking; she
took it up with intense abhorrence; it required
her utmost determination to carry it on. Her
plan had formed itself immediately she had learned
what had happened; her meeting with the Count
that evening and her unexpected solicitude, her
unbidden attention to his injury, were a part of
it.' As time went on she assumed an air that
amazed the man. She meekly accepted his reproaches, she submitted to his abuse; cautiously,
patiently she paved the way to a reconciliation.

It was by no means easy, for she and Henri
had long lived in what was little better than a
state of open hostility, and she had been at no
pains to conceal the utter disregard and contempt
she felt for him. He, of course, had resented it;
her change of demeanor now awoke his suspicion.
He was a vain and shallow person; however; his
conceit was thoroughly Latin, and Hilda's perseverance was in a way rewarded. Slowly, grudg-
ingly he gave ground before her subtle advances—
they were, in fact, less advances on her part than
opportunities for him—he experienced a feeling
of triumph and began to assume a masterful air
that was indeed trying to one of her disposition.
Before his friends he boasted that his energetic
defense of his honor had worked a marvel in his

home; in her presence he made bold to take on a swagger and an authority hitherto unknown.

. Hilda stood it, with what cost no one could possibly understand. In some manner she managed to convey the idea that he dominated her and that she cringed spiritually before him. She permitted him occasionally to surprise a look of bewilderment, almost of fright, in her eyes, and this tickled the man immensely. With a fatuous complacency, thoroughly typical, he told himself that she feared and respected him—was actually falling in love with him all over again. When he felt the impulse to scout this idea he went to his mirror and examined himself critically. Why not? he asked himself. He was very pleasing. Women had always been wax in his hands; he had a personality, an air, an irresistible something that had won him many conquests. It seemed not unlikely that Hilda had been shocked into a new and keener realization of his many admirable qualities and was ready to make up, if, or when, he graciously chose to permit her.

On the very evening that Colonel Cavendish and his wife were discussing Pierce Phillips' affair, Courteau, feeling in a particularly jubilant mood, decided to put the matter to a test; therefore he surprised his wife by walking into her room unannounced.

"My dear," he began, "it's high time we had a talk."

"Indeed!" said she. "What about?"

"About you, about me, about our affairs. Are

we husband and wife or are we not? I ask you."

With a queer flicker of her eyelids she answered: "Why—of course. You have appeared to forget it sometimes, but—"

"No reproaches, please. The past is gone. Neither of us is without blame. You've had your fling, too, but I've shown you that I'm made of stern stuff and will tolerate no further foolishness. I am a different Courteau than you ever knew. I've had my rebirth. Now then, our present mode of life is not pleasing to me, for I'm a fellow of spirit. Think of me—in the attitude of a dependent!"

"I share generously with you. I give you money—"

"The very point," he broke in, excitedly. "You give; I accept. You direct; I obey. It must end now, at once. I cannot play the accompaniment while you sing. Either I close my eyes to your folly and forgive, utterly—either we become man and wife again and I assume leadership—or I make different plans for the future."

"Just what do you propose, Henri?"

The fellow shrugged. "I offer you a reconciliation; that, to begin with. You've had your lesson and I flatter myself that you see me in a new light. The brave can afford to be generous. I—well, I've always had a feeling for you; I've never been blind to your attractions, my dear. Lately I've even experienced something of the—

414

er—the old spell. Understand me? It's a fact. I'm actually taken with you, Hilda; I have the fire of an impetuous lover."

Courteau's eyes gleamed; there was an unusual warmth to his gaze and a vibrance to his tone. He curled his mustache, he swelled his chest, he laughed lightly but deeply. "What do you say, eh? I'm not altogether displeasing. No? You see something in me to admire? I thrill you? Confess."

The wife lowered her eyes. "You have some power—" she murmured.

"Power! Precisely." The Count nodded and there was a growing vivacity and sparkle to him. "That is my quality—a power to charm, a power to achieve, a power to triumph. Well, I choose now to win you again for myself. It is my whim. To rekindle a love which one has lost is a test of any man's power, *n'est-ce pas?* You are fond of me. I see it. Am I not right, my sweet?"

He laid his soft white hands upon his wife's shoulders and bent an ardent gaze upon her. Hilda faced him with an odd smile; her cheeks were white, her ice-blue eyes were very wide and bright and they held a curious expression.

"Come! A kiss!" he persisted. "Oho! You tremble, you shrink like a maiden. I, too, am exhilarated, but—" With a chuckle he folded her in his embrace and she did not resist. After a moment he resumed: "This is quite too amusing. I wish my friends to see and to understand. Put on your prettiest dress—"

"What for?"

"We are going down-town. We shall celebrate our reunion—we shall drink to it publicly. All Dawson shall take note. They have said, 'Courteau is a loafer, a ne'er-do-well, and he permits another to win his wife away from him.' I propose to show them."

"You mean you propose to show me off. Is that it? Another conquest, eh?"

"Have it as you will. I—"

"I won't go," Hilda cried, furiously. She freed herself from his arms. "You know I won't go. You'd like to parade me in the places you frequent —saloons, dance - halls, gambling - houses. The idea!"

"You won't? Tut, tut! What is this?" Courteau cried, angrily. "Rebellious so soon? Is this recent change of demeanor assumed? Have you been fooling me?"

"What change?" the woman parried. "I don't know—"

"Oh yes, you do! For the first time in years you have treated me as a husband should be treated; half-measures will no longer satisfy me. We have arrived at the show-up. Are you a miserable Delilah or—"

"Please don't ask me to go out with you, Henri," the woman pleaded, in genuine distress, now that she saw he was in earnest. "To be paraded like an animal on a chain! Think of my feelings."

"Indeed! Think of mine," he cried. "This

is my hour, my triumph; I propose to make it complete. Now that I carefully consider it, I will put you to the test. You've had a fine time; if you pay a price for it, whose fault is that? No! One must be cruel to be kind."

"Cruel! Kind!" Hilda sneered. "It merely pleases you to humiliate me."

"Very well!" blazed the Count. "If it pleases me, so be it. That is my attitude now and henceforth—my will is to be law. Come! Your prettiest dress and your prettiest smile, for we celebrate. Yes, and money, too; I'm as poverty-ridden as usual. We will treat my friends, we will gamble here and there, we will watch the shows to an accompaniment of popping corks so that every one shall see us and say: 'Yonder is Courteau and his wife. They have made up and she adores him like a mistress. *Parbleu!* The man has a way with women, eh!' It shall be a great night for me."

"Are you really serious?"

Courteau stamped his felt-shod foot. "Anger me no more."

Hilda's face was colorless, her eyes were still glowing with that peculiar light of defiance, of desperation, of curiosity; nevertheless, she turned away and began to dress herself.

Courteau was not disappointed. His appearance in the river-front resorts, accompanied by his wife, created a sensation indeed. And Hilda's bearing, under the circumstances, added to his gratification, for, now that the die was cast, she

surrendered completely, she clung to him as if
feeling a new dependence, and this filled his cup
to overflowing.   It was an outrageous thing to do;
no one save a Courteau would have thought of
subjecting the woman who bore his name to such
a humiliation.   But he was a perverse individual;
his mind ran in crooked courses; he took a bizarre
delight in the unusual, and morality of the common sort he knew not.   To smirch her, even a
little bit, to subject her to seeming disgrace, not
only taught her a lesson, but also united them
more closely, so he told himself.   That he had the
ability to compel her to do anything against her
will immensely tickled his vanity, for her stubborn independence had always been a trial to
him.   He knew that her social status was not of
the highest; nevertheless, her reputation was far
better than his, and among all except the newest
arrivals in Dawson she bore a splendid name.   To
be, himself, the cause of blackening that name,
in order to match his own, gratified his feelings of
resentment.   All in all, it was a night of nights
for him and he was at no pains to conceal his
satisfaction.   From one place to another he led
her, taking malicious enjoyment from the distress
he caused.

Courteau was not loud nor blatant; nevertheless, his triumphant demeanor, his proprietary
air, fairly shouted the fact that he had tamed this
woman and was exhibiting her against her in-
clinations.   At every bar he forced her to drink
with him and with his friends; he even called up

barroom loafers whom he did not know and introduced them with an elaborate flourish. The money he spent was hers, of course, but he squandered it royally, leaving a trail of empty champagne-bottles behind. Champagne, at this time, sold for twenty dollars a quart and, although Hilda saw her earnings melting away with appalling rapidity, she offered no protest. Together they flung their chips broadcast upon the gambling-tables, and their winnings, which were few, went to buy more popularity with the satellites who trailed them.

As time passed and Hilda continued to meet the test, her husband's satisfaction gained a keener edge. He beamed, he strutted, he twisted his mustache to needle-points. She was a thorough-bred, that he assured himself. But, after all, why shouldn't she do this for him? The women with whom he was accustomed to associate would not have counted such an evening as this a sacrifice, and, even had they so considered it, he was in the habit of exacting sacrifices from women. They liked it; it proved their devotion.

Her subjugation was made complete when he led her into a box at the Rialto Theater and insisted upon the two McCaskeys joining them. The brothers at first declined, but by this time Courteau's determination carried all before it.

Joe halted him outside the box door, however, to inquire into the meaning of the affair.

"It means this," the Count informed him. "I have effected a complete reconciliation with my adorable wife. Women are all alike—they fear the iron, they kiss the hand that smites them. . I have made her my obedient slave, *mon ami*. That's what it means."

"It don't look good to me," Joe said, morosely. "She's got an ace buried somewhere."

"Eh? What are you trying to say?"

"I've got a hunch she's salving you, Count. She's stuck on Phillips, like I told you, and she's trying to get a peek at your hole card."

It was characteristic of Courteau that he should take instant offense at this reflection upon his sagacity, this doubt of his ability as a charmer.

"You insult my intelligence," he cried, stiffly, "and, above all, I possess intelligence. You—do not. No. You are coarse, you are gross. I am full of sentiment—"

"Rats!" McCaskey growled. "I get that way myself sometimes. Sentiment like yours costs twenty dollars a quart. But this ain't the time for a spree; we got business on our hands."

The Count eyed his friend with a frown. "It is a personal affair and concerns our business not in the least. I am a revengeful person; I have pride and I exact payment from those who wound it. I brought my wife here as a punishment and I propose to make her drink with you. Your company is not agreeable at any time, my friend, and she does you an honor—"

"Cut out that tony talk," Joe said, roughly. "You're a broken-hipped stiff and you're trying to grab her bank-roll. Don't you s'pose I'm on?

My company was all right until you got your hand in the hotel cash-drawer; now I'm coarse. Maybe she's on the square—she fell for you once —but I bet she's working you. Make sure of this, my high and mighty nobleman"—for emphasis the speaker laid a heavy hand upon the Count's shoulder and thrust his disagreeable face closer—"that you keep your mouth shut. Savvy? Don't let her sweat you—"

The admonitory words ended abruptly, for the door of the box reopened and Joe found the Countess Courteau facing him. For an instant their glances met and in her eyes the man saw an expression uncomfortably reminiscent of that day at Sheep Camp when she had turned public wrath upon his brother Jim's head. But the look was fleeting; she turned it upon her husband, and the Count, with an apology for his delay, entered the box, dragging McCaskey with him.

Frank, it appeared, shared his brother's suspicions; the two exchanged glances as Joe entered; then when the little party had adjusted itself to the cramped quarters they watched the Countess curiously, hoping to analyze her true intent. But in this they were unsuccessful. She treated both of them with a cool, impartial formality, quite natural under the circumstances, but in no other way did she appear conscious of that clash on the Chilkoot trail. It was not a pleasant situation at best, and Joe especially was ill at ease, but Courteau continued his spendthrift rôle, keeping the waiters busy, and under the influence of his potations the elder McCaskey soon regained some of his natural sang-froid. All three men drank liberally, and by the time the lower floor had been cleared for dancing they were in a hilarious mood. They laughed loudly, they shouted greetings across to other patrons of the place, they flung corks at the whirling couples below.

Meanwhile, they forced the woman to imbibe with them. Joe, in spite of his returning confidence, kept such close watch of her that she could not spill her glass into the bucket, except rarely. Hilda hated alcohol and its effect; she was not accustomed to drinking. As she felt her intoxication mounting she became fearful that the very medium upon which she had counted for success would prove to be her undoing. Desperately she battled to retain her wits. More than once, with a reckless defiance utterly foreign to her preconceived plans, she was upon the point of hurling the bubbling contents of her glass into the flushed faces about her and telling these men how completely she was shamming, but she managed to resist the temptation. That she felt such an impulse at all made her fearful of committing some action equally rash, of dropping some word that would prove fatal.

It was a hideous ordeal. She realized that already the cloak of decency, of respectability, which she had been at such pains to preserve during these difficult years, was gone, lost for good and all. She had made herself a Lady Godiva; by this night of conspicuous revelry she had undone everything. Not only had she condoned the sins and the shortcomings of her dissolute husband, but also she had put herself on a level with him and with the fallen women of the town—his customary associates. Courteau had done this to her. It had been his proposal. She could have throttled him where he sat.

The long night dragged on interminably. Like leeches the two McCaskeys clung to their prodigal host, and not until the early hours of morning, when the Count had become sodden, sullen, stupefied, and when they were in a condition little better, did they permit him to leave them. How Hilda got him home she scarcely knew, for she, too, had all but lost command of her senses. There were moments when she fought unavailingly against a mental numbness, a stupor that rolled upward and suffused her like a cloud of noxious vapors, leaving her knees weak, her hands clumsy, her vision blurred; again waves of deathly illness surged over her. Under and through it all, however, her subconscious will to conquer remained firm. Over and over she told herself:

"I'll have the truth and then—I'll make him pay."

Courteau followed his wife into her room, and there his maudlin manner changed. He roused himself and smiled at her fatuously; into his eyes flamed a desire, into his cheeks came a deeper flush. He pawed at her caressingly; he voiced thick, passionate protestations. Hilda had expected nothing less; it was for this that she had bled her flesh and crucified her spirit these many hours.

".You're—wonderful woman," the man mumbled as he swayed with her in his arms. "Got all the old charm and more. Game, too!" He laughed foolishly, then in drunken gravity asserted: "Well, I'm the man, the stronger vessel. To turn hate into love, that—"

".You've taken your price. You've had your hour," she told him. Her head was thrown back, her eyes were closed, her teeth were clenched as if in a final struggle for self-restraint.

Courteau pressed his lips to hers; then in a sudden frenzy he crushed her closer and fell to kissing her cheeks, her neck, her throat. He mistook her shudder of abhorrence for a thrill responsive to his passion, and hiccoughed:

"You're mine again, all mine, and—I'm mad about you. I'm aflame. This is like the night of our marriage, what?"

"Are you satisfied, now that you've made me suffer? Do you still imagine I care for that foolish boy?"

"Phillips? Bah! A noisy swine." Again the Count chuckled, but this time his merriment ran away with him until he shook and until tears came to his eyes.

Without reason Hilda joined in his laughter. Together they stood rocking, giggling, snickering, as if at some excruciating jest.

"He—he tried to steal you—from me. From

me. Imagine it! Then he struck me. Well, where is he now, eh?"

"I never dreamed that you cared enough for me to—do what you did. To risk so much."

"Risk?"

Hilda nodded, and her loose straw-gold hair brushed Courteau's cheek. "Don't pretend any longer. I knew from the start. But you were jealous. When a woman loses the power to excite jealousy it's a sign she's growing old and ugly and losing her fire. She can face anything except that."

"Fire!" Henri exclaimed. "*Parbleu!* Don't I know you to be a volcano?"

"How did you manage the affair—that fellow's ruin? It frightens me to realize that you can accomplish such things."

The Count pushed his wife away. "What are you talking about?" he demanded.

"Oh, very well! Carry it out if you wish," she said, with a careless shrug. "But you're not fooling me in the least. On the contrary, I admire your spirit. Now then, I'm thirsty. And you are, too." With a smile she evaded his outstretched arms and left the room. She was back in a moment with a bottle and two glasses. The latter she filled; her own she raised with a gesture, and Courteau blindly followed suit.

In spite of his deep intoxication the man still retained the embers of suspicion, and when she spoke of Pierce Phillips they began to glow and threatened to burst into flame. Cunningly, per-

sistently she played upon him, however. She en-
ticed, she coquetted, she cajoled; she maddened
him with her advances; she teased him with her
repulses; she drugged him with her smiles, her
fragrant charms. Time and again he was upon
the point of surrender, but caught himself in time.

She won at last. She dragged the story from
him, bit by bit, playing upon his vanity, until he
gabbled boastfully and took a crapulent delight
in repeating the details. It was a tale distorted
and confused, but the truth was there. She
made an excuse to leave him, finally, and remained
out of the room for a long time. When she returned it was to find him sprawled across her bed
and fast asleep.

For a moment she held dizzily to the bedpost
and stared down at him. Her mask had slipped
now, her face was distorted with loathing, and so
deep were her feelings that she could not bear
to touch him, even to cover him over. Leaving
him spread-eagled as he was, she staggered out
of his unclean presence.

Hilda was deathly sick; objects were gyrating
before .her eyes; she felt a hideous nightmare
sensation of unreality, and was filled with an
intense contempt, a tragic disgust for herself.
Pausing at the foot of the stairs, she strove to
gather herself together; then slowly, passionately she cursed the name of Pierce Phillips.

CHAPTER XXVI

TOM LINTON and Jerry Quirk toiled slowly up the trail toward their cabin. Both men were bundled thickly in clothing, both bewhiskered visages bore grotesque breath-masks of ice; even their eyebrows were hoary with frost. The partners were very tired.

Pausing in the chip-littered space before their door, they gazed down the trail to a mound of gravel which stood out raw and red against the universal whiteness. This mound was in the form of a truncated cone and on its level top was a windlass and a pole bucket track. From beneath the windlass issued a cloud of smoke which mounted in billows, as if breathed forth from a concealed chimney—smoke from the smothered drift fires laid against the frozen face of pay dirt forty feet below the surface. Evidently this fire was burning to suit the partners; after watching it a moment, Tom took a buck-saw and fell stiffly to work upon a dry spruce log which lay on the saw-buck; Jerry spat on his mittens and began to split the blocks as they fell.

Darkness was close at hand, but both men were so fagged that they found it impossible to hurry. Neither did they speak. Patiently, silently they sawed and chopped, then carried the wood into the chilly cabin; while one lit the lamp and went for a sack of ice, the other kindled a fire. These tasks accomplished, by mutual consent, but still without exchanging a word, they approached the table. From the window-sill Tom took a coin and balanced it upon his thumb and forefinger; then, in answer to his bleak, inquiring glance, Jerry nodded and he snapped the piece into the air. While it was still spinning Jerry barked, sharply:

"Tails!"

Both gray heads bent and near-sightedly examined the coin.

"Tails she is," Tom announced. He replaced the silver piece, crossed the room to his bunk, seated himself upon it, and remained there while Jerry, with a sudden access of cheerfulness, hustled to the stove, warmed himself, and then began culinary preparations.

These preparations were simple, but precise; also they were deliberate. Jerry cut one slice of ham, he measured out just enough coffee for one person, he opened one can of corn, and he mixed a half-pan of biscuits. Tom watched him from beneath a frown, meanwhile tugging moodily at the icicles which still clung to his lips. His corner of the cabin was cold, hence it was a painful process. When he had disposed of the last lump and when he could no longer restrain his irritation, he broke out:

"Of course you had to make *bread,* didn't you? Just because you know I'm starving."

"It come tails, didn't it?" Jerry inquired, with aggravating pleasantness. "It ain't my fault you're starving, and you got all night to cook what *you* want—after I'm done. *I* don't care if you bake a layer cake and freeze ice-cream. You can put your front feet in the trough and champ your swill; you can root and waller in it, for all of *me.* *I* won't hurry you, not in the least."

"It's come tails every time lately," grumbled the former speaker.

Jerry giggled. "I always was right lucky, except in pickin' pardners," he declared. In a cracked and tuneless voice he began humming a roundelay, evidently intended to ᵗ᷆ᵛ and contentment.

Unable longer to wit᷆'
Tom secured for hʲ
and with this hᵣ
starvation. B᷉
endeavor, fᵣ'
the thing '
testily:
"My ᵣ
phonog᷈
damn'
the iᵣ
"ᶜ
ᵣ
don'
pler
sou

that pilot-bread if your teeth is loose. You can boil yourself a pot of mush—when your turn comes. You got a free hand. As for me, I eat anything I want to and I *sing* anything I want to whenever I want to, and I'd like to see anybody stop me. We don't have to toss up for turns at singin'." More loudly he raised his high-pitched voice; ostentatiously he rattled his dishes.

Tom settled back in exasperated silence, but as time wore on and his hungry nostrils were assailed with the warm, tantalizing odor of frying ham fat he fidgeted nervously.

Having prepared a meal to his liking, Jerry set the table with a single plate, cup, and saucer, then seated himself with a luxurious grunt. He ate sl⌐ ⌐olled every mouthful with relish; ⌐ ⌐alculated deliberation; he blow loudly upon his ounds that in them- an insult to his up his inter- he last scrap,

id-motion, ed, then

light you long

get

fed up and my teeth picked I got all my dishes to wash."

"That wasn't our arrangement."

"It was so."

"You'll eat all night," Tom complained, almost tearfully. "You'll set there and gorge till you bust."

"That's my privilege. I don't aim to swaller my grub whole. I'm shy a few teeth and some of the balance don't meet, so I can't consume vittles like I was a pulp-mill. I didn't start this row—"

"Who did?"

"Now ain't that a fool question?" Jerry leaned back comfortably and began an elaborate vacuum-cleaning process of what teeth he retained. "Who starts all our rows, if I don't? No. I'm as easy-going as a greased eel, and 'most anybody can get along with me, but, tread on my tail and I swop ends, pronto. That's me. I go my own even way, but I live up to my bargains and I see to it that others do the same. You get the hell away from that stove!"

Tom abandoned his purpose, and with the resignation of a martyr returned to teeter upon the edge of his bunk. He remained there, glum, malevolent, watchful, until his cabin-mate had leisurely cleared the table, washed and put away his dishes; then with a sigh of fat repletion, unmistakably intended as a provocation, the tormentor lit his pipe and stretched himself luxuriously upon his bed.

Even then Tom made no move. He merely

glowered at the recumbent figure. Jerry blew a
cloud of smoke, then waved a generous gesture.

"Now then, fly at it, Mr. Linton," he said,
sweetly. "I've et my fill; I've had an ample
sufficiency; I'm through and in for the night."

"Oh no, you ain't! You get up and wash that
skillet."

Mr. Quirk started guiltily.

"Hustle your creaking joints and scrub it
out."

"Pshaw! I only fried a slice—"

"Scrub it!" Linton ordered.

This command Jerry obeyed, although it neces-
sitated heating more water, a procedure which, of
course, he maliciously prolonged. "Waited till I
was all spread out, didn't you," he sneered, as
he stooped over the wood-box. "That's like you.
Some people are so small-calibered they'd rattle
around in a gnat's bladder like a mustard seed in
a bass drum."

"I'm particular who I eat after," Tom said,
"so be sure you scrub it clean."

"Thought you'd spoil my smoke. Well, I can
smoke standin' on my head and enjoy it." There
was a silence, broken only by the sound of Jerry's
labors. At last he spoke: "Once again I repeat
what I told you yesterday. I took the words
out of your own mouth. You said the woman
was a hellion—"

"I never did. Even if I had I wouldn't allow
a comparative stranger to apply such an epithet
to a member of my family."

"You did say it. And she ain't a member of your family."

Tom's jaws snapped. "If patience is a virtue," he declared, in quivering anger, "I'll slide into heaven on skids. Assassination ought not to be a crime; it's warranted, like abating a nuisance; it ain't even a misdemeanor—sometimes. She was a noble woman—"

"Hellion! I got it on the authority of her own husband—you!"

Tom rose and stamped over to the stove; he slammed its door and clattered the coffee-pot to drown this hateful persistence. Having had the last word, as usual, Jerry retreated in satisfaction to his bed and stretched his aching frame upon it.

The dingy cabin was fragrant with the odor of cooking food for a second time that evening when the sound of voices and a knock at the door brought both old men to their feet.

Before they could answer, the door flew open and in and out of the frosty evening came Rouletta Kirby and 'Poleon Doret. The girl's cheeks were rosy, her eyes were sparkling; she warmly greeted first one partner, then the other. Pausing, she sniffed the air hungrily.

"Goody!" she cried. "We're just in time. And we're as hungry as bears."

"Dis gal 'ain't never got 'nough to eat since she's seeck in W'ite 'Orse," 'Poleon laughed. "For las' hour she's been sayin': 'Hurry! Hurry! We goin' be late.' I 'mos' keel dem dog."

Linton's seamed face softened; it cracked into

a smile of genuine pleasure; there was real hospitality and welcome in his voice when he said:

"You're in luck, for sure. Lay off your things and pull up to the fire. It won't take a jiffy to parlay the ham and coffee—one calls three, as they say. No need to ask if you're well; you're prettier than ever, and some folks would call that impossible."

Jerry nodded in vigorous agreement. "You're as sweet as a bunch of jessamine, Letty. Why, you're like a breath of spring! What brought you out to see us, anyhow?"

"Dat's long story," 'Poleon answered. "*Sapré!* We got plenty talkin' to do. Letty she's goin' he'p you mak' de supper now, an' I fix dem dog. We goin' camp wit' you all night. Golly! We have beeg tam."

The new-comers had indeed introduced a breath of new, clean air. Of a sudden the cabin had brightened, it was vitalized, it was filled with a magic purpose and good humor. Rouletta flung aside her furs and bustled into the supper preparations. Soon the meal was ready. The first pause in her chatter came when she set the table for four and when Jerry protested that he had already dined.

The girl paused, plate in hand. "Then we *were* late and you didn't tell us," she pouted, reproachfully.

"No. I got through early, but Tom—he was held up in the traffic. You see, I don't eat much, anyhow. I just nibble around and take a cold snack where I can get it."

"And you let him!" Rouletta turned to chide the other partner. "He'll come down sick, Tom, and you'll have to nurse him again. If you boys won't learn to keep regular meal hours I'll have to come out and run your house for you. Shall I? Speak up. What am I offered?"

Now this was the most insidious flattery. "Boys" indeed! Jerry chuckled, Tom looked up from the stove and his smoke-blue eyes were twinkling.

"I can't offer you more 'n a half-interest in the 'lay.' That's all I own."

"Is dis claim so reech lak people say?" 'Poleon inquired. "Dey're tellin' me you goin' mak' hondred t'ousan' dollar."

"We're just breastin' out—cross-cuttin' the streak, but—looky." Jerry removed a baking-powder can from the window-shelf and out of it he poured a considerable amount of coarse gold which the visitors examined with intense interest. "Them's our paunin's."

"How splendid!" Rouletta cried.

"I been clamorin' to hire some men and take life easy. I say put on a gang and h'ist it out, but"—Jerry shot a glance at his partner—"people tell me I'm vi'lent an' headstrong. They say, 'Prove it up.'"

Linton interrupted by loudly exclaiming, "Come and get it, strangers, or I'll throw it out and wash the skillet."

435

Supper was welcome, but, despite the diners' preoccupation with it, despite Tom's and Jerry's effort to conceal the fact of their estrangement, it became evident that something was amiss. Rouletta finally sat back and, with an accusing glance, demanded to know what was the matter.

The old men met her eyes with an assumption of blank astonishment.

"'Fess up," she persisted. "Have you boys been quarreling again?"

"Who? Us? Why, not exactly—"

"We sort of had words, mebbe."

"What about?"

There was an awkward, an ominous silence. "That," Mr. Linton said, in a harsh and firm voice, "is something I can't discuss. It's a personal matter."

"It ain't personal with me," Jerry announced, carelessly. "We was talkin' about Tom's married life and I happened to say—"

"*Don't!*" Linton's cry of warning held a threat. "Don't spill your indecencies in the presence of this child or—I'll hang the frying-pan around your neck. The truth is," he told Letty, "there's no use trying to live with a horn' toad. I've done my best. I've let him defame me to my face and degrade me before strangers, but he remains hostyle to every impulse in my being; he picks and pesters and poisons me a thousand times a day. And snore! My God! You ought to hear him at night."

Strangely enough, Mr. Quirk did not react to

436

this passionate outburst. On the contrary, he bore it with indications of a deep and genuine satisfaction.

"He's workin' up steam to propose another divorce," said the object of Tom's tirade.

"That I am. Divorce is the word," Linton growled.

"*Whoop-ee!*" Jerry uttered a high-pitched shout. "I been waitin' for that. I wanted him to say it. Now I'm free as air and twice as light. You heard him propose it, didn't you?"

"W'at you goin' do 'bout dis lay?" 'Poleon inquired.

"Split her," yelled Jerry.

"Dis cabin, too?"

"Sure. Slam a partition right through her."

"We won't slam no partition anywhere," Tom declared. "Think I'm going to lay awake every night listening to distant bugles? No. We'll pull her apart, limb from limb, and divvy the logs. It's a pest-house, anyhow. I'll burn my share."

Tom's positive refusal even to permit mention of the cause of the quarrel rendered efforts at a reconciliation difficult; 'Poleon's and Rouletta's attempts at badinage, therefore, were weak failures, and their conversation met with only the barest politeness. Now that the truth had escaped, neither partner could bring himself to a serious consideration of anything except his own injuries. They exchanged evil glances, they came into direct verbal contact only seldom, and when they did it was to clash as flint upon steel. No statement of the one was sufficiently conservative, sufficiently broad, to escape a sneer and an immediate refutation from the other. Evidently the rift was deep and was widening rapidly.

Of course the facts were revealed eventually— Rouletta had a way of winning confidences, a subtle, sweet persuasiveness—they had to do with the former Mrs. Linton, that shadowy female figure which had fallen athwart Tom's early life. It seemed that Jerry had referred to her as a "hellion."

Now the injured husband himself had often applied even more disparaging terms to the lady in question, therefore the visitors were puzzled at his show of rabid resentment; the most they could make out of it was that he claimed the right of disparagement as a personal and exclusive privilege, and considered detraction out of the lips of another a trespass upon his intimate private affairs, an aspersion and an insult. The wife of a man's bosom, he averred, was sacred; any creature who breathed disrespect of her into the ears of her husband was lower than a hole in the ground and lacked the first qualifications of a friend, a gentleman, or a citizen.

Jerry, on the other hand, would not look at the matter in this light. Tom had called the woman a "hellion," therefore he was privileged to do the same, and any denial of that privilege was an iniquitous encroachment upon *his* sacred rights. Those rights he proposed to safeguard, to fight for if necessary. He would shed his last drop of blood in their defense. No cantankerous old grouch could refuse him free speech and get away with it.

"You're not really mad at each other," Rouletta told them.

"*Ain't* we?" they hoarsely chorused.

She shook her head. "You need a change, that's all. As a matter of fact, your devotion to each other is about the most beautiful, the most touching, thing I know. You'd lay down your lives for each other; you're like man and wife, and well you know it."

"Who? *Us?*" Jerry was aghast. "Which one of us is the woman? I been insulted by experts, but none of 'em ever called me 'Mrs. Linton.' She was a tough customer, a regular hellion—"

"He's off again!" Tom growled. "Me lay down *my* life for a squawking parrot! He'll repeat that pet word for the rest of time if I don't wring his neck."

"Mebbe so you lak hear 'bout some other feller's trouble," 'Poleon broke in, diplomatically. "Wal, *ma sœur* she's come to you for help, queeck."

Both old men became instantly alert. "You in trouble?" Tom demanded of the girl. "Who's been hurting you, I'd like to know?"

Jerry, too, leaned forward, and into his widening eyes came a stormy look. "Sure! Has one of them crawlin' worms got fresh with you, Letty? Say—!" He reached up and removed his six-shooter from its nail over his bed.

Rouletta set them upon the right track. Swiftly but earnestly she recited the nature and the circumstances of the misfortune that had over-taken Pierce Phillips, and of the fruitless efforts his friends were making in his behalf. She concluded by asking her hearers to go his bail.

"Why, sure!" Linton exclaimed, with manifest relief. "That's easy. I'll go it, if they'll take me."

"There you are, hoggin' the curtain, as usual," Jerry protested. "I'll go his bail myself. I got him in trouble at Sheep Camp. I owe him—"

"I've known the boy longer than you have. Besides, I'm a family man; I know the anguish of a parent's heart—"

"Lay off that 'family' stuff," howled Mr. Quirk. "You know it riles me. I could of had as much of a family as you had if I'd wanted to. You'd think it give you some sort of privilege. Why, ever since we set up with Letty you've assumed a fatherly air even to her, and you act like I was a plumb outsider. You remind me of a hen—settin' on every loose door-knob you find."

"If you'd lay off the 'family' subject we'd get along better."

Once again the fray was on; it raged inter-mittently throughout the evening; it did not die out until bedtime put an end to it.

Rouletta and her three companions were late in reaching town on the following day, for they awakened to find a storm raging, and in conse-quence the trails were heavy. Out of this white smother they plodded just as the lights of Dawson were beginning to gleam. Leaving the men at the Barracks, the girl proceeded to her hotel. She had changed out of her trail clothes and was upon the point of hurrying down-town to her work when she encountered Hilda Courteau.

"Where in the world have you been?" the latter inquired.

"Nowhere, in the world," Rouletta smiled. "I've been quite out of it." Then she told of her and 'Poleon's trip to the mines and of their success. "Pierce will be at liberty inside of an hour," she declared.

"Well, I've—learned the truth."

Rouletta started; eagerly she clutched at the elder woman. "What? You mean—?"

"Yes. I wrung it out of Courteau. He confessed."

"It *was* a frame-up—a plot? Oh, my dear—!"

"Exactly. But don't get hysterical. I'm the one to do that. What a night, what a day I've put in!" The speaker shuddered, and Rouletta noticed for the first time how pale, how ill she looked.

"Then Pierce is free already? He's out—?"

"Not yet. I'll tell you everything if you'll promise not to breathe a word, not to interfere until Henri has a chance to square himself. I— think I've earned the right to demand that much. I told you the whole thing was counterfeit—was the work of Joe McCaskey. I couldn't believe Henri was up to such villainy. He's dissolute, weak, vain—anything you choose—but he's not

441

voluntarily criminal. Well, I went to work on him. I pretended to—" the Countess again shivered with disgust. "Oh, you saw what I was doing. I hated myself, but there was no choice. Things came to a climax last night. I don't like to talk about it—think about it—but you're bound to hear. I consented to go out with him. He dragged me through the dance-halls and the saloons—made me drink with him, publicly, and with the scum of the town." Noting the expression on her hearer's face, the Countess laughed shortly, mirthlessly. "Shocking, wasn't it? Low, indecent, wretched? That's what everybody is saying. Dawson is humming with it. God! How he humiliated me! But I loosened his tongue. I got most of the details—not all, but enough. It was late, almost daylight, before I succeeded. He slept all day, stupefied, and so did I, when I wasn't too ill.

"He remembered something about it, he had some shadowy recollection of talking too much. When he woke up he sent for me. Then we had it. He denied everything, of course. He lied and he twisted, but I'm the stronger—always have been. I beat him down, as usual. I could have felt sorry for the poor wretch only for what he had put me through. He went out not long ago."

"Where to? Tell me—"

"To the Police—to Colonel Cavendish. I gave him the chance to make a clean breast of everything and save his hide, if possible. If he weakens I'll take the bit in my teeth."

442

Rouletta stood motionless for a moment; then in deep emotion she exclaimed: "I'm so glad! And yet it must have been a terrible sacrifice. I think I understand how you must loathe yourself. It was a very generous thing to do, however. Not many women could have risen to it."

"I—hope he doesn't make me tell. I haven't much pride left, but—I'd like to save what remains, for you can imagine what Cavendish will think. A wife betraying her husband for her—for another man! What a story for those women on the hill!"

Impulsively Rouletta bent forward and kissed the speaker. "Colonel Cavendish will understand. He's a man of honor. But, after all, when a woman really—cares, there's a satisfaction, a compensation, in sacrifice, no matter how great."

Hilda Courteau's eyes were misty, their dark-fringed lids trembled wearily shut. "Yes," she nodded, "I suppose so. Bitter and sweet! When a woman of my sort, my age and experience, lets herself really care, she tastes both. All I can hope is that Pierce never learns what he made me pay for loving him. He wouldn't understand —yet." She opened her eyes again and met the earnest gaze bent upon her. "I dare say you think I feel the same toward him as you do, that I want him, that I'm hungry for him. Well, I'm not. I'm 'way past that. I've been through fire, and fire purifies. Now run along, child. I'm sure everything will come out right."

The earlier snowfall had diminished when

Rouletta stepped out into the night, but a gusty, boisterous wind had risen and this filled the air with blinding clouds of fine, hard particles, whirled up from the streets, and the girl was forced to wade through newly formed drifts that rose over the sidewalks, in places nearly to her knees. The wind flapped her garments and cut her bare cheeks like a knife; when she pushed her way into the Rialto and stamped the snow from her feet her face was wet with tears; but they were frost tears. She dried them quickly and with a song in her heart she hurried back to the lunch-counter and climbed upon her favorite stool. There it was that Doret and his two elderly companions found her.

"Well, we sprung him," Tom announced.

"All we done was sign on the dotted line," Jerry explained. "But, say, if that boy hops out of town he'll cost us a lot of money."

"How's he going to hop out?" Tom demanded. "That's the hell of this country—there's no getting away."

Jerry snorted derisively. "No gettin' away? What are you talkin' about? Ain't the Boundary within ninety miles? 'Ain't plenty of people made get-aways? All they need is a dog-team and a few hours' start of the Police."

"Everyt'ing's all fix'," 'Poleon told his sister. "I had talk wit' Pierce. He ain't comin' back here no more."

"Not coming back?" the girl exclaimed.

Doret met her startled gaze. "Not in dis kin'

of place. He's cut 'em out for good. I mak'
him promise."

"A touch of jail ain't a bad thing for a harum-
scarum kid," Tom volunteered, as he finished
giving his supper order. "It's a cold compress—
takes down the fever—"

"Nothing of the sort," Jerry asserted. "Jails
is a total waste of time. I don't believe in 'em.
You think this boy's tamed, do you? Well, I
talked with him, an' all I got to say is this: keep
Courteau away from him or there's one Count
you'll lose count of. The boy's got pizen in him,
an' I don't blame him none. If I was him I'd
make that Frog hop. You hear me."

'Poleon met Rouletta's worried glance with a
reassuring smile. "I been t'inkin' 'bout dat, too.
W'at you say I go pardners wit' him, eh? I got
dog-team an' fine claim on hilltop. S'pose I
geeve him half-interes' to go wit' me?"

"*Will* you?" eagerly queried the girl.

"Already I spoke it to him. He say mebbe
so, but firs' he's got li'l biznesse here."

"Of course! His case. But that will be cleared
up. Mark what I say. Yes"—Rouletta nodded
happily—"take him with you, 'Poleon—out where
things are clean and healthy and where he can
get a new start. Oh, you make me very happy!"

The woodsman laid a big hand gently over
hers. In a low voice he murmured: "Dat's all I
want, *ma sœur*—to mak' you happy. If dat
claim is wort' million dollar' it ain't too much to
pay, but—I'm scare' she's 'noder bum."

445

The song was still sounding in Rouletta's heart when she sat down at the faro-table, and all through the evening it seemed to her that the revelry round about was but an echo of her gladness. Pierce was free, his name was clean. Probably ere this the whole truth was known to the Mounted Police and by to-morrow it would be made public.

Moreover, he and 'Poleon were to be partners. That generous woodsman, because of his affection for her, proposed to take the young fellow into his heart and make a man of him. That was like him—always giving much and taking little. Well, she was 'Poleon's sister. Who could tell what might result from this new union of interests? Of course, there was no pay out there on that mountain-crest, but hard work, honest poverty, an end of these demoralizing surroundings were bound to affect Pierce only for the better. Rouletta blessed the name of Hilda Courteau, who had made this possible, and of 'Poleon Doret, too—'Poleon of the great heart, who loved her so sincerely, so unselfishly. He never failed her; he was a brother, truly—the best, the cheeriest, the most loyal in the world. Rouletta was amazed to realize what a part in her life the French Canadian had played. His sincere affection was about the biggest thing that had come to her, so it seemed.

Occupied with such comforting thoughts, Rouletta failed to note that the evening had passed more quickly than usual and that it was after midnight. When she did realize that fact, she wondered what could have detained Lucky Broad. Promptness was a habit with him; he and Bridges usually reported at least a half-hour ahead of time.

She caught sight of the pair, finally, through the wide archway, and saw that they were surrounded by an excited crowd, a crowd that grew swiftly as some whisper, some intelligence, spread with electric rapidity through the barroom. Yielding to a premonition that something was amiss, Rouletta asked the lookout to relieve her, and, rising, she hurried into the other hall. Even before she had come within sound of Lucky's voice the cause of the general excitement was made known to her. It came in the form of an exclamation, a word or two snatched out of the air. "Courteau!" "Dead!" "Shot—back street —body just found!"

Fiercely Rouletta fought her way through the press, an unvoiced question trembling upon her lips. Broad turned at her first touch.

"Tough, ain't it?" said he. "Me and the Kid stumbled right over him—kicked him out of the snow. We thought he'd been froze."

"We never dreamed he'd been shot till we got him clean down to the drug-store," Bridges supplemented. "Shot in the back, too."

Questions were flying back and forth now. Profiting by the confusion, Rouletta dragged Broad aside and queried, breathlessly:

"Was he dead—quite dead—?"

"Oh, sure!"

"Who—shot him?" The question came with difficulty. Lucky stared at his interrogator queerly, then he shrugged.

"*Quien sabe?* Nobody seen or heard the shooting. He'd been croaked a long while when we found him."

For a moment the two eyed each other silently. "Do you think—?" Rouletta turned her white face toward the cashier's cage.

"More 'n likely. He was bitter—he made a lot of cracks around the Barracks. The first thing the Police said when we notified 'em was, 'Where's Phillips?' We didn't know the boy was out until that very minute or—we'd 'a' done different. We'd 'a' left the Count in the drift and run Phillips down and framed an alibi. Think of us, his pals, turnin' up the evidence!" Lucky breathed an oath.

"Oh, why—?" moaned the girl. "He— It was so useless. Everything was all right. Perhaps—after all, he didn't do it."

"You know him as well as I do. I'm hoping he had better sense, but—he's got a temper. He was always talking about the disgrace."

"Has he gone? Can't you help him? He might make the Boundary—"

Broad shook his head. "No use. It's too late for that. If he's still here me 'n' the Kid will do our best to swear him out of it."

Rouletta swayed, she groped blindly at the bar rail for support, whereupon her companion cried in a low voice:

448

"Here! Brace up, or you'll tip it all off! If he stands pat, how they going to prove anything? The Count's been dead for hours. He was all drifted—"

Broad was interrupted by the Mocha Kid, who entered out of the night at that instant with the announcement: "Well, they got him! Rock found him, and he denies it, but they've got him at the Barracks, puttin' him through the third degree. I don't mind sayin' that Frenchman needed croakin', bad, and they'd ought to give Phillips a vote of thanks and a bronx tablet."

Mocha's words added to Rouletta's terror, for it showed that other minds ran as did hers. Already, it seemed to her, Pierce Phillips had been adjudged guilty. Through the murk of fright, of apprehension in which her thoughts were racing there came a name—'Poleon Doret. Here was deep trouble, grave peril, a threat to her new-found happiness. 'Poleon, her brother, would know what to do, for his head was clear, his judgment was unerring. He never failed her. Blindly she ran for her wraps, hurriedly she flung them on, then plunged out into the night. As she scurried through the street, panic-stricken, beset, one man's name was in her thoughts, but another's was upon her lips. Over and over she kept repeating:

"'Poleon! Oh, 'Poleon!"

CHAPTER XXVII

THE news of Count Courteau's death traveled fast. 'Poleon Doret was not long in hearing of it, and of course he went at once in search of Rouletta. By the time he found her the girl's momentary panic had been succeeded by a quite unnatural self-possession; her perturbation had changed to an intense but governable agitation, and her mind was working with a clarity and a rapidity more than normal. This power of rising to an emergency she had doubtless inherited from her father. "One-armed" Kirby had been a man of resource, and, so long as he remained sober, he had never lost his head. Swiftly the girl told of the instant suspicion that had attached to Phillips and of his prompt apprehension.

"Who done dat shootin' if he don't?" Doret inquired, quickly.

"Joe McCaskey—or Frank," Rouletta answered with positiveness. 'Poleon started. Through the gloom he stared incredulously at the speaker.

"I'm sure of it, now that I've had time to think," the girl declared. "That's why I ran for you. Now listen! I promised not to tell this, but—I must. Courteau confessed to his wife that he and the McCaskeys trumped up that charge against Pierce. They paid Courteau well for his part—or they promised to—and he perjured himself, as did they. Hilda got the truth out of him while he was drunk. Of course he denied it later, but she broke him down, and this evening, just before we got home, he promised to go to Colonel Cavendish and make a clean breast of everything. He went out for that purpose, but—evidently he lacked courage to go through with it. Otherwise how did he come to be on the back streets? The McCaskeys live somewhere back yonder, don't they?"

"Sure!" 'Poleon meditated, briefly. "Mebbe so you're right," he said, finally.

"I know I'm right," Rouletta cried. "The first thing to do is find them. Where are they?"

"I don' see 'em no place."

"Then we must tell the colonel to look them up."

But Doret's brows remained puckered in thought. "Wait!" he exclaimed. "I got idea of my own. If dem feller kill Courteau dey ain't nowheres roun' here. Dey beat it, firs' t'ing."

"To Hunker? Perhaps—"

"No. For de Boun'ry." 'Poleon slapped his thigh in sudden enlightenment. "By golly! Dat's why I don' see 'em no place. You stay here. I mak' sure."

He turned and strode away, but Rouletta followed at his heels.

"I'm going, too," she stoutly asserted. "Don't argue. I'll bet ten to one we find their cabin empty."

Together they made their way rapidly out of the brightly illuminated portion of the town and into the maze of blank warehouses and snow-banked cabins which lay behind. At this hour of the night few lamps were burning even in private residences, and, inasmuch as these back streets were unlighted, the travelers had to feel their way. The wind was diminishing, but even yet the air was thick with flying flakes, and new drifts seriously impeded progress. Wading knee-deep in places, stumbling in and out of cuts where the late snow had been removed, clambering over treacherous slopes where other snows lay hard packed and slippery, the two pursued their course.

'Poleon came to a pause at length in the shelter of a pole provision-cache and indistinctly took his bearings. Silently he pointed to the premises and vigorously nodded his head; then he craned his neck for a view of the stove-pipe overhead. Neither sparks nor smoke nor heat was rising from it. After a cautious journey of exploration he returned to Rouletta and spoke aloud:

"Dey gone. Sled, dogs, ever't'ing gone."

He pushed open the cache door, and a moment later there came the sound of rending wood as he shouldered his way into the dark cabin, re-gardless of lock and bar. Rouletta was close behind him when he struck a match and held it to a candle which he discovered fixed in its own wax beside the window.

Curiously the interlopers surveyed the unfamiliar premises. Rouletta spoke first, with suppressed excitement:

"You were right. And they left in a hurry, too."

"Sure. Beddin' gone, an'—dey got plenty beddin' on Hunker. Here dey mak' grub-pack, see?" 'Poleon ran his finger through a white dust of flour which lay thick upon the table. Striding to the stove, he laid' his hand upon it; he lifted the lid and felt of the ashes within. "Dey lef' 'bout five hour' ago. Wal, dat's' beeg start. I guess mebbe dey safe enough."

"Don't say that," Rouletta implored. "Rock can overtake them. He's a famous traveler."

"I dunno. Dey got good team—"

"He must catch them! Why, he has ninety miles to do it in! He must, 'Poleon, he *must!* Of course this is evidence, but it isn't proof. Remember, Pierce talked wildly. People are prejudiced against him and—you know the Police. They act on suspicion, and circumstances are certainly strong. Poor boy! If these men get away— who knows what may happen to him? I tell you his very life may be in danger, for the law is an awful thing. I—I've always been afraid of it. So was father, to his dying day. We must send Rock flying. Yes, and without a moment's delay."

"You still got deep feelin' for dat feller?"

'Poleon inquired, gravely. The quick look of anguish, the frank nod of assent that he received, were enough. "*Bien!*" he said, slowly. "I mak' satisfy, dat's all. I never see you so scare' as dis."

"You know how I feel," Rouletta said; then, more curiously: "Why do you need to make sure? Do you think I've changed—?" She hesitated for an instant; there came a faint pucker of apprehension between her brows; into her eyes crept a look of wonder which changed to astonishment, then to incredulity, fright. "Oh—h!" she exclaimed. She raised a faltering hand to her lips as if to stay a further betrayal of the knowledge that had suddenly come to her. "Oh, 'Poleon, my dear! My brother!"

The man smiled painfully as he met her shocked gaze. "I'm fonny feller, *ma sœur*; always dreamin' de mos' foolish t'ing. Don' pay no 'tention."

"I am— I always will be that—your sister. Have I made you unhappy?"

Vigorously he shook his head; his face slowly cleared. "No, no. In dis life one t'ing is give me happiness—one t'ing alone—an' dat is bring you joy. Now come. De grass growin' on our feet."

Together and in silence they hurried back as they had come; then, on the plea that he could make better time alone, 'Poleon left his companion and headed for the Barracks.

Rouletta let him go without protest; her heart was heavier than lead; she could find no words

whatever. A new tragedy, it seemed, had risen
to face her, for she realized now that she had
hurt the man who loved her best of all. That
certainty filled her with such regret, such a feeling of guilt, that she could not bear to think of
it. A very poignant sense of pain troubled her
as she turned into the Rialto, and as a consequence
the lively clatter of the place grated upon her
sensibilities; she felt a miserable, sick desire to
shut her ears to this sound of laughter which
was like ribald applause for the death-blow she
had dealt. Yes, she had dealt a death-blow, and
to one most dear. But how could she have
known? How could she have foreseen such a
wretched complication as this? Who would have
dreamed that gay, careless, laughing 'Poleon Doret
was like other men? Rouletta felt the desire to
bend her head and release those scalding tears
that trembled on her lashes.

Lieutenant Rock was preparing for bed when
'Poleon, after some little difficulty, forced his way
in upon him. The officer listened to his caller's
recital, and even before it was finished he had begun to dress himself in his trail clothes.

"Courteau confessed, eh? And the McCaskeys
have disappeared—taken French leave. Say!
That changes the look of things, for a fact. Of
course they may have merely gone back to
Hunker—"

"In de middle of snow-storm? Dis tam de
night? No. Dey makin' run for de Line an'
it's goin' tak' fas' team for pull 'em down."

"Well, I've got the best dogs in town."

Rock's caller smiled. "*M'sieu'*, dey goin' travel some if dey keep in sight of me."

"*You?*" Rock straightened himself. "Will you go along? Jove! I'd like that!" he cried, heartily. "I've heard you own a lively bunch of mutts."

"I give you tas'e of Injun travel. Better you dress light an' buckle up dat belt, for I got reason to fin' out who keel Courteau. I ain't goin' sleep no more till I know."

The officer smiled as he declared: "That suits me exactly. We may not catch them, but—they'll know they've been in a race before they thumb their hoses at us from across the Boundary. Now see how fast you can harness up."

It was considerably after midnight when 'Poleon swung his dog-team into the lighted space in front of the Rialto; nevertheless, many people were about, for Dawson was a city of sleep-haters. The sight of a racing-team equipped for a flying trip at this hour of the night evoked instant interest and speculation, pointing, as it did, to a new gold discovery and a stampede. Stampedes were frequent, they never failed to create a sensation, therefore the woodsman was soon the center of an inquisitive crowd. Not until he had fully explained the nature of his business was suspicion allayed; then his word that Joe and Frank McCaskey had fled for the Boundary ran up and down the street and caused even greater excitement.

Rouletta came hurrying forth with the others,

and to her 'Poleon made known his intention of accompanying the fleet-footed Rock.

"Nobody is able to catch dem feller but him an' me," he explained. "Dey got too long start."

"You think they may get across?" she queried, apprehensively.

"Five, six hour, dat's beeg edge. But me—" The speaker shrugged. "Forty Mile, Circle, Fort Yukon, Rampart, it mak' no differ. I get 'em some place, if I go plumb to St. Michael's. When I get goin' fas' it tak' me long tam for run down."

Rouletta's eyes opened. "But, 'Poleon—you can't! There's the Boundary. You're not an officer; you have no warrant."

"Dem t'ing is dam' nuisance," he declared. "I don' savvy dis law biznesse. You say get 'em. *Bien!* I do it."

Rouletta stared curiously, wonderingly into the big fellow's face; she was about to put her thoughts into words when a shout arose from the crowd as the Police team streamed into view. Down the street it came at a great pace, flashing through shadows and past glaring lighted fronts, snatching the light hickory sled along behind as if it were a thing of paper. Rock balanced himself upon the runner heels until, with a shout, he put his weight upon the sharp-toothed sled brake and came to a pause near 'Poleon. The rival teams plunged into their collars and set up a pandemonium of yelping, but willing hands held them from flying at one another's throats. Meanwhile,

457

saloon doors were opening, the street was filling; dance-hall girls, white-aproned bartenders, bleary-eyed pedestrians, night-owls—all the queerly assorted devotees of Dawson's vivid and roisterous nocturnal life hastened thither; even the second-story windows framed heads, for this clamor put slumber to flight without delay.

The wind was no longer strong, and already a clearing sky was evidenced by an occasional winking star; nevertheless, it was bitterly cold and those who were not heavily clad were forced to stamp their feet and to whip their arms in order to keep their blood in motion.

Nothing is more exciting, more ominous, than a man-hunt; doubly portentous was this one, the hasty preparations for which went forward in the dead of night. Dawson had seen the start of more than one race for the Boundary and had awaited the outcome with breathless interest. Most of the fugitives overtaken had walked back into town, spent, famished, frost-blackened, but there were some who had returned on their backs, wrapped in robe or canvas and offering mute testimony to the speedy and relentless efficiency of the men from the Barracks. Of that small picked corps Lieutenant Rock was by long odds the favorite. Now, therefore, he was the center of attention, and wagers were laid that he would catch his men, however rapidly they traveled, however great their start. Only a few old-timers —"sour-doughs" from the distant reaches of the Yukon—knew 'Poleon Doret, but those few drew close to him and gave the lieutenant little notice. This French Canadian they regarded as the most tireless traveler in all the North; about him, therefore, they assembled, and to him they addressed their questions and offered their advice.

The dogs were inspired, now, with the full intoxication of the chase; they strained forward fretfully, their gray plumes waving, their tongues lolling, their staccato chorus adding to the general disturbance. When the word came to go, they leaped into their harness, and with a musical jingle of bells they swept down toward the river; over the steep bank they poured, and were gone. A shout of encouragement followed Rock as he was snapped into the blackness, then noisily the crowd bolted for the warm interiors behind them.

Rouletta was slow in leaving; for some time she stood harkening to the swift diminuendo of those tinkling sleigh-bells, staring into the night as if to fix in her mind's eye the picture of what she had last seen, the picture of a mighty man riding the rail of a plunging basket sled. In spite of the biting cold he was stripped down; a thin drill parka sufficed to break the temper of the wind, light fur boots were upon his feet, the cheek pieces of his otter cap were tied above his crown. He had turned to wave at her and to shout a word of encouragement just before he vanished. That was like him, she told herself—eager to spare her even the pain of undue apprehension. The shock of her discovery of an hour ago was still too fresh in Rouletta's memory; it was still too new and too agitating to permit of orderly thought, yet there it stood, stark and dismaying. This woodsman loved her, no longer as a sister, but as the one woman of his choice. As yet she could not reconcile herself to such a state of affairs; her attempts to do so filled her with mixed emotions. Poor 'Poleon! Why had this come to him? Rouletta's throat swelled; tears not of the wind or the cold stood in her eyes once again; an aching tenderness and pity welled up from her heart.

She became conscious finally that her body was growing numb, so she bestirred herself. She had taken but a step or two, however, when some movement in the shadows close at hand arrested her. Peering into the gloom, she discovered a figure. It was Laure.

The girl wore some sort of wrap, evidently snatched at random, but under it she was clad in her dance-hall finery, and she, too, was all but frozen.

Rouletta was about to move on, when the other addressed her through teeth that clicked like castanets.

"I got here—late. Is it true? Have they—gone after Joe and Frank?"

"Yes."

"What happened? I—I haven't heard. Don't they think—Pierce did it?"

"You *know* he didn't do it," Rouletta cried. "Neither did he steal Courteau's money."

"What do you mean, 'I know'?" Laure's voice was harsh, imperative. She clutched at the

THE WINDS OF CHANCE

other girl; then, as Rouletta hesitated, she re-gained control of herself and ran on, in a tone bitterly resentful: "Oh, you'd like to get him out of it—save him for yourself—wouldn't you? But you can't. You can't have him. I won't let you. My God! Letty, he's the only thing I ever cared for! I never had even a dog or a cat or a canary of my own. Think a little bit of me."

Almost dazed by this mingled accusation and appeal, Rouletta at length responded by a question, "Then why haven't you done something to clear him?"

Laure drew her flimsy wrap closer; she was shaking wretchedly. When she spoke her words were spilled from her lips as if by the tremors of her body. "I could help. I would, but—you sha'n't have him. Nobody shall! I'd rather see him dead. I'd— No, no! I don't know what I'm saying. I'd sooner die than hurt him. I'd do my bit, only—McCaskey 'd kill me. Say. Will Rock get him, d'you think? I hear he gets his man every time. But Joe's different; he's not the ordinary kind; he's got the devil in him. Frank—he's a dog, but Joe 'll fight. He'll kill— at the drop of the hat. So will Rock, I suppose. Maybe he'll kill them both, eh? Or maybe they'll kill him and get away. I don't care which way it goes—"

"Don't talk like that!" Rouletta exclaimed.

"I mean it," Laure ran on, crazily. "Yes, Joe'd kill anybody that stood in his way or double-
461

crossed him. I guess I know. Why, he told me so himself! And Courteau knew it, perfectly well—the poor fool!—but look at him now. He got his, didn't he?"

Rouletta laid a cold hand upon the shivering, distracted creature before her. Sternly she said:

"I believe you know who committed that murder. You act as if you did."

"I'm a g-good guesser, but—I can keep my mouth shut. I know when I'm well off. That's more than the Count knew."

"And you probably know something about his robbery, too. I mean that gold-sack—"

Laure cast off the hand that rested upon her; she looked up quickly. "If I did, d'you think I'd tell you? Well, hardly. But I don't. I don't know anything, except that—Pierce is a thief. He stole and gave me the money. He did that regularly, and that's more than he'd do for you. You may as well know the truth. Cavendish knows it. You think he's too good for me, don't you? Well, he isn't. And you're no better than I am, either, for that matter. You've got a nerve to put on airs. God! How I hate you and your superior ways."

"Never mind me. I want to know who killed Count Courteau."

"All right. Wait till Rock comes back and ask him. He thinks he'll find out, but—we'll see. Joe McCaskey 'll be over the Line and away, thank Heaven! If anything happens and they should overtake him—well, he'll fight. He'll never come in alive, never." Turning, the speaker stumbled toward the lights of the saloon, and as she went Rouletta heard her mutter again: "He'll never come in alive, never. Thank God for that!"

CHAPTER XXVIII

FROM Dawson City the Yukon flows in a northwesterly· direction toward the International Boundary, and although the camp is scarcely more than fifty miles due east of American territory, by the river it is ninety. Since the Yukon is the main artery of travel, both winter and summer—there being no roads or trails—it behooved those malefactors who fled the wrath of the Northwest Mounted Police to obtain a liberal start, for ninety miles of dead flat going is no easy run and the Police teams were fleet of foot. Time was when evil-doers had undertaken to escape up-river, or to lose themselves in the hills to the northward, but this was a desperate adventure at best and had issued in such uniform disaster as to discourage its practice. The Police had won the reputation of never leaving a trail, and, in consequence, none but madmen longer risked anything except a dash for American soil, and even then only with a substantial margin of time in their favor.

But the winter winds are moody, the temper of the Arctic is uncertain, hence luck played a large part in these enterprises. Both Rock and

Doret were sufficiently familiar with the hazards and the disappointments of travel at this time of year to feel extremely doubtful of overhauling the two McCaskeys, and so they were by no means sanguine of success as they drove headlong into the night.

Both teams were loaded light; neither driver carried stove, tent, or camp duffle. Sleeping-bags, a little cooked food for themselves, a bundle of dried fish for the dogs, that was the limit the pursuers had allowed themselves. Given good weather, nothing more was needed. In case of a storm, a sudden blizzard, and a drop in temperature, this lack of equipment was apt to prove fatal, but neither traveler permitted himself to think about such things. Burdened thus lightly, the sleds rode high and the malamutes romped along with them. When the late dawn finally came it found them far on their way.

That wind, following the snowfall of the day before, had been a happy circumstance, for in many places it had blown the trail clean, so that daylight showed it winding away into the distance like a thread laid down at random. Here and there, of course, it was hidden; under the lee of bluffs or of wooded bends, for instance, it was drifted deep, completely obliterated, in fact, and in such places even a seasoned musher would have floundered aimlessly, trying to hold it. But 'Poleon Doret possessed a sixth sense, it appeared, and his lead dog, too, had unusual sagacity. Rock, from hi position in the rear,

marveled at the accuracy with which the woodsman's sled followed the narrow, hard-packed
ridge concealed beneath the soft, new covering.
Undoubtedly the fellow knew his business and
the officer congratulated himself upon bringing
him along.

They had been under way for five or six hours
when the tardy daylight came, but even thereafter Doret continued to run with his hand upon
his sled. Seldom did he ride, and then only for
a moment or two when the going was best. For
the most part he maintained a steady, swinging
trot that kept pace with the pattering feet ahead
of him and caused the miles rapidly to drop behind. Through drifts knee-deep, through long,
soft stretches he held to that unfaltering stride;
occasionally he turned his head and flashed a smile
or waved his hand at the man behind.

Along about ten o'clock he halted his team
where a dead spruce overhung the river-bank.
By the time Rock had pulled in behind him he
had clambered up the bank, ax in hand, and was
making the chips fly. He sent the dry top crashing down, then explained:

"Dem dogs go better for l'il rest. We boil de
kettle, eh?"

Rock wiped the sweat from his face. "You're
certainly hitting it off, old man. We've made
good time, but I haven't seen any tracks. Have
you?"

"We see 'em bimeby."

"Kind of a joke if they hadn't come, after all

466

—if they'd really gone out to Hunker. Gee! The laugh would be on us."

"Dey come dis way," 'Poleon stoutly maintained.

Soon a blaze was going; then, while the ice in the blackened tea-bucket was melting, the drivers sliced a slab of bacon into small cubes and fed it sparingly to their animals, after which they carefully examined the dogs' feet and cleaned them of ice and snow pellets.

The tea was gulped, the hardtack swallowed, and the travelers were under way again almost before their sweaty bodies had begun to chill. On they hurried, mile after mile, sweeping past bends, eagerly, hopefully scanning every empty tan· gent that opened up ahead of them. They made fast time indeed, but the immensity of the desolation through which they passed, the tremendous scale upon which this country had been molded, made their progress seem slower than an ant-crawl.

Eventually 'Poleon shouted something and pointed to the trail underfoot. Rock fancied he could detect the faint, fresh markings of sled runners, but into them he could not read much significance. It was an encouragement, to be sure, but, nevertheless, he still had doubts, and those doubts were not dispelled until Doret again halted his team, this time beside the cold embers of a fire. Fresh chips were scattered under the bank, charred fagots had embedded themselves in the ice and were frozen fast, but 'Poleon interpreted the various signs without difficulty.

"Here dey mak' breakfas'—'bout daylight," said he. "Dey go slower as us."

"But they're going pretty fast, for all that. We'll never get them this side of Forty Mile."

"You don' spec' it, do you? Dey got beeg scare, dem feller. Dey runnin' so fas' dey can."

Forty Mile, so called because the river of that name enters the Yukon forty miles above the Boundary, was a considerable camp prior to the Dawson boom, but thereafter it had languished, and this winter it was all but deserted. So, too, was Cudahy, the rival trading-post a half-mile below. It was on the bars of this stream that the earliest pioneers had first found gold. Here at its mouth, during the famine days before the steamboats came, they had cached their supplies; here they had brewed their hootch in the fall and held high carnival to celebrate their good luck or to drown their ill-fortune.

Rock and his companion pulled up the bank and in among the windowless cabins during the afternoon; they had halted their dogs before the Mounted Police station, only to find the building locked and cold. The few faithful Forty-Milers who came out to exchange greetings explained that both occupants of the barracks had gone down-river to succor some sick Indians.

Rock was disgusted, but his next question elicited information that cheered him. Yes, a pair of strangers had just passed through, one of them an active, heavy-set fellow, the other a tall, dark, sinister man with black eyes and a stormy demeanor. They had come fast and they had tarried only long enough to feed their dogs and to make some inquiries. Upon learning that the local police were on the main river somewhere below, they had held a consultation and then had headed up the Forty Mile.

"*Up* Forty Mile?" Rock cried, in surprise. "Are you sure?"

"We seen 'em go," his informant declared. "That's what made us think there was something wrong. That's why we been on the lookout for you. We figgered they was on the dodge and hard pressed, but we couldn't do nothing about it. You see, it's only about twenty-three miles to the Line up Forty Mile. Down the Yukon it's forty. They been gone 'most two hours, now."

"What do you want 'em for?" another by-stander inquired.

"Murder," Rock exclaimed, shortly; then he heaved his sled into motion once more, for 'Poleon had started his team and was making off through the town. Down into the bed of the smaller stream the pursuers made their way and up this they turned. Again they urged their dogs into a run. It took some effort to maintain a galloping pace now, for the teams were tiring, and after some mental calculations Rock shook his head doubtfully. Of course, his quarry was at a disadvantage, there being two men to one sled, but —twenty-three miles, with a two-hour start! It was altogether too great a handicap. The lieutenant had figured on that last forty miles, the

469

last five or ten, in fact, but this change of direction had upset all his plans and his estimates. Evidently the McCaskeys cared not how nor where they crossed the Line, so long as they crossed it quickly and got Canadian territory behind them. Barring accident, therefore, which was extremely unlikely, Rock told himself regretfully that they were as good as gone. Two hours! It was too much. On the other hand, he and 'Poleon now had a fresh trail to follow, while the fleeing brothers had unbroken snow ahead of them, and that meant that they must take turns ahead of their dogs. Then, too, fifty miles over drifted trails at this season of the year was a heavy day's work, and the McCaskeys must be very tired by now, for neither was in the best of condition. In the spring, when the snows were wet and sled runners ran as if upon grease, such a journey would have been no great effort, but in this temperature the steel shoes creaked and a man's muscles did not work freely. Men had been known to play out unexpectedly. After all, there was a possibility of pulling them down, and as long as there was that possibility the Mounted Policeman refused to quit.

Rock assured himself that this flight had established one thing, at least, and that was Pierce Phillips' innocence 'of the Courteau killing. The murderers were here; there could be no doubt of it. Their frantic haste confessed their guilt. Friendship for the boy, pride in his own reputation, the memory of that ovation he had received upon leaving, gave the officer new strength and determination, so he shut his teeth and spurred his rebellious limbs into swifter action. There was no longer any opportunity of riding the sled, even where the trail was hard, for some of the Police dogs were limping and loafing in their collars. This was indeed a race, a Marathon, a twenty-three-mile test of courage and endurance, and victory would go to him who could call into fullest response his last uttermost ounce of reserve power.

Doret had promised that he would show his trail-mate how to travel, and that promise he had made good; all day he had held the lead, and without assistance from the lash. Even now his dogs, while not fresh, were far from exhausted. As for the man himself, Rock began to feel a conviction that the fellow could go on at this rate eternally.

Luck finally seemed to break in favor of the pursuers; accident appeared to work in their behalf. The day was done, night was again upon them, when Doret sent back a cry of warning, and, leaping upon his sled, turned his leader at right angles toward the bank.

His companion understood the meaning of that move, but the Police team was less responsive to command, and before Rock could swing them he felt his feet sink into soft slush.

"Dam' overflow!" Doret panted when the two teams were safely out upon the bank. "You wet your feet, eh?"

Apprehensively the officer felt of his moccasins; they were wet to the touch, but as yet no moisture had penetrated his socks. "You yelled in the nick of time," he declared, as he dried his soles in the loose snow.

"Dem feller got in it ankle-deep. I bet we fin' camp-fire soon."

This prediction came true. As the travelers rounded the next bluff they smelled the odor of burning spruce and came upon a trampled bed of boughs beside which some embers were still smoldering.

"Jove! That gives us a chance, doesn't it?" Rock panted.

His companion smiled. "We goin' start travel now, for sure. Dey can't be more 'n a mile or two ahead."

Down upon the river-bed the teams rushed. With biting lash and sharp commands the drivers urged them into a swifter run. Rock was forcing his dogs now; he made the smoke fly from their hides when they lagged. He vowed that he would not permit this French Canadian to out-distance him. He swore a good deal at his mala-mutes; he cursed himself as a weakling, a quitter; anger at his fatigue ran through him.

The travelers were up among the hills by now. Occasionally they passed a deserted cabin, home of some early gold-digger. Valleys dark with night opened up to right and to left as the Forty Mile wound higher, deeper into the maze of round-ed domes: the Boundary was close at hand. The hillsides hid their feet in black thickets of spruce, but their slopes were thinly timbered, their crests were nearly bare, and the white snow gave off a dim radiance that made traveling possible even after the twilight had deepened. By and by it grew lighter and the north horizon took on a rosy flush that spread into a tremendous flare. The night was still, clear, crackly; it was surcharged with some static force, and so calm was the air, so deathlike the hush, that the empty valley rang like a bell. That mysterious illumination in the north grew more and more impressive; great ribbons, long pathways of quivering light, unrolled themselves and streamed across the sky; they flamed and flickered, they writhed and melted, disappearing, reappearing, rising, falling. It was as if the lid had been lifted from some stupendous caldron and the heavens reflected the radiance from its white-hot contents. Mighty fingers, like the beams of polar search-lights, groped through the voids overhead; tumbling waves of color rushed up and dashed themselves away into space; the whole arch of the night was lit as from a world in flames. Red, yellow, orange, violet, ultra-violet—the tints merged with one another bewilderingly and the snows threw back their flicker until coarse print would have been readable. Against that war of clashing colors the mountain-crests stood out in silhouette and the fringe of lonely wind-twisted trunks high up on their saddles were etched in blackest ink.

It was a weird, an unearthly effect; it was exciting, too. As always when the Aurora is in full play, the onlookers marveled that such a tremendous exhibition of energy could continue in such silence. That was the oddest, the most impressive feature of all, for the crash of avalanches, the rumble of thunder, the diapason of a hundred Niagaras, should have accompanied such appalling phenomena. It seemed odd indeed that the whine of sled runners, the scuff of moccasins, the panting of dogs, should be the only audible sounds.

There were other overflows underfoot now, but the cold had frozen them and the going was getting constantly better. The snow was thin and in places the sleds slewed sidewise and the dogs ran on slack traces across long stretches of bare glare ice. It was while negotiating such a place as this that Rock paid the price of his earlier carelessness. Doret's dry moose-skin soles had a sure grip, hence he never hesitated, but the lieutenant's moccasins were like a pair of tin shoes now and, without warning, he lost his footing. He was running swiftly at the moment; he strove to save himself, to twist in midair, but he failed. 'Poleon heard a cry of pain and dismay, so he halted his team and came striding back. Rock raised himself, then took a step, but faltered and clung helplessly to the handle-bars. He began to curse furiously; he undertook to estimate the extent of his injury, then explained:

"My foot doubled under me and I came down

474

on it hke a ton of bricks. By Heavens! I believe something broke!"

'Poleon was solicitous. He blamed himself, too. "It's dem wet moccasin'. I should have stop' an' mak' you change," said he.

"We can't stop," Rock groaned. "I'll be all right as soon as—" The words ended in another explosive oath as he again put his weight upon the injured member. Blasphemy poured from his lips as repeatedly he tried to force his foot to carry him. He cursed himself for a clumsy, blundering ass; he shouted at his dogs; he sent his sled forward and lurched along behind it, half supporting himself, until 'Poleon finally halted him.

"It's no good mak' bad t'ing worse, *M'sieu'*," the woodsman declared. "You bus' him for sure, an' it's no use goin' furder. S'pose mebbe we boil de kettle, eh?"

"And let them get away clean? When we had 'em? They can't be a mile ahead. Let 'em slip between our fingers?" raved the officer. "I can't. I won't—"

"We mak' li'l fire an' look him over dat foot. Me, I t'ink you don' walk no more for two, t'ree week'."

"You go! I'll deputize you! Get 'em, Doret, quick! You can do it! I'll wait! Go ahead!"

The other nodded. "Sure, I can get 'em! I never have no doubt 'bout dat in de least, but it's better we fix you comfor'ble."

"They'll be across, I tell you—over the Line—"

31   475

"I came pas' dat place more 'n once or twice" —the French Canadian grinned—"an' I never seen it no Line." He forced his companion to lower himself upon the sled, then swung it toward the river-bank, calling upon his own lead dog to follow. Up and into the shelter of the spruce he drove the Police team; quickly he felled dry wood and kindled a fire. This took but a few moments, but Rock was wet with sweat and in consequence he was shivering wretchedly; his teeth were chattering even before the blaze had taken hold. 'Poleon continued to work with what speed he could, and in a surprisingly short time he had built a snug wickiup and filled it with boughs. This done, he unhitched and fed both teams, spread Rock's sleeping-bag under the shelter, and set a pail of snow to melt. By the light of the fire he examined the latter's injury, but could make little of it, for already it was badly swollen and every manipulation caused its owner extreme pain. There were no remedies available; there was not even a vessel of sufficient size in which to bathe the foot; hence 'Poleon contented himself by bandaging it and helping his trail-mate into bed.

Not since leaving Dawson had either man tasted hot food, but their hunger was as nothing to their thirst. Even in this length of time their bodies had shrunk, withered, inside their clothing, and for perhaps an hour they took turns greedily draining the pail of its tepid contents. Under intense cold the human body consumes itself at a rapid rate. Once it has burned itself out it preys upon those deep-hidden forces which nature holds in reserve, and the process of recuperation waits upon a restoration of a normal balance of moisture.

Both men were weighed down by an aching, nightmare fatigue, and as they sat gulping hot water, absorbing heat from within and without, their muscles set and they felt as if their limbs had turned to stone.

But, once the first mad craving for drink had been assuaged, they fried bacon and made tea. Like wolves they fell upon the salt meat; they dipped the hot grease up in their spoons and swallowed it with relish; they crunched their hardtack and washed the powdery mouthfuls down with copious draughts from the blackened pail. When the tea was gone they brewed another scalding bucketful.

Rock lay back, finally, but the movement caused him to bare his teeth in agony. At 'Poleon's quick inquiry he shook his head.

"I'm all right," he declared. "Good for the night. You can pull out any time you want to."

"Dere's plenty tam." 'Poleon lit his pipe and reached again for the tea-bucket.

"Better go before you stiffen up."

"I go bimeby—sooner I get li'l drinkin' done."

"They'll fight," Rock announced, after a silence of perhaps five minutes. "I feel pretty rotten, playing out like this."

"You done firs' rate," the woodsman told him.

477

"If I come alone I catch 'em ten mile below, but —li'l tam, more less, don' mak' no differ."

"I believe you *would* have got 'em," the officer acknowledged. After a time he persisted: "They'll put up a battle, Doret. You'll need to be careful."

'Poleon was squatted Indian fashion over the blaze; he was staring fixedly into the flames, and an aboriginal reticence had settled upon him. After a long time he answered: "Mebbe so I keel de beeg feller. I dunno. So long one is lef' I mak' him clear dat boy Phillips."

"Decent of you to take a chance like that for Pierce," Rock resumed. "It's different with me; I have to do it. Just the same, I wouldn't care to follow those fellows over the Boundary. I don't think you'd better try it."

In spite of his suffering, the lieutenant fell into a doze; whether he slept ten minutes or an hour he never knew, but he awoke, groaning, to find the big woodsman still bulked over the campfire, still smoking, still sipping tea. Rock ate and drank some more; again he slept. For a second time his pain roused him, and once more he marveled to discover 'Poleon occupied as before. It seemed to him that the fellow would never satisfy himself. Eventually, however, the latter arose and made preparations to leave.

The Northern Lights had flickered out now; the empty sky was sprinkled with a million stars which glittered like scintillating frost jewels frozen into the dome of heaven; there were no sounds whatever to break the deathlike silence of the night, for the Arctic wastes are all but lifeless. There were no bird-calls, no sounds of insects, not even the whisper of running water, for the river was locked deep beneath its icy armor.

"You got 'nough wood to las' long tam," 'Poleon declared. "If I don' come back, dem Forty Mile Police is sure to pick you up."

"I can go in alone if I have to," the injured man declared. "*Au revoir* and good luck."

'Poleon made no attempt to hurry his tired team; for several miles he plodded along behind them, guiding them to right or left by a low-spoken word. Years before, he had rocked on the bars of this stream; therefore its landmarks were familiar to him, and in spite of the darkness he readily identified them. In time he made out the monuments marking the International Boundary, and a short distance beyond that point he unhitched his dogs, then took a carbine from his sled and slipped it full of shells. Next he removed his lash rope, coiled it, and placed it in his pocket, after which he resumed his journey alone.

Occasionally he dimly glimpsed deserted cabins, habitations built by the gold-diggers of other days. Carefully he followed the all but indistinguishable sled tracks ahead of him until they swerved abruptly in toward the bank. Here he paused, pulled a mitten, and, moistening a finger, held it up to test the wind. What movement there was to the air seemed to satisfy him, for, step by step, he mounted the steep slope until his head finally rose over its crest. Against the sky-line he now made out a small clearing; straining his eyes, he could see the black square of a cabin wall. No light shone from it, therefore he argued that his men had supped and were asleep. He had assumed that they would not, could not, go far beyond the Boundary; he had purposely allowed them sufficient time in which to overcome the first agony of fatigue and to fall asleep. He wondered apprehensively where they had put their dogs, and if by any evil chance the McCaskey team included an "outside" dog of the watchful, barking variety.

Gingerly he stepped out, and found that the snow underfoot gave off only the faintest whisper. Like a shadow he stole closer to the hut, keeping the imperceptible night breeze in his face.

So noiseless was his approach that the tired dogs, snugly curled each in its own deep bed of snow, did not hear him—your malamutes that are broken to harness are bad watch-dogs at best. Not until he had melted into the gloom beneath the wide overhang above the cabin door did the first disturbance come. Then something started into life and the silence was broken.

'Poleon saw that a canvas sled-cover had been used to curtain the door opening, and during the instant following the alarm he brushed the tarpaulin aside and stepped into the pitch-black interior.

It had been a swift maneuver, the result of a

lightning-like decision, and not so reckless as it appeared.

He stood now with his back to the rough log wall, every muscle in his body taut, his ears strained for some sound, some challenge. He had been prepared for a shot out of the darkness, but nothing came. His lungs were filling with the first deep breath of relief when a sleepy voice spoke:

"That you, Frank?" 'Poleon remained fixed in his tracks. "Frank!" There was a moment's pause, then, "*Frank!*"

Followed a rustle as of a body turning, then a startled mumble in answer.

"Was that you?" Joe McCaskey's voice again demanded.

"Me? What—?"

"Was you outside?"

"Outside?"

"I heard the dogs rowing. They're stirring now. Hear 'em? I'll swear I saw that fly drop—" McCaskey's words died out and again the interior of the cabin became soundless.

"Who's there?" the former speaker suddenly barked.

When another moment had dragged by, a sulphur match was struck. For a second or two it shed a sickly blue radiance sufficient only to silhouette a pair of hands cupped over it; then, as the flame ignited the tiny shaft, it burst into a yellow glow and sent the shadows of the cabin leaping.

Joe McCaskey uttered a cry, a scream. The flame was crushed in his palms and again the cabin was ink black. It remained as silent as before except for a dry rattling of breath in the elder brother's throat.

"Wha—what 'd you—see?" the younger one gasped. Both men were now fully awake, but, disregarding the question, Joe cried, wildly:

"Who are you? What d'you want?" And then, when no answer came: "Christ! *Say* something."

'Poleon could hear the wretch moisten his dry lips; he could picture both men sitting bolt upright in their sleeping-bags; he could feel the terror that was creeping over them.

"Who'd you see?" Frank whispered again.

"S-something big! Right there! By God! Something's in here!"

Joe's tone was firmer now; nevertheless, fright still held him motionless, paralyzed. He was staring with blind eyes into the velvet blackness, and his flesh was rippling with a superstitious horror of that formless creature he had glimpsed. What was it that had walked in out of the night and now crouched ready to spring? Nothing human, nothing natural, that was sure.

Similar thoughts raced madly through his brother's brain, and the latter let forth a thin wail—almost a sob. The sound set Joe into motion. Swiftly but clumsily he fumbled through the dry grass with which his bunk was filled. He uttered a throaty curse, for he had laid his

482

revolver by his side, right where his hand would fall upon it. Where was the thing—?

Joe's body turned rigid, his shaking fingers grew stiff and useless, when out of the darkness came a sigh—faint but unmistakable; whence it issued neither brother could tell.

With another shriek Frank fell back and burrowed into his sleeping-bag.

CHAPTER XXIX

ROULETTA KIRBY spent an anxious and a thoughtful night. The more she dwelt upon Laure's peculiar behavior the more it roused her suspicions and the more she felt justified in seeking an interview with Colonel Cavendish. She rose early, therefore, and went to Police Headquarters.

Two people were in the office when she entered, one a redcoat, evidently acting in some clerical capacity; the other a girl whom Rouletta had never seen. The colonel was engaged, so Rouletta was told, and she sat down to wait. With furtive curiosity she began to study this other young woman. It was plain that the latter was a privileged person, for she made herself perfectly at home and appeared to be not in the least chilled by the official formality of her surroundings. She wandered restlessly about the room, humming a tune under her breath; she readjusted the window-curtains to her liking; she idly thumbed the books upon the shelves; finally she perched herself upon the table in the midst of the documents upon which the officer was engaged, and began a low-voiced conversation with him.

Rouletta was not a little impressed by this stranger. She had never seen a finer, healthier, cleaner-cut girl. Here for once was a "nice" woman of the town who did not stare at her with open and offensive curiosity. She was not surprised when she overheard the Police officer address her as "Miss Cavendish." No wonder this girl had poise and breeding—the Cavendishes were the best people in the community. With a jealous pang the caller reflected that the colonel's daughter was very much what she herself would like to be, very much her ideal, so far as she could judge.

When, eventually, the commandant himself emerged from his sanctum, he paused for a moment at his daughter's side; then he approached Rouletta.

Very briefly the latter made known the reason of her presence, and the colonel nodded.

"You did quite right in coming here," he declared, "and I'm sure this dance-hall girl knows more than she has told. In fact, I was on the point of sending for her. Please wait until she arrives. Perhaps we can straighten out this whole unpleasant affair informally. I'll need Phillips, too. Meanwhile, there's a friend of yours inside." Stepping to the inner door, he spoke to some one, and an instant later the Countess Courteau came forth.

Rouletta had not seen the Countess alone since early the previous evening. She went swiftly to her now and placed an arm about her shoulders.

Hilda responded to this mark of sympathy with a weary smile.

"Well, I had to go through with it to the bitter end," she said, in a low voice. "Henri didn't spare me even that."

Rouletta pressed her closer, murmuring: "Colonel Cavendish is a fine man—I'm sure he understands. You've undergone a dreadful ordeal, but —it's nearly over. He's sending for Laure now. She can tell a good deal, if she will."

"About the theft, yes. But what about the —murder? Joe McCaskey did it. There's no doubt about that. Henri weakened, after I gave him his chance. He got to drinking, I hear, and evidently he conceived the notion of telling those men. He may have gone to warn them, to appeal to them. I don't know. Then they must have quarreled. It's all clear enough when you understand the inside facts. Without knowing them, it was natural to suspect Pierce, so—I did what I had to do. I doubt if Laure knows anything about this part of the affair."

The two women were still talking when Laure entered, in company with the Mounted Police officer who had been sent to fetch her. At sight of them she halted; a sudden pallor came into her cheeks; she cast a glance of alarm about her as if seeking retreat; but Colonel Cavendish grimly invited her to follow him, and stepped into his private office. The new-comer faltered; then with a defiant toss of her head and with lips curled in disdain she obeyed; the door closed behind her.

486

Rouletta and the Countess Courteau fell silent now. They found nothing to talk about, and in spite of themselves they strained their ears for some sound from the other room. Even Miss Cavendish seemed vaguely to feel the suspense, for she finally took her stand beside a frost-rimed window and engaged herself in tracing patterns thereon with the tip of her finger. An occasional stormy murmur of voices, deadened by the thick log partition, indicated that Laure and her inquisitor were not getting on well together.

Suddenly the girl at the window started; her apathy vanished; her expression of boredom gave place to one of such lively anticipation as to draw the attention of the two other women. A magic change came over her; she became suddenly animated, alive, atingle in every nerve; her eyes sparkled and a new color flooded her cheeks. The alteration interested her observers; they were mystified as to its cause until a quick step sounded in the entry and the door opened to admit Pierce Phillips.

It was natural that he should first see Miss Cavendish, and that he should greet her before recognizing the other occupants of the room. It was natural, too, that he should be a trifle nonplussed at finding Hilda here; nevertheless, he managed to cover his lack of ease. Not so, however, when, a moment later, the door to Colonel Cavendish's office opened and Laure, of all persons, appeared therein. Quickly Pierce inferred the reason for his summons, but, happily for him,

487

he was spared further embarrassment. Cavendish called to him, took him by the hand in the friendliest manner, and again disappeared into his retreat, drawing the young man with him.

Brief as had been the interruption, both Hilda and Rouletta had gathered much from it; their inference was borne out when Laure paused before them and in a voice subdued by the very force of her agitation exclaimed:

"Well, I hope you're satisfied! I got it, and got it good." Her face was livid, her dark eyes were blazing wrathfully. She outthrust a shaking hand and unclenched her fingers, displaying therein a crumpled sheet of pink paper, a printed official form, the telltale tint of which indicated its fateful character. Both of her hearers were familiar with the so-called "pink tickets" of the Mounted Police; every one in the Northwest Territory, in fact, knew what they were—deportation orders. But in a tone hoarse and suppressed Laure read, "'—leave by the first safe conveyance!' That's what it says—the first safe conveyance. I suppose you'd like it better if it were a blue ticket and I had to leave in twenty-four hours. You put it over, but I won't forget. I'll get even with you."

"We had nothing to do with that," the Countess declared, quietly. "I'm sorry you take it so hard, but—it serves you right."

"Who wouldn't take it hard? To be expelled, fired out like a thief, a—" The girl's voice broke; then she pulled herself together and uttered a quavering, artificial laugh. She tossed her head again, with an obvious attempt at defiance. "Oh, it takes more than a pink ticket to down me! Anyhow, I'm sick of this place, sick of the people. I hate them." With a vicious fling of her shoulders she swept on to a seat as far from them as possible and sank into it.

So the girl had confessed, Hilda reflected. She was glad, for Pierce's sake, that this miserable complication was in process of clearing up and that he would be finally and completely exonerated; she was glad, too, that her efforts in his behalf, her humiliation, had borne fruit. He would never know how high he had made her pay, but that was all right. She felt very gently toward him at this moment, and experienced a certain wistful desire that he might understand how unselfish had been her part. It might make a difference; probably it would. Things now were not as they had been. She was a free woman. This thought obtruded itself insistently into the midst of her meditations. Yes, Courteau was gone; there was no reason now why she could not look any man honestly in the eye. Of course, there was the same disparity in years between her and Pierce which she had recognized from the beginning, but, after all, was that necessarily fatal? He had loved her genuinely enough at one time. Hilda recalled that windy night on the shores of Linderman when the whimper of a rising storm came out of the darkness, when the tree-tops tossed their branches to the sky, and when her own soul had broken its fetters and defied restraint. She thrilled at memory of those strong young arms about her, those hot lips pressing hers. That was a moment to remember always. And those dreamy, magic days that had followed, the more delightful, the more unreal because she had deliberately drugged her conscience. Then that night at White Horse! He had told her bitterly, broken-heartedly, that he could never forget. Perhaps even yet— With an effort Hilda Courteau roused herself. Never forget? Why, he had forgotten the very next day, as was quite natural. No, she was a foolish sentimentalist, and he—well, he was just one whom fate had cast for a lover's rôle, one destined to excite affection in women, good and bad. Some day he would find his mate and—Hilda believed she loved him well enough to rejoice in his happiness when it came. There spoke the maternal instinct which Phillips had the knack of rousing; for want of something better, she determined she would cherish that.

Meanwhile Laure sat in her corner, her head bowed, her very soul in revolt. She was tasting failure, disappointment, balked desire, and it was like gall in her mouth. She could have cried out aloud in her rage. She hated these other women whom she blamed for her undoing; she hated Cavendish, Pierce Phillips, herself.

"It serves me right," she told herself, furiously. "I deserve the pink ticket for making a fool of myself. Yes, a *fool!* What has Pierce ever done

490

for me? Nothing. And I—?" Before her mind's eye came a vision of the opportunities she had let slip, the chances she had ignored. She knew full well that she could have had the pick of many men—the new-made millionaires of Dawson—but instead she had chosen him. And why? Merely because he had a way, a smile, a warm and pleasing personality—some magnetic appeal too intangible to identify. It was like her to make the wrong choice—she always did. She had come North with but one desire, one determination—namely, to make money, to reap to the full her share of this free harvest. She had given up the life she liked, the people she knew, the comforts she craved, for that and for nothing else, and what a mess she had made of the venture! Other girls not half so smart, not half so pretty as she, had feathered their nests right here before her eyes, while she was wasting her time. They had kept their heads, and they would go out in the spring, first class, with good clothes and a bank-roll in the purser's safe. Some of them were married and respectable. "Never again!" she whispered to herself. "The next one will pay." Chagrin at the treatment she had suffered filled her with a poisonous hatred of all mankind, and soundlessly she cursed Phillips as the cause of her present plight.

Such thoughts as these ran tumbling through the girl's mind; her rage and her resentment were real enough; nevertheless, through this overtone there ran another note; a small voice was speaking in the midst of all her tumult—a small voice which she refused to listen to. "What I ever saw in him I don't know," she sneered, goading herself to further bitterness and stiffening her courage. "I never really cared for him; I'm too wise for that. I don't care for him now. I detest the poor, simple-minded fool. I—*hate* him." So she fought with herself, drowning the persistent piping of that other voice. Then her eyes dropped to that fatal paper in her lap and suddenly venom fled from her. She wondered if Cavendish would tell Pierce that he had given her the pink ticket. Probably not. The Mounted Police were usually close-mouthed about such things, and yet— Laure crushed the paper into a crumpled ball and furtively hid it in the pocket of her coat; then she raised wild, apprehensive eyes to the door. If only she dared slip out now, before Pierce reappeared, before he had a chance to see her. It seemed as if she could not bear to have him know, but—Cavendish had ordered her to wait. "My God!" the girl whispered. "I'll die, if he knows! I'll die!" She began to tremble wretchedly and to wring her hands; she could not remove her gaze from the door.

This waiting-room at the Barracks had housed people of divers and many sorts during its brief history; it had harbored strained faces, it had been the scene of strong emotional conflicts, but never, perhaps, had its narrow walls encompassed emotions in wider contrast than those experienced by the four silent women who waited there at this moment. One object of interest dominated the thoughts of each of them. These thoughts were similar in nature and sprang from the same starting-point. Curiously enough, however, they took channels as wide apart as the poles.

Josephine Cavendish had heard just enough about the incidents of the previous night to awaken her apprehensions and to stir her feeling of loyalty to the depths. The suggestion that Pierce Phillips was in the slightest degree responsible for the death of Count Courteau had roused her indignation and her fighting-blood. Unable to endure the suspense of idle waiting, she had sought relief by assuming a sort of sentinel post where she could watch developments. It was something to be close to his affairs. It was next to being close to him; hence the reason of her presence and her insistence upon remaining.

In her mind there had never been the slightest question of Pierce's innocence; any doubt of it, expressed or implied, awoke in her a sharp and bitter antagonism quite remarkable; no bird could have flown quicker to the aid of her chick, no wolf mother could have bristled more ferociously at threat to her cub, than did this serene, inexperienced girl-woman at hint of peril to Pierce Phillips. And yet, on the surface, at least, she and Pierce were only friends. He had never voiced a word of love to her. But—of what use are words when hearts are full and when confession lurks in every glance, every gesture; when every commonplace is thrilling and significant?

In her eyes no disgrace whatever attached to him as a result of the notoriety he had suffered. On the contrary, she considered him a martyr, a hero, the object of a deep conspiracy, and his wrongs smarted her. He was, in short, a romantic figure. Moreover, she had recently begun to believe that this entire situation was contrived purely for the purpose of bringing them together, of acquainting them with each other, and of testing the strength of their mutual regard. These other women, whom she saw to-day for the first time, she considered merely extra figures in the drama of which she and Pierce played the leads—witnesses in the case deserving no attention. She would be grateful to them, of course, if they succeeded in helping him, but, at best, they were minor characters, supers in the cast. Once Pierce himself strode into the scene, she forgot them entirely.

What a picture her lover made, she reflected; how he filled her eye! What importance he possessed! Surely the world must see and feel how dominant, how splendid he was. It must recognize how impossible it would be for him to do wrong. The mere sight of him had set her to vibrating, and now inspired in her a certain reckless abandon; guilty or innocent, he was her mate and she would have followed him at a word. But—he was innocent; it was her part to wait here as patiently as she could until the fact was proved and until he could ask that question which forever trembled between them.

Such thoughts as these were impossible to conceal; they were mirrored upon the face of the colonel's daughter as she stood raptly gazing at the door through which Pierce Phillips had disappeared. Her lips were parted; the shadow of the smile his coming had evoked still lingered upon them; her soul was in her shining eyes. Unknown to her, at least one of the other women present had read her sudden emotions and now watched her curiously, with an intent and growing astonishment.

Rouletta Kirby had been as quick as the Countess to correctly interpret Laure's chagrin, and she, too, had experienced a tremendous relief. Oddly enough, however, she had felt no such fierce and jealous exultation as she had anticipated; there had been no selfish thrill such as she had expected. What ailed her? she wondered. While groping for an answer, her attention had been challenged by the expression upon Miss Cavendish's face, and vaguely she began to comprehend the truth. Breathlessly now she watched the girl; slowly conviction grew into certainty.

So! That was why the colonel's daughter was here. That was why, at sound of a certain step, she had become glorified. That was why Pierce had been blind to her own and Hilda's presence in the room.

It would be untrue to say that Rouletta was not shocked by this discovery. It came like a thunderclap, and its very unexpectedness jolted her mind out of the ruts it had been following these many days. But, astonishing to relate, it caused her no anguish. After the first moment or two of dizzy bewilderment had passed she found that her whole being was galvanized into new life and that the eyes of her soul were opened to a new light. With understanding came a peculiar emotional let-down, a sudden, welcome relaxation—almost a sensation of relief.

Rouletta asked herself, over and over, what could be the matter with her; why she felt no twinge, no jealousy; why the sight of that eager, breathless girl with the rapturous face failed to cause her a heartache. She was amazed at herself. It could not be that she no longer cared for Pierce, that she had mistaken her feelings toward him. No, he was what he had always been—her ideal—the finest, the most lovable, the dearest creature she had ever met; just the sort of fellow she had always longed to know; the kind any girl would crave for lover, friend, brother. She felt very tender toward him. She was not greatly surprised that the nicest girl in Dawson had recognized his charm and had surrendered to it. Well, he deserved the nicest girl in the world.

Rouletta was startled at the direction her thoughts were taking. Did she love Pierce Phillips as she had believed she did, or had she merely fallen in love with his good qualities? Certainly he had never been dearer to her than he was at this moment, and yet— Rouletta abandoned the problem of self-analysis and al-

CE AND JOSEPHINE TURN AWAY, HAND IN HAND, THEIR HEADS CLOS
TOGETHER

lowed her bubbling relief at the turn events had taken to remain a mystery for the time being.

The door to the commandant's office opened without warning. Pierce stood framed in it. His head was up, his shoulders were back, his countenance was alight; with confident tread he entered the big room and crossed it directly to the girl who stood waiting beside the table. He held out his two hands to her and with a flash of her clear blue eyes she placed hers in his. Gladness, trust, blind faith, and adoration were in her face. She murmured something which Rouletta did not hear, for at that instant Colonel Cavendish appeared with the curt announcement:

"That is all, ladies. You needn't remain longer."

Blindly, confusedly, Rouletta rose and fumbled with her wraps. She saw the colonel go to Laure and speak with her in a stiff, formal way. She saw Pierce and Josephine turn away hand in hand, their heads close together—he had not even glanced in her direction; then Cavendish was speaking to her directly.

At first she did not understand him, but finally made out that he was telling her that everything had been cleared up, including even the mystery of Count Courteau's gold-sack.

"Laure confessed that she got a duplicate key to the cashier's cage," she heard the colonel say. "Got it from Pierce. It was she who put the evidence in there during the confusion. Pretty ingenious, I call it, and pretty spiteful."

"Did she—have anything to say about the—the murder?" Rouletta inquired.

"No. But the Countess has that figured out right, I'm sure. We'll have the proof when Rock brings back his prisoners."

As Rouletta moved toward the door Pierce stopped her. There was a ring in his voice as he said:

"Rouletta, I want you to meet Miss Cavendish. I want the two nicest girls in the world to know each other. Josephine, this is Miss Kirby, of whom I've said so much." Then without reason he laughed joyously, and so did the colonel's daughter.

The latter took Rouletta's hand in a warm and friendly clasp. Her smiling lips were tremulous. Engagingly, shyly, she said:

"Pierce has told me how splendid you've been to him, and I'm sure you're as happy as we are, but—things always come out right if we wish for them hard enough. Don't you think so?"

The Countess Courteau was walking slowly when Rouletta overtook her a block or so down the street. She looked up as the younger woman joined her.

"Well," she said, "I presume you saw. Not a look, not a thought for any one but her—that other girl."

"Yes, I saw." There was a pause, then: "She's wonderful. I think I'm very glad."

"Glad?" Hilda raised her brows; she glanced curiously at the speaker.

"If I had a brother I'd want him to love a girl like that."

"But—you have no brother, outside of 'Poleon Doret." Hilda was more than ever amazed when her companion laughed softly, contentedly.

"I know, but if I had one, I'd want him to be like—Pierce. I— My dear, something has changed in me, oh, surprisingly! I scarcely know what it is, but—I'm walking on air and my eyes are open for the first time. And you? We've been honest with each other—how do you feel?"

"I?" The Countess smiled wistfully. "Why —it doesn't matter how I feel! The boy has found himself, and nothing else is of the least importance."

CHAPTER XXX

JOE McCASKEY was not a coward, neither was he a superstitious man, but he had imagination. The steady strain of his and Frank's long flight, the certainty of pursuit close behind, had frayed his nerve and rendered him jumpy. For a man in his condition to be awakened out of a trancelike sleep by an intruder at once invisible, dumb; to feel the presence of that mysterious visitor and actually to see him—it—bulked dim and formless among the darting shadows cast by a blazing match—was a test indeed. It was too much for Joe.

As for Frank, he had actually seen nothing, heard nothing except his brother's voice, and then—that sigh. For that very reason his terror was, if anything, even greater than his brother's.

During what seemed an age there was no sound except the stertorous breathing of the McCaskeys themselves and the stir of the dogs outside. The pale square of the single window, over which a bleached-out cotton flour-sack had been tacked, let in only enough light to intensify the gloom. Within the cabin was a blackness thick, tangible, oppressive; the brothers stared into it with bulg-

ing eyes and listened with ear-drums strained to
the point of rupture. Oddly enough, this utter
silence augmented their agitation. Unable finally
to smother the evidence of his steadily growing
fright, Frank uttered a half-audible moan. Joe
in the next bunk put it down as a new and threatening phenomenon. What sort of thing was it
that sighed and moaned thus? As evidence of
the direction Joe's mind was taking, he wondered
if these sounds could be the complaint of Courteau's unshriven spirit. It was a shocking thought,
but involuntarily he gasped the dead man's name.

A guilty conscience is a proven coward-maker;
so, too, is a quick, imaginative mind. It took
only a moment or two to convince Joe that this
nocturnal interloper was not a creature of flesh
and blood, but some enormous, unmentionable,
creeping thing come out of the other world—out
of the cold earth—to visit punishment upon him
for his crime. He could hear it stirring, finally,
now here, now there; he could make out the
rustle of its grave-clothes. There is no doubt
that the cabin was full of half-distinguishable
sounds—so is any warm habitation—but to Joe's
panicky imagination the nature of these particular
sounds indicated that they could not come from
any normal, living being. There was, for instance, a slow, asthmatic wheezing, like the
breath of a sorely wounded man; a stretching and
straining as of a body racked with mortal agony;
even a faint bubbling choke like a death-rattle
heard in an adjoining chamber. These and others

as horribly suggestive. Joe's wild agitation distorted all of them, no matter whether they came from his brother Frank, from the poorly seasoned pole rafters overhead, or from the sleepy dogs outside, and 'Poleon Doret, with a grim internal chuckle, took advantage of the fact.

When finally the elder McCaskey heard his own name whispered, the last shred of self-control left to him was whipped away; his wits went skittering, and for a second time he groped with frantic, twitching fingers for his revolver. He raised it and, with a yell, fired at random into the blackness, meanwhile covering his eyes with his left arm for fear of beholding in the sulphurous flash that bloodless, fleshless menace, whatever it might be.

Somehow he managed to get out of bed and to place his back against the wall, and there he cowered until he heard his brother's body threshing about the floor. As a matter of fact, that shot had sent Frank sprawling from his bunk, and he was striving to kick off the hampering folds of his sleeping-bag, nothing more; but the thumping of his knees and elbows bore a dreadful significance to the terrified listener. Evidently the Thing had closed in—had grappled with Frank. Its hands, damp with death sweat, even now were groping for him, Joe. The thought was unbearable.

Blindly the elder brother thrust his revolver at full length in front of him and pulled the trigger; Frank shrieked, but again and again Joe fired, and when the last cartridge was spent he continued to snap the weapon. He desisted only when he heard a voice, faint, but hoarse with agony, crying:

"O God! You've shot me, Joe! You've shot me!"

Then and not until then, did a sort of sanity come to the wretch. The revolver slipped from his fingers; he felt his bones dissolving into water; a horror ten times greater than he had previously suffered fell upon him. He tried to speak, to throw off this hideous nightmare, but his voice came only as a dry, reedy whisper.

Frank was still now; he did not respond to his brother's incoherencies except with a deep groaning that momentarily became more alarming.

"I—I—didn't— Christ! I didn't shoot you ... Frank! ... Answer me! Say something. ..." Even yet the dread of that hobgoblin presence lay like ice upon the elder brother; he feared to move lest he encounter it, lest he touch it and it enfold him; but when Frank's twitching body became still he fell to his knees and went groping forward on all-fours in search of it. Death was here now. He had slain his brother and *there was no light!*

Joe began to sob and to chatter in a maudlin hysteria of fright and apprehension. He succeeded in finding Frank by the sound of his breathing, and he was pawing at him and wildly calling his name when at his back a match was struck.

The sound, the flare, brought a scream from his

throat. He cringed and cowered; the pallid face
he raised was slack-jawed, his gaze was that of
a crazy man.

Slowly, very slowly his dementia left him. His
eyes were still distended, to be sure, but into them
sanity, recognition, began to creep. He stared
dazedly about him, and at last he managed to
speak Doret's name.

"Wh-what you doing—here?" he breathed.

"Me? I come to tak' you back."

Joe shook his head weakly. "You can't.
We're across—safe." His eyes dropped to the
prostrate body beside which he knelt, and a new
thought swiftly flooded his vacant mind. "Look!
You— Now I understand. *You* did it! *You*
shot him. I never— *By God!*" The fellow's
insane vehemence, the panting eagerness with
which he undertook to absolve himself from the
hideous results of his deed, argued that he loved
his brother. He rose slowly to his feet, his countenance flaming, his gaze fixed in an arresting
expression of mingled rage and horror upon the
woodsman's face. "You did it, damn you! Shot
him, in the dark, asleep! Now you want me. . . .
Take me back, eh? You can't do it. I'm safe
. . . safe . . . !" .

'Poleon uttered a grunt. He leaned his carbine against the wall behind him, and from his
pocket he drew a thin cotton sled-rope. With
this in his hand he advanced upon the slayer.

McCaskey retreated. Weakly at first he fought
off his captor; then, as fear overwhelmed him, he

became possessed of a phrenetic energy and struggled with the strength of two men. He struck,
he bit, he clawed, he kicked. It was like the
battle of a man with a beast—ferocious, merciless
—while it lasted. They rocked about the cabin,
heedless of the wounded man; the stove came
crashing down and they trampled the pipe under
their feet.

But McCaskey collapsed as suddenly as he had
flown to action. When 'Poleon trussed him up
he had neither strength nor spirit either for resistance or for resentment. He was as spineless
as a wet sáck. With anguished eyes he watched
his captor lift Frank into a bunk and then pro-
ceed to do what remained to be done. Bleak of
face, lifeless of voice, hopeless of expression, he
answered the questions put to him and made no
feeblest effort at concealment. He was, in fact,
no longer capable of any resistance, mental or
physical.

Frank died as the first ashen streaks of dawn
came through the window and lit the sickly face
of the brother who had slain him. There was no
longer need of the rope; in fact, Joe implored his
captor with such earnestness not to leave him
alone that 'Poleon untied his hands, feeling sure
that he was impotent. Joe followed him outside,
and stood near by while he harnessed the dogs;
he accompanied every step the woodsman took—
wild horses could not have dragged him away in
his present frame of mind—and finally, when they
set out back toward the Canadian Line, he sham-

bled along ahead of the team with head down and
eyes averted from the gruesome bundle that lay
in the sled. His punishment had overtaken him
and he was unequal to it.

Dawson was in ferment, for the news of another
"strike" had come in and a stampede was under
way. Discoveries of gold, or rumors of them,
had been common. The camp had thrilled to
many Arabian Nights tales, but this one was
quite the most sensational of all. So amazing,
so unbelievable was it, in truth, that those who
had been too often fooled laughed at it and declared it impossible on its face. Some wood-
cutters on the hills above El Dorado had been
getting out dry timber for the drift fires, so ran
the report, and in shooting the tree-trunks down
into the valley they had discovered a deposit of
wash gravel. One of them, possessed of the pros-
pector's instinct, had gophered a capful of the
gravel from off the rim where the plunging tree-
trunks had dug through the snow and exposed the
outcropping bedrock, and, to satisfy his curiosity,
had taken it down to camp for a test. He had
thawed and panned it; to his amazement, he had
discovered that it carried an astonishing value in
gold—coarse, rough gold—exactly like that in the
creek pay-streak, except with less signs of abrasion
and erosion. Rumor placed the contents of that
first prospect at ten dollars. Ten cents would have
meant the riches of Aladdin, but—ten dollars!
No wonder the wiseacres shook their heads. Ten

dollars to the pan, on a hilltop! Absurd! How did metal of that specific gravity get up there? How could there be wash gravel on the crest of a mountain? There was no sense to such a proposition.

But such old California placer miners as chanced to hear of it lost no time in hitting the trail. They were familiar with high bars, prehistoric river-beds, and they went as fast as their old legs would carry them.

More faith was put in the story when it became known that the diggings were being deserted and that the men of El Dorado and Bonanza were quitting their jobs, actually leaving their thawed drifts to freeze while they scattered over the domes and saddles round about, staking claims. That settled matters, so far as Dawson was concerned; men who had dogs hitched them up, those who had none rolled their packs; soon the trail up the Klondike was black and the recorder's office prepared for riotous activity.

Those who had set out thus late met excited travelers hastening townward, and from them obtained confirmation. Yes, the story was true, more than true! The half had not been told as yet. Gold lay under the grass roots where anybody could see it; it was more plentiful than in the creeks—this was the richest thing ever known. "Frenchman's Hill," the discovery had been named, but all the ground for miles round about had been already staked and now men were going even further afield. It was well to hurry.

A frenzy took possession of the hearers, and they pressed on more rapidly. This was like the rush of the autumn previous, from Dyea to the Chilkoot, only here dogs flew under snapping lashes; pedestrians, when shouldered aside, abandoned their burdens and sacrificed all to speed. At the Forks the new arrivals scattered up over the hills, and that night road-houses, cabins, tents, were crowded; men slept on chairs, on floors; they stood around open fires.

Dawson awoke, on the second morning, to behold a long queue of fur-clad miners waiting outside the Gold Commissioner's office; the town took on an electric liveliness. This signified big things; it gave permanence; it meant that Dawson was to be the world's first placer camp. Business picked up, the saloons became thronged, on every corner knots of gossiping men assembled. There began a considerable speculation in claims on Frenchman's Hill; merchants planned larger stocks for the next season; the price of town lots doubled.

Late that afternoon through the streets ran a cry that took every foot-free man hurrying to the river-front. "Rock was coming!" In a jiffy the vantage-points were crowded. Sure enough, far down the Yukon two teams were approaching; with the smoke of Dawson in their nostrils they were coming on the run, and soon the more keen-eyed spectators announced that they could make out 'Poleon Doret. The lieutenant himself, however, was not in evidence. Instantly speculation became rife. Here was a sensation indeed, and when the second runner was identified beyond question as Joe McCaskey, excitement doubled. Where was Rock? Where was the other fugitive? What, in the name of all that was unexpected, had occurred?

A shout of relief issued from the crowd when the teams drew in under the bank and Rock sat up, waving a mittened hand; the shout was quickly hushed as the lookers-on saw what sort of burden Joe McCaskey was driving.

Up into the main street came the cavalcade. The crowd fell in alongside and ran with it to the Barracks, clamoring for details, pouring questions upon the returning travelers. Joe McCaskey, of course, was speechless, this ordeal proving, as a matter of fact, scarcely less trying than that other one at Sheep Camp when he had run the gauntlet. As for Rock and the French Canadian, neither had much to say, and as a result sensational stories soon spread through the resorts. The Mounted Policeman had got his men, as usual, but only after a desperate affray in which Frank McCaskey had fallen and the officer himself had been wounded—so ran the first account. Those who had gone as far as the Barracks returned with a fanciful tale of a siege in the snow and of Rock's single-handed conquest of the two fugitives. These conflicting reports were confusing and served to set the town so completely agog that it awaited fuller details with the most feverish impatience. One thing only was certain

—the lieutenant had again made himself a hero; he had put a new feather in his cap. Men lifted glasses to him and to the Force. Such efficiency as this commanded their deepest respect and admiration.

Pierce Phillips, of course, was the most eager member of that welcoming throng. At the earliest moment he bore 'Poleon away to his cabin, and there, when the last morbid curiosity-seeker had been shaken off and the dogs had been attended to, he heard the story.

"You don' got no more worry," 'Poleon told him, with a smile. "Joe keel' de Count."

"He confessed? Really?"

"Rouletta figger' it out jus' right. By golly! Dat's de smartes' gal!"

"She is indeed. But Frank? What happened? How did you manage—?"

'Poleon hesitated. There was a reason why he did not wish the details of that affair on the upper Forty Mile to become public. Joe McCaskey was beginning to talk loudly about his outraged rights, his citizenship, international law, and such incomprehensible things—but stronger by far than any fear of consequences to himself, remote at best, 'Poleon felt a desire to help his friend, the Police lieutenant. Rock was deeply humiliated at his weak failure in living up to his reputation; he felt that he had cut a very sorry figure indeed; and, although he had undertaken to conceal that feeling from 'Poleon, the latter had read him like a book and had secretly made up his mind to give

510

full credit to the officer, eliminating himself as much as possible. There was no reason why the actual facts should be made public, so far as he could see, and, once an artfully colored account of the exploit had gained currency, Rock could not well contradict it. He might, undoubtedly would, make a truthful report to his superiors, but 'Poleon determined that in the eyes of the hero-worshiping people of Dawson the fellow should still remain a hero and stand for one hundred per cent. efficiency. That was quite as it should be.

It was not difficult to distort the story enough to reverse the rôles he and the officer had played, and, when he had finished, Pierce was loud in his praise of the Mounted Policeman.

"Well, things happened here, too," the youth declared. Succinctly he told the story of Laure's delayed confession proving that he had been the victim of a deliberate conspiracy. "Believe me, I'm glad it has all come out so well," he said. "People didn't actually accuse me, but I was conscious of their suspicion, their doubt. I had talked too much. Then, too, there was that beastly rumor about the Countess and me. It was fierce! Appearances were strong. I'd—have gone on the stampede, only I didn't have the heart. You've heard about that, of course? The new strike?" When 'Poleon shook his head the young man's eyes kindled. "Why, man," he broke out, "the town's crazy! dippy! It's the biggest thing ever! Frenchman's Hill, it's called. Get that? Frenchman's Hill!"

"Some French feller mak' lucky strike, eh?"
'Poleon was not greatly interested. "Where de
place is? Who dis Frenchman?"

"It's a high bar somewhere above El Dorado—
a mountain of pay gravel—an old river-bed or
something. They say it's where all the gold
came from, the mother lode. You can see it
right at the grass roots—"

'Poleon started and his mouth opened; then he
shook his head.

"By Gar! Dat's fonny! I seen gravel up
dere, but me—I'm onlucky. Never I quite get
not'in'; always I'm close by when 'noder feller
mak' strike."

Pierce still managed to control himself enough
to explain: "They were shooting dead timber
down into the gulch and they wore the snow off
where the rim cropped out. It happened to be
staked ground right there." Pierce's excitement,
the odd light in his dancing eyes, bore to 'Poleon
a significance. "Some Frenchman had taken it
up, so they called it Frenchman's Hill."

Doret's blank, confounded stare caused the
speaker finally to blurt out: "Good Heavens!
man, wake up! I'm trying to break the news
gently that you're a millionaire—the Frenchman
of Frenchman's Hill. I don't want you to faint.
First time in history a miner ever left his claim
and another fellow came along—"

Doret uttered a feeble cry and rose to his feet.
"*Ma sœur!*" he exclaimed. "She's got claim up
dere—I stake it for her. For me, I don' care if

512

I lose mine—plenty tam I come jus' so close as
dis; but if dem feller jump her groun'—"

"Wait, wait! There's no question of anything
like that. Nobody has jumped your claim, or
hers, either. The law wouldn't let 'em. I wonder if she knows— Why, she *can't* know! I left
her not two hours ago—"

"She don' know?"

Pierce shook his head. "She doesn't dream.
I wish *I'd* known. I'd have loved to tell her."

'Poleon Doret gazed fixedly, curiously at the
speaker. He nodded his head. A peculiar, set,
hopeless look crept into his eyes; his broad shoulders sagged wearily. He had traveled far and
swiftly on this young man's affairs; he had slept
but little; and now a great fatigue mastered him.
Oddly enough, too, that fierce, consuming desire
to see Rouletta which had hourly gnawed at him
was gone; all at once he felt that she was quite
the last person he wished to face. This weakness,
this smallness of spirit, was only temporary, he
assured himself; it would soon pass, and then he
would find the strength to go to her with his customary smile, his mask in place. Now, however,
he was empty, cheerless, frightened by the por-
tent of this new thing. It could have but one significance—it meant that he would lose his "sister,"
that she would have no further need of him.

Well, that was all right. It was something like
this that he had worked for. Why cherish a mean
envy of this happy boy? Why permit a narrow
selfishness to mar this supreme moment?

Doret was not a grudging giver; he straightened himself finally, and into his tired eyes there came the gleam that Phillips had been waiting for.

"*Bien!*" he breathed. "My li'l bird goin' wear de plumage she deserve. She's goin' be reech an' happy all her life. By golly! Dat's nice, for fac'. I feel lak gettin' drunk."

"She'd never stand for that."

"I spec' you tol' her you an' me is pardners on dis Frenchman' Hill, eh? An' she's glad 'bout dat—"

"Oh, see here!" Pierce's tone changed abruptly. "Of course I didn't tell her. That's cold; it's off. D'you think I'd permit—" The boy choked and stammered. "D'you imagine for a minute that I'd let you go through with a proposition like that? I understand why you made it— to get me away from the life I've been leading. It was bully of you, but—well, hardly. I'm not that sort. No, I've laid off the old stuff, absolutely—straightened out. I've lived ten years in the last ten days. Wait and see. 'Poleon, I'm the happiest, the most deliriously happy man you ever saw. I only want one thing. That's work and lots of it—the harder the better, so long as it's honest and self-respecting. What d'you think of that?"

"W'at I t'ink?" the woodsman said, warmly. "I t'ink dat's de bes' news of all. *Mon ami*, you got reecher pay-streak in you as Frenchman' Hill, if only you work 'im hard. But you need pardner to get 'im out." He winked meaningly. "I guess mebbe you fin' dat pardner, eh?"

Pierce flushed; he nodded vigorously and laughed in the purest, frankest joy. "You're a good guesser. A partner — life partner! I— She— Oh, my Lord! I'm overflowing! I'm— Funny thing, I've never said a word to her; she doesn't know—"

"Ho, ho!" cried the elder man.

"Oh, she does know, of course. If she didn't I wouldn't feel as I do, but we've never actually mentioned it. I've got to prove myself, understand? It came to me of a sudden, struck me all in a heap, I can tell you. I saw what a fool I'd made of myself. What a damnable thing chance is, anyhow! It makes you, breaks you; carries you along and leaves you stranded finally, then sweeps you on again. Fortunately, she's big enough to understand and make allowances. If she weren't, I'd die. I wouldn't want to live and not make good. It's ecstasy and it's—pain. I'm frightened, too, at my own unworthiness—" Abruptly the speaker's voice ceased and he bowed his head.

'Poleon wet his dry lips and essayed to speak, but he could find nothing to say. Of course Rouletta was big enough to understand and make allowance for any human shortcomings. She was the sanest, the most liberal, the most charitable of girls. And it was true, too, that love came unbidden. He had learned that, to his cost. It was pretty hard to stand quietly and lend a sympathetic ear to this lucky devil; it took an effort to maintain a smile, to keep a friendly gaze fixed

515

upon Phillips' face. The big fellow was growing weary of forever fighting himself. It would be a relief to get away and to yield to his misery.

But with a lover's fatuous absorption in his own affairs Pierce resumed: "I've been thinking lately how I came to this country looking for Life, the big adventure. Everything that happened, good or bad, was part of a stage play. I've been two people in one—the fellow who did things and the fellow who looked on and applauded—actor and audience. It was tremendously interesting in an unreal sort of way, and I jotted everything down mentally. I was stocking up with experience. Understand? Well, the whole thing has suddenly become very different. I'm not in the gallery now, not in the theater at all, not acting. And I thank God for it. I don't imagine that I make myself plain in the least—"

Evidently he had not; evidently, too, his auditor's mind had strayed slightly, for the latter said:

"I s'pose you t'inkin' all at once 'bout gettin'—marry, eh?"

Phillips paled; he uttered a panicky denial. "Not yet! Oh no—! That is, I've *thought* about it a good deal—can't think of anything else—but it's too early yet. I'm in no position; I must make good first."

"For why it's too early? Mebbe dis gal goin' tak' lot of fun in he'p you mak' good."

"I wonder—"

"Sure t'ing. All women is lak dat. You goin'

t'ink of her after dis, not yourse'f. She's got money—''

"Oh yes. That makes it hard, still—''

"Wal, you ain't broke, my frien', not wit' half interes' in Discovery on Frenchman' Hill."

"Once and for all," Pierce protested, in extreme agitation, "I tell you I won't take it. My Lord! that's generous! You're a princely fellow, Doret, but—the most you can give me is a job. Work? Yes, I'll eat that up."

"All right. We talk 'bout dat 'noder tam. Now, mebbe so she lak hear de lates' news from you. Dere's plenty for tellin' her—'bout Joe McCaskey an' all de res'. You can spoke now, lak hones' man. *Sapré!* Don' you s'pose she's waitin' to hear you say you love her? An' how you goin' mak' big success? By Gar! I keeck you out dis cabin if you keep her waitin' some more!"

With a cry, half of trepidation, half of exultance, Phillips crushed his cap upon his head. "I—I've a notion to. I can *almost* say it; anyhow, I can say enough so she'll understand. Gad! I will! I just needed you to stiffen me up." Fiercely he wrung the woodsman's hand, and, forgetful of all else but his new determination, moved toward the door. "Thanks for all you've done for me, old man, and all you've offered to do."

"Frenchman' Hill is nice place for two nestin' doves—fine place for sing an' be happy," the other reminded him.

In a choking voice Pierce exclaimed: "You're a prince, Doret, and I won't forget! A prince!"

He was gone; the cabin door had slammed shut with a crash. 'Poleon sank to a seat and with a long sigh bowed his head.

It was over; he had done his bit. For a long while he remained there inert, his patient, haggard face bent, his eyes fixed upon the floor. He felt very old, very much used up, and the labor of thinking was unbearable. When the fire had died and a chill had crept into the room he roused himself to note that it had grown dark. Manifestly, this would not do; there was the problem of living still to face. Sooner or later this very evening he must go to Rouletta and pretend to a joyousness he could never again know. That meant more smiles, more effort; it would take all he had in him to carry it off, and, meanwhile, the more he let his mind dwell upon her the more unbearable became his thoughts. This solitude was playing tricks with him. Enough of it! He must get out into the lights; he must hear voices and regain the mastery of himself through contact with sane people. Perhaps in the saloons, the restaurants, he could absorb enough laughter to make safe the mockery he purposed; perhaps it would enable him to stamp a grin upon his features.

But his impulse was futile; in spite of himself he shrank from people and hid himself unobtrusively in a corner of the first place he entered. He was hurt, wounded, sick to death; he longed to creep away somewhere and be alone with his pain.

In order that he might the sooner be free to do so, he rose finally and slunk out upon the street. It would soon be time for Rouletta to go to work. He would get it over with.

Cap in hand, his heart beating heavily at the prospect of merely seeing her, he came on noiseless soles to her door. He could hear her stirring inside, so he took a deep breath and rapped softly.

She uttered a cry when she saw him standing there; then a sudden pallor crept into her cheeks, a queer constraint enveloped her. Nevertheless, she put both her hands in his and drew him across the threshold. She said something which neither of them understood.

'Poleon's ears were roaring, but after a few moments he discovered that she was gently chiding him. Where had he been? Why had he delayed so long, knowing all the time that she was dying to see him and to hear his story? He could not understand her embarrassment, her shyness, the fact that she seemed hurt.

"Wal, I'm tucker' out wit' travelin'," he declared. "Dat's hardes' trip ever I mak'. You hear 'bout 'im, eh?—'bout how McCaskey tell de truth?"

. Rouletta nodded, with a curious little smile upon her lips. "Yes. I heard all about it, the first thing—how Rock ran down those fellows—everything. The town was ringing with his name inside of an hour. Of course, I went to the Barracks, finally, looking for you. I'm just back.

I saw the lieutenant and—he told me the true story."

'Poleon stirred uncomfortably.

"He swore at you roundly and said he'd take it out of your skin as soon as he was able—giving him the credit. He told me it was you who did it all—how you followed those men over the Line, alone, after he played out; how Joe McCaskey killed his own brother in trying to kill you. But the whole thing is public now. I heard it as I came back. You're quite a famous character in Dawson to-night, 'Poleon dear, what with this and with Frenchman's Hill."

"Ho! Dat Frenchman' Hill," the man broke out, hurriedly. "It's beeg s'prise for us, eh? Pierce told you 'bout dat?"

"Pierce?" The girl shook her head vaguely.

"You 'member I stake two claim', one for you, one for me. By golly! *ma sœur*, you're millionaire."

"I remembered, of course," Rouletta said, faintly. "I—" She closed her eyes. "I couldn't believe it, however. At first I didn't understand where the strike had been made; then I couldn't credit it. I thought I was dreaming—"

"You dream as much as you can," 'Poleon said, warmly. "Dey all come true now. What? Everyt'ing come out nice, eh?"

Rouletta opened her eyes. They were shining; so, too, was her face. "Yes, my dream has come true—that is, my biggest, finest dream. I'm— the happiest girl in the world, 'Poleon."

"*Ma sœur!*" the man cried brokenly and with a depth of feeling that even Rouletta could not fathom. "I give my life to hear you say dose word', to see dat light in your eye. No price too high for dat."

A silence, throbbing, intense, fell between them. Rouletta felt her heart-beats swaying her. She opened her lips, but no sound issued. The figure before her was growing misty and she had to wink the tears back into place.

"'*Ma sœur!*'" shee choed, faintly. "I love to hear you say that, dear. It has grown to be a caress, a—kiss, when you say it. But I've something to tell you—"

"I know."

"Something you don't know and would never guess. I've found another brother." When he stared at her in open bewilderment she repeated: "Yes, another brother. I took him for something altogether different, but—" She laughed happily. "What do you think of a girl who doesn't know her own mind? Who lets the one man, the real man, go away? She doesn't deserve much, does she?"

"*Ma sœur! Ma sœur!*" the big fellow cried, hoarsely. He had fallen all atremble now; he could have believed himself demented only for something in Rouletta's face. "You mean— him? W'at's dis you sayin'?"

"I mean him—you. Who else could I mean? He doesn't care for me. but for another, and I'm— oh, so glad!"

"*Mon Dieu!*" 'Poleon gasped. "For why you look at me lak dat? Don'—don'—!" His cry was one of pain, of reproach; he closed his eyes the while he strove to still his working features. He opened them with a snap when a small, warm, tremulous hand closed over his.

"You wouldn't mind if he called me his sister, if—if you called me—something else, would you, dear?"

"Oh, *ma sœur!*" he whispered. "I'm poor, ignorant feller. I ain't no good. But you—de bes' man in all de worl' would love you."

"He does, but he won't say so," Rouletta declared. "Come, must I say it for him?"

One last protest the fellow voiced. "Me, I'm rough-neck man. I scarcely read an' write. But you—"

"I'm a gambler's daughter, nothing more—a bold and forward creature. But I'm done with dealing. I'm tired of the game and henceforth I'm going to be the 'lookout'—your 'lookout,' dear." With a choking little laugh the girl drew nearer, and, lifting his hands, she crept inside his arms. Then as life, vigor, fire succeeded his paralysis, she swayed closer, until her breast was against his.

With a wordless, hungry cry of ecstasy, so keen that it was akin to agony, 'Poleon Doret enfolded her in his great embrace. "Don' spoke no more," he implored her. "I'll be wakin' up too soon."

They stood so for a long time before she raised her dewy lips to his.

THE END

Lightning Source UK Ltd.
Milton Keynes UK
UKHW020600120219

337137UK00005B/835/P